The Most Passionate Story of Star-Crossed Lovers Since *Doctor Zhivago*!

Forbidden to marry the noble officer she loves, forbidden to love the gentle Englishman whose bed she shares . . .

IMPERIAL NIGHTS, set in the splendor and ruin of the final days of Tsarist Russia, is the unforgettable story of the illegitimate daughter of a noble family—a woman at once high-born and marked with shame. Anastasia. Ana! A woman you will always remember, whose love leads her to a life of romance and adventure you will never forget!

IMPERIAL NIGHTS
by the bestselling author of
INDIGO NIGHTS,
OLIVIA O'NEILL

Berkley Books by Olivia O'Neill

IMPERIAL NIGHTS
INDIGO NIGHTS

OLIVIA O'NEILL

A BERKLEY BOOK
published by
BERKLEY PUBLISHING CORPORATION

This Berkley book contains the complete
text of the original hardcover edition.
It has been completely reset in a type face
designed for easy reading, and was printed
from new film.

IMPERIAL NIGHTS

A Berkley Book / published by arrangement with
Futura Publications, Ltd.

PRINTING HISTORY
Futura edition published 1979
Berkley edition / December 1979

For information address: Berkley Publishing Corporation,
200 Madison Avenue, New York, New York 10016.

ISBN: 0-425-04233-2

A BERKLEY BOOK® TM 757,375
PRINTED IN THE UNITED STATES OF AMERICA

Cast of Characters

ANASTASIA *Stanya*

TAMARA GALZINSKI *Anastasia's mother*

COUNT ARKADY KHARKOV *Kadya, Anastasia's father*

COUNTESS OLGA KHARKOV *Anastasia's stepmother; Kadya's wife*

VALERIAN RADEK *Olga's son by her first marriage*

ANDREI KHARKOV *First son of Olga and Kadya*

PETROUSHKA KHARKOV *Second son of Olga and Kadya*

LOUISA SUTHERLAND *An English governess*

NICHOLAS II *Tsar of All the Russias*

ALEXANDRA *His wife, the Empress*

VARVARA DUBROVINA *Daughter of a minor Russian official*

FATHER GRIGORI EFIMOVITCH *Rasputin, a Holy Man*

ANTHONY MILES *British diplomat*

AUGUSTUS FINDLAY *An artist*

FRANCOIS SOULIER *An Egyptologist*

SUSANNA MACDONALD *A Scottish missionary doctor*

REVEREND ELIAS ARMSTRONG *A Scottish missionary*

MARTHA *His wife*

LIN TONG *A Chinese peasant*

SYBIL DUNWOODY *An English girl*

HEINRICH VON STUCKEL *A German officer*

BORIS MILUIKOFF *A Bolshevik*

VALENTIN RADEK *Son of Valerian Radek and Susanna Macdonald*

GUY RICKARD *Commander of a submarine*

YURI *A Russian peasant*

O who can hold a fire in his hand
By thinking on the frosty Caucasus?
Or cloy the hungry edge of appetite
By bare imagination of a feast?

—William Shakespeare
Richard II
Act I, Scene iii

Imperial Nights

Prologue

CASIMIRVEK, POLAND
1888

When the green-eyed girl in the outmoded white muslin dress saw her governess' head loll forward, an incredulous smile lifted the corners of her wide, willful mouth. It was Frau Sturmer's gentle snores she was hearing, mingled with the hum of bees and the dreamy coo of wood-pigeons. The soul of vigilance asleep? Such a thing had never happened before. It must have been due to the heat and the wine Madam had drunk to ward off a migraine.

"Frau Sturmer . . .?" she whispered intently.

When a contented gurgle was the only response, the girl's smile broadened. Eyes sparkling with mischief, she rolled quickly over in a flurry of beribboned petticoats and tugged at the sleeve of the dark-haired young officer who lay propped on one elbow a few feet away, lazily teasing an ant with a blade of grass. His splendid blue and gold tunic was unbuttoned and his face darkly flushed with wine and heat.

"What is it, cherie?" he drawled sleepily. Then, as his eyes followed her pointing finger, a sudden grin transformed his aristocratic features.

"She's fast asleep," the girl whispered excitedly. "We can go and pick strawberries now—there's nothing to stop us."

The young man looked around the peaceful, sunlit glade. His glance moved quickly over the wooden cart propped with its shafts pointing skyward, the empty picnic hampers neatly stacked beside it, and to the two fat horses tethered beneath a chestnut tree's spreading branches, their tails swishing rhythmically against the flies. Beside them sat the old Polish coachman and his own Russian orderly, all differences forgotten in a blue haze of tobacco smoke, as they solemnly gambled for melon pips, deaf and blind to the rest of the world.

With a swift movement the girl was on her feet, kicking off her tight shoes and heading uphill.

"Come on!"

She padded softly up the winding path, and after a moment's indecision he rose and followed. Stifling their laughter like naughty children, they scrambled up the steep track between huge boulders polished smooth by countless spring spates, beside a dancing stream, inviting them on to the rocky pools higher up. It was the first time they had been alone together.

Once out of sight of the picnic glade they both collapsed, gasping and giggling. Mirages shimmered in the hot air like the landscape of a dream. How handsome he is, she thought. How different from those clumsy, tongue-tied boys my brother brings home. All *they* can talk about is how to drive the Russians out of our homeland. If Stepan tells me once more that Kadya's an enemy and I must stop seeing him, I shall scream.

She sprang to her feet, ready to climb again, but Kadya put out a protesting hand.

"This is far enough, cherie," he said. "No one can see us here. Let's sit in the shade of these rocks and I'll tell you more about life at Court."

For a moment she was tempted. She loved hearing him talk about the Imperial Court, far away in St. Petersburg, about England, France, Italy... To a young girl from a remote Polish village, he seemed the epitome of cosmopolitan sophistication, but now when he tried to draw her down beside him, she pulled away impatiently.

"No! We'll never get another chance like this. I want to find the first strawberries."

Despite his tall, athletic figure he had no love of exercise, and plodding uphill on a sweltering afternoon held little charm for him. "It's too hot, cherie. I'll die of exhaustion," he groaned.

"Then I'll go on without you," she teased, and skipped nimbly out of his reach.

"Such energy..." Nevertheless, he followed her uphill, admiring the sway of her neatly rounded rump and the long, slim legs outlined by clinging folds of muslin. What a figure she had! Even in that prim, old-fashioned dress with its high-buttoned collar and ridiculous leg o' mutton sleeves, she excited and tantalized him more than any of the chic little ballet dancers whose haunts he frequented in St. Petersburg; and a thousand times more than his wife, with her flat chest, her long, serious horse's face and her millions of roubles.

The air freshened as they climbed higher, but his shirt clung stickily to his back, and as much to slow down the girl—who was now several yards ahead—as because he wanted an answer, he called:

"What if Madam wakes and finds we've gone?"

The girl's laughing face turned fleetingly toward him. "She can't tell on us! If I should mention to my mother that Frau Sturmer got drunk, she would soon be looking for another job—and without a reference. How clever you were to keep filling her glass with wine!"

He accepted the compliment with a smile and tried to slip his arm around her waist, but once more she evaded him and skipped away. "Come, on, Kadya! We're nearly there and you can rest at the top."

But when they rounded the last bend and stood in the high mountain meadow carpeted with strawberry vines, where the stream broadened into a pool fed by a foaming waterfall, the girl gave a cry of disappointment.

"Oh! We're too early!"

Patches of white flowers showed among the strawberry leaves, but of fruit there was still no sign. The green-eyed girl looked ready to cry. He put a consoling arm around her shoulders. Through the thin muslin he could feel the heat of her body and it excited him almost unbearably. "*Don't* do that!" Again she forced his arm away. "It's too hot." As she flopped down on the bank of the stream, pushing loose strands of hair back into the knot at the nape of her neck, he sat beside her.

"All right," he said. "If we can't pick strawberries,at least we can swim."

She stared at him, stunned.

"I suppose you're shocked by the idea," said the Russian, with a maddening superior smile. "All the Court ladies enjoy bathing, of course. I'd forgotten that things were bound to be different here."

"The Court ladies bathe?"

"Oh, yes. It's quite the fashion during the summer," he said casually. "I believe even the Empress takes to the water now and then . . . Of course,"—he shrugged—"it takes time for new ideas, new fashions, to reach a country place like this."

She wasn't going to admit she was shocked. She couldn't bear it if he thought her old-fashioned. She knew that her shabby, outdated clothes amused him—there was nothing she could do about that. But he mustn't be allowed to think of her as provincial. Surely if the Empress Alexandra bathed, she could do the same?

With just the right degree of nonchalance she said, "Of course. We find that bathing is really the only way to cool off during the summer."

The Russian hid his amusement. "You mean to tell me you can swim?"

"Not exactly," she admitted reluctantly.

"Let me have the pleasure of teaching you," he said with a smile.

She was in a quandary. If she refused, he would consider her a prude. That was the last thing she wanted. If she accepted, it would mean committing herself to closer physical contact than she had ever had with any man—and she was not sure she wanted that either. She had the feeling that she had been skillfully maneuvered into a position from which it might prove difficult to retreat, and just for a second she longed for the fussy, familiar presence of Frau Sturmer to protect her from having to make a decision.

The heavy silence stretched out between them while she hesitated, and he watched her with secret amusement.

"Of course, if you're scared . . ." he shrugged.

"Why should I be scared?" she said coldly. "I was only hesitating because—because I'm not sure if it's deep enough to swim here."

The Russian laughed. "Of course it is. Look, you can undress behind these rocks. I promise I won't watch."

Gallantly he turned away and waited while she struggled with buttons and hooks. "Do you need any help?" he asked at last, tiring of the delay.

A flushed, embarrassed face peeped out from behind the rocks. "It's these fasteners at the back," she explained. "I can't reach them and I can't see what I'm doing."

With an effort he overcame the temptation to rip the whole flimsy mass of material from her shoulders, and started to fiddle with the tiny hooks. Two or three resisted him so doggedly that he pulled them off, but at last the job was done and the girl, clad only in her drawers and shift, stepped gingerly into the water.

"It—it's l-l-lovely," she shuddered, clinging to a rock, submerged up to her neck. The wide green eyes in her pointed face reminded him of a startled kitten's.

"I'm coming in." The Russian stripped to his underpants and plunged into the pool head-first, then paddled over to her, pushing the wet hair out of his eyes. "Now I'll teach you to swim."

At first she was brave, and allowed him to tow her into deeper water with one hand under her chin and the other firmly supporting her midriff. But as soon as she put down a foot and found that the bottom was beyond her reach, she panicked and her arms flashed out to clutch him around the neck.

"I'm sinking! I'm drowning!" she shrieked.

"No, you're not." He took the opportunity to run his hands over the small pointed breasts still clammily swathed in folds of wet linen shift. "There—you see what a good hold I've got on you? I won't let you go: I promise. Now kick your legs about in the water. You're perfectly safe."

Gently he lowered her back into the water. She splashed about conscientiously until he slipped on a rock and fell, losing his grip on his pupil. The girl gave a strangled yelp of terror and disappeared below the surface.

She came up gasping, spluttering insults.

"You wretch, you're trying to drown me! I should never have trusted a Russian. You promised you wouldn't let go and then you dropped me into the water to sink like a stone. Take me out," she moaned, clinging to him like a limpet. "Hold me tight. Don't let me go again."

He stumbled across the wet rocks toward the shallows, carrying her in his arms. She wouldn't let go even when he laid her down on the grassy bank and stretched out beside her.

"You're safe now, cherie," he said huskily.

Shudders ran through her slim body and he held her closely, with excitement mounting in him. The fright had demolished all her defenses; he was master now and she was his for the taking. She seemed unaware that his hands had moved beneath the sodden shift, pulling it off her shoulders and peeling it down to uncover her breasts and the smooth swell of her hips. The sun struck their naked bodies and the still, sultry air enfolded them. He pulled her to him and kissed her eyes and mouth, pushing the wet, tangled hair away from her forehead, and she made no effort to resist him.

"I love you, cherie," he said softly. "Didn't you know that? How could you imagine I'd let you drown?"

She shivered, pressing closer to him. "I—I didn't really; but it was so frightening. The water was dark and cold and I couldn't see you. I couldn't breathe. It was horrible. Oh Kadya . . . do you really love me? I can't believe it."

"From the moment I first set eyes on you in the snow. You were wearing white furs and Janusz drove you in the troika with gilded runners. I was watching from the guardroom window, and I was transfixed."

"So long ago!" A blush mounted to her cheeks and she said wonderingly, "What about all those other girls—the ones you told me about. The Court ladies you taught to swim?"

"Oh, them!" He dismissed them all with a wave.

"Do you love me more than them?"

"A thousand times more," he said absently, his fingers busy with the tapes that fastened her drawers.

She laughed, her eyes crinkling like those of a satisfied cat. "Ah, Kadya, that's easy to say. How do I know it's true?"

"I'll give you a token," he vowed recklessly. The girl had already recovered from her fright and soon would realize the danger as well as the impropriety of lying naked beside a young man in the sunlight; he must seize his opportunity before it fled.

"Easing the heavy gold wolf's-head ring from his little finger, he slipped it onto the fourth finger of her right hand.

"Now you are mine and I am yours forever." He stroked her warm, smooth shoulders, aware even as he spoke that his wife's sharp eyes would soon notice the absence of the ring which had once belonged to her first husband. He'd never liked it: he'd simply pretend he'd lost it.

The girl smiled, turning her hand to and fro, making the gold flash in the sun. "Oh, thank you," she exclaimed, hugging him impulsively. "It's beautiful—I'll keep it forever and ever." She stared up at the handsome features that had so often haunted her dreams, then sighed as a shadow crossed her face. Pulling away a little, she murmured, "Kadya . . . does Colonel Solokov know how often we meet?"

His white teeth flashed in a grin. "Of course, the old fox. He knows everything that goes on in this town."

"Does he . . . does he mind?"

"Why should he? He's glad to see a little friendship between Poles and Russians for a change."

She frowned, still uneasy. "Friendship, yes. But *this* . . ." Her thoughts were running along dangerous lines and for a moment—but only for a moment—he wondered if he should tell her the truth. No. His stirring of conscience died stillborn. The present was all he cared about. Let the future look after itself.

"Don't let's think about Solokov, cherie," he murmured, kissing her eyelids. "We love each other—that's all that matters. No one— not even a general—can come between us now. You've got my ring to prove it."

"But I have nothing to give you in return."

"How about a kiss?"

"That's not much," she laughed, and wound her arms about his neck. The feel of her pliant young body against him, of her mouth seeking his, scattered the remnants of his self-control.

"You're all I want," he said huskily. "I love you—I want you now. Don't you understand what you're doing to me? You're driving me crazy . . ."

Dimly a warning sounded at the back of her brain, but she ignored it, entranced by her unexpected power over him, the new sensations aroused by his caressing hands, hypnotized by his narrowed, burning eyes that stared at her while he murmured the endearments she longed to hear. "I love you . . . You're so beautiful . . ."

It no longer astonished her that his face was only inches from hers while his strong brown hands gently stroked her breasts. Those hands that had pulled her out of the terrifying dark depths would explore every inch of her body, and she didn't even want to stop them.

"Can I go with you to Petersburg?" she whispered.

"Anywhere! Oh, cherie . . ."

The warning in her brain sounded louder now. She tried belatedly to push him away, but suddenly his hands were no longer gentle and his breathing had become loud and harsh. She realized with a shock of fear that he was actually hurting her, pinning her to the ground with his full weight, sending a tearing, stabbing pain through her vitals that made her cry out loud.

"Oh, stop it! Let me go! Kadya, you're hurting me!"

He stared down at her as if she was a stranger. Her dream was fast becoming a nightmare. She squirmed under the cruel, stabbing thrusts, but his fingers dug into her shoulders and beside his strength she knew she was powerless.

"Help me!"

The scream came faintly to Frau Sturmer's ears as she toiled up the mountain path, with fear clutching at her heart. Moments later, sobbing for breath after a final frantic scramble, she rounded the last corner and looked down into the waterfall pool. The first thing that caught her eye was her charge's frilled white dress, dropped carelessly over a rock; the second was two naked bodies sprawled gracefully, shamelessly, like sated animals in the sun beside the mountain stream. The Russian's dark head was pillowed on the green-eyed girl's breast; their limbs were closely entwined and her tumbled hair spread out like a yellow fan across the strawberry plants. There was no mistaking the significance of their attitude of utter relaxation, complete fulfillment.

Frau Sturmer groaned and covered her eyes in a helpless gesture. The worst had already happened and she was too late to prevent it!

Part One

Chapter One

POLAND
1903

"Send the priest away," whispered Tamara Galzinski in her harsh, strained voice. "I don't want a priest. I want revenge."

The little group of women gathered around her bed sighed and moaned. Old Marisya, who had nursed Tamara since the day she was born, sobbed and flung her apron over her head. She couldn't bear to watch Tamara—her sweet nursling— set out to meet her Maker with vengeance in her heart and mortal sin on her soul.

It seemed only the blink of an eye since Tamara had been a pretty, willful girl full of life and laughter, with teasing green eyes and a waist you could span with your hands. What evil magician had transformed her into this bitter, white-faced woman with nervously twitching hands and two bright patches of unhealthy color high in her cheeks? But then we are all changed, thought Marisya sadly; and it is not the blink of an eye but eleven long years since disaster struck the house of Galzinski, and our sorrows began. The only ones unchanged are those that are dead: old Prince Marek and Princess Galzinski, who dreamed of freeing Poland from the Russian yoke; and that reckless young hothead Prince Stepan, Tamara's brother, whom Marisya had loved as her own son.

Death's hand had been hovering over Tamara for ten days now, ever since that scoundrel doctor had declared that her case was hopeless and pocketed his fee. Nothing was keeping her alive except her sinful yearning for vengeance on the man who had betrayed her; and when Death gathered her in, the ancient house of Galzinski, ennobled by Casimir and Wenceslas and once the greatest landowners in Poland, would be finally extinguished.

Except for Anastasia.

Marisya dried her eyes and gazed thoughtfully at the coltish child with the mane of lint-fair hair who stood quietly by the window: Anastasia, Tamara's daughter; the only new life to come out of the whirlwind of death and destruction that had eclipsed the Galzinskis.

Anastasia was not crying for the mother who had never cared for her; on the contrary she was trying hard to suppress a definite sense of relief. It could not be long now. She felt as if the black cloud that had hovered over her all her life was slowly melting away, letting in the sun at last. Without Mama's uneasy presence, how happy this little household would be! She couldn't understand why fat, good-natured Katya Gulyas was crying so bitterly for the woman who had treated her generosity with such scorn.

Anastasia loved Katya, who was soft and cuddly and would hug and slap and laugh at and scold her all in the space of a couple of minutes; and she loved nut-brown, wrinkled old Marisya, who could sometimes be persuaded to while away winter evenings with tales of the old days in Poland, when Anastasia's own grandfather owned fifty coaches and two hundred fine horses, besides all the land between Khust and Casimirvek.

Anastasia did not love her mother at all. It was never any use trying to cajole stories from Marisya when Mama was sitting with them. Mama would look angry and tell Marisya sharply to hold her tongue if she ever mentioned the past glory of the Galzinskis. Luckily Mama was more often busy upstairs in the little office attached to the workroom, where a dozen hardworking seamstresses snipped and pinned and measured and sewed the glowing silks and satins, fine, soft lawns and pretty figured muslins to be made into dresses for Katya Gulyas' customers.

Even when the day's work was done and the sewing-machines stood on the long tables like silent shrouded ghosts, Mama would stay in her office, working at long columns of figures and allocating the tasks to be done next day, until Marisya, grumbling, climbed the steep stairs to beg her to come and eat her supper. Soon after the meal, Mama would retire to her own room, silent and aloof, while in the cosy, cheerful kitchen her daughter plagued Marisya for a bedtime story.

Two other people told her stories, and them she loved most of all. She had only to seek out old Janusz, the coachman, as he sat smoking by his small stove in the corner of the harness-room, where a single set of perfectly polished harnesses hung on the wall, and complain that she had no one to play with, and he would settle down to tell her tales of the giants and trolls who lived in the great dark forests surrounding the town of Casimirvek. If Ivan Ivanovitch, the stocky, flat-faced Tartar who had once been a Russian orderly, came to join them and rest from his unending battle against the garden weeds, he would contribute magical tales of far-off Russia, where birds and beasts spoke like men and often outwitted them, too. Vanya told her of fairy castles and enchanted lakes; of kings who built palaces entirely of diamonds and had daughters who could turn themselves into geese whenever they pleased, and Anastasia listened enthralled, her dark-lashed green eyes fixed unwinking on his weatherbeaten face.

Mama had summoned Vanya, to her room the day before yesterday; an hour later the old man had emerged shaking his head and muttering. Later on, Anastasia had caught puzzling snatches of his conversation with Marisya.

"... got my orders, I'll have to do as she wants. *She* says it's all for the best, but I'm not so sure... A long journey—six weeks at least—and the spring mud's always hard on a horse... Sometimes I wonder if she's still quite all there... Memory plays funny tricks..."

Then he had tapped his forehead in a special way and Marisya, noticing Anastasia's interest, had told her sharply to run along and play.

Now, two days later, Tamara stirred restlessly in the white-painted iron bed. "Go away, all of you," she ordered in her breathy whisper, "and take that greasy priest with you. He'll do no good by waiting here. I want to talk to my daughter alone. Come closer, Anastasia."

Reluctantly the child moved a few inches nearer to the bed, while the women shuffled out of the room, casting anxious glances over their shoulders. Tamara did not speak until the sound of their footsteps died away, then she demanded:

"What do you know of your father, Anastasia?"

"He was a brave soldier who died before I was born, fighting for his homeland against the cruel Russians." She added,

"Marisya makes me pray for his soul every night before I go to sleep."

"A brave soldier!" Tamara laughed bitterly. "Marisya told you that—yes? What would you say if *I* told you that your father is alive? That he is a Russian officer who seduced me when I was only a young girl, just a few years older than you are now? That he ruined our family and ran away to Russia before you were born. What would you say to that?"

The idea was too strange for Anastasia to take in. Her father a *Russian*? Surely Mama's mind must be wandering, she thought, remembering Vanya's significant tap at his forehead.

"Answer me!" said Tamara impatiently.

"I—shouldn't believe you, Mama," she faltered.

"You'd call me a liar? You are certainly your father's child. Listen, and I'll prove to you that what I say is true. I wanted to tell you when you were older, but I have not long to live, so there is no choice. It must be now..."

As if in a dream, Anastasia listened to the breathless voice recounting the circumstances of her birth, but her mother's story seemed to have no more relevance than one of old Janusz' fairy tales. What if her father *was* a Russian officer and not the brave dead Polish soldier for whose soul she had been taught to pray? What did it matter now? Russia was almost as far away as heaven, and the long-ago wrong he had done her mother had no power to rouse indignation in her.

She listened in silence as Tamara told of that bitter betrayal. Years of brooding had blotted from her memory all traces of her own part in the affair, and she remembered nothing of her own eagerness. The lover she now described was a monster of deceit who had taken cruel advantage of her innocence even while he used her as a bait to destroy her family's political aspirations.

When the bitter recital ended, Tamara lay back against her pillows, exhausted, and still Anastasia was silent.

"Well, have you nothing to say?"

"I—I am sorry, Mama." The child fidgeted, uncomfortable in the austere room permeated by a cloying aura of sickness, despite the wide-open window.

"Sorry?" exclaimed Tamara in disgust. Through slitted eyes she regarded her daughter with something akin to hatred. "I prayed for a son to avenge me," she said with deadly softness. "When *you* were born, I knew for certain that there is no God, and all I'd been told about Him was nothing but a pack of lies. I had to work to live—I, who had never so much as dressed myself before—and I helped that fat fool Katya Gulyas build up her business for one reason, and one reason only. I wanted to make enough money to travel to Russia and seek out Arkady Kharkov. That is your father's name and you must never forget it. Count Arkady Kharkov. When I found him, I wanted to draw him away from the safety of his wife and home and make him my slave. I could have done it, too! I could have twisted him around my little finger and made him spend every rouble he possessed for my pleasure. Then, when I had ruined him as once he ruined me, I would have killed him, and laughed as I did so. But first I needed money—lots of money." Her voice died away and she began to cough.

"Come away," hissed Marisya from the doorway. "You are tiring your mother, little one."

Anastasia wanted nothing more than to escape, but as she turned to go, Tamara's thin white hand shot out and fastened on her wrist.

"Wait!" she gasped between fits of coughing. "You haven't... yet heard what you... have to do. I am—going to die. You must kill him for me."

The child stared at her mother, terrified. She knew in that instant that her mother was mad. "I—I can't kill."

"Yes, yes... you can. You are the last of the Galzinskis. Remember that. It is your solemn duty to avenge your mother and all your family. If you refuse I shall be eternally dishonored and from my grave I shall curse you. Now swear that you will avenge me, Anastasia. Swear it!"

"Leave the child alone," begged old Marisya, but she withered under Tamara's glare.

"Swear it!"

"I don't know what to say." A growing sense of unreality had possessed Anastasia. The darkening room, the lamp smoking in the draught from the window—all seemed to shrink and fade until she was aware of nothing but the hypnotic power of her mother's burning green eyes, shining cat-like in the gloom, willing a response from her lips.

Tamara fumbled beneath her pillow, then placed something cold and hard in her daughter's hand.

"This is your father's ring, with which he swore to be true to me. Because he broke his oath, you shall swear on it to kill him. Say after me: 'I, Anastasia Arkadeivna...'"

"I, Anastasia Arkadeivna..." The high, childish voice stumbled over the strange name.

"...do swear that with my own hand I will kill my father, Count Arkady Kharkov..."

"...Count Arkady Kharkov..." The words seemed to be dragged from her, no matter how strongly her mind repudiated them.

When the oath had been spoken to her satisfaction, Tamara relaxed and lay back on her pillows. "As soon as I am dead, you must take the money I have saved and go to your father. Vanya knows where to find him, for he was once his servant. Tell him who you are, and if he tries to deny it, give him back his ring. I shall be watching over you, and should you forget your oath I shall show you no mercy, for only when Arkady Kharkov has paid for his crime shall I rest quiet in my grave. Now go, child, and remember what I have said."

It was the last time that Anastasia saw her mother alive. The will to live left Tamara as soon as she laid the legacy of vengeance upon her daughter, and two days later Katya Gulyas found Tamara kneeling by the open window, struggling vainly for breath. She died quietly that night, and as she expired the burden with which she had charged her daughter descended on Anastasia's slight, childlike shoulders.

Anastasia's nightmares dated from the night of her mother's death, and nothing Marisya said or did had the power to drive them away.

Chapter Two

RUSSIA
1902

Ivan Ivanovitch clucked and whistled to the chestnut horse as it jogged steadily along the white dust road. On either side stretched cherry orchards, heavy with fruit, as far as the eye could see, and the short grass of the Russian verge was sprinkled with vivid wildflowers.

Vanya was glad to be going home at last. In the past year or two, as his joints grew stiffer, and tending the Widow Gulyas' walled garden became more of a burden, his thoughts had turned with increasing frequency to his own little cottage on Count Kharkov's estate. He dreamed with longing of the small patch where melons and tomatoes ripened against a sunny bank while chickens scratched industriously in the dirt. He even entertained warm feelings about his tubby little wife, Natasha.

He had been away from home for twelve years now. Perhaps there were grandchildren in the mud-walled cottage; he would like to see them before he died. At the thought of death he shifted uneasily in the driving seat and a crease appeared between his slanted eyebrows. He hoped that Count Arkady would not blame him for Princess Tamara's death. Truly, he had done his best to fulfill the young master's charge, and tried to protect her and make her happy as he had ordered, but it hadn't been easy. Now she was safe in God's care, and if she wasn't happy there she was even harder to please than Vanya had supposed.

Her daughter, now, that was another matter. Vanya's frown melted away as he looked at Anastasia, who sat sideways on one shaft, her back propped against the front of the cart, swinging her long legs as her busy fingers plaited buttercups, and daisies into a necklace. She bore a strong physical resemblance to her father, and the likeness didn't end there. Just like Arkady, she knew how to laugh— though since her mother's death they'd heard less of her laughter than before—and she knew how to get her own way.

He would have liked to bring her home in grander style—in a coach pulled by four white horses, maybe, with hatboxes and good leather valises strapped on the roof, but after Princess Tamara had been given the kind of funeral that Marisya thought fitted to her birth, the money she'd saved away hadn't amounted to much.

It had bought some dry stores for their long journey; a warm hooded cloak lined with fur for Anastasia, and bedding for the nights when they'd have to sleep in the cart. Sacha, the chestnut horse, had been a parting gift from the widow Gulyas; with tears in his faded blue eyes, Janusz had harnessed him for the last time in the shining brass and leather on which he'd spent so much loving care. Sacha was getting long in the tooth now, no longer the impulsive, fiery animal he'd been in his youth, but he still put in an honest day's work, and pulled the loaded cart easily enough.

Vanya reckoned that another ten days on the road should see them home. Already he was beginning to recognize certain landmarks from his soldiering days, and he had quite lost his early fear that he would spend months wandering hopelessly in the vastness of Russia, unable to find the way home.

"Hey," he called back to Anastasia, who had dropped down from the shaft in order to replenish her supply of wildflowers, "don't get left behind. We'll stop overnight in that little wood yonder—I remember there's a stream with fish in it. And you can pick all the flowers you want while I catch our supper."

"All right," said Anastasia, scrambling aboard again. But secretly she wished with all her heart that she could be left behind. The nearer they drew to the end of their journey, the more frightened she became. Sometimes at night the memory of her vow lay so heavy on her that she woke up gasping, drenched in sweat, feeling herself near suffocation. How had it all happened? Two months ago she had been a happy, carefree child, the pet and spoiled darling of those she looked on as her family. She'd had no father then, nor felt the need of one.

Now, as swiftly as if some evil magician had waved his wand, her happy security had vanished. Like a fledgling tipped roughly from its nest, she had been driven away from those who loved her, into the bleak unknown where the sinister figure of a father she'd never seen loomed ever larger on her horizon.

Mama can't have meant me to kill him right away, thought Anastasia. She must have known that I can't—I'm not strong enough. But every time the signet ring bumped against her bony chest, she seemed to see again her mother's set white face and fanatical eyes. The thought of Mama turning restlessly in her grave during the long years it took Anastasia to grow up, or rising horridly from it to remind her of her promise, made the child's skin crawl with fear. If only none of this had happened! If only she could go back to believing herself the daughter of a brave, dead, patriotic Polish soldier once more!

"Why did you lie to me about my father?" she asked Vanya, as they sat by their fire grilling the fish he had caught. "You, and Janusz, and even Marisya lied to me, for you all knew who my father really is."

"We thought it was for the best, little one," Vanya said soothingly.

Anastasia poked the fire furiously, making it flare. "How can lies be for the best?"

"You are right to be angry, but your mother had suffered so much, we could not bear to see you suffer too. As you grew older we would have told you little by little, I swear," pleaded Vanya. "How could we know the Princess would die so young?"

"Now you must tell me about my father." There was no fear, no uncertainty, in her voice, and Vanya was happy to obey. He lit his pipe and sat late by the glowing embers, recounting all he remembered of his young master's boyhood at the Imperial Court, how he had outdanced, outskated, outridden all the other courtiers until he was chosen to be the Tsarevitch's very own companion; his reckless hunts after dangerous wolves and bears, his daring as a soldier. To Vanya, at least, Arkady Kharkov was a superman, a paragon of courtly manners and military prowess, and staring sleepily at the red embers, Anastasia was infected with his hero-worship.

Slowly the image of the wily, ruthless seducer that her mother had painted began to fade from her mind to be replaced by Vanya's portrait, but Anastasia's problem remained the same: how could she, a child, single-handedly bring down the finest swordsman in the Imperial Armies? Surely, from her perch up in heaven, Tamara must see that she'd set her daughter an impossible task?

"Yes, little rabbit, you have a father to be proud of," concluded Vanya, before rising stiffly to tuck her blankets around her in the cart and heap the fire high with logs.

From the surrounding darkness, covetous eyes watched closely as the old soldier took a last swig of vodka from his leather bottle and settled down to rest, his back against the trunk of a tree. But under the cart's canvas hood Anastasia lay sleepless for a long time, brooding on what he had told her about Arkady Kharkov in an attempt to keep nightmares at bay until the sun rose, and daylight dispeled her fears.

But it was no use: tired by the long hours of travel, her eyelids closed and at once the dream-demons pounced. She tossed and twisted in their cruel grip.

She was running down a winding path through the snowy forest, trying to reach an enchanted castle made of diamonds which sparkled in the distance, but the faster she ran the farther it receded from her. She knew she must keep running, but her legs were heavy as lead, and all the time a pack of wolves howled as they trailed her, urged on by a tall, dark-cloaked figure she knew to be her father, Arkady Kharkov, riding a huge horse and carrying a long, snaking whip. When at last she could run no farther she turned and confronted him, and saw that where his face should be there was nothing but a blank, eyeless mask. At that moment she tripped over a tree root and fell heavily.

The jolt that woke her was no dream; instantly she sensed that something was wrong. The cart she lay in was moving slowly, stealthily, its wheels creaking over the rutted ground of the clearing. And the figure on the driving seat was not Vanya but a great hulk of a man shrouded in sheepskin whom she had never seen before.

In an instant Anastasia was wide awake, throwing aside her blankets with a scream of terror.

"Vanya! Come quickly—help! He's stealing our cart!"

She tried to pluck the reins from the driver's grasp, but a hard hand instantly clamped over her mouth and nose.

"Quiet now, little lady," growled her captor. "You're coming with us. We could do with a nice girl like you to keep us warm at night. Ah! You little vixen!"

He had spoken in Russina, which she understood imperfectly, but he released her momentarily as her sharp teeth fastened on his thumb, and Anastasia drew in her breath and screamed again.

"Help, Vanya! Help!"

This time the old soldier heard her and lumbered blearily to his feet with an angry bellow. The man at the reins cursed and, abandoning any attempt at stealth, he lashed at Sacha with his heavy Cossack knout. "Giddup there!" he shouted.

Astonished by this treatment, the chestnut horse stood stock-still for an instant, then plunged forward at a mad gallop. Anastasia clung to the sides of the cart, whimpering.

The Cossack sawed at the bit, trying to steer Sacha between two birch trees, but he had been drinking and underestimated the gap. With a bone-cracking jolt, the wheels of the cart caught against the tree trunks and both traces snapped like rotten string. Sacha, freed, careered off into the night; the axle broke and the cart tipped over on one side, flinging Anastasia and the thief out in a heap. His head hit the tree with a crack, but the sheepskin coat he wore cushioned Anastasia's fall and in a second she was on her feet crying: "Vanya, where are you? Come quickly!"

Puffing and gasping, the old man ran over to the wrecked vehicle, waving his long sword. He beat savagely with the flat of it at the unconscious thief.

"Dirty Cossack—thieving scum! I'll give you a hiding you won't forget... Trying to steal my horse..."

"Don't, Vanya; you'll kill him," pleaded the child, trying to pull him away. "Oh, look out! There's one behind you!"

Vanya whirled around just in time and struck the second man a heavy blow on the arm. The intruder made a halfhearted attempt to fight back, but Vanya—despite his age— was too strong for him. Howling, with blood streaming from his wounded arm, the second thief turned and fled.

Anastasia turned back to the tree where a moment ago the stunned Cossack had lain but he, too, had melted into the shadows. The fight was over.

"We must find the horse," panted Vanya, wiping his sword on the grass and carefully replacing it in the scabbard.

"I'll do that while you rest." Anastasia was alarmed at his shortness of breath.

"No, we must stay together. Who knows how many more of

those vile animals are hiding here?" He kept one hand on Anastasia's wrist and the other on his sword as they hurried in the direction Sacha had taken.

It was dawn before they caught up with the frightened horse and managed to grab hold of the trailing reins. "Whoa, boy; stand now," soothed Vanya, examining him for cuts and scratches. "He's all right, but it's a good job he didn't wait around for those Cossacks to catch him, or we'd never have laid eyes on him again." He boosted Anastasia onto the tired horse's back, and together they trudged across the wide fields to the clearing where they'd made their ill-fated camp.

The cart was still where they'd left it, wedged between the birch trees, but all their possessions—food, clothes, and bedding—had vanished.

"Just as I expected," said Vanya bitterly. "Don't cry, little rabbit. Be thankful that we've got the horse and we're still alive. That axle's a fine old mess, but it certainly saved your life."

"Can you mend it?" she said anxiously.

"Yes. But it'll take a day or two. First I must find a safe place to stay while I work on it and that won't be easy, because the peasants around here are a scurvy lot and suspicious of strangers."

It took all their remaining money to get the cart repaired and buy food and clothes to replace what they'd lost. Vanya complained that the wheelwright who helped him was no better than a common thief, and he was further alarmed by the attention paid to Anastasia by the wheelwright's pock-marked assistant. It was all too clear that he found the child attractive, though luckily she didn't understand half he said.

"Simple, is she?" he asked with a leer.

"Certainly not. Get on with your work," snapped Vanya. "And you, child, stay close to me."

Anastasia obeyed readily; she didn't like the way the young man kept touching her, and putting his face so close to hers that his onion-laden breath nearly choked her.

Vanya groaned, considering the implications of this unforeseen complication. At the first town they came to after leaving the wheelwright's yard, he bought a large pair of scissors. To Anastasia's delight he cut off her long fair hair in a ragged crop, and dressed her in the jerkin, smock, and baggy trousers of a peasant boy.

"Oh, my head feels lovely—all light and free!" she exclaimed, capering barefoot beside the cart and shaking her short locks. "How I wish I'd been born a boy." Even the thought that her mother had so passionately wished the same could not dampen her spirits.

Vanya grinned, admiring his handiwork. It was a rough enough disguise, but he hoped it would serve to protect her from lustful roving Cossacks and others during the last stages of their journey.

It was not until their battered little equipage trotted up the Kharkovs' sweeping drive that he began to regret his brilliant stroke. Burnt brown as any peasant child, her bare legs scratched and dirty, her ragged hair bleached white-gold by the summer sun and plentifully coated with dust, Anastasia looked in no way a daughter whom the fashionable Count Kharkov would be proud to acknowledge.

At the sight of Vanya's doubtful face, the last remnants of Anastasia's self-confidence vanished.

"Don't let's stay here," she urged in a small voice, tugging at Vanya's sleeve. "It's all so grand, it scares me. Let's go away quickly."

But it was too late. The rumble of wheels on gravel had alerted the household. The front door flew open to reveal the black-clad, tightly corseted figure of Valentina Vladimirova, the housekeeper, standing at the head of a double row of peeping, giggling, white-aproned maids.

Valentina advanced onto the doorstep, staring incredulously at the gaunt horse and dusty cart whose occupants emphatically were not the travelers she was expecting.

"How dare you come to the front door, you dirty rascals?" she shrilled. "Be off with you before I call the dogs to speed you on your way!"

Stiffly Vanya rose to his full, imposing height. "Hold your tongue, Valentina Vladirmirova," he announced grandly. "You should give an old friend a better welcome than that. Don't you remember me? In the old days, you used to steal my watermelons. I am Ivan Ivanovitch, home from many long years in Poland, and this—" he laid a hand on Anastasia's dusty head, "this is the master's daughter!"

Anastasia never forgot the consternation that Vanya's words created in that sedate, well-ordered regiment of servants. The stately housekeeper was suddenly struck dumb, though her eyes bulged alarmingly. Then a tubby little woman with a scarf bound tightly about her head broke from the ranks of housemaids and ran forward, sobbing: "Vanya—my Vanya! Oh, I can't believe it. Is it *really* you?"

The next moment the cart was surrounded by a laughing, jostling crowd, helping them out and swinging up their baggage, unharnessing Sacha and leading him away to the stables, hugging Vanya and thumping him on the back; and all the time staring at her so that she wished she could hide by sinking into the earth. They jabbered away so fast that her rudimentary Russian was quite inadequate to follow what they were saying. Vanya grinned, preened himself and answered their questions as best he could.

Was that funny little creature really the Count's daughter, they asked. Yes, but the Count had never seen her. The Count didn't know she existed. But when her mother died, far away in Poland, what else could Vanya do but bring her home?

The servants nodded wisely, understanding his point of view.

But, they wondered, would the Countess regard an illegitimate daughter in the same way that they did? Vanya shrugged; he'd cross that bridge when he came to it. He'd done his duty as far as he could, now it was up to others to assume responsibility for the motherless child. Perhaps, he admitted cautiously, he should not have brought the secret of Anastasia's parentage into the open quite so soon, but when Valentina Vladimirova tried to drive him away like a common thief, he'd been so angry that he'd said the first words that came into his head. They happened to be the truth, of course; but now it might be a good thing if the servants were to forget what he'd said in the heat of the moment. It would be common knowledge soon enough, he was sure.

The servants nodded and promised to forget—for the moment. They stared even harder at Anastasia, promising themselves a splendid gossip that evening. They'd have the full story out of Vanya before nightfall, never fear! So that odd-looking scrap was the Count's daughter! She looked as if she could do with a bath and a meal, poor mite, suggested the housekeeper, eager to atone for her earlier mistake. The household was holding itself in readiness for the master's arrival, she explained. He was coming and bringing friends with him, but as usual he hadn't told them whether he would arrive today or tomorrow, so of course when they heard the cart drive up . . .

"Of course," said Vanya, smiling forgiveness at her. "After all, you'd have needed an angel from heaven to tell you that I was coming home today after twelve long years! Ah, but it's good to be back. Everything's just the way I remember."

Over an enormous meal in the housekeeper's room, they told him the family news. The old Count had died and now Kadya was Count Kharkov. He and the Countess, Olga Feodorovna, had two boys now as well as Valerian Radek, her son by her first marriage.

"And daughters?" inquired Vanya, with a touch of anxiety.

No daughters, they reassured him. The Countess often said she longed for a daughter, but she'd been so ill after the birth of little Petroushka, the younger boy, that the doctor had advised her to have no more children.

The Count and Countess slept in separate rooms, murmured the housekeeper—after a quick glance to see that the youngest housemaids could not hear her, and they led widely different lives. The Countess was a model of piety, kept a strict accounting of the souls of her servants, and strongly disapproved of her husband's gambling and drinking. It was rumored that he kept a ballerina from the Imperial Ballet in a pretty little house by the Pavlovsk Palace, but of course, living here in the country, hundreds of miles from Petersburg, none of them could be certain if this was more than a rumor. When the Count came home to Kharkov, his behavior toward his wife was always impeccable. They were expecting the arrival of the Countess and the two little boys sometime during the next few days.

Vanya relaxed and let out his belt, nodding and smiling. He was confident that his adored Anastasia would quickly win the austere heart of Olga Feodorovna, and that the Countess could soon be persuaded to overlook any irregularity in the circumstances of her birth.

The scrunch of hoofs on the gravel outside put a sudden end to the convivial party in the housekeeper's room. Pushing their chairs back hurriedly, and leaving their meal half eaten on the table, the servants ran outside to greet their master and his guests. Anastasia was left dozing in a curiously carved little rocking chair which stood in a shadowed alcove beside the roaring fire. The clock ticked loudly in the suddenly deserted room.

In the distance she heard shouting and bustle. Doors banged, hoofs clattered over cobbles, Valentina Vladimirova's voice issued shrill commands to her army of maids, but the excitement meant little to Anastasia. She was warm, well fed, and clean for the first time in months, and so sleepy that even the thought that the dreaded meeting with her father might be at hand had no power to rouse her. In a trance of comfort, she gazed into the firelit shadows and waited for Vanya to return.

Suddenly, the door burst open and a strange man stood on the threshold. Anastasia caught her breath and shrank further back into her chair, her heart thudding like a frightened rabbit's. Her father must have come to find her at once, and now there was no Vanya at hand to support her and give her confidence. All the Russian words she knew had vanished at once, and her mouth felt dry with fright. She shut her eyes tightly, hoping against hope that the man in the doorway would not notice her in the shadowed alcove beside the fire.

But he did, and crossed the room in two long strides. "What are *you* doing in my chair, boy?" he asked.

It was the last question she'd expected. Cautiously, Anastasia opened her eyes. Then her mouth fell slowly open as she stared at the newcomer. She thought he was the most handsome man she had ever seen. From his dark, silky hair to his gleaming boots, everything about him seemed to shine: his tunic, with its rows of buttons and gold braid, his sword-belt, the silver-mounted pistols thrust into his sash, the twinkling spurs; but brighter than any of these were the brown eyes that gazed down at her, alert and vividly alive, expecting an answer. His magnificence almost stunned her, but she realized with a surge of pure relief that this man could not possibly be her father: he was much too young.

"Well, boy?" he repeated, with a touch of impatience.

Anastasia continued to stare silently at the stranger, taking in every detail of his appearance. He was eighteen or nineteen, she guessed, tall and slender as a whiplash but with an air of strength and confidence—pride, even—that belonged more naturally to an older man. His black hair curled forward onto high cheekbones, and his face seemed to be all fine, slanting lines, with eyebrows that winged upward away from the straight, high-bridged nose with its flaring nostrils, and a long, well-modeled mouth whose lower lip curved upward. His complexion was pale, which gave even greater definition to his brows and bright-brown slanting eyes. Pale, too, was the strong long-fingered hand which he now laid on Anastasia's shoulder.

"Don't look so scared, little fellow," he said gently. "I'm not going to eat you. I was only curious to know who you are, and why you've chosen to sit in my old rocking-chair. My father had it made for me when I was even younger than you are. He had my name carved on it—look..."

He took her hand and carefully traced the graceful Cyrillic letters: Валерьян Радек. "Valerian," he said, smiling. "That's my name: Valerian Vassilievitch Radek. What's yours?"

Forgetting her peasant boy's garb, Anastasia stood up and curtsied carefully, bobbing her head and bending her knees as Marisya had taught her to do.

"I am Anastasia Arkadeivna Kharkova," she said slowly in her clear, high voice. "You see, I am not a boy at all. Vanya brought me here after my mother died far away in Poland. I am sorry I didn't ask before I sat in your chair, but I think..." a sudden mischievous gleam lit up her green eyes—"I think that you are much too big for it now, Valerian Vassilievitch."

Valerian was so taken aback by this speech that for a moment he couldn't think of a suitable reply. Anastasia, the daughter of Kadya—it couldn't be true! He looked more closely at the dignified little figure standing so stiffly before him, and his eyes fastened on the heavy gold signet ring that swung on a ribbon around her thin neck. Noticing his stare, the child's hand closed protectively over the metal.

"What's that ring you're wearing?" he said. "Let me look at it."

Gently he prized her fingers away and examined the ring with its deeply engraved crest. His eyebrows drew together, and when he spoke his voice was suddenly harsh.

"Where did you steal this, you thieving Pole?" he demanded.

Anastasia gasped and stepped back, jerking the ring from his grasp. "I didn't steal it!" she said hotly. "It was my mother's. She told me to take it to my father, to prove... to prove..." She choked on the thought.

"Your father gave it to your mother—is that right?"

Crimson-faced, she nodded.

Suddenly Valerian flung back his head and laughed. She watched him uncertainly, baffled by his swift changes of mood. He put his arm around her thin shoulders and hugged her to him. "My apologies, Anastasia Arkadeivna!" he said gaily. "I've always wanted to know what happened to that ring; I never dreamed it would come back to me by such a roundabout route! It's mine, you see. My mother was foolish enough to entrust it to my stepfather for safekeeping, in the early days of their marriage, before she realized what sort of a man he was. He told her that he'd lost it in Poland. Well, I suppose that was true, up to a point. He must have given it to your mother, no doubt with a promise of eternal fidelity, and she— poor soul—sent it back with you."

"You mean, it wasn't his to give?" She struggled to absorb this puzzling information.

"Certainly not. It's the Radek wolf. Your father has no more right to it than you have. I'll take it back now, if I may."

He held out his hand, but Anastasia backed away, her eyes enormous in her pale face. "N—no," she stammered. "I can't —it's all I've got . . . to prove I'm his daughter. Mama said . . ."

"Doesn't your father know you're here yet?" asked Valerian curiously.

The child said bleakly, "He doesn't even know I exist. Vanya says he'll be pleased to see me, but I think he may be very angry."

Valerian was inclined to agree with her. He knew his stepfather's sudden, alarming rages when things didn't go as he pleased. All the same, he thought with an inward laugh, it would be amusing to tease him a little . . . to hold this delicious scandal over his head and see him twist himself into knots . . .

Peremptorily, he said, "Give me the ring. I'll see that your father isn't angry with you. I know exactly what to say to him. Leave it all to me."

Anastasia gazed adoringly at this young god who was clearly as kind as he was magnificent. She said hesitantly, "If I give you the ring, will you look after me?"

"Of course I will," he said impatiently, holding out his hand again. He took the ring and dropped it into a pocket. "I mean, I'll see that my mother takes care of you," he amended. "I myself am a soldier, you see. I don't come here except when I'm on leave. But my mother's a good woman—sometimes I think she's almost a saint. She loves children, and she'll look after you."

Anastasia had a daunting vision of a woman wearing a gold halo, hands folded and eyes turned up to heaven. She seemed a dull substitute for this superb soldier. Doubtfully, Anastasia said, "Your mother is the Countess, Olga Feodorovna? Do you think she will love the child of another woman?"

"When she hears your story, she won't be able to help loving you," said Valerian, with a confidence he was far from feeling. It was true that Olga Feodorovna had often expressed a wish for a daughter, but to find her wish translated into such an unexpected and solid reality might prove more than her Christian charity would welcome. Well, thought Valerian, we must hope for the best. It's Kadya's problem, after all, and Kadya must find a solution. Unfortunately, Kadya had an astonishing ability to side-step responsibility, leaving it to be shouldered by others. His stepson firmly resolved to interfere in this particular problem only if it became apparent that the child would suffer if he didn't.

Thinking of a way to express her gratitude, Anastasia led him toward the long table. "I'm sure you are hungry after your journey," she said, in a fair imitation of the widow Gulyas offering refreshment to her more important clients. "Won't you eat something? The pelmeni are excellent."

Valerian was unused to eating leftovers from the servants' table. Good-naturedly, however, he picked up a handful of pelmeni. "Thank you, but that's enough," he said, as she offered more. "I shall dine later. I came here looking for Natasha, my old nurse. She always wants to hear the news from Petersburg . . . Ah, here's Vanya."

The old soldier's look of consternation at finding the two of them together was almost comical.

"So you have found her! Please say nothing to the master until I can speak to him," Vanya begged. "It is too difficult now—he's busy with his friends. He hasn't time to talk to old Vanya."

Valerian could imagine the scene so well: the tall figure of his stepfather, resplendent in his long, dark-red tight-fitting coat, a black felt *burka* slung from one shoulder, his fur hat adding six inches to his height, swaggering through the press of servants, laughing loudly, shouting also to his friends, patting a head here or asking a question there, but never listening to the answers. Valerian sensed the old man's hurt and patted him on the shoulder.

"Later he will have more time," he agreed. "You must speak to him privately, Vanya, for the news that you have brought his daughter home will be a shock to him. I will see that he calls you in after he has eaten."

Vanya shook his shaggy head slowly from side to side. "You

think it will be a shock? Did I do wrong to bring the little one home? Should we have stayed in Poland to starve?"

Anastasia glanced sharply from one man to the other, trying to understand. It was her own future they were discussing, and she could see that Vanya was scared of her father—as scared, perhaps, as she herself was. She was appalled to find that Vanya, who had always seemed a tower of strength and confidence, could also look worried and helpless. Had they been wrong to come? With a sudden rush of homesickness, she longed to be back in the dark old house on Varsovie Avenue, warm and safe, curled up in Marisya's ample lap. Everything here was so strange and unfriendly, and she was oh, so tired. Her lip trembled. She was on the verge of tears, and Valerian noticed at once.

"Put the little one to bed now, Vanya," he said. "In the morning we can decide what's to be done. Don't worry. I'll make certain that the master listens to your story."

It was late that night before Kadya summoned Vanya to him. The old servant found his master in the library, standing before a blazing fire, for the June night was chilly.

"So you have come home at last, old friend," said Kadya genially, but there was a hint of wariness in his eyes. "Did you tire of drinking slivovitz after all? Tell me, what of Princess Tamara? Is she well?" The Count hesitated and then added abruptly, "Has she married?"

"No, master."

"They why have you left her? Didn't I tell you to stay and look after her welfare?"

"She is dead, master. She died two months ago, in the spring. It was God's will," said Vanya, as if to disclaim responsibility for the tragedy.

"I understand." Kadya bowed his head, not wishing Vanya to see the relief that flowed through him at this news. So she was dead—lovely, green-eyed Tamara, his wild Polish mistress. Yes, he had loved her, but from this distance he could see how wise Colonel Solokov had been to separate them. In the intervening years Kadya's career had prospered and so had his estates, thanks to his wife's money and her influence with the young Tsarina, whose rigid principles and unswerving devotion to God, family, and duty coincided so exactly with Olga Feodorovna's. Kadya knew well that the Tsarina disapproved of him, but he realized shrewdly that so long as she remained intimate friends with his wife, his future was assured. The revival of the affair with his lovely, willful Polish beauty, delightful though it might have been initially, could easily have jeopardized his career, because the Tsar—on whom all promotions depended—was completely under the thumb of his wife . . . All in all, it was probably for the best that any dreams of seeing Tamara again must now be banished.

"You did right to come home, old friend," Kadya said solemnly. "I am glad to see you and so is your wife, I'm sure. It is sad to hear of the Princess' death, but you have done your duty as a soldier should and you shall be rewarded."

"Thank you, *barin*," said Vanya, looking stolidly in front of him, though his heart was quaking at what he must next announce. "I knew it was also my duty to bring your daughter home to you."

Kadya, who turned back to the fire anticipating the interview's end, swung violently around to face his servant. His cheeks were ashen. *"My daughter?"*

"Yes, master. She has no other home."

"Don't talk rubbish, man," snapped Kadya. "I have no daughter. How can you talk about my daughter when you know perfectly well I haven't one?"

Vanya said with dignity, "Anastasia is truly your daughter. You have only to look at her to know it. How she was begotten, you know better than I. But I remember a warm spring day when Frau Sturmer slept and you went to pick strawberries with Princess Tamara. Janusz and I both said that it was early for strawberries . . ."

"Hold your tongue, insolent serf!" shouted Kadya in a rage. "Have you forgotten how it feels to have the knout sting your fat back? I can soon refresh your memory."

Vanya refused to be cowed. "Say what you like, master: you cannot deny that Anastasia is your daughter, for she wears the ring you gave her mother. With her dying breath, Princess Tamara made me swear to bring the child to you."

Kadya drew in his breath with a hiss. His eyes were suddenly as cold as chips of solid black ice. "Very well, Vanya," he said softly, "you've fulfilled your promise to Princess Tamara. Now you can take *my daughter* away again."

"You can't turn the child away without even seeing her! She

has nowhere else to go. The Countess..." Vanya was frantic with worry.

"I forbid you to trouble the Countess. Before she arrives here, both you and the child must be gone." Kadya thought rapidly. "I shall arrange for the girl to be brought up in the home of some decent peasant and his wife—perhaps on my Crimean estate. You shall drive her there and then forget all about her."

"She knows who she is—she wears your ring around her neck. You can't send her away like a stray dog. She's your daughter."

"You're quite right, Vanya. I hadn't thought of that. She mustn't go away wearing my ring," agreed Kadya. "Where is the child? Perhaps I should take one look at her after all."

"She is asleep."

"All the better. Take me to her at once."

If Vanya hoped that the sight of the sleeping child would soften his master's heart, he was doomed to bitter disappointment. Kadya looked down at the lamplit face of his daughter without showing a flicker of emotion, then reached out a casual hand toward the ribbon she still wore around her neck.

There was no ring attached to it. Eyebrows raised, Kadya turned to Vanya, and as he did so his hand brushed against the child's skin. Instantly Anastasia's eyes were open.

For a long moment father and daughter stared at each other. Then Arkady stepped back as though a snake had struck him. He was more shaken than he could admit to himself to see Tamara's long, sea-green eyes set in a face so unmistakably his own. He made no further attempt to find the ring, but stalked swiftly from the room. An onrush of poignance made him determined to drown his memories in vodka.

With narrowed eyes, Vanya watched him go. A few moments later the servant was tapping gently at the door of Valerian's bedroom.

Chapter Three

"I met a lovely girl last night," said Valerian, breezing into the dining room, fresh and glowing from an early gallop. He flung himself into a chair opposite his stepfather,who was pecking listlessly at some food. Flecks of gray showed more clearly in Kadya's dark hair where the strong sunlight struck it, and beneath his eyes the skin was unhealthily pouched. He grunted noncommitally without looking up.

"She was a real charmer, little father—not one of the local girls, either..."

"Don't call me little father, you impertinent cub," growled Kadya, who had spent a miserable night wrestling with memories of Tamara wreathed in mists of vodka. "And kindly keep the details of your amorous conquests to yourself, at least until my stomach feels a little stronger. Where are Boris and Grigori?"

"Riding in the forest, as you should be doing. It's a splendid tonic for the liver, if you've had a heavy night of drinking," said the irrepressible Valerian. "I went out with them—not because I'd been drinking, of course, but I felt like some exercise. But I took a shortcut home, because I wanted a word in private with you, Kadya."

"*Not* Kadya either, damn you. Why can't you show a little respect for your elders... and betters?"

"I show respect to those I feel respect for," Valerian grinned, and ducked the bread roll his stepfather aimed at him. "As I was saying, I want a few quiet words with you, so I came back early."

"All right, all right. Get on with it then and leave me alone," groaned Kadya. "This happens every year: I come down here for some peace and quiet after working like a dog in Petersburg, and what do I get but nag, nag, nag, from one person after another! Why can't you deal with your own problems instead of running to me with every little difficulty you encounter? Well, out with it. What do you want this time?"

Valerian was enjoying himself. He pretended to hesitate, then said with carefully feigned diffidence, "It's about this young lady, you see. I hardly know how to begin. . . ."

"Oho," said Kadya, looking up sharply. "You want to get married, do you? I don't advise it, old boy, not at your age. You know the saying: 'Marry in haste, repent at leisure'? It's all too true, believe me. I'm not saying a word against your . . . uh, mind—she's a wonderful woman, as we both know, but I do sometimes feel that if I hadn't been pushed into an arranged marriage with your mother at the age of eighteen, I might have been a happier man."

"Of course. You'd also have been a much poorer one," Valerian pointed out.

"Oh—money!" said Kadya, with a fine show of disdain. "Never fall into the trap of believing that money can buy happiness, my boy. Still . . . it has its uses. You want to marry an heiress, then, do you? Shall I hazard a guess: Ekaterina Sonneberg, eh? Not a bad choice, I'd say. You could do worse, far worse."

"Of course, it's fascinating for me to hear your innermost thoughts about marriage," said Valerian politely, "but I may be misleading you. *I'm* not proposing to marry anyone just yet."

Kadya was disconcerted. "What about this young lady, then?"

"That's the point I'm trying to make. This girl is a *very* young lady—far too young to marry, although I'm sure she'll be a beauty one day, and possibly rich as well. But at the moment she's only a child. I met her purely by chance in the housekeeper's room last night, and she told me that her name is Anastasia Arka . . . Is anything wrong?"

Kadya had choked on a mouthful of cucumber in yogurt. Solicitously, his stepson thumped him on the back. When he had recovered enough to speak, he said savagely, "I'll see Vanya dance in hell for telling you that. And you will dance too, Valerian, if a single whisper about that child's existence ever reaches your mother's ears."

"Old Vanya had nothing to do with it," said Valerian quickly. "As I said, it was purely accidental that I met the child. And isn't telling my mother the best possible thing you can do?"

"Of course not. The child is deranged. She's got nothing to do with me or any of the Kharkov family. It's a great pity that Vanya was foolish enough to listen to her story and bring her here to trouble us. I'm sending her away tomorrow to my estate at Chertovitze, where she'll be properly cared for. And I'd be obliged if you'd forget that you ever met her."

Valerian laughed. "You're the rottenest liar I know, little father. That child is the image of you—how can you deny that she's yours? Now listen to me: you'd much better tell my mother the truth. You can't send your daughter away to live in some peasant's cottage and pretend she doesn't exist. I know your reputation for ducking your responsibilities, but that's downright barbaric and I won't stand for it."

"*You* won't stand for it!" Kadya flushed a dull red. "What the devil makes it any of your business?"

"It's my business because I choose to make it my business," said Valerian imperturbably. "That child isn't going to be deprived of her rights merely because you're afraid to face my mother with the true story of how she entered the world."

Kadya stared at his stepson's implacable face, heard the determination in his voice, and decided to compromise. Even he could see that his chances of concealing Anastasia's existence were becoming increasingly remote, as each new person was admitted to the secret, but he still shied away from a direct confrontation with his wife. "All right," he agreed, "but I'm not going to tell her now. I'll let the truth out gradually—it'll be less of a shock that way."

"Why not do it at once? The servants know who the girl is; they saw her arrive yesterday with Vanya. My valet tells me they're talking of nothing else. You can't put locks on the tongues of fifty servants."

Kadya swore. No matter how he tried to avoid it, the trap seemed to be closing. He gazed in near desperation at his arrogant stepson, only a dozen years younger than he was but with twice the intelligence and ten times the will power. Their personalities had clashed as soon as Kadya had tried to take the place of old Vassily Radek, the father Valerian remembered with such pride. Ever since, he seemed to take pleasure in showing up his stepfather as a fool. Trust Valerian to place him in this intolerable position, he thought. If the wretched boy hadn't gone into the housekeeper's room—where he had absolutely no business to be, Anastasia would be gone by now and no one but Vanya any the wiser.

"How can I tell your mother now?" Kadya said. "I've always been so careful . . . She still believes I've always been faithful . . ."

Rubbish, thought Valerian, but he loved his mother too much to say it aloud. Instead he suggested: "Then why not let me do it for you?"

There was a long pause while Kadya considered this escape route.

His wife adored her eldest son. Therefore, Kadya reasoned, she would be predisposed to believe whatever he told her. If Valerian were to soften the facts a little . . . and present Anastasia as the daughter of a Polish princess who had been an old friend of Kadya's . . . an orphan, say . . . Yes, that sounded good. The mere fact that the story came form Valerian improved its chances for acceptance, whatever she decided to believe. For there was still one major problem: Anastasia's face. Nothing could disguise the girl's disturbing resemblance to her father.

Kadya groaned. "She will never forgive me."

Oh yes, she will, thought Valerian. She'll always forgive you, just as she deliberately blinds herself to your faults and infidelities and tries so hard to believe that you love her fully as much as she loves you. Look at you! Any other man so debauched would resemble a ruin, but not my stepfather. Valerian wondered sometimes if Kadya had sold his soul to the devil in return for perpetual youth. Certainly his fairy godmother had blessed him with looks no excesses could mar. Even after a sleepless night and half a gallon of vodka, Kadya merely appeared pale and interesting, whereas another man would be half dead. Poor Mama loves you for your handsome face, Valerian had often silently informed his stepparent; it can't be for any other reason.

Aloud he said briskly: "We haven't much time. If you want me to help you, you'll have to make up your mind. Soon Boris and Grigori will come in from their ride."

Kadya raised two despairing eyes. "Yes, please help me," he said with a humility that his stepson found repulsive. "But can't you, somehow, make her believe that it wasn't my fault? . . . Tell her I was betrayed . . . misled . . . whatever . . ." His voice trailed away.

"Go away on a hunting trip for a few days, Kadya, and leave Mama to me. *I'm* not afraid of her."

No, because she's always spoiled you rotten, thought Arkady viciously, but he had the good sense to hold his tongue.

"I'll be obliged to tell her privately that the girl's your daughter, of course," continued Valerian, delighted by his stepfather's embarrassment. "But don't worry. I'll put you on the side of the angels. More sinned against than sinning. I'll say that her poor, innocent husband was seduced by a ruthless Polish adventuress when he was no more than a callow boy, pining for his homeland. I'll beg her to forgive you. I'll explain that you're much too ashamed to face her yourself. I'll say . . ."

"You'll make me sound like a fool," said Kadya.

Valerian grinned. "I can't help telling the truth, little father. You'll have to put up with a few trifling blows to your self-esteem. Anyway, that's my offer. Take it or leave it." Ostentatiously, he turned his attention to the morning mail, ignoring Kadya's furious glares.

There was a testy silence. Valerian was on the point of leaving the room when his stepfather finally spoke.

"All right," he muttered. "But don't expect to be thanked, you interfering son of—"

"'Of your beloved wife,' were you going to say?" inquired Valerian gently, getting to his feet with menacing speed as the dining room door was shoved open.

"Ah, here are Boris and Grigori at last," exclaimed Valerian, relaxing his stance. "Let's tell them about the lovely hunting party you're planning for them, little father."

As his friends stamped boisterously into the room with dusty boots and jingling spurs, Kadya's smile resembled a snarl. But he knew he had no choice. With a marked lack of enthusiasm, he began to outline the proposed expedition to the two cavalry officers.

Although she tried very hard, like her friend the Tsarina, to put aside personal vanity and concentrate on higher things, Olga Feodorovna could not help being aware that spectacles were especially unbecoming to her long sallow face, with its high forehead and narrow jaw. Without them, she could at times look aristocratic, even noble; with them she looked like a horse with blinkers. Her large dark eyes were her best feature, and if she obscured them with steel or even gold-rimmed spectacles, she hid her one claim to passable looks and became, in her own hypercritical estimation, downright ugly.

But now, peering short-sightedly at the thin little waif whose nut-brown complexion consorted oddly with the frilly white dress and sunbonnet she wore, the Countess earnestly wished that her spectacles were not lying hidden at the bottom of her dressing-case. She would have liked a clearer view.

So that's one of Kadya's bastards, she thought. I've often wondered what that handsome face of his would look like on a girl. Poor little creature: she's scared to death of me, and no wonder. I suppose I should thank the good Lord that she didn't bring her mother as well. I don't think I could have managed that. How she stares at Valerian!

She tried to concentrate on the details of the complicated story that the tall dark son, who had towered over her since his fourteenth birthday, was telling her with, his brow earnestly furrowed. What a pack of lies the naughty boy has invented, she thought in wry amusement. Does he really expect me to believe a tale so fraught with coincidence and peppered with Polish names, so extravagantly unlikely? Why, anyway, was *he* the one chosen to spin me this ridiculous yarn? Why should Valerian, of all people, be covering up for my foolish Adonis of a husband?

It was one of Olga Feodorovna's great secret sorrows that her husband and eldest son were not better friends. When she married Kadya, only a year after the death of her first husband, she had dismissed Valerian's resentment as mere childish pique. But when this attitude persisted into Valerian's teens and worsened with each passing year, the Countess could barely hide her concern.

Valerian was old for his years and self-assured. Whereas Kadya, at heart, was a little boy who had never grown up. The gap between them was too enormous to bridge; they would never, she knew, be friends, only rivals. And Olga Feodorovna, who loved them both, had to use all her wiles to prevent their mutual jealousy from erupting into open warfare.

Now here, amazingly, was Valerian endeavoring to conceal a serious—and obvious—misdemeanor of Kadya's. Had they finally reached a truce and agreed to pull together instead of in opposite directions, whatever their feelings? With all her heart she hoped so. Whatever had forged this unlikely coalition, and however tiresome its raison d'être, from her point of view, Olga felt that she must not allow her own feelings of outrage to spoil this first delicate blossom of peace between the two most important men in her life. She must banish her pride, and summon up her Christian charity... Besides, it might even prove amusing. She was tired of sons; they grew up too quickly and became so rough and rebellious. She might be able to enjoy a ready-made daughter, whom she could dress in pretty clothes and have at her beck and call—especially if the daughter arrived minus the painful chore of childbirth. Her funny little Andrei, now staring at the Polish girl as if he'd like to kill her, did his best to take a daughter's place, but he couldn't do so much longer. He was growing up; soon his voice would change and he'd be nothing but a man like the rest of them.

Sometimes she'd thought that Andrei really believed himself a girl. It couldn't be merely to amuse her that he was always hanging about her bedroom when the other boys were out at play, begging to be allowed to wear her jewels or strut ridiculously in her high-heeled slippers. He loved to put a few stitches into her latest embroidery, or sing duets with her in his high, pure boy's soprano.

Of course, his nurse must often have told him how his mother had received the news that her second child was also a boy.

"Take him away!" she had cried out. "I don't want another son. I wanted a daughter this time. I've made everything ready for a dear little girl, and that's what I'm going to have."

So Andrei had spent his babyhood in a cradle lined with pink silk. Until he was over five years old, he wore frilly white dresses threaded with pink ribbons. Much to his own distress, these were replaced with sailor suits at his father's insistence.

But although this marked one of the rare occasions when the Countess gave in to her husband, she continued to treat Andrei more like a girl than a boy, encouraging him to wear fancy clothes and listening solemnly to his advice on fashions and hair styles. He was a clever child, and possessive about his mother.

Now, as he watched her inspect the odd little waif whom Valerian was trying to foist on the family, Andrei felt the first chill breath of a threat to his own position in his mother's affections.

Concealed by her wide skirts from all but Anastasia's gaze, he deliberately stuck out his tongue. The Countess turned from her painful examination of the little girl in the sunbonnet and smiled at Valerian, who had run out of explanations and was anxiously awaiting her reaction.

"What a sad life she has had, poor child," said Olga, in her high, misleadingly vague drawl. "We must somehow make her happier here. You say she has traveled all the way from Poland because her mother died last spring? Whatever became of her father, then?"

"No one knows," said Valerian with a quelling glance at Anastasia. She had been severely instructed to say nothing unless he addressed her directly. To smile, to curtsy, to kiss the nice lady's hand, but not to speak. The servants, too, had entered readily into the conspiracy: they were used to concealing their master's peccadillos, as well as their own, from his capricious, autocratic wife.

"So you believe there is no danger that her father will return and claim the child?"

"None whatsoever, Mama."

"How can you be so certain?"

Valerian threw an anguished glance at Vanya, who stepped forward and declared in his placid, respectful voice: "He was a soldier, *barina*, who went off to fight many years ago and did not return to his family. I do not think he will come back now to look for his daughter."

They're all in on it, thought the Countess—all except the one person directly involved. How typical of Kadya. Having persuaded others to take up his child's cause, he vanishes on a hunting party, leaving his accomplices to carry on as best they can! Nevertheless, she was determined to cement the miraculous new relations between Kadya and Valerian.

"Will you... *can*... you care for her, Mama?" asked Valerian. "She is now all alone in the world."

An imp of mischief prompted the Countess to tease. "Of course. Willingly—if only I could be certain that your stepfather would approve of my accepting such a responsibility. He is the head of the household, after all. I really should consult him before agreeing to adopt the child. What a pity he isn't here! When will he return?"

"Tomorrow, Mama. He... he told me before he left that he

was perfectly agreeable to the adoption if it would not put too great a burden on you," Valerian assured her. Beads of sweat had appeared on his forehead and Olga wondered again why he cared so much. For one dreadful moment, before the resemblance to Kadya reassured her, the Countess had wondered if the child could possibly be Valerian's. Even allowing for the precocity of the males in the Radek family, however, she realized that Valerian could hardly have begotten a child at the tender age of eight. It was time she stopped tormenting the poor boy and let him know she was willing to play the new part.

"I'm delighted that you and Kadya discussed the matter and came to such a sensible conclusion," she said, looking him straight in the eye. "So much can be achieved if all the parties concerned act *responsibly* together, instead of squabbling over trifles."

Valerian looked at the ground.

The Countess smiled. "Of course I'll adopt the child. I've always wanted a daughter, haven't I, Andrei? Now you will be able to ride and shoot and play with the other boys, and forget all about your poor mother."

Andrei's scowl deepened and he scuffed at the floor with one foot, but Valerian's face lit up with sudden relief and he bent impulsively to kiss his mother's cheek.

"Dearest Mama, now I am convinced that you are a saint! I'm sure you'll never regret your decision, and that Anastasia will be the best daughter a mother could ever wish for." He turned to the child, and spoke slowly and clearly:

"You are going to live with this kind lady, Anastasia, and be her daughter. Now come over here and kiss her hand."

Anastasia moved forward obediently, but the Countess noticed with a small, unpleasant shock that even as she knelt to kiss the hand of her benefactress, the child's striking sea-green eyes were still fixed in worship on Valerian's dark and mobile face.

It wasn't until a week later, when the train bound for Petersburg carried Valerian away to join his regiment, that the full sense of her isolation reached Anastasia. Bewildered by her sudden change in status from a peasant child, who ate and conversed on equal terms with old Vanya, to an aristocratic young lady-in-the-making, she felt herself totally lost, stripped of her old identity and unable to fit into the one newly thrust upon her.

Valerian had been her emissary between the two worlds. While he was there to protect her from the jealousy of her new stepbrothers, and the thousand and one blunders she made daily in her speech, manners, and deportment—which Andrei, in particular, was delighted to exploit, Anastasia felt she had a chance of learning to overcome them. Both boys admired their soldier stepbrother, and ceased their baiting when so ordered by him.

Anastasia was equally anxious to please her benefactress, but the stiff, haughty manner in which the Countess customarily addressed her failed to inspire confidence in the newly adopted daughter. Valerian always knew how to bring a smile to his mother's face, or persuade her that it was better for the children to ride in the forest on their ponies, or swim among the shy waterbirds in the turquoise waters of the lake, than to spend every sunny morning at their books.

While Valerian was on leave, the rambling old house seemed full of sunlight and laughter. Dashing young men in striped suits and pretty girls with parasols and long white dresses drove up from neighboring houses to visit. They played tennis on the newly mown court, bribing the children with sweets to search for lost balls in the damp gloom of the shrubbery. As night fell, they called in Nikolai the goatherd to scrape away at his fiddle as they danced on the verandah.

Anastasia would lean out of her little window under the eaves to watch the glowing tips of the men's cigars and the pale, ghostly shadows of the long white dresses swaying to the music, or leaning on the balustrade talking the night away. She longed to be grown-up, to be rid of Andrei's sly taunts and pinches beneath the schoolroom table. If only she could skip the intervening years of childhood and be instantly transformed into a young woman like those below her window, laughing and flirting and waving graceful fans, able to gaze into Valerian's eyes as they revolved slowly on the moonlit verandah together. Valerian... always Valerian! The sight of his arms around another woman's waist sent such a pang of anguished jealousy through Anastasia that she became physically sick. He was her hero, her partner, her anchor in an uncertain world, and she loved him with all the strength of her passionate nature. She knew, of course, that her devotion meant no more to him than the wagging tail of his favorite dog. Everyone loved Valerian: he seemed to attract affection from every person he met—except his stepfather. Never mind, thought Anastasia, when she turned at last from the window. One day I'll grow up and then I'll show him how much I love him . . .

With Valerian's departure a different—and far less agreeable—atmosphere descended on the Kharkov dacha. The Countess had been profoundly shocked to discover that Anastasia could neither read nor write. Something of a bluestocking herself, she believed passionately in the education of women, and decided that this vacuum in her adopted daughter's upbringing must be remedied without delay. Accordingly, she interviewed and engaged Nadya Tereshkova, a thick-set young woman with burning eyes and severely combed dark hair swept back in a bun, to teach Anastasia the rudiments of learning. When the family returned to Petersburg in the autumn, she thought, Anastasia could have music and language masters, could be taught to speak English and French—as well as a little Latin and Greek if she showed any aptitude for learning, but for the moment it would suffice to teach her the letters and numbers she should have been made familiar with long ago.

Because the Countess also decided that it would do Andrei, the elder of Kadya's sons, no harm to join the lessons, every morning after breakfast the two children reluctantly climbed the stairs to the old schoolroom where Nadya Tereshkova awaited them. The Countess herself retired then to the office where her husband should have worked, and tried to bring order into the chaotic accounts of his estate as well as her own.

Unfortunately, Olga Feodorovna was a poor judge of character and far too trusting of her employees. If she had ever witnessed Nadya's teaching methods, she would have dismissed the instructor immediately. Nadya was a plain, embittered young woman who held advanced political views. The daughter of a petty official who had died in jail, she nursed a grudge against the Russian aristocracy who had been responsible for sending him there, and she saw her appointment as governess to the Kharkov children as a heaven-sent opportunity to revenge herself on the offspring of those she most hated. Nine-year-old

Andrei was no problem. He was a sycophantic little boy who already knew most of what she could teach him, and the slavish way in which he obeyed her gratified her pride. But Anastasia was another matter. It enraged Nadya, who had been obliged to fight for her own education, to see this adopted waif being given all the advantages which should have been hers. The governess was determined, therefore, to insure she got no joy from them.

With systematic cruelty she undermined Anastasia's morale and made her lessons a torment. Over and over again, the child copied her letters only to have the exercise torn up before her eyes. When verbal baiting and criticism no longer reduced her pupil to tears, Nadya took to slapping and hair-pulling, standing the child in the corner and rapping her knuckles with a heavy ruler.

At first Anastasia tried to please her governess, but her sense of injustice grew daily. When she discovered that the harder she worked the more savage her punishments became, she lapsed into sullenness and refused to put pen to paper in spite of her teacher's furious threats.

One morning, in desperation, she defied her tormentor and refused pointblank to take her place for lessons. Andrei licked his lips in delight. He sat up straighter at his end of the table, paper and pencil neatly aligned, and waited for the punishment to begin.

"Sit down at once and write out your alphabet three times. Otherwise you'll have bread and water for your lunch again," said Nadya.

"I won't."

"Then I'll make you," said Nadya grimly. She seized the child's bony shoulders and forced her to sit at the table, but the moment she lifted the pressure, Anastasia quickly stood up again.

Andrei laughed, then clapped his hand over his mouth. Nadya lost her temper completely. She forgot that she was dealing with a child belonging to the most powerful family in the district; all she saw was a rebellious girl, whose spirit must be broken at once.

"I'll teach you to do what I say!" she exclaimed, lashing out at Anastasia with a heavy ruler. A long red welt appeared on Anastasia's cheek. The force of the blow had knocked her to the floor. For a moment she lay there, half stunned. Nadya, suddenly frightened at what she had done, bent over her charge, then took a quick step backward as Anastasia sprang up, eyes blazing, and raked her nails across her tormentor's face. Such was the fury of her assault that the governess was required to pick up a chair and hold it in front of her body like a shield.

"Stop it!" she commanded, in a trembling voice. "Stop it at once!"

But Anastasia couldn't stop. She was, by now, beyond pain or fear. So long as she was able to hurt her governess, she didn't care what happened to herself. With surprising strength she wrenched the chair from the woman's grasp. As Nadya tried to defend herself, she tripped over her skirt. Catching her off balance, Anastasia pulled her down onto the floor, seated herself quickly on top of the brawny shoulders, wound her small fists in Tereshkova's thick bun of hair and thumped her head vigorously against the carpet.

Unable to unseat the savage little demon she had provoked, Nadya moaned feebly. Andrei, who had anticipated a different outcome to the rout, burst into tears and rushed downstairs where he ran headlong into his father, dressed for riding and carrying a whip.

"Papa, Papa, come at once," he sobbed. "Anastasia is killing the governess!"

"*Anastasia?* That's impossible!" Kadya ran up the stairs to the schoolroom. Books and papers were scattered all over, the carpet was a mess and chairs had been overturned by Nadya's flailing legs, but Anastasia was still on top and the governess, though her body lay still, appeared to be yet among the living.

As she raised her tormentor's head for a final triumphant thump on the floor, Kadya seized his daughter's arms.

"What is the meaning of this?" he roared, although he could hardly contain his laughter. The whole situation was too absurd: the stout governess prone on the carpet— showing an unseemly expanse of petticoat and thick white leg; the towheaded little savage who was his daughter triumphantly astride her shoulders. How often, Kadya wondered, had he longed to knock a hole in the head of some stuffy professor, but never dared to do it? He felt a glow of pride for his daughter, but under the circumstances it was hardly an emotion he could admit to.

"Stop that at once," he said, yanking Anastasia away from her victim. "Go to your room and wait there for me." He shoved his daughter out of the schoolroom, then turned his attention to the prostrate figure of Nadya Tereshkova. Blood was streaming down her nose, and hair down her back.

"That wicked girl tried to kill me," she moaned. "She's a mean, terrible girl."

Her employer could only recoil in revulsion. After muttering, that he would send the housekeeper to attend her, he escaped from the untidy schoolroom. Still holding his riding whip, he marched up another flight of stairs to Anastasia's small bedroom. It was fortunate, he thought, that the Countess had chosen to drive into Kharkov that morning to consult the doctor. If he acted quickly, the whole disgraceful episode could be kept from her ears. Anastasia must be punished, that was plain, but her silence must also be bought...

When he entered the room there was no sign of the girl, but a movement by the window caught his eye. But when he looked outside, he saw the thick creeper swaying wildly as Anastasia attempted to climb down it to the verandah below. Kadya remembered trying to do the same thing himself as a youngster—not to escape punishment, but to meet a girl in the woods—and a sudden sympathy for his rebellious young daughter made him say:

"You won't get down that way, you know. The creeper goes around the corner and out of reach before you get to the verandah. I know, because I've tried it. Come back in, young lady. You and I have some business to settle."

The disconcerting green eyes looked him over carefully before Anastasia climbed back over the window sill. She realized with amazement, that this ogre, her father, wasn't angry at all. He was only pretending to be, and the break in his voice sounded suspiciously like suppressed laughter. Well, she thought, it *had* been funny to see stout Nadya Tereshkova, that unpleasant self-important bully, flat on the floor with her skirt hiked up to show her laddered stockings, a sight well worth a beating.

"What are you grinning about?" demanded Kadya. "It is no joke, I assure you, to attack your governess like an animal. Now I've got to beat you, to teach you better manners."

His face assumed a stern expression. He bent the child across his knee and administered a few half-hearted swishes of his whip in the general area of her pantaloons. Through her several petticoats, however, she scarcely felt them. When he released her and threw down the whip with a sigh of relief, Anastasia turned a surprised face up to him.

"Nadya beats me much harder than that," she exclaimed.

"Your governess beats you?"

"Anastasia nodded.

"How dare she?" said Kadya. "Is that how it started? Had you not done your lessons well?"

Anastasia nodded with a little sigh of resignation. "It doesn't matter if I do them well or badly, she still beats me."

"Then, by God, she'll leave this house tomorrow. How dare that peasant raise a hand against my daughter?"

There, he had said it. The words slipped out before he could control them, and as they did so the heavy weight of guilt that had lain on Kadya since the child's arrival suddenly lifted. He smiled. Why *not* admit it, after all? Vanya was right; Anastasia might well grow into a daughter he could be proud of.

For her part, Anastasia was more surprised by his indignation than his admission of paternity. Could it be true that he really didn't know what went on behind the schoolroom door? The hope that someone might, after all, care what happened to her fueled a small glow of comfort in her heart.

"Am I your daughter?" Her green eyes searched his face intently.

"Well, my adopted daughter . . ." When he saw the hope fade from her expression, he exclaimed, "No, damm it! You're old enough to know the truth, but it must be a secret between us. Can you keep a secret? You are my daughter, but I wasn't married to your mother. I fell in love with her when I was in Poland. But then . . . then we were separated and I never saw her again. I left Vanya to take care of her, but Vanya didn't tell me about you . . ."

"Vanya can't write," she said. "He would have told you if he could, but my mother forbade it."

There was a silence while they both considered the past, endeavoring to glimpse what the other's life must have been. At last Anastasia asked shyly, "Does the Countess know that you loved my mother?"

"No." Arkady's denial was immediate and firm. "And she must never know, because her health is delicate and any shock might be dangerous. Can I trust you not to tell her?"

She nodded, her eyes solemn.

"So!" he said cheerfully. "Now we can be friends. I'll see that Nadya Tereshkova never troubles you again. You'll have to change your dress and make yourself presentable, however, before you come downstairs. I was about to go riding—perhaps you'd like to join me?"

To his dismay she burst into tears.

"I want to go home," she sobbed. "I don't want to stay here."

Awkwardly, Kadya patted her arm. "Don't start crying just when we're getting to know each other," he said. "This is your home now. You needn't be afraid of Nadya Tereshkova any more."

She shook her head fiercely, as tears streamed down her cheeks. "It isn't Nadya Tereshkova. It's you. How can I . . . kill you . . . if I don't hate you any more?"

"Kill *me*?" Kadya was profoundly shocked. "Why do you want to kill me?"

"I don't want to," she choked, trying to swallow her tears.

"Well then, what's the matter? You can tell me. I promise I won't be angry."

Anastasia looked at him doubtfully, then decided to risk it. Having gone so far she could hardly refuse to explain the worry that was making her nights as wretched as her days.

"Mama made me swear to kill you. Every night, she comes in my dreams, to ask why I haven't avenged her yet. I try not to sleep but I can't help it, and then she sits on my bed and tells me to keep my promise," Anastasia said. "She wanted her baby to be a boy who would kill you for ruining the house of Galzinski. Now I have to do it."

"Revenge, betrayal, they're all a lot of nonsense," grunted Arkady, annoyed to find a small chill running down his spine. It was always disconcerting to discover hatred from an unexpected quarter. "You've got the story wrong, Anastasia. It wasn't like that at all, as your mother knew perfectly well. You melodramatic Poles always over-dramatize, and make out that you've been wronged when, if the truth were known, it's nobody's fault but your own."

"Poles, yes; but *I* am half a Russian," declared Anastasia proudly.

Kadya couldn't help laughing. "True enough, you monkey. So you knew that all along, did you? Well, now you must let the sensible Russian side of your nature take command, and forget all this Polish nonsense."

"Then you didn't betray my mother?"

"If anyone was betrayed, it was *me*," said Kadya hotly. "I loved your mother, but her blasted family did their level best to get me killed. I'll tell you all about it some day, and you'll see what I mean. There were faults, certainly, but they were on both sides . . ."

"If my mother was mistaken, then I needn't kill you," said Anastasia, much relieved. "Perhaps God will explain to her that you were not to blame, and she will stop disturbing my dreams."

Half amused, half exasperated, Kadya took his daughter by both hands. "Listen to me, child. Killing isn't as easy as you seem to think, and a murder doesn't end with the victim's death. What do you suppose would happen if the Countess found out that the little Polish viper she'd taken into her house had killed her husband? She'd die of a broken heart, and then what would become of Andrei and Petroushka? Ah, I'll bet you hadn't thought of that. Now, if your mother comes to pester your dreams, tell her she won't stay in heaven long unless she learns to forgive her enemies—not that I was ever her enemy."

Anastasia nodded. "Can't you tell me what really happened?"

Arkady shook his head. He had no wish to put himself too much in the hands of this volatile child. "Someday, perhaps. When you've proved to me that you've grown into a sensible girl, instead of a little wildcat who fights with her governess. Until then you'll have to be patient. Now, let's go out for a breath of fresh air. And remember, not a word of all this to your foster-mother. It would only upset her health."

As she was coming back from the doctor's, still worried about the pain in her chest which sometimes made it difficult to breathe, Olga's mood lightened when she saw Kadya and Anastasia galloping down the tree-lined avenue toward her. He's still only a boy, she thought indulgently, as whooping in triumph, he leaned out of the saddle to snatch the cockade off Anastasia's hat. What a mercy he's stopped this pretense of not caring for the child!

But oddly enough, the sight of their flushed, laughing faces, in all respects except coloring so absurdly alike, brought the pain back to her chest, and she called to the coachman to drive on quickly. Back at the house a thousand matters awaited her attention.

Though the Countess pooh-poohed any suggestion that the trouble in her throat and chest had any connection with her fondness for fat Egyptian cigarettes, in the spring she was persuaded to try the fashionable mares'-milk cure at Samara. During her absence Kadya took it upon himself to select an English governess for Anastasia.

It would have been hard to imagine a greater contrast than that between the grim, draconian Nadya and the ebullient young Scotswoman Kadya chose to replace her. Mademoiselle Froissart, a plain, elderly Frenchwoman whom Anastasia liked, had already taught her charge to converse in tolerable French, but Kadya was determined that his daughter should be fluent in English as well. He interviewed half a dozen hopefuls before engaging the best-looking of them.

Miss Louisa Sutherland was nineteen years old. Her large, soulful brown eyes reminded Anastasia of a spaniel. She had a radiant milk-and-roses complexion, and wore her springy dark hair with copper glints parted in the center then drawn closely down over her temples; looping behind her ears, it then exploded in an exuberant cascade of curls that no pins could ever control. She seemed always to be laughing, and Kadya was delighted with his choice. He admired the way her well-proportioned figure was always dressed in the height of fashion, for Miss Louisa was a clever dressmaker who could copy the latest French styles. It did not worry him in the least that as a teacher she was completely inexperienced.

Nor, indeed, did this seem to matter much. Since she was a voluble talker who spoke neither French nor Russian with any fluency, Miss Louisa was obliged to converse with her pupil in English, and from her incessant chatter Anastasia soon learned, almost without realizing it, a good deal of English. Though her accent was reinforced by a strong Lowland burr, imitated from the governess, Anastasia made astonishingly rapid progress in the language, and could soon gabble away to Miss Louisa at a great rate, much to her father's satisfaction.

The physical attractions of this new addition to his household did not, of course, escape Kadya's roving eye. It was perhaps inevitable that, as soon as he noticed his stepfather's marked attentions to Miss Louisa, Valerian should determine to put a little competition in his way.

As the Countess lingered in Samara, the two men embarked on an unacknowledged battle for Miss Louisa's affections. Blithely, she encouraged each of them in turn.

Whatever Kadya did to please her, Valerian did one better. Miss Louisa was musically gifted: she danced and sang and played several instruments. Accordingly, Kadya developed a sudden passion for ballet and opera. On the pretext of broadening Anastasia's cultural education, he took a box at the opera for the entire season and escorted the two girls himself when they attended.

Valerian countered by taking them to supper in the cheerfully Bohemian atmosphere of the *cafés chantants* along the Kamenno-Ostrovsky, where young aristocrats mingled with artists and writers, whose company Anastasia much preferred to the grandeur of the opera house.

For Miss Louisa's birthday, Kadya gave her a miniature grand piano, only four inches high, with real ivory keys and gold pedals, made by Carl Fabergé, jeweler to the Imperial Court. Valerian examined this masterpiece with admiration, waited until the end of Lent, and then retaliated by presenting to the governess a Fabergé Easter egg which opened to display an entire miniature orchestra, perfect in every tiny detail, the musicians and their instruments all modeled in gold, enamel and semi-precious stones.

A girl far more level-headed than Miss Louisa might well have had her head turned by the attentions of these two good-looking noblemen of apparently limitless means. Scatter-brained as she was, the Scots girl dimly realized the danger of flirting with a married man who was also her employer, and gradually she began to accord most of her favor to Valerian. This made Kadya all the more determined to win her with increasingly extravagant presents and treats.

For Anastasia, it was delightful to have both father and Valerian, constantly in and out of the schoolroom. She was totally unaware that it was Miss Louisa's company they were seeking. But when the Countess at last returned from Samara, she took in the situation at a glance. She decided—somewhat reluctantly, since Anastasia's English had made such progress since Miss Louisa's arrival—that the pretty governess would have to be replaced by one of a rather more sober character.

On the morning of Anastasia's birthday, the Countess decided not to spoil her party by announcing the departure of her English governess until it was over. After a brief interview, in which she explained firmly to Miss Louisa just why her services were no longer required, she thanked her for the way she'd taught Anastasia to speak her language, and gave her a handsome present of money in lieu of notice.

Any sensible girl would have quietly packed her bags and gone to stay in the English hostel while she looked around for another job; but not Miss Louisa. Believing herself to be in the throes of a grand amour, and totally misunderstanding Valerian's motives in paying court to her, she stormed up to his bedroom, flung herself into his arms, and cried that she would jump from the Troisky Bridge into the icy waters of the Neva if he was heartless enough to turn her away.

"I have lost my job, my home, my character, and all for your sake!" she exclaimed dramatically. "I am friendless now and alone in a foreign country. Surely you cannot betray me!"

Valerian, who was extremely susceptible to beautiful young women weeping on his shoulder—and who knew nothing of the money his mother had just given Miss Louisa, chose the most direct way he knew to comfort her.

"Don't cry, little pigeon," he said caressingly, drawing her down onto the bed. "Nothing is ever as bad as it seems. Of course I'll look after you."

Downstairs, Anastasia waited impatiently for the last of her guests to arrive. Valerian had promised to come to her party, but already the hands of the clock showed the half hour, and there was still no sign of him.

On the long table in the dining room, presents wrapped in snow-white tissue paper bound with gaily colored ribbon were heaped in tantalizing profusion. There was also an enormous cake with her name spelled out in pink icing—Mademoiselle Froissart's handiwork—and old Stephania the cook's offerings of little birds and animals made of her favorite almond paste, wafer-thin sandwiches, sugar biscuits, and quivering mounds of jewel-bright jellies. Servants hurried to and fro with loaded plates, while Anastasia and her stepmother greeted the guests and Mademoiselle Froissart organized games to occupy the time until the feast should begin. The younger children were already beginning to fidget and eye the food hungrily, but Valerian had not appeared.

"Anastasia!" said the Countess. "Call your guests to the table. It is time to open your presents."

"But we can't start without Valya," objected Anastasia.

"We'll have to. He must have been delayed. Never mind—I'm sure he'll come as quickly as he can. Now you must think of your other guests."

Anastasia, who had been watching from the window as the servants prepared for the party, knew that Valerian had returned to the house at least an hour before. Could he have forgotten her party altogether, and fallen asleep instead in his room? Or perhaps he was working, writing one of the stories which he laughingly told her would never be published. When he was writing, he often lost all sense of time.

When the Countess' back was turned for a moment as she summoned the children to the table, Anastasia slipped from the room and ran quickly upstairs.

Valerian's door was closed. She paused for a moment outside it. He was certainly there, but he might be ill. She could hear fast, heavy breathing and then a small moan.

"Valya?" she said softly. She opened the door and stepped into the room, but no one answered. The setting sun was streaming through the uncurtained window, throwing the bed into strong relief. Valerian's naked back was toward her, and the sun highlighted every sinew and ridge of muscle in his powerful shoulders. His arms were around the soft white shape of a woman... Irresistibly, Anastasia's eye traveled to the carelessly discarded heap of clothing by the bed, and with a shock of horror she recognized Miss Louisa's blue silk gown.

As Valerian's hands slid down to cup the woman's breasts and draw her closer to him, a hot tide of longing seemed to surge through Anastasia's whole being. She was transfixed, unable to tear her eyes away from the dark figures writhing on the bed.

Miss Louisa gave another moan of pleasure.

"More," she murmured huskily. "Oh, darling, give me more! Oh, Valerian, I love you so."

Helplessly, Anastasia struggled with strange new emotions. In her mind, it was not Miss Louisa's white breasts that Valerian caressed but her own. The body that moved so voluptuously against his spare, muscular frame, seeming to mold its curves into his own planes and angles, was not Miss Louisa's but hers. A shudder shook her body from head to foot, and her breath came short and fast as if she'd run a mile without stopping. Every nerve seemed to tingle separately with intense new longing. She was aware of an emptiness that craved fulfillment, a bitter sense of betrayal.

"Now!" begged Miss Louisa's hoarse whisper, and Valerian rose above her, enormous against the light.

Suddenly, Anastasia fled.

Trembling all over, she softly closed the door. She felt giddy and sick. Could it be? Valya—her Valya—and Miss Louisa! It seemed impossible... and yet she had seen it. What a fool she had been. What a blind fool not to have seen where those swaying hips and fluttering eyelashes had been directed! And Valerian, too! Why hadn't she realized that all his visits to the schoolroom, his presence on walks and sleighrides, hadn't been for *her* company, but Miss Louisa's?

Even if she'd discovered their liaison, however, she would never have imagined this. The brutal sight of their nakedly entwined bodies was etched indelibly on her mind. Though she now closed her eyes, she could still see every detail...

I love you, Miss Louisa had said, in a voice tormented, quite unlike her usual light, musical tone. But that wasn't Love, not the Love that Anastasia knew.

Could this fearful thing be Love? No; there must be some mistake. Miss Louisa didn't love Valerian. She had no right to love him. The jealousy that Anastasia now felt against the Scots governess was worlds removed from the vague and childish envy she'd experienced watching Valerian stroll with wide-skirted country girls in the scented moonlight. That had been bad enough, but it was nothing beside this new and bitter knowledge: Valerian—her Valerian—lying naked in Miss Louisa's arms.

A dreadful curiosity possessed her. How did the one become the other? By what dark mysterious stages did courtship progress from strolling in the moonlight fully clothed, which was respectable, to naked grappling on a bed, which was not? Clothes were not shed like the petals of a flower. There were buttons and hooks, belts and suspenders. She couldn't imagine fashion-conscious Miss Louisa allowing her clothes to be torn from her body: and it was equally hard to visualize the governess undressing herself, while Valerian watched her. Had he asked her consent? Had she laughed and joked, or cried and protested? Or had the whole horrifying, undignified ritual been conducted in silence—apart from those hoarse, urgent whispers and that heavy indecent breathing?

Anastasia could not answer her questions. But on one thing she was determined: no one must ever guess either where she had been or what she had seen.

How long she stood in the passage, shocked and sickened, she didn't know exactly, but gradually her breathing slowed and she remembered why she had come to look for Valerian...

Her party! The guests would be waiting, and wondering what had become of their hostess. Her foster-mother, too, would be waiting...

With a sudden sense of urgency, almost of fear, she tiptoed into a bathroom, closed the door and leaned against it. Valerian had betrayed her—oh, how he had betrayed her. "Valya, Valya." She began to croon to herself, "why did you do it?"

After a while, with an effort, she mastered her tears and looked in a mirror. A stranger's face gazed back at her: it had wide, shocked eyes, dilated pupils and a trembling mouth. Hastily she splashed stinging cold water on her cheeks and scrubbed them dry again.

From downstairs, she could hear them calling her. "Anastasia! Anastasia!"

Feet pattered on the stairs, then Andrei showed up, breathless and self-important. "Come *on*, Stanya! What are you doing up here? We're starving to death and Mama's getting angry. She won't have time to dress for the opera tonight unless we begin the party now." He looked closely at her face. "Why are you crying?"

She wanted to tell him to go away and leave her alone. What did she care about a silly old party when her heart had just broken? Then self-respect came to her rescue. No one must ever know what she had seen—least of all Andrei, with his sly, hypocritical smile.

"Crying?" she said cooly. "You silly boy, why should I cry on my birthday? I'm coming. I can't imagine why you're making such a fuss. Can't I even wash my hands without being bothered?"

Head high, she followed him down the curving staircase to rejoin her guests.

* * *

A crumbling tower leaned at an angle over a rocky chasm that marked the boundary of the park at Ostrovskoye. It exercised a powerful fascination for the Kharkov children when they visited Valerian's estate in the Crimea.

"They say that Valya's ancestor, Yildiz Khan, trained his horse to climb up all the steps to the platform at the top. From there, he could keep a good lookout for his enemies, in case they tried to creep up and attack him," said Petroushka self-importantly, showing Anastasia this feature of the estate.

"No horse could walk up there, silly" jeered Andrei. "It's much too steep. Anyway, Yildiz Khan would have had a servant to keep watch for him. I'll bet he never went up there himself."

Petya flushed angrily. "He did so! I know because Valya told me."

"Poor little Petya—Valya was teasing you," mocked Andrei.

"He wasn't! He said that when the enemies *did* come, Yildiz Khan jumped his horse right across the chasm and escaped, because none of them dared to follow."

Andrei lay down on his stomach and peered into the gloomy depths. "Then he's a liar. This chasm is much too wide for a horse to jump."

"No, it isn't. Valerian told me that he tried it himself when he was twelve, and it's not a big jump if the horse is bold and you don't let yourself look down." Airily, he added, "I'm twelve now. I might try it soon myself. It should be exciting."

"You wouldn't dare." Andrei turned green at the thought. Unlike his younger brother, who didn't know the meaning of fear, Andrei was a physical coward, who imagined pain even before he felt it. Since he was far too proud to admit to this weakness, his furious strivings to outdo his brother at games and sports led him into painful situations he could easily have avoided.

"Just wait and see," said Petya.

Early in the year, while Petersburg still lay in the iron grip of winter, the Countess liked to bring her family south to enjoy the warm spring at Ostrovskoye. Of all the family's estates, this was Anastasia's favorite. She loved the sensation of waking in her snug bunk in the special train, and looking out of the window to find that during the night winter had been left behind. Peach and almond blossoms were shedding showers of pink petals onto the fresh young grass beside the railroad tracks.

The intense blue of the sea, and the rocky coastline scented with pine and thyme, were sheer delight after the icy gray slush of the Petersburg streets. So was the freedom to wander at will all over the huge estate, riding unescorted through villages where smiling peasant women held up their babies to catch a glimpse of the *barinushki*, while the Kharkov children dug into their pockets for sweets to throw.

"Come with me, Stanya," commanded Petya in a mysterious way, about a month after he'd shown her the old watchtower. "I want to show you something."

Andrei glanced up quickly, then pretended he hadn't heard. Petya and Stanya were always going off secretly without him. Usually he didn't care, but today, he decided, he wasn't going to be left out of something special. As Anastasia and Petroushka rode along the tracks carpeted with sweet-smelling pine needles, Andrei followed at a careful distance.

"Tie up your horse and watch me," said Petya when they reached the foot of the watchtower. His face was glowing with a mixture of excitement and apprehension.

"You're not going to ride up the steps!" exclaimed Stanya. "They're too steep. You'll fall."

Petya grinned. "Don't worry. I've been practicing."

He turned his horse toward the steps. Obediently the animal walked up the first flight.

"That's as far as we've gone so far," Petya shouted down to his half-sister, "but today I'll try to get him up to the top."

"Oh no, Petya. Come back. It's too dangerous," she called. From where she stood, the second flight of steps looked very steep, and the tower seemed to sway with the horse's weight as the animal placed each hoof carefully on the old worn steps. Anastasia held her breath, but they reached the top safely. Petya waved a triumphant hand.

"Well done!" she shouted, cupping her hands around her mouth. "But—how—are—you—going—to—get—down?"

Apparently Petya had not considered this problem in advance. The steps he had climbed grew steep toward the top. Although mounting them on top of a horse was relatively simple, it would be difficult to persuade an animal to walk back down.

As Petya hesitated, trying to make his horse turn round in the confined space of the platform, Stanya heard hoofbeats behind her and turned to see Andrei cantering toward the tower.

Petya spotted him at the same time, and immediately decided on a dramatic way out of his difficulty. Wheeling his horse to face the chasm ahead, he urged it forward with hands and heels.

For a second the bay mare hesitated, then her powerful quarters bunched and she sprang from the platform far out across the ravine, landing lightly and safely on the smooth turf below.

"Bravo!" cheered Anastasia, shouting. "Can I try it too?"

Petya cantered back to the edge of the ravine, delighted with himself and his horse. "It's quite easy," he said. "The steps are the trickiest part, but then the jump is nothing. Your pony can easily do it. I'll stay on this side to encourage him."

"After me," said Andrei, riding suddenly to the foot of the tower. "I'm going first." They stared at him in amazement.

Savagely, he said, "You think you're so clever, always trying to do things better than me. Well, I'm not going to be beaten by my younger brother."

"Don't be silly, Andrei. I'm not trying to beat you," said Petya. "We're only having fun. Besides, your horse won't be able to get up the steps—he's too big and clumsy."

"You're only saying that because you want to tell Valerian that you've jumped from Yildiz Khan's tower and I haven't. Well, you're not the only one who can do it. I'm not afraid."

He was working himself into a rage.

"You *look* simply terrified," said Stanya tactlessly.

If Andrei was doubtful before, he was determined now. He gave her a furious scowl. "I'll tell mother you said that and then you'll be sorry," he promised, and urged his horse forward. Taken by surprise, the animal scrambled clumsily up the first flight of steps and stood there trembling.

"Don't go any further," pleaded Stanya. "It's not safe for you."

"If he was safe, why shouldn't I be?" said Andrei.

He struck the balking horse savagely with his whip and the animal leaped halfway up the second flight of steps, then reared and attempted to turn. Andrei, caught off balance, clutched desperately at the reins to save himself. He pulled the horse over backwards on top of himself and together they struck the ground with a horrifying jar.

"Get him off!" he screamed.

After jumping off her pony, Anastasia did her best. But the horse was winded and she was not sufficiently strong to roll him off of Andrei's inert body, and Petya, still on the wrong side of the ravine, could do nothing to assist her.

"Stay there. I'll go for help," he shouted, and was gone like the wind in the direction of the house, which lay some distance away across the park.

By the time his horse had recovered enough to roll off, Andrei had fainted. His legs stuck out from his body at an unnatural angle. Stanya did her best to make him comfortable, rolling her jacket into a pillow and placing it under his head, but it seemed an eternity before Petya returned, accompanied by his father and half a dozen servants.

"How did this happen?" exclaimed Kadya in horror, when he saw the motionless figure of his son spread-eagled on the grass. "No; don't tell me now. Lift him carefully, you men. And Kolya, take the fastest horse in the stables and ride for the doctor. Tell him to come at once. There's been a terrible accident."

When the Countess heard from the doctor that Andrei's legs were paralyzed, and that he would never walk unaided again, her rage and grief made the whole household tremble. Andrei's horse was instantly shot. Although the animal had sustained no injury in the fall, the Countess could not tolerate letting it live. Both Stanya and Petya were soundly whipped for their part in the tragedy.

Left to herself, the Countess would have banished her foster-daughter from her home forever, but Valerian, returning unexpectedly to the grief-stricken household, intervened to save her from this fate.

"You can't be so unjust, Mama," he said. "We've all heard the story, and there's no doubt in my mind that Andrei himself was entirely to blame for the accident. Stanya says she tried to stop him but he wouldn't listen, and Petya backs her up."

"Of course, they're both lying. She says that to save her own skin. That wretched girl has been nothing but trouble ever since I was fool enough to take her in. She's an ungrateful, rebellious brat, and a shocking influence on Petya. I don't care what you say, I'm determined to get rid of her once and for all."

"As you got rid of Andrei's horse, and the puppy who bit Petya's finger when he teased it, and the maid who answered back when you accused her of lying?" said Valerian. His dark face was determined. "I warn you, Mama. If you turn Stanya out of your house to starve, *I* shall take her in. She's a good-looking girl, even if she is only fourteen, and you may imagine what a scandal it will cause when the story gets around—as I promise it shall."

The Countess knew her son too well to believe that he was bluffing. "So you prefer to side against your own mother," she said bitterly. "Very well, then, she may stay. But this is her last chance, I warn you. If she's ever involved in trouble again, Anastasia must go."

Chapter Four

ST. PETERSBURG
1904

Two years later Count Kharkov sat at the library window of his great house on the outskirts of St. Petersburg. His straight right leg was supported by cushions in front of him as he cursed the fate that had saddled him with a stepson like Valerian Radek.

On the frozen lake below the house, sleighs were racing, bells jingling, their paint and gilding vivid against the freshly fallen snow. Faintly the excited yells of the contestants were borne to Kadya's ears. Petulantly, he hunched his shoulders, trying to ignore the sounds of merriment in the manner of a child who, unexpectedly confined to bed, begrudges the pastimes of his playmates.

Damn this leg, he thought bitterly, and double damn Valerian! I'd never have broken it if the confounded boy hadn't challenged me to that ridiculous skating game. How could I refuse? Conveniently, Kadya forgot his own eagerness to demonstrate to Eva Furtseva, the blonde actress with the spectacular bosom whom he was currently pursuing, that he was a better skater *and* a better lover than his stepson.

They had arranged a course round the lake, zigzagging between poles and under arches and ending with a daring leap over an obstacle of lined-up barrels. As the giggling Eva held a stopwatch and the children cheered them on, Kadya and Valerian in turn tried to clip a few seconds off the other's time around this obstacle course. They were the best skaters in the group.

On the third attempt, Kadya, growing careless, had jumped too soon and landed awkwardly athwart the barrels, smashing his shin in two places. As though determined to add insult to injury, the fickle Eva then lost no time in transferring all her interest to Valerian. Even now Arkady could see her, blonde hair shining against the vivid green of her *palto*, clapping ecstatically as Valerian's sleigh crossed the finish line ahead of his four remaining rivals.

She ran forward today, as Valya pulled up his horses, and planted a kiss on both of the victor's cheeks. Kadya, observing through the window, could hardly bear to watch. Stupid, promiscuous bitch, he thought, I can't imagine how I ever found her attractive. He picked up a book from the table beside him, but the print seemed to dance in front of his eyes and before long he was glancing out of the window again.

The tall, slender figure at Eva's side, who watched the oblivious Valerian with quite as much interest, was well wrapped in sables against the biting cold. She was taller than the rotund little actress by four inches or more. Kadya's mood lightened as he regarded Anastasia. No one, he thought, would recognize in this graceful, accomplished young lady of fashion the crop-haired wildcat he'd found fighting her governess in the schoolroom at Kharkov. He had to admit that the Countess had worked wonders with her adopted daughter.

This year would see Anastasia's presentation at Court; perhaps next year would see a brilliant match—who could tell? From time to time, Kadya remembered that Anastasia was still only fifteen, although everyone except Valerian believed her to be two years older.

Perhaps he ought to take steps to delay that brilliant match a little longer. He decided to find an objection to every one of Stanya's suitors until she was sixteen at least. One way to achieve this objective would be to take her abroad—to London, Paris, maybe even New York. That might be an agreeable way to further her education. Kadya fell to wondering which diplomatic posts were at present vacant—or could be rendered vacant by a skillful word from his wife in the ear of the Tsarina . . .

A sudden stir among the brightly-dressed crowd by the lake heralded the arrival of members of the Imperial Family, eager to see the races. Kadya soon caught a glimpse of the Tsar, stiffly erect, walking through a lane formed by his subjects, who knelt as he passed them, like corn flattening in the path of the wind. At his heels trotted two little Grand Duchesses, Olga and Tatiana, their hands thrust deep into white fur muffs. Then the sturdy backs of Cossacks forming the Imperial Bodyguard hid the short-bearded Emperor from the Count's view.

Kadya fidgeted, and wondered if his leg would survive without protest the short hop across the rug to the window seat, from which he would be able to see much better. Before he could reach a decision, however, heavy steps crunched on the snow-covered drive, voices murmured respectfully and the Count heard the front door swing open. Smiling, he sank back into his chair.

A few moments later Nicholas II, Tsar of All the Russias, marched with military briskness into the library, waving to his bodyguard to stay outside. He halted in front of the invalid's chair, a smile on his bearded lips.

"Well, well, my old friend, what's this I hear you've done to yourself? Will you never learn to resist a challenge, Kadya Pavlovitch? No—" as Arkady struggled to rise—"no ceremony, I beg of you. Stay where you are, or that leg will never mend. Since Mohammed could not come to the mountain, I reasoned that the mountain must go to Mohammed—and here I am."

Beneath the joviality, Kadya could detect a definite unease in his sovereign's manner. But then, he thought, when was poor Nicky ever wholly at ease? The anxious little boy, tortured by shyness, whom Kadya remembered from their schooldays, was now hidden—though not very deeply—beneath the trappings of the most powerful man in Russia. Even Nicky's father, that stern old reactionary Alexander III, had felt that his heir should learn to adopt a more sanguine attitude toward life in general and his sacred duty in particular. That was partly why he had picked out the happy-go-lucky Kadya to be the Tsarevitch's playmate, but the plan had misfired. For Nicholas hero-worshipped the bigger, stronger boy, and suffered such torments of anxiety when Kadya got into trouble—as he frequently did—that it was almost as though he himself were being punished.

Now, although he was the all-powerful Tsar and Kadya merely a cavalry officer whose career was stagnating because he was too lazy to be ambitious, the shadow of that hero worship still lay on the Tsar's heart. More than anything, Nicholas longed to surprise and please his friend.

Now he said: "I wanted to speak to you before my Committee of the Far East meets this week. As usual, General Kuropatkin is dragging his feet. He doesn't think we should go to war over this business of trade in Manchuria, although it's perfectly clear that the Japanese are damaging our interests there. He doesn't approve my appointment of Admiral Alexieff as my representative in the Extreme East. He complains that it would be impracticable to fight a war—even a war against Japan!—five thousand miles from his base. You know what he's like: if there aren't any real difficulties he invents them."

The Tsar's tone was peevish. Oho, thought Arkady, so now the great General Kuropatkin is in the Little Father's bad books! I wonder why . . .

The reason soon became clear: Nicholas hesitated, then added, "I wanted to get *you* elected to the Committee. I know you'd have supported me against Kuropatkin and his clique, but they wouldn't have it . . . Gromykov, Komarovsky, Kuropatkin himself—they were all against me, I don't know why." Honest and bewildered, his pleading dark eyes seemed to beg Arkady to understand that he'd done his best for his friend.

In fact, Kadya understood several things only too well. First, his wife and the Tsarina had been intriguing on his behalf again. Olga refused to accept the fact that her dear husband was simply too lazy to enjoy responsibility, and since he wouldn't seek promotion himself, she undertook to do it for him.

Second, General Kuropatkin had foiled their scheme. This neither surprised nor worried Kadya. The Minister for War was a soldier of the old school, a stickler for military discipline. In a lofty, thoroughly respectable manner, he was devoted to Olga, having been a lifelong friend of her first husband's, but he neither liked nor approved of her second one. The fact that General Kuropatkin had recently attached Valerian to his Staff in no way softened his feeling toward Kadya, whom he despised as a gambler and a frivolous fool who had no business on any military council, let alone the Committee of the Far East. Rumors that war with Japan was about to be declared had been circulating in the army for months now. By January, relations between the two countries over the matter of trade in Manchuria were delicate and highly volatile. The Japanese were showing unexpectedly stiff opposition to the gradual extension of Russian influence in the Far East.

Two years earlier, Japan and Britain—that interfering little island whose foreign policy seemed directed solely at the provocation and harassment of Russia—had signed an agreement which affirmed their desire to maintain the status quo in the Extreme East. They agreed also to support the independence and territorial integrity of China and Korea—an aim which made them view with increasing disapproval Russia's stealthy advance eastward across the continent of Asia.

A clash appeared inevitable, sooner or later, and during the past year Russia had been building up her military power in Manchuria in readiness for the coming conflict.

Neither the Tsar nor Kadya was worried about the outcome of the struggle, nor doubted the rightness of Russia's cause. Nicholas was proud of his settlements in Manchuria, and the prosperity they and the new railroad had brought to the formerly desolate region. Stories concerning the plight of native nomads who sold their grazing lands to Russian settlers—and then were forced deeper into the arid interior—were only faint echoes by the time they reached the Imperial Court. And in the Tsar's opinion, they were a thoroughly insufficient reason to deprive the rest of Manchuria of the many benefits that Russian trade and culture would provide.

On the military side, Russia's millions of people surely had nothing to fear from little Japan, whose armed forces at the end of her war with China, ten years before, numbered only sixty-seven thousand men.

With such numerical superiority, it had been simple in 1894 for Russia, backed by Germany and France, to intervene and deprive Japan of most of the fruits of her hard-won victory. Bowing to overwhelming forces, the Emperor of Japan had been obliged to withdraw his troops from the Liautung Peninsula. But behind the smooth Oriental acceptance of such humiliation seethed a savage rancor which intensified as the Emperor saw Russia installing herself in the very places she had insisted the Japanese should vacate. Had the Tsar known what dramatic improvements, what a build-up of men and armor the past decade had seen within the Japanese army, he might not have felt so complacent.

"Kuropatkin's an old woman," Nicholas said now, when Kadya had repeatedly assured him that he'd never even thought of being invited to join the Far East Committee; although, of course, he was surprised, honored, and deeply grateful for the Imperial efforts on his behalf. "He got his way over the

Committee in the end, but he couldn't stop me appointing you Military Governor at Irkutsk. It's an important post, you know," the Tsar added anxiously, seeing Kadya's jaw drop. "I'll need a man I can trust on the Manchurian border, now that Sobiriev's resigned, and who better than you? So many generals try to hide things from me, but you'll always tell me the truth—eh, Kadya? Anyway, it's time you were promoted; you've been waiting long enough. Well, what do you say?"

What *could* he say? Kadya thought desperately. He no longer felt any desire to laugh. Olga's interference had done it for him this time, and no mistake. Why couldn't she leave him in the happy obscurity that suited him so well? It was unthinkable now that he should presume to refuse what any other officer would sell his soul to get—instant promotion, a remote command of enormous strategic importance, an invitation to send uncensored reports direct to the Tsar—and he knew that refusal would be seen by his friend as a personal betrayal. Any soldier with a grain of ambition would fling himself at his Imperial master's feet, kissing his hands and babbling thanks at such a mark of favor, but Kadya sat rooted to this chair while one moment of silence stretched on and on and on.

"Well?" prompted Nicholas, his smile beginning to fade.

Kadya rallied. "You're far too good to me, sir" he murmured deferentially. "I feel quite . . . quite overcome by your generosity. I only hope I can prove worthy of your trust."

It was sufficient to reassure Nicholas, who relaxed and became expansive. "Of course you will, my dear fellow. I wouldn't have appointed you otherwise." The Tsar clapped a friendly hand on Kadya's shoulder. "Perhaps I was wrong to spring the news on you so suddenly, but I wanted to surprise you . . . I hope your wife won't feel too far from cosmopolitan delights on the Manchurian border. I'm told that the summer climate there is altogether is agreeable. And besides, you can console her for the lack of theaters and museums by pointing out that you are at the very heart of the war—the nerve center of our communications between St. Petersburg and our eastern seaboard."

Kadya looked up sharply, suspecting his friend of irony, but nothing was farther from Nicholas' straightforward mind. How little he understands me, thought Kadya, if he imagines that Olga is the one who'll be reluctant to leave Petersburg and all its fun!

"I only wish I could be nearer the scene of action myself," continued Nicholas, "but alas, my duty lies here. I shall expect your reports to keep me in direct touch with my regiments, though... We're building a chain of new blockhouses for the troops all along the line of the railway, and our first task is to complete them. You'll be in charge of the most important section of all, where the line crosses the border..."

A sudden burst of cheering interrupted his speech and the attention of both men was drawn to the window. The smile of a proud parent lit up the Tsar's bearded face as he saw his two small daughters driving around the lake in Valerian's sleigh, acknowledging the cheering crowd with smiles and waves.

"I knew they wouldn't be happy until your stepson gave them a ride in his troika. How they'll enjoy telling their mother when we get home! It's strange how children seem to adore that young man."

"Not only children," said Arkady in secret disgust. Eva's defection to Valerian still rankled. The Tsar, who was himself not attracted to large-bosomed actresses, smiled and clapped him on the shoulder.

"I must leave you now, and wish you good fortune in your new appointment," he said, marching to the door.

As best he could from his seated position, Kadya bowed and stammered the incoherent thanks expected of him. But when his Imperial visitor was gone, he picked up the book from the table beside him and deliberately hurled it at the mantelpiece, breaking two vases and knocking an enameled egg by Fabergé—which the Tsar himself had given him—into the smouldering fire.

Delighted by the Emperor's informal visit, and even more pleased to know that her scheme to get her husband promoted had succeeded so triumphantly, the Countess set about preparing for their departure to Eastern Siberia at once. For years she had dreamed of separating Kadya from the thousand and one temptations St. Petersburg had to offer. She had never begrudged him the money he spent so freely, drawing upon her fortune with the same reckless abandon that had exhausted his own. She loved his high spirits and talent for enjoying himself and felt, with the poet, that no matter how unfair it seemed, it was the eternal law that first in Beauty should be first in Might.

Keenly aware of her own unprepossessing appearance, Olga

took pride and pleasure in Kadya's good looks. She liked watching his mobile face with its flashing changes of expression, his quick, graceful gestures and rapid shifts of mood. At the same time she was well aware of how much of his time and her money he squandered on a succession of petites amies from the lower ranks of the Petersburg *demimonde*—well-upholstered girls with painted lips and crudely dyed hair who tortured their sturdy Russian figures into extravagant fashions which they fondly imagined were Parisian, all low-cut bosoms and tightly-pinched waists.

When Kadya filled his town house with these creatures for weeks on end, giving all-night gaming parties and banquets, their raucous voices and showy clothes grated on Olga's nerves, and it was only with an effort that she could bring herself to be smilingly civil to her husband's female guests. She knew they laughed at her among themselves, calling her "Old Horseface," and "The Dowager," but she also knew that they would never dare insult her in Kadya's presence. Although he was physically unfaithful to her with every little soubrette or showgirl who caught his roving eye, his fancy could be lost as easily as it was attracted, and Olga knew these girls posed no real threat to her marriage.

On her bad days, though, when the pain in her chest cut like a knife and the mirror reflected her long, sallow face unflinchingly, Olga wished that Kadya would finally grow up. He was now in his thirties, but in St. Petersburg especially, he still behaved like a boy.

At home, in Spassnoye, outside Kharkov, on the other hand, it was as if the stern presence of his father still hung about the rambling *dacha*, ready to pounce on any sign of irresponsibility in the son. Obedient to this presence, Kadya became a different person while he lived there, hunting and shooting over his lands like any country gentleman, nodding over his wine and falling asleep in his armchair at ten every night. Growing bronzed and fit, he soon lost the eye pouches and incipient paunchiness that sometimes put years on his appearance, and became once more the handsome young man she had married.

If only he could have been content to live the year round at Spassnoye; if only he took a minimal interest in the management of his estates! But no: Arkady looked on Spassnoye strictly as a holiday haven, whose lands fed his purse just as the wholesome life recharged his physical batteries. Once they were replenished, he was off to the bright lights again, and the excuse he always used when Olga sought to detain him was "my career."

"My career is at a standstill while I enjoy myself here in the country," he would say with his disarming smile. "You know as well as I do that only those close to the Tsar get promoted. When he's looking for a new military governor, he's unlikely to remember an officer who chooses to retire to the back of beyond. That's what I'd like to be, of course. Military governor of some region where there's plenty of shooting and fishing. The more remote the better, as far as I'm concerned. But that sort of appointment doesn't grow on trees, you know. I don't see myself attaining that happy position quite yet. We'll just have to keep hoping. And meantime—" he'd heave a brave, resigned sigh—"meantime it's Petersburg for us, I'm afraid."

Olga had often suspected this bucolic desire, often expressed, to be mere window-dressing, designed to pacify any intention she might have of nudging his career. Well, she'd finally called his bluff. Thanks to the influence of the Tsarina, dear Alexandra Feodorovna—now expecting her fifth child, whose generosity toward the few people she admitted to her confidence knew no bounds, Kadya was going to get the very post he said he longed for. It was up to his wife to see that he filled the post successfully.

Little as he liked the prospect of leaving the capital at the height of the winter Season, when invitations to balls and dinners littered his otherwise unused desk, Kadya realized that he had been outmaneuvered at last by his wife. After the first shock he accepted his banishment to Siberia with somewhat rueful grace, offering up a silent prayer that the appointment would be brief. But when Anatasia was given the news, she set up a mighty protest.

"Before my Ball? Before my presentation? I won't do it! You cannot make me go. I refuse to be dragged off to the wilds of Siberia just because it suits the whim of his Imperial Majesty to send you to look after some Godforsaken barracks."

Kadya had chosen to announce his new appointment to the assembled family as they breakfasted in the English style, in imitation of the Tsarina, who had acquired the habit of eating a substantial morning meal on her visits to the Court of her grandmother, the English Queen Victoria. As he saw his daughter's green eyes smoulder dangerously, her mouth set in a straight, mutinous line, Kadya hastily wiped his mustache on a napkin, muttered excuses about an urgent summons to attend his Colonel, and escaped from the room.

The Countess looked after him and sighed. "Really, Anastasia, you are not to speak of His Imperial Highness in that tone of voice," she reproved sharply. "After the kindness with which he's always treated you, it does you no credit. And it sets a very poor example to your brothers."

Andrei smirked, and gentle Petya, who hated to see anyone in disgrace, sent forth an appeal from his dark eyes, silently willing her to abandon the argument. His mother continued, "I know it's disappointing to have to postpone your Season, but you won't lose it altogether. It'll only be a postponement. Anyway, with the threat of war hanging over us, I doubt if this year's Season will be either brilliant or particularly enjoyable. Believe me, it will be far better to delay your Ball until we've won the war, and taught those yellow monkeys a lesson they won't forget. Until then, all the young officers will have matters more important than dancing on their minds."

Normally Anastasia knew better than to argue with her stepmother, but disappointment made her reckless. "It's easy enough for you to say that," she exclaimed hotly. "*You've* been to a thousand balls, and so many levees that you're tired of them. No wonder *you* don't mind being carted off to oblivion in the Land of Sleep. It's different for me, and I won't go, I tell you. I've waited so long to start going to parties and having fun. *Please*, can't I stay here just a few months longer and join you in the summer? Aunt Vera would let me live with her, I'm sure."

"Certainly not!" Olga's tone was sharp. "Vera will have quite enough to do, looking after Andrei and Petya, without being burdened with a willful girl like you to chaperone. Come now, Anastasia, surely you realize that the Tsar has done my husband a great honor in appointing him to this command? Surely you can forget your own selfish pleasure for once and help him succeed."

Anastasia was silent. The matter might have ended there had not Andrei, from his wheelchair, ever alert for an opportunity to put Anastasia in the wrong, said maliciously, "You ought to be glad to go. I wish *I* had the chance to visit the new Russian settlements in Manchuria. My professor says they're simply fascinating, and well worth going all that distance to see, the way the settlers are bringing trade and prosperity to our eastern possessions."

"Then you'd better swap places with me, you sanctimonious little hypocrite," muttered Anastasia.

"I don't know why you're calling *me* names," said Andrei, in a tone of injured innocence. "If anyone's a hypocrite, it's you. When you talk to Valerian, you always pretend you're so eager to see more of the world, and now, when you're offered the opportunity, you don't want to go."

"How dare you eavesdrop when I talk to Valerian, you meddling, long-eared prig!"

The Countess was shocked. "Anastasia! Apologize to your brother at once. I won't allow you to use such language."

Petya looked agonized. He fidgeted unhappily, trying to think of a way to distract his mother's attention. He achieved this object accidentally by upsetting a glass of scalding tea into his lap. The Countess led him howling from the room, whereupon Anastasia turned fiercely on Andrei. "You'll be sorry you poked your interfering nose into my business," she promised. "What else did you hear me say to Valerian? Tell me, before I shake the teeth from your head."

"N-n-nothing. Really, nothing," stammered Andrei in alarm. While his mother was in the room, he felt safe enough to bait Anastasia; it was a different matter when he was alone with her.

"Come on, *what did you hear*?" Standing behind him, she shook him backwards and forwards until his wheelchair threatened to topple.

"Nothing, I tell you. Honest, Stanya, can't you take a joke? I was only teasing, because you're always trying to drag Valerian off on your own to tell him all those boring things you think are fascinating."

"They're not boring and he likes to listen," said Anastasia, but with less conviction. A horrid little worm of doubt was twisting in her mind. Did Valerian find her conversation boring? Had he—dreadful thought—admitted as much to Andrei?

Andrei pressed his advantage. He could hear his mother's voice now, from just outside the breakfast-room door. He knew that a yelp from him would bring swift retribution down on Anastasia's head. She heard the voice of Olga, too. After releasing Andrei's shoulders, she began to tiptoe back to her place.

But Andrei wasn't through. He sneered. "Valya only listens because he's too kind to tell you how bored he is. You're nothing but a poor little Polish peasant and Valya feels sorry for you. I don't know why Mama and Poppa adopted you. You've forgotten what you looked like when Vanya brought you to Spassnoye, but I haven't. Your hair! It was enough to make a cat laugh."

Anastasia went white with anger. "Take that back, you rotten little liar," she said in a low, furious voice. "You don't know what you're talking about. My mother was a Princess and my father—"

"Was a dirty rebel who was hanged for fighting against the Tsar," jeered Andrei.

"He wasn't! My father is the same as yours! My father is Kadya Pavlovitch! There! Now you know everything, and you can stop your dirty hints that I'm not as good as you are. Valerian knows, and it's only because you're a stupid little fool that you didn't learn the truth long ago. You're a nasty, rotten, slimy—"

"That will do, Anastasia," said the Countess, sweeping through the door. "You've said quite enough—more than enough. I hope you realize that you've damaged your own character quite as much as you've damaged my husband's. Now put on your hat and coat at once. I'm driving to the hospital for a committee meeting and I wish to speak to you as we go. Be so good as to get ready now."

As the well-matched chestnuts trotted briskly through the snowy streets, Anastasia was unusally subdued. She wished she had bitten off her tongue, before uttering the words that must have shattered the Countess' illusions. In her own capricious way, her stepmother, she knew, had done much more than mere Duty called for.

Why had she sought a cheap victory over the obnoxious Andrei by confronting him with a truth far better left buried? Now surely, she would be sent far away. Ingratitude, the Countess had often told here, was the deadliest of sins, and Anastasia saw with painful clarity just how ungratefully she had behaved. Miserably she twisted her hands in her lap and stole a glance sideways at the Countess' bony profile, which appeared to be contemplating some inward joke. But as soon as she realized she was being watched, Olga composed her features into their usual severe lines and spoke brusquely:

"Well then, Anastasia. What have you got to say for yourself?"

The girl swallowed her nervousness. "I'm very sorry. Truly I am," she said humbly. "I really didn't mean to speak as I did, but I was so angry I forgot what I was saying."

"Do you deny that you spoke the truth?"

Sudden tears stung Anastasia's eyes as she stared straight ahead through the curved tips of the horses' ears, glinting like gold in the sun. "No," she said.

"And both my husband and Valerian know it?"

"Yes."

"Look at me, Anastasia." The Countess' voice was more gentle. "I am thankful that you're not compounding your misdemeanors by attempting to lie to me. That I would have found distressing. You have shown a disgraceful lack of control and demonstrated all too clearly that you are not yet mature enough to go about in Society."

The blow had fallen. All hope Anastasia had clung to of cajoling her father into permitting her to remain in Petersburg during the winter Season now vanished like the morning dew. When the Countess put her foot down in earnest, Kadya never dared to oppose her. Blinking away the tears, Anastasia sat up straighter, inwardly cursed her errant tongue.

"You must grow out of this habit of bickering with Andrei once and for all," continued the Countess. "It is most unbecoming. If you wish to be treated as a young lady, you will have to behave like one. I know it wasn't all your fault," she added, holding up a gloved hand to forestall Anastasia's protest. "Boys can be very tiresome at times, particularly when they feel that a newcomer is usurping a part of their parents' affection. Andrei's disability must be allowed for as well. You are the elder by some years, however, and you must prevent such quarrels from developing."

"Yes, Mama. I do try, but—"

"Then you must try harder. Now listen to me. You will no doubt be surprised to hear that what you so rashly told Andrei this morning was not news to me. I'm not so blind as you think, child—" a rare and unexpectedly sweet smile curved her mouth—"and the resemblance between you and my husband is . . . *striking* . . . to say the least. I've known you were his daughter since I first set eyes on you, but I had no wish that Andrei and Petya should know. The servants have been instructed not to gossip, for I was afraid that my sons' respect for their father might be damaged."

Astonished as she was by this revelation, Anastasia couldn't hide her amusement entirely. *"Respect?"*

"Yes, respect," the Countess said firmly, but her widening smile had more than a hint of conspiracy in it. "Boys ought to respect their father," she added, almost as if to convince herself. "Even if he is as . . . well . . . *indulgent* toward them as Kadya has always shown himself. It would undermine the very fabric of our family if Andrei and Petya had occasion to question his moral standards."

Anastasia digested this. She tried to locate any hint during the past years that the Countess was not telling the truth, but of course there was none. It was, of course, typical of Olga that, having decided on a course of action, she had pursued it single-mindedly, protecting her husband's reputation even though there was little enough left to protect. Neither scandal nor gossip could make the least dent in her convictions. Suddenly Anastasia seemed to hear again Valerian's half-laughing, half-guilty exclamation on that long-ago day at Spassnoye, as she cowered under her frilly sunbonnet waiting for her fate to be decided: "Dearest Mama, now I am convinced that you are a saint!"

Saints, Anastasia decided, could be uncomfortable people to live with. She cried impulsively, "Oh, if only you had told me! I've been so wretched, thinking you you were deceived. I could have kept the secret from Andrei and Petya, just as the servants have, if only you'd trusted me!"

"Trusted you to keep a secret?" Olga's voice was mocking, but she took her stepdaughter's hand and patted it briefly. "No one should expect a child to keep secrets; it never crossed my mind to do so. In many ways you're still a child, my dear. And although my husband wanted to present you at Court this year, I myself have never thought it wise to expose my daughter so young to all the temptations of Society. This morning's events merely confirm my opinion, so that's all there is to be said."

But Anastasia refused to give up her cherished dreams so easily. For years she had visualized herself liberated from the schoolroom, transformed overnight—by the magic ceremony of being presented to the Tsar—into one of the glamorous, self-assured creatures who hung on Valerian's arm at parties and picnics, or swept elegantly through crowded ballrooms at his side. All tossing ringlets and powdered white shoulders and bosoms, they floated on warm billows of exotic fragrance, laughing and chattering above the swish of their silken skirts. They seemed to live in a world apart from the restricted horizon of the schoolroom, and Stanya longed with all her heart to be one of them, to giggle and exchange gossip unhampered by their companions and chaperones, who spent the evenings drinking tea in another room, away from the exciting rhythms of the band and out of sight of couples drifting languorously arm-in-arm about the moonlit terraces.

She couldn't wait another twelve whole months to taste these delights—twelve months fraught with the ever-present fear that what the Countess had postponed once she might postpone again.

"Since Irina Mikhailovna is being presented at Court this year," Anastasia countered, despairingly, "wouldn't it save you trouble to let me stay with her and go to the parties that way. I know Aunt Vera would agree, and then you'd be free to give all your attention to your work in Siberia."

For a moment Olga was tempted. It was true that she had no great taste for parties herself. She had regarded the coming Season of festivities as a chore that must be endured for Anastasia's sake. It was equally true that Vera would be happy to chaperone two girls instead of one, and it would certainly be agreeable to spend a few months alone with her husband...

Then she thought of Irina—a black-eyed, tempestuous beauty of seventeen, who had been turning men's heads since she left the schoolroom. Who could tell what mischief she and the headstrong Anastasia might not get into together? It would hardly be fair to place responsibility for two such lively and willful maidens on poor, ineffectual Vera.

"No," she said firmly. "I cannot allow it, so please do not argue any more. You'll be grateful to me one day, my dear."

She doesn't believe a word I say, Olga thought, observing the sulky droop of Stanya's full lower lip. She added: "I'm torn in both directions, you see, for if I stay with you in Petersburg I'll be failing in my duty to my husband, and also to Valerian. If

Valya should be sent to the eastern front, I would want him to know he had a home to come to, at no great distance from the theater of war."

Anastasia's heart leapt. This was very welcome news, and suddenly Siberia turned from a land of exile into a magical world of excitement and mystery.

"Valerian will be with us in Siberia?" She tried hard to keep her tone neutral—to make the question as casual as possible, but the telltale blood rose to her cheeks.

The Countess noted the blush. That was another pitfall she must somehow avoid. Nothing would be more annoying—or more unsuitable—than to have Anastasia fall in love with Valerian. She knew very well that her son was no saint where women were concerned, and Stanya's looks had improved dramatically in the past year or so. The high cheekbones and strong jaw that had looked out of place on a small girl now gave her face a touch of drama, accentuated by the long green eyes with their dark lashes, and the generous, full-lipped mouth. Her childish hero worship could so easily turn into something more serious, and the last thing the Countess wanted was to see Valya enslaved by the daughter of a Polish adventuress.

Olga sighed. What a difficult business it was to bring up a girl—especially an attractive one! Dangers lurked at every step. To let Anastasia know that she was displeased with her forwardness, Olga frowned. Naturally, he will visit us sometimes," she said, then called to the coachman to make haste, or she would miss the start of her committee meeting.

Anastasia said no more but hugged herself in secret delight, forgetting all about the Petersburg Season. She could hardly wait to get to Siberia, and to start finding new opportunities of being alone with Valerian...

Chapter Five

SIBERIA

Kadya's departure from St. Petersburg brought flocks of his friends and relations to the railway station to see him off on the long journey to Irkutsk. They came in sleighs laden with food and whine, bearing presents of fur hats and sable cloaks for the travelers. Uncle Vladimir Nicholaevitch, who had once given a party for twenty thousand friends, even brought his private orchestra to send his nephew off in style, the musicians all dressed alike in yellow silk blouses and green breeches. Chattering like brilliant, exotic birds, Count Kharkov's friends shouldered aside the other passengers, while the orchestra did its best to drown the train's engine. Soon the crowded platform began to look like a ballroom.

The trains that now ran four times a week to Manchuria were often packed with military personnel but women passengers were a rarity, and Anastasia attracted many admiring glances as she kissed her brothers and cousins good-bye. She wore a saucy little hat of reddish fox fur and a *palto* of heavy green cloth that emphasized her slim height.

"My heart is broken! My world is in ruins! I shall never love anyone else as I love you, dearest Kadya!" wailed Irina Markova, Kadya's latest flame. "I shall count every minute until you return to my arms."

"You'd better count the lovers you take before I see you again," said Kadya, who had a realistic opinion of her fidelity. He was in high spirits, the center of attention as he liked to be, his white teeth flashing, his tall, broad-shouldered figure displayed to advantage by the well-cut military greatcoat and high boots.

He thinks it's all a party, the start of a new adventure, thought Olga, watching him through the smoke of her Egyptian cigarette. He's still just a boy; he has no idea of what responsibility means. But once we're away from Petersburg he'll learn. I'm sure of it. She signaled to Anastasia to leave the group of young officers who clustered around her like wasps round a jam jar.

"We will board the train now," she commanded. Reluctantly Anastasia mounted the high steps, turning to wave to the laughing faces turned up to her. From her vantage point she suddenly noticed an unfamiliar figure, his face obliquely lighted by one of the station lamps, a giant of a man, bareheaded, his fair hair tightly curled, his alert, flashing eyes appearing to watch her movements with more than casual interest. There was something indefinably foreign about the cut of his clothes; something faintly disturbing about his intent gaze, and she tossed her head, wondering fleetingly who he was and why he stared so. Then a billow of smoke blew up from beneath the train and erased him from her view.

It was strange and exciting to be starting a journey late at night. As the engineers examined the couplings between cars, their burning flares gave their sweating faces the aspect of devils in an inferno. She waved to Andrei, a pale figure in his wheelchair, and blew a kiss to Petya, who was fighting to control his tears as he stood beside his Aunt Vera. The boys were to remain at school in Petersburg and rejoin the family in Siberia in the summer.

Valerian had shouldered his way through the crowd and into the carriage. "I'm supposed to be on duty at the Palace," he said gaily, "but I couldn't let you go without wishing you godspeed, little sister. Have a good journey and don't break too many hearts."

Anastasia looked at him in despair. When would he stop calling her "little sister"? They weren't even related! When would he see her as a woman instead of a schoolgirl to be teased or ignored, instructed or given treats as the fancy took him? Her hair was worn up, and her clothes were the height of fashion. Other men immediately treated her as an adult. Why was Valya—the only man she cared about—so provokingly blind?

"I'm *not* your sister," she said, "nor am I little. And I don't like being patronized and spoken to like a ten-year-old."

Valerian looked as surprised as if his pet dog had bitten him. He gave a shout of laughter. "Pray forgive me, mademoiselle. I find it difficult to keep pace with such fashionable young females. One day you're climbing trees like a tomboy, and the next you're as unapproachable as the Venus de Milo—though I'm glad to see that you're more sensibly dressed for the climate than she." He looked approvingly at her new green coat. "You should wear that color more often. It suits you very well. Now, let's start over again . . . My dear sister, allow me to extend my warmest wishes for an agreeable journey and a speedy. . . ."

"No, no, no, no!" Anastasia stamped her booted foot. She was furious. "I'm not your sister. Don't you understand?"

"Surely you won't deny me the right to call you my sister? After all, you're the only one I have. Please allow me that small pleasure—even if we agree that it's only a courtesy title."

"All right," conceded Anastasia. "But remember! I'm not related to you *in any way*."

"Alas for me," he said solemnly, and there was nothing in his face to show if he was laughing at her or not.

She smiled. For once she'd had her way. "When will we see you again, Valya? Will you visit us on your way to the Extreme East?"

"That's for my general to say, I'm afraid. I'm only a lowly staff officer, doing what I'm told. . . . However, he's planning to make an inspection of our new blockhouses along the Trans-Siberian Railway before the spring thaw, so maybe I can visit you then. I'll come as soon as I get an opportunity. I can hardly wait to see my revered stepfather holding a key strategic position in the Imperial forces. It should be funnier than watching a monkey play chess."

Anastasia was shocked. She knew that Valerian had a low opinion of Kadya's military capability, but she couldn't help being taken aback by such open disloyalty.

Valerian laughed. "Don't look like that, my pet. And don't bother to defend him either. He's not worth it. I'm only telling you what every other member of the Committee of the Far East has been whispering ever since your father's appointment. Nobody else dares to say it out loud, that's all."

"You're jealous," she teased.

"Oh, no. I've got better things to do than build blockhouses in Siberia, but if I *were* to be made a military governor I can tell you I'd make a better job of it than poor Kadya ever could. Ah well, at least my mother will be happy to have him with her for a few months."

"You don't think we'll be in Siberia longer than that?" asked Anastasia.

"I don't think the war will last any longer. And when the Japanese—whom he despises so much—start chasing us out of Manchuria, you can bet that Kadya Pavlovitch won't be there fighting a rear-guard action on his own."

For a moment Anastasia was too astonished by this prediction to do more than stare at him. Valerian gazed out at the crowded platform where Kadya now stood with an arm around one girl while he whispered to another. "That buffoon!" Valerian murmured, as if to himself. His dark, fine-boned face wore an expression of angry frustration that Anastasia had never seen there before. She laid a hand on his sleeve and shook it gently.

"Valya, what are you saying? The Japanese chase us? Why, that's impossible! Are you teasing me again?"

His face was still averted, but his expression softened. "No, little sister; I was never more serious. Consider the difficulty of fighting a war five thousand miles from your base. Just think: we have no access by sea to the Liautung Peninsula. Our Mediterranean fleet is boxed up helplessly in that narrow harbor at Port Arthur, which means that every item of food, equipment and ammunition—not to mention coal for all those useless ships—has to be brought to our army in Manchuria by means of a single line of rail. And even that's not complete yet, since it's broken at Lake Baikal. All our goods have to be loaded on steamers or icebreakers to cross the lake, and of course that means even more delay." He shook his head sadly.

"But Papa—"

"Exactly. Your father. How do you think General Kuropatkin feels, knowing that the weakest link in this long and damnably fragile chain will be entirely at the mercy of that well-known gambler and playboy Count Kharkov: administrative experience—zero; plain common sense—nil? A man whose military career began and ended in a remote Polish garrison town way back in 1890."

"Oh, please don't go on," she begged. "I'm certain you're quite wrong. Surely Papa will succeed, once he sees what should be done."

"Spoken like a loyal daughter. Well, I hope I'm wrong. However—" Now the old mischievous sparkle lit his dark eyes—"you're far too pretty to worry your head about war, and supply lines. I apologize for alarming you."

He had said she was pretty! Anastasia's heart was pounding; she immediately forgot everything else. This was what she wanted to hear; never before had he said as much.

"Do you *really* think I'm pretty?" she couldn't help asking.

"The prettiest little sister a man could wish for," he said absently, and put a casual arm round her shoulders as he bent to kiss her cheek. "It wrings my heart to say good-bye, little one."

Anastasia knew a moment's rage. When would he realize she was no longer a child? As his lips brushed her cheek she turned her head quickly so that her mouth met his, and at the same time tilted back her head to gaze provocatively at him through her lashes. He stiffened, his dark eyes narrowing, and she was afraid he would pull away. For a long moment he scanned her face. Then slowly, deliberately, he bent his head again to kiss her on the mouth.

Ecstasy, not unmixed with triumph, swept through her body as his arms tightened around her, crushing her hard against his gold-encrusted tunic. She felt the round buttons pressing against her flesh even through her coat. His mouth on hers was fierce, demanding—so unlike the chaste, brotherly pecks she was accustomed to receiving from him. She was almost frightened at the demon she had aroused. His strong, long fingered hands moved caressingly over her shoulders. Fleetingly, her mind jumped back in time to another occasion, when she'd merely seen his hands stroke a woman's skin . . . when she'd heard that husky foreign voice murmuring, "More, Valya, more."

With an effort she pushed away the ghost of Miss Louisa and concentrated on the pleasure of being at last in Valya's arms.

The pleasure was short-lived. Almost immediately he detached himself firmly from her clinging arms and hands and patted her behind in a brisk, thoroughly unlover-like way.

"Good-bye then, little sister," he said, much louder than the occasion warranted. And already he had turned to watch his mother being helped aboard the train by her personal maid. Their moment of solitude was over.

The Countess' face was shining with excitement and emotion, and Anastasia realized with relief that she was far too preoccupied to have noticed the earlier embrace.

"Valya, darling," she exclaimed, "please go and tell Vera to take the two boys back to bed. I can't bear to listen to poor Petya's laments, and if I have to look at his woebegone face again I shall feel obliged to whisk him aboard and take him with us—and never mind what happens to his education. Andrei is quite happy to stay behind, but my poor baby! He's the picture of misery. Vera should never have brought him to the station."

"I'll see what I can do," promised Valerian. He kissed his mother and received her blessing, then jumped lightly down from the train without another glance at Anastasia.

The Countess removed her hat and sank thankfully down into her luxurious seat. Closing her eyes, she laid her head back against the plush cushions and sighed deeply.

"What a tiresome business traveling is! How I wish we could have the whole family together in Siberia, but I suppose the boys' schooling must come first. Oh, why won't the train start and put an end to this horrible waiting?"

Anastasia had never seen her stepmother so agitated. Rarely demonstrative toward her sons, Olga was nonetheless finding the leavetaking unexpectedly difficult. Watching Valerian's blue-and-gold back disappear into the crowd on the platform, Anastasia, too, felt sudden tears flooding her eyes. Siberia was so far away... What if Valerian was killed in the war and she never saw him again...?

"Cheer up! This is a party, not a wake!" Kadya stomped into the warmth of the carriage, snow still attached to his boots. His arm was around the shoulders of the fair-haired foreigner Anastasia had noticed earlier on the platform. In fact, it looked suspiciously as if the tall stranger was holding Count Kharkov upright. The two male bodies seemed to fill all the space in the carriage.

"May I present my English friend, Mr. Anthony Mills?" said Kadya, taking elaborate care to pronounce the name correctly. He had consumed a lot of vodka in the course of making his farewells.

Blinking away her tears, Anastasia regarded the Englishman with interest. He had a strong, square-jawed face with prominent cheekbones, and eyes of a clear light blue. His complexion was smoothly tanned, a shade lighter than olive, in contrast to his arresting fair hair, which curled closely all over his head somewhat like that of a newborn lamb. But there was nothing in the least lamblike about his intense blue gaze. Anastasia realized that he was looking her over with a curiosity equal to hers. His straight, regular features would have been classically handsome were it not for a slight misalignment of his high-bridged nose. At some time it had evidently sustained a blow heavy enough to drive it a fraction away from its orignal straight line—an injury which lent his face a touch of originality.

Anastasia remembered that she'd done nothing to arrange her hair since Valerian's kiss. Had the kiss, she wondered, been visible from the platform? Slowly the color rose in her cheeks.

"Mr. Mills was introduced to me by Prince Tchernikov," said Kadya, his speech more confident as he reverted to French. "He has been authorized to observe the war in the Extreme East and will be giving us his company as far as Irkutsk, where we leave the train."

The Countess extended her hand. "Any friend of Prince Tchernikov's is a friend of mine," she declared graciously, then broke off with a little gasp, staring at her husband. "War! You said war—" she exclaimed. "But Valerian told me—"

Kadya wore the pleased expression of a man who knows his news to be the very latest—and from an unimpeachable source. "Valerian likes to imagine he knows everything," he said. "He's only a very junior officer, however, and not always privy to the latest news. I've no wish to alarm you, my dear, but I have it from His Imperial Majesty himself that the Japanese have withdrawn their ambassador from Petersburg." He paused portentously to guarantee his audience's full attention before producing his trump. "Yes, my dear, I regret to inform you that further negotiations with those little yellow monkeys have proved fruitless. We are at war!"

Disappointingly, the fair-haired Mr. Mills seemed unsurprised at this pronouncement. He nodded thoughtfully and murmured, "So I believe," in an understated fashion that was, Kadya thought, typically British. The two women, on the other hand, shrieked and exclaimed and begged him to deny what he had just said in a most satisfyingly histrionic manner.

In the midst of their confusion the train pulled majestically out of the station to the accompaniment of cheers and tears, while the wailing violins of Vladimir Nicholaevitch's orchestra struggled to follow the melody of "Will Ye Not Come Back Again?", which had been hastily transcribed for them by

"Scottie" McFarlane, the Highland governess he employed who, unfortunately, had never fully mastered the intricacies of musical form.

Olga scarcely noticed their departure, so shaken was she by the news that the long-awaited war had actually, and finally, begun. So, she thought, all General Kuropatkin's protests had been in vain, and the Tsar had preferred the counsel of the warmongers! She lay back in her seat and tried to assess what this development meant to her family.

Kadya would be safe enough, of course. But unless she moved swiftly to prevent it, Valerian would certainly see action at the front. Her brain whirled with plans to secure his exemption from active service. Wasn't there a law that gave only sons the right to stay at home in order to feed the family? Perhaps if she wrote at once to the Tsarina...

Deep in her thoughts, Olga paid little attention to the way in which Anastasia had begun to chatter to her husband's young English friend—chatter which, at any other time, she would have considered unbecomingly forward.

"Are you a reporter for an English newspaper, Mr. Mills,?" asked Anastasia. She was eager to put to the test the conversational English which so many governesses, from Miss Louisa onward, had drummed into her over the past five years. She was pleased when the Englishman answered seriously, as if to a proper grown-up lady!

"No, I'm in the diplomatic service. I'm traveling to the front merely as an observer, although my superiors may haul me back to Petersburg before I complete my journey. But you, I understand, are not going quite so far? Tell me, is this your first experience on the famous Trans-Siberian Railway? You have certainly chosen the most comfortable way to travel!"

She noted again the elegantly furnished private carriage, with its blue silk curtains and deep armchairs upholstered in dark blue leather. A suite of sleeping compartments—whose monogrammed sheets and down pillows were for the exclusive use of the Kharkov family—joined the carriage at one end; the other was linked to a private dining room and well-equipped kitchen, where Olga's traveling chef held sway over half a dozen underlings who were, already, working nonstop, washing and chopping and slicing and peeling, before donning white gloves to serve the family's meals.

Accustomed though she was to the luxurious way in which the Countess always traveled, Anastasia was nonetheless aware of the degree of irony in Mr. Mills' voice.

"I can assure you that Prince Youssoupov's carriage is far grander than ours," she said defensively. "When *he* travels, he takes his whole aviary of rare birds with him in the observation car."

"Whereas I take nothing that cannot fit into a single valise."

"Oh, any fool can be uncomfortable," said Anastasia, with a touch of scorn.

For a second Mr. Mills was taken aback. Then he laughed. "You're right, of course. But I don't do too badly, and traveling light gives me a greater degree of mobility. How on earth did Count Kharkov persuade the authorities to let him bring such a circus to war with him?"

Anastasia neither knew nor cared that three wagonloads of munitions destined for the Eastern Front had been delayed a whole day so that Count Kharkov and his retinue could be suitably accommodated, and she disliked being referred to as part of a circus. She was about to say so in her most chilling tone when Olga raised a languid cautionary hand. A moment later, Kadya beckoned the Englishman into the small cabin which served as his traveling study. It contained neither books nor papers, but rods, rifles, and shotguns stood in their canvas and leather cases beside a cupboard plentifully supplied with wine and spirits.

Neither man had emerged from this private sanctum when the ladies retired to bed. Anastasia lay awake for a long time listening to the steady clatter of wheels and the occasional mournful hoot as the train chugged eastward. Staring into the darkness, she remembered the touch of Valerian's lips and his strong, gentle fingers as they caressed her shoulders. Oddly enough, when at last she fell asleep she saw in her dreams not Valerian's slanting dark eyes and the fine-drawn features she had loved so long, but the amused, slightly mocking face of the Englishman, Anthony Mills.

Life on the train soon settled into a comfortable routine—not so very different from that in the Kharkov's great house in St. Petersburg. Anastasia might well have found herself becoming bored had it not been for Anthony's companionship.

He seemed to have nothing more important to do than entertain her. He had, besides, a strange knack of being on the spot whenever some incident broke the monotony of their journey. In the splendid isolation of their private carriages, cushioned in luxury, she would have missed all the small excitements of train life if Anthony hadn't involved her in them.

She was playing bezique—a game she detested—with her stepmother one dark afternoon when the Countess' maid timidly entered the carriage where they sat.

"What is it, Natasha?" asked the Countess, surveying her cards carefully. "I didn't ring."

"Oh, my lady, my lady," cried Natasha in agitation, "there's a poor woman here whose child's fallen off the train. He was looking out of the window and he fell."

"What in the world does she expect me to do about it?" asked the Countess, with a marked lack of sympathy. "If she lets her child lean out of the windows, she must expect the child to fall."

At that moment the distracted mother pushed her way into the carriage and knelt at the Countess' feet. Tears streamed down her broad face.

"Barina, please stop the train," she begged. "My Volodya has fallen into the snow. He will die if you don't stop the train!"

"I expect he's dead already," said the Countess callously. "Why have you come to me?"

"The conductor will not listen to me, but you are a great lady and he will have to stop if you command it," beseeched the wretched woman. "Oh, for the love of God, barina, stop the train!"

With an expression of distaste, the Countess pulled her skirt away from the clutching fingers. "Vladimir! Natasha! Take this woman away," she commanded.

"Oh, Mama, please do as she asks," pleaded Anastasia.

The door of the study opened.

"What's all the commotion about?" demanded Kadya. Anthony Mills, who topped the Russian by several inches, stared over his shoulder.

Icily, the Countess said, "I fail to see why I should delay our train still further just because this woman has been careless enough to allow her child to fall out of an open window."

"Oh, but surely that is impossible . . ."

"A child on the tracks?" Anthony's mouth tightened into a

grim line and he strode from the carriage. Before Anastasia could do more than wonder where he had gone, she heard the engine groan and felt the shudder of the brakes being applied.

Then, led by the Englishman, a party of volunteers carrying spades and torches hurried back down the tracks. They returned an hour later with a bawling, apple-cheeked toddler, whose fall had been broken by the deep snow and the thick fur coat he wore. Though frightened by his experience, he was none the worse for it, and the gratitude of his mother was almost overwhelming. She laughed and cried and kissed Anthony's hands, calling down blessings on him until the Countess told her sharply to go away.

"You have made quite enough of a nuisance of yourself already," she said crisply. "The English barin does not want your dirty kisses ruining his coat. Be off now, and take that howling brat with you. Mr. Mills," she added graciously, "perhaps you would care for a hand of bezique? Anastasia seems quite unable to grasp the game..."

As the journey continued, there were more unscheduled stops and delays.

When the first engine proved unable to surmount a steep gradient, it was Anthony who summoned Anastasia to the drama of watching a second one attached. And during the frequent halts to clear snow that had drifted across the tracks, he would often grab a shovel and join the muffled, booted figures of the workmen clearing the blockage—much to the amusement of the Russian officers aboard the train.

"You seem more anxious than we to reach Vladivostok," joked Kadya, offering the sweating Englishman a glass of wine as the engines groaned uphill again after the most recent such halt.

"I enjoy the exercise," said the Englishman. "I don't understand how you can go day after day without stretching your legs at all."

Kadya smiled. He had not stirred from the luxurious cocoon provided by his private suite since the train had left Petersburg. "I have everything I want here," he said gently.

Overhearing this exchange, Anastasia reflected that it would be hard to imagine two men less alike in temperament. Her father, dark, handsome, and indolent—who accepted as inalienable his right to be waited on hand and foot, would never understand Anthony's insatiable curiosity and restless energy which made it a penance for him to sit still for more than half an hour at a time, or watch others doing something he could do himself. Despite this contrast, however, they were united in their love of gambling, happily whiling away the long evenings on the train with cards or backgammon, while Anastasia watched and advised and fiddled with her embroidery, and the Countess reread the books on Egyptology which were her new passion.

The days fell quickly into a pattern. Anastasia would take breakfast with Miss Catherine Lonsdale, her current English governess, a haughty lady of uncertain age whose main recommendation was the fact that she roused no ardor in Kadya's susceptible breast, and the faithful old Frenchwoman, Mlle. Froissart. Her lessons would follow, at the Countess' insistence, and then Anastasia was free to take a walk through the train to see how Anthony was employed.

He introduced her to the gymnasium, with its elaborate exercising equipment. But, to her disappointment, the dark-room for developing photographs was closed; since the declaration of hostilities it had been forbidden to take photographs from the train.

When the train stopped, as it frequently did, she lost no time in jumping out to buy delicious homemade meatballs and hot, spiced pancakes stuffed with aromatic fillings, offered for sale by peasant women so padded and enveloped in quilted coats and petticoats that they looked like stuffed toys themselves. She could always be sure that Anthony Mills would soon be there beside her.

Anastasia was surprised to discover that he could speak fluent Russian. Although his lofty disregard of gender and case would send the peasant vendors into gales of laughter, he seemed not in the least abashed. Indeed, she sometimes suspected that half his mistakes were deliberately made for the purpose of unbuttoning his listeners' tongues and distracting them from the real drift of his questions. How had the harvest been? How did the war in the East affect their lives? How many sons had gone to the Front from this or that village?

Certainly, on the rare occasions when Anthony spoke Russian with her, his command of the language seemed to improve dramatically. But normally, because the Countess preferred it, they conversed in English or French. She, who had seen more than either Valerian or Anastasia suspected of their embrace in the carriage, watched with approval the friendship between her adopted daughter and the young blond English giant.

Now there, she thought, was an eminently suitable match. Although he worked for his living, Mr. Mills was clearly a gentleman, and since it was well known that the English cared nothing for noble quarterings, the slight ambiguity concerning Anastasia's parentage should not, in itself, constitute a drawback to marriage, either in his eyes or those of his family. He was physically attractive, laughed readily, and had a pleasantly cosmopolitan assurance and ease of manner that was rarely found in Englishmen. So much she could see for herself, but when, with the most delicate circumspection, she tried to discover more about Mr Mills' origins, she found she could learn surprisingly little.

He appeared to answer her oblique but persistent questions with perfect frankness, but he had a disconcerting ability to turn her inquiries into questions of his own, so that at the end of an hour's conversation she would find she knew very little more about him, than she had to begin with, though she had given him a great deal of information about herself.

On his side, Anthony soon divined her intentions, and took a naughty pleasure in frustrating them.

But Olga could be stubborn, too. She issued him an open invitation to their private carriage, plied him with food and drink, and persisted with her questions. Little by little she built up a dossier.

He was twenty-three years old and this was his first diplomatic posting. He had been privately educated at a number of different schools in a number of different countries. His parents were alive and lived a quiet country life not far from Oxford. He was the eldest of four children and had a married sister living in London. He thought Russia was a wonderful country and was looking forward to seeing her great army in action. But when the Countess tried to penetrate beyond these meager and mundane facts, she encountered a polite barrier of silence.

Where, precisely, did his parents live?

"Oh, it's just a tiny Cotswold village, madame. I doubt if you've heard of it."

"I happen to know that part of England very well, Mr. Mills.

I have many friends living there. Perhaps I have even visited your village."

But when she heard that the tiny hamlet's undistinguished name was Lower Middleton, and that Sir Dymoke Mills—who had been one of her mother's oldest friends—was only a remote cousin of Anthony's father, she was obliged to admit defeat. Nor did she find it any easier to determine by oblique questioning either the nature of his father's business or the extent of his possessions.

"That young man has been in and out of here for six days now, and I cannot even be sure if he is married or not," she said to Anastasia one evening, as Anthony politely bade them good night.

"I know he isn't, because I asked him," said Anastasia at once. "He said that he travels fastest who travels alone. And that he has no desire to burden himself with a wife until it becomes necessary to his career." She didn't add that she had been disappointed, even annoyed, at so decisive an answer.

The Countess regarded her thoughtfully. "A hardheaded young man, indeed," she observed disapprovingly. She wished she could place him more precisely. As a fervent Anglophile, it was her pride to know exactly who was who among the British landed gentry—as well as in political and diplomatic circles. For years she had maintained a voluminous correspondence with English friends. Perhaps Milly Dartmoor will know who he is, she thought with sudden inspiration. I've been meaning to write to her for months. She called for her writing case and embarked on an affectionate scrawl to her old friend, the Dowager Countess of Dartmoor.

Anastasia had no such reservations about enjoying Anthony's company. Strolling along a moonlit provincial platform at his side, the crisp new snow crunching under her felt-soled boots, she laughed as he responded to the good-natured banter of the soldiers lounging through the train's open doors and windows.

"Coming to fight for us in the East, Englishman?"

"You should tell your government it's backed the wrong side this time."

"I wish *I'd* had the sense to bring a pretty girl to the front," shouted a languid young officer in the splendid Uhlan uniform, regarding Anastasia with the eye of a connoisseur. She blushed and drew closer to Anthony as they wove their way through the crowd.

"Is Britain really going to fight against us?" she asked the Englishman shyly. "It seems so strange. Here we are, walking together, talking your language, while Mama is writing one of her enormous letters to England, and my father is hoping the war will be over in time for him to shoot grouse in Scotland. Yet—"

"You feel we should behave like enemies? It will be very disagreeable for me if others follow your example," said Anthony, smiling down at her. "But I know what you mean, and it does appear strange until you learn to think of international diplomacy as a game of chess on a grand scale. Do you play chess? Of course—all Russians do. Well, then: these wars and treaties and agreements are all moves in the chess game played by our heads of state. They are all aimed at making sure that throughout our world the balance of power is evenly maintained. Do you understand? When one country takes more than its share of land, the others are quick to weigh in against the offender. And if mere threats are not enough to bring him to heel, the next step is war."

Anastasia thought this over, then said indignantly, "But it is our *right* to bring trade and civilization to those poor Manchurians! Why should the British interfere in a matter which has nothing to do with them?"

"It has a great deal to do with us. The Japanese are our allies, you know. In their view, trade with Manchuria is a Japanese prerogative, not a Russian one. It went against their grain to surrender all they had won during their war with China, ten years ago, but *then* they had to bow to Russia's command. Now they're determined that Russia shall not grab what they were obliged to give up."

"But it's ours!" cried Anastasia. "Our settlers are bringing prosperity to a country which has never known it before. My father says so."

"Without asking if the Manchurians want it."

"Don't be silly. Of course they must want it."

"I'm not so certain. You Russians tend to forget that the Chinese were producing their finest works of art when your ancestors—and mine, for that matter—were still living in caves and eating raw flesh. To them, the civilization you're so proud of seems a mere parvenu; I doubt if they have the smallest wish to have it thrust upon them."

With some amusement he observed the stormy look fade from Anastasia's long green eyes to be replaced by a very thoughtful expression. Clearly she didn't relish having her ideas upset, but she was shrewd enough to realize that she was, as yet, poorly equipped to argue with him.

The engine hooted, whistles blew, and there was the usual scramble to board the train. As Anthony escorted Anastasia back to her carriage, his fingers squeezed hers gently.

"Don't look so worried," he murmured. "Russia's not the first nation to go to war for the wrong reason. And I doubt very much that she'll be the last."

Winter still held the Sleeping Land in its iron grip when the train dragged its length into Irkutsk, where the trucks were to be loaded onto ice-breakers for the crossing of Lake Baikal. Gangs of railway laborers were working hard to complete the section of line around the lake, so that troop trains could run without interruption to Vladivostok, but in the bitter weather progress was slow. There seemed no hope of completing the link before summer. Meanwhile the loading, trans-shipping, and reloading delayed every consignment of munitions and goods for the front and it was the new military governor's most important task to see that these delays were reduced to a minimum.

With some regret, Anastasia watched the sturdy vessels carrying the train that had been her home for the past ten days chug away down the channel they had cut through the ice, taking Anthony with them. She wondered how he would fare at the front, and what his restless curiosity would garner to fill those slim morocco notebooks over the pages of which his pen moved so rapidly. To her, at least, he'd never concealed the low opinion he had of the ponderous Russian war machine, or his admiration for the well-armed and resourceful Japanese. At the front, she imagined, such outspokenness could get him into trouble.

"Half the trouble with your army is that your high command is overloaded with senile brasshats," he'd exclaimed once, when she mentioned the Countess' old friend Admiral Alexieff, now the most powerful man in the East of Russia. "Yes, I know all about old Alexy's distinguished career, but the fact remains that he's an old man, and so are most of the others. Elderly generals are not noted for their flexibility, as we found to our cost in the Crimea."

Sorry though she was to lose Anthony's company, it was a relief to reach the end of their long journey—even if the military governor's house at Nicholasgnad, near Irkutsk, seemed strangely lacking in comfort to be the official home of a high-ranking officer. The previous occupant had been a hardy bachelor, with a deep distrust of modern inventions and a scorn for soft living.

To Kadya's dismay, the two-story wooden building, guarded by high iron gates, was in a ruinous condition, with rotten floorboards in every room and peeling paint outside. The furniture, heavy and primitive, had been locally made, and the extensive garden was little better than a jungle.

"What a place to invite one's friends!" he exclaimed in disgust, surveying the damp, dismal entrance hall. He made up his mind at once to spend as little time in his official residence as he possibly could.

It didn't help matters that the first war dispatch he received reported a naval disaster. Even before the Tsar's formal declaration of war, on February 10, the Japanese fleet under Admiral Togo had made a daring night attack on the Russian squadron lying in the Chinese waterways outside Port Arthur. Unhindered by patrol boats, nets, or any other defensive precautions, the Japanese torpedo boats had delivered a sudden mine attack, damaging the battleships *Tsareivitch* and *Retvisan* as well as the cruiser *Pallada*. On the following day, the Japanese consolidated their success by crippling another battleship, the *Poltava*, two first-class cruisers and one second-class. Not only had the Russian fleet failed to protect itself from surprise attack on a clear, calm night of excellent visibility, it had compounded the error by turning on searchlights, creating silhouetted outlines and perfect targets for their attackers.

Kadya wadded up the sheet of paper containing this dismal news and flung it into the wastepaper basket. "Oh, well," he said to his wife and daughter, optimistic as ever, "they'll simply have to learn by their mistakes. One battle—even a sea battle—doesn't make a war. Just wait until those yellow monkeys come ashore. Then they'll find out what the Russian man is made of. They'll be scampering for their trees so fast that we won't be able to catch them. What we've got to do is get the rail link completed. That's the best way we can help..."

Anastasia couldn't be sure, but she thought she heard her stepmother sigh.

For the next three months Kadya flung himself enthusiastically into his work. Winter turned to spring while the new military governor inspected military installations in his district, harried his subordinates by ordering parades at unexpected hours, and issued a stream of directives designed to speed up the completion of the Circum-Baikal Rail Link.

But gradually his natural indolence reasserted itself. As the short Siberian summer warmed the countryside, those who had groaned and cursed him for insisting on perfection in every military detail were alowed to relax almost imperceptibly into their old slapdash ways. Kadya's thoughts turned toward lighter diversions, such as hunting and cards and bringing a little Petersburg dazzle into the lives of the local girls.

Not that there were many girls to dazzle. Apart from Varvara Danilova Dubrovina, the fat, giggling daughter of a minor official who lived near the military governor's residence, Anastasia found herself with no companions of her own age. At times she even longed for the prickly presence of her half-brother Andrei, or young Petrushka with whom she could argue and fight, gallop over the wide steppe and swim in the countryside's clear lakes in a way neither Varvara nor her governesses were prepared to do.

Varvara was obsessed by men. She thought of nothing else. A lack of competition and an elaborate system of fantasy had convinced her that she was the belle of the district, and she rolled her prominent brown eyes at every male she encountered, from the military governor down to his youngest subaltern. Anastasia found her the least stimulating of companions, but it was impossible to avoid her company altogether since the Countess, worried by her stepdaughter's isolation, invited the fat girl to join them on every possible occasion. Both Varvara and her even sillier mother, who saw this as an opportunity for social advancement, took such full advantage of the invitation that Anastasia was soon longing for solitude again.

"Did you see how Lieutenant Mishchenko watched me during the races yesterday?" giggled Varvara, fanning herself as they sat on the lawn one warm summer afternoon.

"No, I was watching the horses," said Anastasia truthfully.

Varvara pouted. "Oh, but you must have noticed. Everyone was talking about it. Mama said he couldn't take his eyes off me. I was wearing that new green muslin with the gold ribbons threaded through the bodice. Mama says it shows off my complexion to such advantage. Ivan must have thought so too—the way he kept staring! I hardly knew where to look. They say his father has enormous estates in the Crimea, and his brother's a member of the Tsar's own bodyguard!"

She simpered, clearly imagining herself mistress already of the lieutenant's broad acres, sweeping her curtsy to the Imperial family. Anastasia, who privately thought that the pale, obese lieutenant would make a fine match for Varvara, refrained from pointing out that his presence in this remote Siberian outpost was due to his gambling excesses, which had long ago outstripped the meager allowance doled out to him by a close-fisted father.

"Yes, I believe I've met Captain Mishchenko of the Garde Equipage," she agreed, yawning. "He may be Ivan's brother, for all I know."

It was a tactical mistake. A faint sparkle lit Varvara's dull brown eyes and she pounced eagerly on the opportunity to question Anastasia about Court life in faraway Petersburg. It had been impossible to conceal from Varvara the Countess' connection with the Imperial family, since she regularly received letters from the Tsarina herself. Incoming envelopes embossed with the double-eagle crest soon told their own tale.

Varvara glanced over her shoulder and lowered her voice as she always did when about to impart a secret, though the servants bringing tea trays out to where they sat were well out of earshot.

"I hear your mama received an interesting letter today. Is it true that the Tsarina has given birth to another girl? Our servants were saying last night that she had gone into labor a week early. They say that's always a sign that the baby will be a girl."

Anastasia had not heard the news. She was silent, unwilling to admit as much to Varvara.

"Tell me!" the fat girl whined. "You don't know how lucky you are to have a mother who gets all the news from Court."

"There's nothing to tell you. *I* haven't heard anything, but if it's true we'll all know soon enough. Anyway, I hope your servants are wrong—servants usually are."

Stiff and unpopular though the Empress was, with many of her subjects and most of her husband's family, she had always been kind to Anastasia, who shared her stepmother's opinion that the shy, sensitive woman was often unfairly maligned in Court circles.

"She had a bad time with her last one, didn't she?" giggled Varvara.

"What do you mean?"

"*You* know! With four daughters already, you'd have thought Her Imperial Majesty could tell the difference between a real pregnancy and a false one. Wasn't it the Archimandrite Theophan himself who told her she was being punished for listening to heretics, when she asked him why the baby hadn't arrived? She had to make a pilgrimage to the tomb of some saint or other to pray for forgiveness."

"You seem to know all about it," said Anastasia. "But it sounds like the most ridiculous gossip to me."

Varvara bridled. "It certainly isn't gossip! I know for a fact that she *did* make the pilgrimage. What's more, she fell into the holy well. So there! It must have been a scream. They say her skirts floated right up over her head. Her ladies had to jump in and wrap a towel around her body before anyone saw..."

"I don't believe a word of it," said Anastasia cooly. "You're making up the whole thing. But Mama is certain to know the truth. I'll tell her what you just said and see what she makes of it."

"Oh, no, don't do that!" Varvara realized belatedly that her love of gossip had betrayed her into saying too much. She was greatly in awe of the Countess and feared her displeasure. "Can't you take a joke, Anastasia? I thought you'd be amused to hear what silly things some people say."

"I doubt if the Countess would find them funny. We all know that Her Imperial Highness wants a son to succeed his father. But if women were allowed to rule in Russia—as they are in England, for example—it wouldn't matter if the Tsarina gave birth to a dozen daughters in a row."

This was an idea she had picked up from Anthony Mills. As she had expected, Varvara was profoundly shocked.

"A woman to rule Russia! Oh, that would be impossible."

"Why? It wasn't impossible for the Empress Elizabeth, or Anna, or Catherine the Great. All it needs is a ukase from the Tsar, revoking the decree that no woman can succeed to the Imperial throne," pointed out Anastasia, enjoying the fat girl's consternation. She was about to elaborate on her theme when she caught sight of the Countess hurrying toward them across the lawn. A sheet of paper fluttered in her hand.

"Oh, my dears, such splendid news! Just guess what's happened!"

"We've chased the yellow monkeys out of Manchuria!" cried Anastasia hopefully.

"No, no—better than that, even. Her Imperial Highness has been safely delivered of a son, and all Russia is rejoicing. We must thank God that the Romanov succession is safe at last!"

Chapter Six

In spite of the loneliness and her constant yearning for news of Valerian, Anastasia found that summer in Siberia had its compensations. The wide, wild steppe, its thin grass stirring gently in the morning breeze beneath the boundless blue arc of the sky, held a strange fascination for her. She loved to ride with her father as he visited the soldiers on summer maneuvers, or inspected the blockhouses under construction along the thin line of rail that stretched away into the distance—a silver thread that was now her only link with Valerian.

At first she had written to him—effusive schoolgirlish letters in her round, loopy scrawl, pouring out her impressions of this vast, untamed country and faithfully recounting the family's daily activities. But there was so little to relate. Day after day went by with no incident to distinguish it from its fellows, until she grew afraid of boring him with written trivia, as Andrei had accused her of boring him with small talk. And Valerian, harassed and overworked as the war went from bad to worse, found few opportunities to respond.

She could not blame him. He was busy. His duties as ADC to the Minister for War kept him shuttling to and fro, hither and yon, on matters of high importance. How could he find the time—if he had the inclination—to write to a bored, lonely girl he still considered a child, far away in remote Siberia?

Kadya, too, was becoming restless as the novelty of his new command wore off and he realized both the isolation and the responsibility of his position. He felt cut off from his friends and out of touch with the progress of the war, but for him there was a remedy denied to Anastasia.

Leaving his wife and family to fend for themselves, and his work in the charge of Captain Costalinsky, his bottle-nosed second-in-command, Kadya took the train to Vladivostok, ostensibly for the purpose of seeing for himself how the Russian armies were faring in the field.

"I can't go on kicking up my heels in safety while our brave lads are giving their lives out there on the Liautung Peninsula," he said gravely to the Countess. "I must do my bit to help them, though naturally it's a sacrifice for me to leave you here alone for a month or two."

"We'll manage all right, my dearest," Olga assured him, "but must you stay so long? You say you've every confidence in Captain Costalinsky, but if you ask me, that young man drinks. I believe it would be unwise to leave him in charge for more than a week, at most."

"Oh, a fortnight, a month—what does it matter?" Kadya waved an impatient hand. "Nothing can go wrong here. I've given all the necessary orders—you really must take my word for it. A child could take command of a dead-end place like this, now that I've organized it properly. Don't worry, I'll have my finger on the pulse all the time. Costalinsky's been told to make his reports to me, wherever I am. The important thing now is to understand the *broad outlines* of our strategy at the front. Then I can give the Emperor a true picture of what's going on. You know how those old generals try to pull the wool over his eyes. If you're worried about Costalinsky, my dear, why not keep an eye on him youself? He's quite an obliging lad if you handle him right, even if he is too fond of the bottle."

He kissed her blithely and departed, together with six of their eight servants and a sleigh piled high with baggage, just as the first snow of winter began to fall.

Needless to say, his visit to the theater of war took him nowhere near the front, but he enjoyed himself immensely among old friends and comrades, and picked up a great deal of scandalous gossip—for which he'd been pining—about goings-on among the Petersburg aristocracy. Refreshed and invigorated, Kadya took the train directly back to the capital to make his personal report to the Emperor.

Winter came early to Siberia. The light snow that had been falling as Kadya left his post at Nicholasgrad, near Irkutsk, turned to blizzards before he had been gone a fortnight.

Snowdrifts cut off the village from the town. Olga developed a severe cold. Whenever she was tired or worried, the strain would affect her throat; it was the chink in her physical armor, she sometimes said, her Achilles heel. First she'd become aware of soreness, as if a prickly hedge had sprung up at the back of her mouth, and every time she swallowed the thorns dug into her throat. Next her voice would disappear, leaving only a pathetic whisper in place of her usual incisive tones.

At this point she could usually be persuaded to take to her bed. Although she hated admitting any weakness, she was sensible enough to realize when enough was enough. But with Arkady gone and his troops visibly sliding into slackness, Olga felt a responsibility too heavy to allow the behavior of an invalid. Day after icy day she struggled to keep on her feet, to chivvy Kadya's officers as she chivvied her servants, and make certain that Captain Costalinsky did not neglect his duty. Despite her efforts, however, the building of the new blockhouses slowed gradually down until finally, as the iron frost caused machinery to seize up and tools to snap like twigs, it came to a complete standstill.

"Do stay in bed today, Mama," pleaded Anastasia one bitter morning just before Christmas. She had found the Countess ashen-faced, coughing as she struggled to rise from her pillows. "I'll get Vera to bring you a honey drink for your sore throat. You can't possibly go out in this weather, and you know as well as I do what Doctor Zinoviev told you: look after a cold from the beginning, and it'll cure itself in half the time."

"Old Zinoviev is nothing but a prophet of doom. His ideas were out of date in 1800," said the Countess, with an attempt at her usual briskness although her voice was nothing but a whisper. "I've got far too much to do today to lie in bed."

"Let me do it for you."

"Nonsense, Stanya. Go off to your lessons and don't worry about me."

"I won't go unless you promise to stay indoors," said Anastasia firmly. "Make Peter Stepanovitch bring his report to you. Why should he snuggle up to his stove while you freeze in a sleigh going to see him. Will you promise?"

Olga sighed. "I wish I could, but you know as well as I do what Peter is like. He'll swear that everything is fine when nothing's being done at all. The only way to keep him working is to supervise him personally. It's a great pity that he's the senior officer here; Lieutenant Malin is far more reliable. But then, so many officers were obliged to accompany your dear father... As he pointed out, it would have looked very odd for a military governor to travel virtually unattended."

"I don't see why he had to take six of the servants," said Anastasia, glancing around the untidy room. "We've hardly enough to clean the house, let alone keeping Miss Catherine's fires going. Why can't she be content with a stove, like everyone else?"

"My dear girl, she comes from a country where they know nothing about stoves. She doesn't think a room is warm unless she can see the flames."

"It's high time she learned, then," said Anastasia. Miss Catherine's refusal to adapt to local conditions was a sore point with the whole household.

Painfully, the Countess suppressed a cough. "Let me get dressed now, dear," she said. "I've asked the Dubrovs and their daughter over for a game of cards this evening, so you'll have a nice little party to look forward to."

To Anastasia, the prospect of yet another evening in Varvara's company was anything but alluring. But hours before their guests arrived, the fever that Olga had held at bay for days suddenly gained the upper hand. She collapsed in Captain Costalinsky's overheated office just as he was explaining why he hadn't visited the new blockhouses for a whole week. The alarmed coachman drove her home in the sleigh and summoned Anastasia from her lessons. Together with a twittering Mademoiselle Froissart they carried her upstairs and laid her on the big bed.

"Go at once for the doctor, Sergei," ordered Anastasia. "Tell him it's urgent." She felt the weight of responsibility settle heavily on her shoulders. To whom could she turn for help? Miss Catherine was no use at all: muttering darkly about infection, she had retired to stoke up the roaring fire in her bedroom. Mademoiselle Froissart, though willing, was frail and elderly herself, with a history of heart trouble. It would hardly be fair to ask her to help with the nursing which the Countess clearly needed, and the two remaining servant girls were slow and stupid.

There's no one but Sergei, thought Anastasia. Imagine Sergei as a lady's maid! Still. There was no choice. Nearly seven feet tall, dressed in countless layers of shirts and coats and exuding a powerful indoor odor, the coachman looked thoroughly out of place in the Countess' boudoir, with its delicate rosewood furniture. Her treasured collection of porcelain seemed in imminent peril every time he moved.

As she lay under the great bearskin rug taken from the sleigh, the Countess' breathing was fast and shallow, and her hands felt icy although her face burned with fever. Left alone with her stepmother, Anastasia prayed that Sergei and the doctor would hurry. But when at last the burly coachman returned, he was alone.

A military train had been derailed a few miles from Irkutsk that morning, and the doctor had been summoned to the hospital to help those injured in the crash.

"Then we must take Mama to him!" cried Anastasia, but Sergei shook his grizzled head.

"The roads are too bad, miss. I can't get my horses through the drifts and the mistress isn't fit to travel."

Anastasia was forced to agree. Such a journey might do more harm than good. It might even be fatal. Like it or not, Olga would have to be nursed without the doctor's aid.

Unexpectedly, help arrived in the form of Varvara, who came with her parents for the promised game of cards. After only a little prompting from her mother, she offered to help nurse the patient.

"Varvara has been training at the hospital for over a month," her mother said proudly. "This will be a good chance for her to practice."

Gratefully, Anastasia agreed. For the next week, she and Varvara took turns nursing the tossing, fever-racked Countess, feeding her cooling drinks and replacing the covers thrown off by her burning, restless body. In spite of all their care, however, the patient didn't improve—nor did the doctor return. A fresh fall of snow had blocked the road from Irkutsk to Nicholasgrad, and in any case he had plenty to keep him busy at the hospital. A number of high-ranking officers had been on the military train that crashed; the Minister for War, General Kuropatkin himself, had escaped only because he moved to the carriage behind in order to speak to his ADC. Now that he was temporarily stranded in this Siberian backwater, the general decided to inspect the military installations in the area—and in particular the blockhouses under construction along the road to Nicholasgrad.

While he was there, he thought, how pleasant it would be to pay a visit to his old friend Olga, and see how her fool of a husband was coping with his new way of life. At once, he ordered a passage to be dug through the snowdrifts that obstructed the road.

"What can we do?"

Anastasia, pale and heavy-eyed after another sleepless night, stared at Varvara across the bed. The Countess' head turned weakly from side to side on the pillow, as if seeking a cooler place. Although her eyes were open, she was delirious and recognized neither girl.

"She's so *thin*!" said Anastasia. "She's getting worse every day, not better. I'm scared. I'm afraid she'll die if we don't get help."

She gazed out of the heavily curtained window, as if to summon the doctor's sleigh by magic. But now it was snowing again, thick soft flakes covering the trampled slush of yesterday with a pure white blanket.

Varvara licked her lips, and gave the customary glance over her shoulder which always preceded a dramatic revelation.

"There's only one thing to do," she said importantly. "We must ask the holy man to heal her."

"Oh, no," said Anastasia. "Mama would be horrified." Unlike the Tsarina, the Countess fiercely rejected mystical manifestations and messages from other worlds.

"The Countess will know nothing about it," pointed out Varvara.

Anastasia considered the matter. Drastic steps were clearly called for. Since conventional methods seemed to have no good effect, perhaps it was time to adopt unconventional ones. After all, what was there to lose? The holy man might be a charlatan; most of them were. But he could hardly make the Countess any worse. If only she had someone to advise her, someone she trusted! Sick with fear as well as pity, she looked again at the emaciated figure on the bed. If she did nothing, Mama would die—she was certain of it.

Abruptly she reached a decision. "Who is this holy man? Is he a priest?"

"Hush, not so loud. You could get into trouble," warned

Varvara, shivering with pleasure, her protruberant brown eyes rolling. "His followers must take a terrible oath of silence."

"Don't be silly. There's no one here to overhear us except Mademoiselle Froissart, and you know what *her* Russian's like," said Anastasia contemptuously. "Anyway, I'm not one of his followers—or likely to become one."

"You'll have to become one if you want his help."

"Are *you* a follower?"

Varvara looked sly. "That's a secret."

"Oh. I see... That means you are. Oh, what does it matter, anyway? All right, if this holy man can do anything to cure Mama, I'll willingly become a follower. Who cares if Father Ignatiev disapproves? A lot he's done to help!"

"You don't know what you're saying." A singularly unattractive smile, at once triumphant and secretive, creased Varvara's quivering cheeks.

"Yes, I do. Now hurry, please, Varvara. Go find this holy man of yours and tell him to come quickly—it's urgent. Tell him I'll pay him well for his trouble."

Varvara opened her mouth to speak, thought better of it and departed into the snow with remarkably little fuss. Anastasia cleaned up the sickroom as best she could and stroked up the potbellied stove. Because wood was getting short in the governor's residence, Anastasia wished she had the authority to send Captain Costalinsky and his card-playing soldiers out to search for fuel. It was the general's fault that the Countess was ill, she thought angrily, and a large part of her anger was directed at her absent father, who had so lightly abandoned his family to the cruel Siberian winter.

She returned to the bedside. For the moment her patient lay still, breathing so quietly that for a panicky instant Anastasia believed that the Countess had already died. Then she saw that her patient was merely asleep. With a sigh of relief, Anastasia collapsed into an armchair and fell at once into a doze.

She awoke suddenly, with the strange impression that someone had been shining bright points of light onto her eyelids. The room was dim; the icon lamp cast only a faint glow. As her vision focused, Anastasia saw the long shape of a strange man's face not two feet from her own. The bright points of light came from his deepset, luminous eyes, which seemed to bore right into her head. She tried to jump up from the chair, but the eyes held her captive, chaining her unwilling gaze so strongly that she could not even move them to focus on the rest of the man's features. With a great effort, she turned her whole head to one side, away from that burning scrutiny, and the spell was broken.

"Look at me again, little sister," said a deep, resonant voice with the same rough accent as Sergei's but a thousand times more authority.

Anastasia very nearly obeyed, but some tough inner core that loathed a dictator warned her to screw her eyes shut before the spell could overwhelm her once more. She got up hastily, putting out a hand to steady her giddy head.

"It's so...so hot," she murmured. "I must have fallen asleep."

"This is Father Grigori," said Varvara from the doorway. She looked excited and animated, almost attractive, thought Anastasia in surprise. Now that her head had cleared, she could see that the holy man was tall and lean, his long dark hair parted in the middle, and tumbling straight down over his temples to accentuate a narrow, strong-featured face with a great beak of a nose. His ankle-length black robe had a monkish look, but as she covertly studied the wide, sensual mouth half hidden by a straggly beard, Anastasia realized instinctively that not all the monastic vows would figure in this man's philosophy. Poverty, yes; obedience, possibly; chastity, never. He exuded a powerful masculine aura, to which Varvara's fluttering eyelashes and heaving bosom showed she was very much aware. Anastasia herself felt the power of his personality, but it didn't attract her. On the contrary, she resented the way this man—a stranger—had so arrogantly stared at her and sought to dominate her will.

Avoiding those magnetic eyes, she said rather coldly: "It is good of you to come, Father Grigori. As you see, the Countess is ill and there is no doctor to help her. Can you do anything?"

"I will cure her through the power of God better than any doctor could," said the holy man, with a deep, booming laugh that sounded out of place in a sickroom. "Be silent and watch, little sister, while I intercede for your mother at the Throne of the Most High."

A medley of confused emotions filled Anastasia's heart as she watched the tall, black-clad figure move to the Countess' bedside and stand, head bowed, arms upraised like the wings of some huge bird of prey about to capture its quarry. Anger at the brash self-confidence of this rough peasant, who spoke of God as an equal, was mixed with a strange, unreasoning fear such as she had never known before. All her instincts told her that whatever power this man possessed stemmed from the Prince of Darkness rather than the God Whose Name he was invoking. Suddenly, she felt that she had stepped out of the safe, sure world she knew into a whirling vertiginous blackness where unknown horrors lay in wait to devour her body. Yet, as he prayed, she saw to her astonishment that the figure on the bed had stopped its restless tossing from side to side and appeared to be listening:

"Sister! Sister! Look at me!" commanded the strong, vibrant voice. "Open your eyes."

In the glow of the lamp, Anastasia could see rivulets of sweat coursing down Father Grigori's forehead and cheeks, and feel the power of his will beamed like a shaft of concentrated energy at the woman he addressed. A current of magnetism so strong it was almost tangible linked them together.

"Sister, sister! Open your eyes and look at me."

The Countess' eyelids fluttered and her pupils, wide and unfocused, gazed straight at Father Grigori. A moment later she smiled and raised her shoulders from the pillow.

"Mama!" Anastasia started forward with a glad cry, but Varvara caught at her sleeve.

"Wait!" she hissed. "Let him finish."

Father Grigori bent forward, and now his voice was low and soothing. "You have been ill, sister, very ill. God sent this illness as a punishment for your sins, but now He has forgiven you and sent me to heal you. You are tired, very tired, and your eyes are heavy, but the evil has left you. Sleep now, sister, and when you wake you will be well again."

Now a new fear gripped Anastasia. What if the Countess should wake from the trance and find this rough, unkempt peasant addressing her so familiarly? She who had always scoffed at the mystics and prophets who thronged the Tsarina's apartments! Her anger would be terrible if she were to discover that in her helplessness she had been treated by some unlettered Siberian *starets* who claimed to have taken away her sins. But Anastasia's fears were short-lived. With a deep sigh of contentment, the sick woman lay back against her pillows and one thin hand curled gently beneath her chin in an attitude of utter peace.

"So... tired," she sighed. "You're right, I am so tired..."

Father Grigori bowed his head a moment longer, watching her, then he turned and herded the two girls out of the room.

"Wine," he muttered hoarsely. "Bring me wine—quickly." Without waiting for an invitation he sank onto the Countess' chaise lounge. As he propped his heavy felt boots on its embroidered cushions, his dirty, calloused hand and grimy nails spread on the delicate gold armrest where the Countess' manicured fingers so often rested, Anastasia had a wild desire to giggle. It couldn't be true: what she had just witnessed must be the result of lightheadedness after too many sleepless nights. But no—it was real all right. Here was Varvara with a decanter of Madeira dredged up from heaven knew where, fussing over the dirty figure of the holy man just as if she, and not Anastasia, were the daughter of the house.

The wine quickly restored Father Grigori. Tossing back his tangled reddish-brown mane of hair, he swung his boots off the chaise lounge, blessed the girls briskly, and left by the back stairway before Anastasia could even mention the delicate subject of payment.

Barely two minutes later the burly, stovepipe-hatted form of Father Ignatiev was admitted to the house. Anastasia felt certain that it was the village priest's imminent arrival which had prompted Father Grigori not to linger over his wine. From where the holy man had been sitting, it was certainly possible to see anyone approaching the front door from the snowy street outside. But why all the secrecy, she wondered. Surely a holy man with Father Grigori's powers should not have to scuttle away from the presence of a simple village priest.

When Father Ignatiev at last took his leave, after finishing the Madeira, she tried to question Varvara, but the fat girl, quivering with self-importance, would only return such mysterious and evasive answers that Anastasia soon gave up in disgust.

"I promised to pay him. Why did he hurry away like that?"

"Father Grigori does not want money."

"How do you know?"

"Never mind how I know," said Varvara maddeningly. "All Father Grigori asks is that you should come and pray with him tonight."

"I can't leave Mama tonight."

"Ask Mademoiselle to sit with her. She'll be all right. Didn't

Father Grigori say she was going to get well?"

"Yes, but . . . Oh, all right then. I'll come with you, if that's really all Father Grigori wants, but it seems very strange to me. I've never heard of a holy man turning down an offer of good roubles before."

"Don't tell anyone where you're going," warned Varvara, "and wear dark clothes—the simpler the better."

"Where are we going?"

"You'll know soon enough, Anastasia Arkadeivna."

Their destination turned out to be a cellar, dug in the side of a hill beneath a large barn belonging to Varvara's uncle. They went on foot, muffled in thick dark cloaks, and Varvara insisted on slipping from one path of shadow to another with what Anastasia considered ridiculously exaggerated caution. Varvara stopped frequently to glance behind and listen for footsteps.

"No one's watching us," Anastasia protested, her teeth chattering. "Do come on. Anyone with a grain of sense is indoors by the stove on a night like this. Why can't we walk down the street in the usual way? We're not criminals, after all. Lurking about in the shadows is surely the best way of attracting attention."

Among the dark trees a few hundred yards beyond the village's last dwelling, Varvara stopped at last. With a final furtive glance over her shoulder she pulled Anastasia down a concealed flight of steps cut roughly in the earth at one side of a large barn.

"Here we are. This is my uncle's old barn," she said.

She knocked three times on the stout wooden door at the bottom of the steps. She paused, then knocked again. The door swung open so smoothly and suddenly that Anastasia took a startled step backwards, and Varvara caught her by the sleeve.

"Welcome, sisters," said the tall figure in the doorway, and Anastasia recognized Father Grigori.

Varvara retained her firm grip as they stepped into the dark cellar. But for its support Anastasia would have fallen as she stumbled onto the unexpectedly deep pile of a carpet that covered the floor. Apart from this, the cellar was unfurnished, though candlelit icons glowed dimly against the walls. As her eyes grew accustomed to the gloom, Anastasia saw a dozen people present besides the holy man. Most of them were women, stout, respectable middle-aged matrons wearing headscarves and somber clothes; she counted three men besides Father Grigori. As they chatted quietly among themselves, there was an air of suppressed excitement in the looks they gave the newcomers.

The cellar was warm; Anastasia loosened her cloak. When the hood slipped back, revealing the pale gleam of her hair in the candlelight, one man grunted appreciatively. Then she felt rather than saw Father Grigori beside her again. His long fingers grasped her hand, palm against palm, and a wave of magnetism flowed through the joined limbs like the tingling of an electric current. Suddenly uneasy, she jerked her hand away and heard the holy man's deep chuckle. But he made no further attempt to touch her. Instead he opened his arms in a wide, embracing gesture, inviting the people to gather around him.

"Brothers and sisters, let us pray," he intoned.

As his rich voice rose and fell in the familiar prayers she had known from childhood. Anastasia's anxiety began to fade. Of course it was strange that a holy man should prefer that she pay her debt by attending a quasi-religious service in an underground crypt rather than in good money. But, then, holy men *were* strange. God had touched them with a little of His power, and you couldn't expect them to behave like others did. The furtive arrival was probably due more to Varvara's morbid love of secrecy than any necessity. Even an orthodox fanatic like Father Ignatiev would find it hard to locate heresy in the words with which the holy man was exhorting his little congregation to love God, to love Christ, to love one another as they loved Him...

Father Grigori's voice was remarkable; there was no doubt about that. Deep, rich and caressing, it seemed—though he addressed them as a group—to be speaking to each in private. Anastasia could tell by the rapt, ecstatic faces of the women, and the faint sheen of sweat on the faces of the men, that each was experiencing some deeply significant stirring of the soul, for which the holy man's simple words could not wholly account. The man beside her was breathing quickly, as if he'd been running, and his hands moved to fumble with the front of his baggy trousers. Anastasia herself felt a strange sensation of freedom—a *blurring*, as if the clear lines between Right and Wrong were no longer distinct.

With difficulty she pulled her eyes away from the priest's tall figure and surveyed her companions. Irina, Varvara's mother, licked her lips; her bulging brown eyes—so like her daughter's—were half closed in bliss. Her sister Sophia, whose husband owned the barn above, plucked nervously at her throat. A thin thread of saliva hung suspended from her slack mouth. Madame Galina, the dressmaker, was swaying rapturously as she clutched the hand of one-eyed Sergei Ilyitch, the ex-soldier who now worked on the Spasskys' farm. Even if Anastasia found Father Grigori disturbing, the sight of so many familiar and respectable faces was enough to reassure her. What harm could come to her in their presence?

"Love ye one another! See that ye love one another as Christ loved you," repeated the holy man. He raised his arms, lifting his tattered dark robe like the wings of a giant bird. Then, with a sudden sharp gesture, he tore it apart and stood naked before them, his phallus fully erect. A sigh which was almost a groan came from his assembled followers.

They linked hands and began to circle him, slowly at first and then faster, faster, until the cellar blurred before Anastasia's eyes. The only point on which she could focus herself was the priest's sexual organ, which seemed to grow larger and larger until it filled the whole room.

With a loud, frenzied cry, Varvara's mother broke away from the circle and began to tear off her clothes. Before she was free of them, she flung herself on her knees before Father Grigori, clasping his legs and kissing the object of her adoration in an ecstasy of surrender. Seconds later her sister, also half naked, was trying to usurp her place.

Anastasia's eyes widened in horror. She tried to step back, tried vainly to free her hands from the sweaty grip of her companions on either side. Then many of the devotees were breaking ranks. The women fell either on the priest or on the other men, who now lay groaning in corners of the cellar, each of them striving to accommodate two or three women at once.

A wave of nausea brought Anastasia to her senses. The secrecy, Varvara's sly hints and excited eyes, the care with which she had prepared this trap, were all suddenly plain to her. She had been led to the den where the Khlisti—a sect whose sexual orgies were whispered about all over Siberia—celebrated their profane rites. Father Grigori must be their leader: no wonder he had avoided a meeting with the orthodox priest. No wonder she had felt disturbed by his strange, magnetic attraction, which had no holiness in it. Shuddering, she detached herself from Varvara's sweaty grasp and dodged the long arm with which Sergei Ilyitch sought to draw her closer to him.

Anastasia flattened herself against the cellar's rough walls. Then, taking care to avoid contact with any of the writhing naked forms, she edged toward the door. Varvara's mother, a mound of pale, flabby flesh, lay sprawled and sated against it. Father Grigori was already coupling with a second wild-eyed matron, while two other women, waiting their turn, stroked his back and loins with trembling hands.

If she could only escape while they were thus engaged. If she could only draw the heavy bolts securing the door and flee into the clean cold night, surely no one would notice her departure? She reached the door and pulled back first the top bolt and then the lower one. They slid aside easily, testifying to recent oiling, but when she grasped the handle, the door would not budge. In dismay, Anastisia remembered seeing Father Grigori lock the door just after she and Varvara entered. The key had vanished beneath his dark robe, which now lay in a tumbled heap beside him. Without it, there was no way to escape.

"It's a disgrace," muttered the Minister for War. "A disgrace to the Russian Army and an insult to His Imperial Majesty. Do you hear me, Valerian?"

"Sir!" said Valerian, wooden-faced.

General Kuropatkin, his jowls growing steadily redder in startling contrast to his silver hair, shuffled on through the corridor. A dozen alarmed soldiers, filthy rags showing through the burst seams of their boots, were hastily shoveling snow, heaped high against the walls of their half-built blockhouse. Captain Costalinsky cursed steadily as he urged them on. He looked like a man whose worst nightmares had sprung to horrible life. How could he have guessed that a trainload of the very top brass—on its way to visit the front, together with an escort of fawning journalists, photographers and foreign observers—would be derailed at Chertovalinsk and forced to stay a week while the line was repaired?

How could he have seen into the restive mind of the Minister for War and divined that he would choose today to inspect the soldiers' quarters in the new town of Nicholasgrad, quarters which were supposed to be the model on which future barracks would be built?

Captain Costalinsky was honest enough to admit that even if the general had chosen the second blue moon a year from now to pay his visit, the blockhouse situation would have been much the same. It was the lack of warning that rankled, being left in the lurch by that pampered ass Count Kharkov. The Count should have been here, taking the blame for his own shortcomings, instead of leaving his subordinate to face the music alone.

So Costalinsky cursed and shouted at his men until they felt as ill-used as he did. In silence they endured the stinging reprimand which the General delivered before mounting his sleigh to drive on to the next unfinished fortification.

Long before his tour was complete, the Minister for War had dismissed all the non-military personnel in his retinue. It was, as he remarked bitterly to his ADC, doing nothing but harm to the image of "Russia Armed for the Conflict," with which he had been trying to impress both foreign newsmen and the national press. Now their rumblings of discontent about the way the war was being conducted would be louder than ever. Looking at the disreputably undernourished soldiers, at their rusty weapons and hangdog faces, General Kuropatkin cursed Count Kharkov from the bottom of his heart.

Other officers made more successful efforts than Captain Costalinsky had to explain why military installations in the district were so poorly maintained, but Kuropatkin was no fool. He soon had a very accurate idea of where the blame lay for the ruinous state of affairs. As darkness put an end to his tour, he ordered his sleigh to drive back to Nicholasgrad.

"I shall have to see how your poor mother is faring before we continue our journey," he explained wearily to Valerian. "No doubt you wish to see her as well. Poor lady, what a place to spend the winter! I did all I could to oppose your stepfather's appointment to this post, but His Imperial Majesty was quite determined that he should have it. Perhaps he'll change his mind when I make my report . . ." The grim set of his mouth relaxed suddenly and he gave his iron-gray mustache an almost skittish upward flick. "All the same, it will be agreeable to see Olga. It doesn't hurt to combine duty with pleasure, eh?"

"Duty, sir?"

The General grimaced. "I have the honor to be acting as the Imperial errand boy," he explained. "The Empress insisted that I must, with my own hands, present your mother with a miniature of herself with the little Grand Duchesses and a special receipt for cough linctus compounded by some old witch at the Danish Court. Can you imagine?"

Valerian grinned sympathetically. The Tsarina's highhanded habit of using distinguished officers and diplomats to run her personal errands was well known at Court.

"I'm sure my mother will be delighted to receive you, sir," he said tactfully. "She remarked in her last letter how much she longs for news from Petersburg." He himself could not suppress an odd lift of the heart at the thought of seeing Anastasia again. That fleeting embrace in the train had remained in his memory more poignantly than most of his fleeting embraces. Valerian, who prided himself on his ability to keep heart and head firmly detached in his numerous *affaires du coeur*, had to admit that in this case they had moved perilously close to one another. He had begun the kiss as a brother might, and somehow it had turned into a lover's embrace. *Lovers'* embrace, he corrected himself, remembering her eager response. Passion had flared between them in that single brief contact before his mother entered the carriage. Despite his efforts, he could not forget the feel of Anastasia's warm, soft lips against his, the sight of the long lashes sweeping her cheeks in crescent moons as she closed her eyes in ecstasy, that taut, firm body pressed against him.

It was absurd, of course. Absurd and almost incestuous. Not only was Anastasia a child, she was also his sister. It was unworthy of him to think of her in any other light. Still, he couldn't dismiss the memory of her husky voice, with an intonation yet not wholly Russian, saying with suppressed passion: "I'm *not* your sister, nor am I little."

Yes, it would be very pleasant to see Anastasia again.

But when, after beating repeatedly on doors and gates, the general had been helped down from the sleigh and ushered inside by a distraught Miss Catherine Lonsdale, pins cascading from her disordered hair, nose bright red above the many shawls in which she was nursing a heavy cold, Anastasia was nowhere to be seen.

"Oh, dear, I'm so sorry . . . We didn't know you were coming. There's nothing in the house . . . nothing to eat," gabbled the flustered governess.

Valerian looked around in horror at the cold, dirty hall of the house. General Kuropatkin, cheated of the warmth and comfort he'd been anticipating after a long, cold and frustrating day, sat on a hard bench in numbed consternation.

"Where is my mother? Where is Anastasia? Where are all the servants?" Valerian demanded. "What's the matter, woman? Don't cry. I'm not going to eat you. What is happening here? Why is the house so cold?"

Slowly the plaintive story emerged. Count Kharkov had left nearly a month ago, taking most of the servants with him. The snow had fallen. The Countess got sick, and there was no one but Miss Anastasia to nurse her...

"Why couldn't you nurse her?" Valerian's voice was harsh.

Miss Catherine drew herself up. "I am a governess, not a sickroom attendant."

Valerian suppressed his urge to dismiss this ignoble creature on the spot. "Did Mademoiselle Froissart interpret her duty in the same way?" he asked, barely able to keep from shaking her.

No, the Frenchwoman had done what she could, though that was little enough. It was so difficult to keep the house warm. There was no one to carry wood for the stoves, and now the kitchen maid had left...

Abruptly Valerian abandoned his questioning. Action was what was needed; explanations could wait until later.

"You say my mother is better? Take me to her."

He turned to the general, huddling in his overcoat on the bench. "Excuse me a moment, sir, while I find someone to attend to your comfort. Sergei! Valentin! Get wood from the stables and start fires in those stoves. This place is like an icehouse. And you, Yuri, see what you can find to eat in the kitchen."

As the soldiers scurried around, the dismal house seemed to spring to life. Yuri Potopkin, the Tartar cook who had been known to feed ten officers—and feed them well—from a couple of scrawny chickens, found enough odds and ends to make a savory stew. And Valerian's hand fell unerringly on the key to his stepfather's private supply of spirits.

Leaving the general to down as much cognac and vodka as he needed, Valerian entered his mother's bedroom. Her room, he was glad to note, was at least warm and clean. The Countess was sleeping, but when she opened her eyes and saw her son standing over her, she gave a little cry.

"Valya! My dearest boy, is it really you—or is it a dream? I've had so many dreams... Oh, tell me it's true and you've come to help Anastasia. Poor child, she's had so much to do since your father went away."

"He's no father of mine," growled Valerian, as he bent and kissed her. "It's me all right, Mama. And your old admirer General Kuropatkin. We've come to visit you on our way to the front. He's got all sorts of presents and messages for you from the Empress . . . I'll bring him up to see you, but first we must set the house to rights."

"The house?" She looked around vaguely. "The house is all right. The servants all see to that, darling. Don't worry about the house. Mademoiselle! Go and tell the cook to prepare dinner at once for the general! Sit down, Valya, and tell me the news from Petersburg. Have you seen the little Tsarevitch yet?"

He realized that she was very weak and quite unaware of the state of the house.

"Later, Mama," he said gently. "First I must show the general to his room. He's had a hard day. Then I want to talk with Anastasia. Where is she?"

Neither the Countess nor Mlle. Froissart could tell him.

"She sleeps, perhaps? *Pauvre petite*, for many nights while madame is so ill she sleeps not at all. Wait, and I shall find her."

Valerian waited downstairs in his stepfather's study—whose desktop, he noted, overflowed with neglected correspondence. The clatter of pans and cutlery told him that the kitchen brigade was buckling down to work, and upstairs in the best bedroom the general's valet was tenderly ministering to his master's needs. Faintly, far off, he could hear Mlle. Froissart's voice twittering like a bird's.

"Anastasia? Anastasia? Where are you, cherie?"

"Anastasia!" echoed Miss Lonsdale's deeper tones.

Silly old bitches, he thought savagely. What have they been doing? How on earth can they have lost the girl they are supposed to be taking care of? She's only fifteen, after all; she's still a child. He strained his ears for Anastasia's reply, but there was no response to the increasingly frantic calls.

At last Mlle. Froissart, trembling, came to him and murmured, "*Je regrette* . . . I am very sorry, Monsieur le Comte, but Mademoiselle is not in the house. I do not know, for she told me nothing, but I think perhaps she go with her friend, Varvara . . ."

"Alone? At night?" With a great effort Valerian controlled his urge to shake the frail Frenchwoman until her teeth rattled. Grimly he said, "Direct me to Varvara's house at once!"

Chapter Seven

Inch by inch, Anastasia crawled across the thick carpet toward the dark heap of clothing discarded by Father Grigori. The key must be there. It *must*. She refused to even think about her fate if he had hidden it elsewhere—behind an icon, perhaps, or in a crevice. She had no time to search for other hiding places, she knew this with absolute conviction. Although the other men in the cellar were beginning to flag in their efforts to satisfy the women who clutched at them, Father Grigori's sexual appetite seemed to be freshly stimulated by each new female.

Now he was coupled with Varvara. The sight of her pale plump thighs locked round the holy man's straining body sent a fresh wave of revulsion through Anastasia. Another girl—young, her dark hair streaming down her back, an expression of ecstasy on her face—caressed his neck and shoulders, drawing strands of his hair through her hands as she waited her turn.

I shall be next, thought Anastasia in terror. When he has finished with Varvara, he will look for me. I must hurry.

Madame Galina was sprawled half across the holy man's clothing. She seemed barely conscious, however, and didn't resist when Anastasia pulled it free. A pungent, throat-catching aroma, rose from the holy man's garments. She was afraid that they were infested with lice and other vermin. But as her fingers felt the hard cold iron of the key, hidden in the deep folds of material, thankfulness made her body sway dizzily. As she crawled toward the door, her head was reeling. She had already pulled back the bolts, but in order to turn the key it was necessary to stand. Hardly had she risen to her feet when she heard Father Grigori's hoarse, rasping voice.

"Don't go yet, little sister. You still haven't paid me. Let me finish with this one and then..."

"No!" she whispered, her throat dry with terror. "Oh, no!" With all her strength, she struggled to turn the key. For an instant, as she pushed too hard, it jammed. Despair clutched her heart. Then she eased the pressure and the key turned smoothly, setting her free.

"Wait!" shouted the holy man as the door swung open, letting a blast of icy air into the fetid cellar. "Stop her!" he roared. "She'll betray us!"

He tried to reach her, but Varvara and the other girl, murmuring incoherently, clung so desperately to his body that he had to struggle to escape them. It was just the edge that Anastasia needed. Made fleet by fear, she leapt up the cellar steps and over the crunchy snow like a deer, dodging between the dark trunks of firs as she took the shortest way back to the safety of the familiar village street.

A hundred yards behind her, Father Grigori ran silently, a look of grim purpose on his saturnine features. His robe, put on in haste, flapped like the wings of a crow. Farther back still, Sergei Ilyitch, the one-eyed soldier, roused from his post-coital torpor, stumbled along in his wake.

Reaching the first house, gasping, Anastasia slowed her pace. Surely, *surely* now she was safe? A stitch jabbed painfully in her side. Surely he wouldn't dare pursue her here? But the long row of houses turned blank, shuttered windows toward her. A glance back at the holy man, as he followed in hot pursuit, lent fresh wings to her feet.

Suddenly light blazed from a single house set back from the street. A door had opened, spilling a glow onto the street, Anastasia sped toward it. Father Grigori was now so close behind that she could hear him panting, all but feel his strong talons clutching at her body... She twisted in his grasp, trying to tear herself free, but the hateful face was close to hers, so close that she caught the terrible odor of his unwashed hair...

Then with a shock that knocked all the breath from her body, she ran full tilt into a group of men emerging from the lighted doorway. They were like a brick wall; she dropped in a crumpled heap at their feet.

"What the hell...?" exclaimed an angry voice. The men gathered around her, bending over, blotting out the stars.

"Leave the girl alone. She's mine!" snarled Father Grigori. He thrust through the crowd and jerked Anastasia to her feet again. She sagged against him, helpless in his grasp. He pulled the hood forward to conceal her face. Her lungs were burning, straining for air which the unexpected blow had driven from her body. Though her mouth opened and closed, she couldn't utter a sound of protest.

Supporting her easily, the monk began walking away. "She's drunk. I'll take her home," he muttered.

"Wait a minute," said Valerian, pushing through the crowd. He caught the holy man by the shoulder and swung him around to face the light from the open doorway. "Who are you, man? Why were you chasing this girl through the streets? Does she want to go home with you?"

Angrily Father Grigori shook off the restraining hand. As the light fell on his swarthy face, the headman of the village, who was standing beside Valerian, gave a grunt of annoyed surprise.

"So it's you again, Grigori Efimovitch! Didn't I tell you to get out of town? Didn't I say that if I ever caught you practicing your obscene rites here again, I'd lock you up?"

The holy man's deepset eyes slid quickly from man to man, reading hostility in every face. He dropped Anastasia's body and stepped back hastily. By now the rest of General Kuropatkin's bodyguard had arrived, and Father Grigori was surrounded.

"I wasn't doing anything, Your Excellency," he blustered.

"This young lady wanted to hear about the Blessed Virgin of Kazan who appeared to me when I was . . ."

"Throw the fornicating blasphemer out of town!" shouted a rough voice at the back of the crowd. "Let him preach his gospel to the Siberian wolves, and leave our wives and daughters alone."

There was a general threatening move toward Father Grigori, but he stood his ground, stretching out two fingers in the age-old sign against the evil eye.

"Whoever lays a hand on me shall be accursed, I swear it!" he shouted, and the murmuring crowd fell back.

Valerian had bent over the crumpled figure on the ground.

"Give her air. The girl has fainted," he said. "Carry her into the house. Careful, now, Stepan . . ."

As soldiers raised the limp body, the hood fell back and Valerian recognized Anastasia. A blinding rage such as he'd never known engulfed him. He thrust his way through the still muttering crowd and confronted the holy man face to face.

"Don't touch me," warned Father Grigori, observing the fury in Valerian's eyes. "I am the Anointed of God. Evil will befall him who strikes at the Lord's Anointed."

"What have you done to my sister?" demanded Valerian in a terrible voice.

A spasm of fear crossed Father Grigori's swarthy features. "I called on your sister to cleanse herself through the mercy and love of God. To cast out false pride and open her heart to the healing grace of the Holy Spirit—"

"And open her legs for the benefit of Father Grigori..." shouted one man.

Valerian's self-control snapped. "Then say your prayers, Father Grigori," he roared, "because I am going to kill you."

The monk bared his teeth in a snarl that was almost inhuman, and fumbled under his robe. But before he could withdraw his knife, Valerian's fist shot out and caught him on the point of the chin. His head snapped back, his long arms flailed as they clutched the air, and Father Grigori toppled sideways like an artificial cross. Valerian caught him before he touched the hard-packed snow, hauled him upright again and smashed twice more at the bearded face before becoming aware of the headman's voice entreating him to stop.

"My lord, my lord! Don't dirty your hands with that tramp. Leave him to me. I'll put him in prison. Then we'll beat him and throw him out of town."

Two of Valerian's own men were holding his arms by now, thus preventing him from bludgeoning the blaspheming charlatan in monk's clothing who had dared to lay hands on Anastasia, on his own little sister... Gradually the red mist of rage cleared away from Valerian's eyes and he realized that he had almost fulfilled his promise. The holy man lay face down in the trampled snow. A dark stain of red spread around his head, soaking his tangled hair.

"All right," said Valerian. "Let me go. I'm not going to hit him any more. But if he's violated my sister, I'll see that he hangs."

Relieved, the headman poked at the fallen *starets* with his foot. Father Grigori did not stir. "We'll lock him up for the night and get him out of town tomorrow," he promised. "I warned him before not to stir up trouble."

"Who is he?" asked Valerian, rubbing his bruised knuckles.

"Where does he come from?"

"He has a wife and children in Pokrovskoye, by all accounts—not that they see much of him," grunted the headman. "A few years ago Father Grigori took it into his head to go wandering. He's been up and down the countryside causing trouble ever since. He even went to Petersburg, last year, and we thought we'd seen the last of him. But no—here he is again, stirring up a lot of silly women, making them do what they shouldn't... begging your pardon, sir, and meaning no disrespect to your sister," he added hastily. "As to his name, why they call him Rasputin, the Dissolute One. And the bastard is proud of the title, I've heard."

"Rasputin..." said Valerian thoughtfully. "Yes, I'll remember that name. And he, no doubt, will remember me."

Anastasia knew she was dreaming but she didn't want to wake up. Nothing but a dream could have conjured up Valerian, just when she needed him most. If, by keeping her eyes closed, she could preserve that dream, she was determined never to open them again.

The trouble was, Valya was shaking her, gently at first and then harder. And in the end she had to steal a glimpse from beneath her lashes, even though she knew it might end her dream. When she did, the miracle happened, for Valya was still there, bending over her body. A lock of black hair had fallen across his forehead. His face, she thought, looked very pale in the lamplight. He shook her again.

"Anastasia! Little sister! Wake up. Tell me you're all right."

Convinced at last that he was real, she sat up smiling. "Oh Valya! I thought I must be dreaming. How wonderful to find it is really you! How on earth did you get here?" She put her hand on her head, trying to remember. "I was running and that terrible man was trying to catch me... Did that really happen, or was it a dream? I must have hit my head, because suddenly everything went black, as if a lamp had been blown out. Oh!" she said, as a new thought struck her. "Perhaps I've died and gone to heaven."

"I'm not an angel, I assure you," said Valerian, grinning. He put his arms around her in a bear hug, squeezing till her ribs ached. But when she tried to turn her mouth to his, he pushed her gently, but firmly, aside. "None of that, now. I want the full story of how that man came to be chasing you. Why did you go away without telling Mademoiselle Froissart, who was sick with worry? Why did Kadya leave you and my poor mother with hardly a servant in the house—*and* the barracks in a shambles? Here, have a sip of this before you begin."

Anastasia sipped the brandy. Then she did her best to explain Kadya's departure, the Countess' illness and finally the visit of Father Grigori. As the stories progressed, Valerian's handsome face grew murderous.

"Damn them all to hell!" he shouted. "Kadya Pavlovitch, your friend Varvara, and that greasy charlatan of a monk as well. Monk? Multiple rapist would be closer to the truth. I want to go straight to the headman with the evidence you've given me."

"But the women liked it," she protested. "It was horrible, but they liked it. They encouraged him in everything he did. It was only because I was frightened—"

"He didn't harm you?" asked Valerian, desperate for reassurance.

Anastasia blushed, but answered steadily, "No. I opened the door and ran before... before it was my turn. He would have caught me, though, if you hadn't been there. Oh, Valya, I've been so scared... Please stay with us till Papa comes back. You don't know what it was like, with the snow falling day after day and no one to tell me how to make Mama better. Don't go away and leave me again." She began to cry. With a sigh, he took her in his arms to comfort her as he had when she was a child.

"Hush, little sister. Don't worry. Everything will be all right. I'm here now... Don't cry any more."

Racked by indigestion after his makeshift dinner the night before, shivering with cold and burning with indignation, General Kuropatkin was more than ready to grant his ADC a week's compassionate leave.

"Put those idle rascals to work, Valerian," he spluttered, mopping his whiskers following a series of sneezes. "Clean this place up—it's a disgrace. You have my personal authority to summon the military surgeon from—what in the hell is that place called, Tiusakrovskoye?—to attend your mother. He's a splendid man—did wonders for a lady of my acquaintance who suffered with her lungs. Get him here and see what he can do. And *I'll* see that His Imperial Majesty hears how his wonderful friend Count Kharkov has betrayed his trust here. Leave that to me."

He climbed stiffly into his sleigh. The coachman fastened the bearskin rug across his knees, and the retinue fell in behind. With a crack of the whip and another heroic sneeze, the general departed.

"Good-bye! Good-bye!" Anastasia hugged herself beneath her heavy cloak, almost dancing with delight. The general was gone. Now there would be no Andrei to pester her, no ever-present Mama to call her back to her needlework. For the first time in her life she had a chance to be alone for seven whole days with Valerian.

Watching her radiant face, as the winter sun made golden lights in the shining coils of blonde hair, her stepbrother felt a sudden misgiving. He loved women as much as they loved him. He enjoyed their company, understood their strengths and frailties, and appreciated their beauty. He also possessed a strong sexual drive, and saw no reason for not sleeping with any woman who attracted him sufficiently. He had previously taken his little stepsister's adoration for granted. Now he was uncomfortably aware that although her adoration remained the same, her feelings were now a woman's. Since he had last seen Anastasia, the shy chrysalis had been transformed by some magic into a beautiful butterfly. The gangling child with prominent cheekbones had blossomed into a lovely girl whose freshness and innocence contrasted sharply to the charms of the sultry, sophisticated sirens at the Imperial Court. And she wasn't as she had taken pains to point out to him, truly his sister. She was no blood relation at all.

It was going to be very difficult to keep their relationship platonic, especially when her proudly carried head and laughing, provoking green eyes inflamed and tempted him. Already, her taut young breasts and strong, slender legs seemed to invite his caresses.

But to succumb to these temptations would be to betray his mother's trust—and betray Anastasia herself, who must be quite unaware of the havoc she caused in men of Valerian's susceptible nature.

He decided to be very careful. A week could be a short time or a long one, depending how you looked at it. In this case, Valerian decided, it was going to be short, too short to allow him to lose his head over the lovely butterfly that had hatched so unexpectedly in the cruel Siberian winter.

Had she been aware of his elaborate plans to protect her, Anastasia would have been amused. In fact, she would have been surprised to know that he thought her innocent. She was already confident that she knew all there was to know about the Tender Passion—admittedly at second hand. But in a city like St. Petersburg, with a father like Kadya Kharkov, it was impossible for a girl of her age to be ignorant not only of the broad, well-trodden thoroughfares of sex, but of its secret alleys and hidden byways as well. To the bored *jeunesse doree* of St. Petersburg, gossip, experiment, and sensation were the staff of life, and nothing provided a richer field for sensation, experiment, and gossip than the many aspects of love.

Of course, her love for Valerian was of the highest, purest and noblest kind. But Anastasia's passionate blood made her keenly aware that what she wanted from her stepbrother went much farther than a simple affair of the spirit.

During that long, snow-bound week in the wilds of Siberia, thrown so unexpectedly into one another's company, Anastasia knew moments of supreme irritation when Valerian blithely refused to unbend. Much as she loved looking at him and listening to his deep, warm voice, she often wished that he would stop talking about war. About the folly of generals who were leading the Russian Army into one catastrophe after another, and the admirals who had already lost the best of Russia's battleships. Of course she was interested; of course she regretted as much as he did any reverses the Russian's might suffer, but why couldn't he forget the war for this one precious week while they were together?

"You never used to criticize our leaders," she complained. "I thought you were proud of our army. Now you seem to hate it. You used to say you were tired of being a peacetime soldier. What's made you change your mind?"

Valerian's laugh had little amusement in it. "What a fool I must have been! I don't hate our army, but I often wonder how it can fight at all under such generals."

It was an echo of Anthony Mills' opinion. But coming from Valerian the words seemed doubly shocking. "Our generals haven't had much practice in fighting lately," Anastasia said defensively. She was eager to show that she knew something of recent history. "There was the war against Turkey—didn't we win that?"

"No," he said bitterly, "it was another of our military disasters. Another mismanaged, ill-advised attempt by our glorious Emperor to increase his empire which is already, God knows, far too big for a single autocrat to administer. Panslavism is a myth—a convenient myth for those who want to stir up trouble in the Balkans. The Tsar should have known better than to listen to that fool Nelidov in 1896, just as he should never listen to feather-brained firebrands such as Count Arkady Kharkov today."

The Countess raised herself from her pillows. "Really, Valerian, I cannot allow you to speak of His Imperial Majesty in that disrespectful way—nor of my husband either. You should be ashamed of yourself. However strong your opinions, keep them to yourself. Such seditious talk is hardly suitable for Anastasia's ears, and of no great interest to her either."

"I'm sorry, Mama," said Valerian with a grin. "I thought you were asleep."

"Then watch your tongue, my boy, for I am sleeping less with each passing day," she replied tartly. Still weak after her illness, she spent much of each day in bed. But the prophecy of the Dissolute One had proved accurate; she had not relapsed into fever since his visit—of which, fortunately, she remembered nothing. Anastasia was unable to decide whether the fever had broken naturally before the monk made his appearance, or whether she had witnessed a miraculous cure.

"He prayed, and called her name three times," she told Valerian privately. "And suddenly Mama opened her eyes."

"Fakirs have half a dozen tricks of that kind," he said. "The man's a charlatan, there's no doubt about it. A good flogging was what he deserved. I doubt if he'll show his face around here again."

"Do you think *we'll* be here much longer?" she asked wistfully. "It seems to have been winter forever. When you're here, the house is warm and the servants do their work properly, but when you leave . . ." Her voice trailed away.

Valerian looked at her in quick sympathy. "Poor little Stanya. It must be dreary for you, so far from your friends. Can't you persuade Mama to send you back to Petersburg?"

"She might listen to you," said Anastasia hopefully.

The week of Valerian's leave was slipping by much too fast. Even if he cajoled his mother into sending her back to Aunt Vera's, she would never have this opportunity to be alone with him so often. In Petersburg, she realized, there were many Court beauties more gifted, more sophisticated, more intelligent than she was. How could she compete with them? How could she wrest Valerian from their voluptuous arms and glue him to her side? If only they shared some secret, some memory which a vision of her would always evoke for him.

She knew that he was attracted to her, although he fought against it here, in the wilds of Siberia. She could read it in the careful way he refused to touch her; in the many times she glanced up to find him watching her, hunger in his dark eyes. It was a look she had no difficulty in interpreting, but she knew that Valerian would always bow to his mother's wishes. These did not include marriage to a penniless orphan whose real mother had disgraced her family name, however proud that name had once been. To satisfy his mother, Valerian would have to marry a Grand Duchess, or, failing that, a Princess at least.

As the day of his departure raced nearer, a kind of desperation gripped her. What could she do to break down this barrier between them? On their last evening together, when more snow fell, she prayed that the road to Irkutsk would be blocked again. But Sergei, entering at ten—when the samovar was brought—to ask for tomorrow's orders, shattered this hope.

"The road is clear, Excellency, and I can see the stars. Would you like the horses brought around at eight? It may take us two hours or more to reach the town in such weather."

"Oh, Valya, must you really go so soon?" asked the Countess.

"Yes, indeed—if I'm to get you both out of this wretched hole by spring," said Valerian cheerfully. Rested and refreshed by a week's leave, he was keen to see action again. "Very good, Sergei. We'll have the horses at eight. Good night to you."

"Then we'll play a last hand of picquet," said the Countess, who had a weakness for this game. "Go to bed, child," she urged Anastasia. "You look worn out."

Sensing that she wanted her son to herself, Anastasia rose obediently and kissed her stepmother. She didn't feel tired at all and sleep was the last thing she wanted.

"Good night, Valya," she said. He ignored the pleading look in her eyes and gave her cheek the briefest, most perfunctory caress.

"Sleep well, little sister," he said casually, his hands already shuffling the cards.

"Little sister" again! Her eyes blazed with rage and disappointment as she swept out of the room. Had this week changed nothing? Did he still think of her as a child, to be packed off to bed before the grownups could enjoy themselves? Neither Valerian nor the Countess noticed the door slam as she made her angry exit.

The candles had burned low by the time Valerian finished the game with his mother and received her blessing. He yawned after she left the room, and kicked the logs in the fireplace into a blaze. Then he poured himself a last glass of his stepfather's excellent cognac and sat down at Kadya's littered desk.

Poor little Stanya, he thought. She wanted me to kiss her good night, but how could I in front of Mama? Stanya's such a one for theatrics, poor child. But with a face and figure so lovely, I expect she'll be able to get away with it.

For a few moments he indulged his imagination, breaking the strict bonds he had imposed on it all week long. How would it feel to run her heavy golden tresses through his fingers? To gather up great handfuls of its thick, warm silkiness? To kiss those curving lips with their secret, tantalizing smile, and feel her soft breasts crushed against his chest, as they'd been for that one brief instant in the train leaving Petersburg...?

Valerian sighed, then drained his glass. There was no point in dreaming of what could never be—must never be. Anastasia needed a husband. She would never be the kind of girl to indulge in lighthearted, casual affairs; he knew that instinctively. She felt things too deeply. She needed a man whose abiding love would give her the security she'd always lacked—the sort of love which Valerian knew would bore him rigid within a month of the wedding. He grinned. One day she'd thank him for keeping his distance this whole frustrating week!

He got up, surprised to find the room not quite as firmly grounded as he'd expected. Steadying himself at the mantel-shelf, he saw for an instant his own face reflected in the mirror above it. What kind of an officer do I look like now?, he thought, grinning at his image. Hair messed up, cheeks flushed, eyes too bright, coat unbuttoned... The general would have fifty fits! But his valet, who had been slightly injured in the train crash, was recuperating in the hospital at Irkutsk.

Valerian ran his fingers through his tousled dark hair and carefully navigated his way to the stairs. He must have put away more of his stepfather's cognac than he'd meant to. His mother's door was closed; no light showed under it. None of the servants had waited up for him either; Valerian was glad. Grunting, he jacked off his boots and dropped the rest of his clothes in a heap on the floor. Then he blew out the candle and reached a careless hand beneath the pillow for his nightshirt.

Immediately he regretted the loss of the candle, because the nightshirt was not there. Damn these interfering maids, he thought. Why can't they leave a man's clothes alone instead of carrying them off to wash and iron, then failing to put them back in place? Despite the fire in the stove, the bedroom was bitterly cold. He swore, gave up the search and slipped quickly under the covers, thanking heaven that the bed, at least, was warm. Moments later he was fast asleep.

Women crowded his dreams. It had been over a month since he'd last seen Ludmila, his gypsy mistress, whose wildness stirred the coldest loins. During his weeks at the front, dancing attendance on the general, Valerian had found it easy enough to resist the wiles of the local girls, but now he needed a woman.

Restlessly, he tossed. His dreams were curiously vivid, almost tangible. Was it his imagination, or was there actually warm soft breath on his cheek, and the vague, indefinable presence that suggested he was not alone? Sleepily he reached out and moved his hands over the slim length that had somehow come to life beside him. She was much more enticing than Ludmila. If he could exchange this woman of his dreams for the gypsy, he need never again suffer her gypsy tantrums. What an economy that would be! All I have to do is fill my body with cognac and dream of a woman, and there she'll be in bed beside me. I wonder which woman I've conjured up tonight...

"Ludmila?" he teased. "Is that you, darling?"

Her body curled into a tight ball in the cold expanse of Valerian's bed, Anastasia shivered. Had she made a terrible mistake? An hour had passed since her pride had brought her running to his room, planning to talk to him alone. She was determined to wring from him something she could treasure through the long, dreary months ahead.

At first she had wandered about his room, examining his belongings in growing impatience, trying to coax a little more heat from the fire, wondering why he didn't hurry. He had an early start tomorrow; surely he would soon come to bed? But the minutes dragged on and still there was no Valerian.

Her eyes grew heavy, and she lay down on his bed to rest. I'll be certain to hear him coming up the stairs, she thought. There'll be plenty of time to go to the chair and pretend I've been sitting up waiting for him.

It was cold on top of the bed. She shivered. Perhaps if she slid under the covers for a few minutes her feet would warm up a little. His nightshirt lay on the pillow; she pushed it to the floor and snuggled her head down where it had lain. Suddenly, the bodice of her dress felt too tight for comfort. One by one she eased the buttons undone and sighed with relief. That was better: surely he'd be here soon? It was getting late and she was oh, so sleepy . . .

She awoke with a jump. The room seemed much darker. The fire was almost dead now and the air was growing rapidly colder. Snug in the nest her body had made, she was reluctant to move, though she could now hear heavy, uncertain footsteps approaching in the hall. That can't be Valerian, she thought sleepily, he never walks as slowly as that. It must be one of the servants coming in drunk and using the hall as a shortcut to his room. I hope Mama doesn't hear him! She lay motionless in the dark, waiting for the footsteps to pass. To her horror, they stopped. The door was flung open with a crash. In the dim light from the passage she saw a tall figure swaying on the threshold, a candle flickering in his hand. She had waited too long to get out of the bed. Valerian had arrived and she was trapped!

Suddenly the idea of invading his privacy seemed childish and rude. Valerian believed he was alone. How would he like finding his stepsister in his bed, spying on his actions. Her throat was dry. Somehow she couldn't summon up the courage to indicate her presence. With every second that passed, it seemed harder to do. He was undressing already, dropping his clothes carelessly on the floor. She cringed across to the farthest edge of the bed, wondering if she could sneak out of the room after he had gone to sleep. She remembered with a chill that Valerian was a soldier about to return to active service. What if he kept a revolver in his bedroom? What if he took her for an enemy before she could escape? In the cold air she could smell the brandy fumes that had entered the room with him and realized from his blundering movements that he was far from sober. Oh, why had she ever conceived this mad plan of trying to catch him alone?

Minutes later, to her great relief, Valerian belw out the candle, but almost immediately he muttered a curse when he failed to find the nightshirt she had thoughtlessly pushed on to the floor. Would he relight the candle to search for it?

No. The bedclothes were suddenly heaved aside and then the springy mattress dipped as it took his weight. He was in bed only inches away from her—*naked*! Alexia lay absolutely rigid with alarm, unable to move a muscle for fear of discovery. This was the most awkward situation her impulsive nature had ever landed her in: she knew that if she spoke to him now she would risk earning his undying contempt—perhaps even hatred. If only he would go to sleep quickly, she might be able to escape to her own room.

It could have been hours or minutes—she had no means of telling—before his slow, even breathing told her that he'd at last succumbed to the combination of fatigue and strong drink. Very gently, very gradually, careful not to make a sound, she began to ease herself off the bed. One foot was already touching the floor when Valerian sighed and turned towards her, ande his hand reached over unerringly in the dark and descended on her breast.

"Ludmila?" he whispered. "Is that you, darling?"

She'd been so sure that he was safely asleep that the sound of his voice, slurred with drink, was doubly shocking. Then common sense came to her rescue. Valerian must be still asleep, dreaming of a mistress in faraway St. Petersburg. So long as she kept silent he need not discover her presence. But how could she remain silent when his hands were straying boldly all over her body, slipping inside her unbuttoned bodice and nudging her thighs apart? Her whole face felt as if it was on fire with shame. Somehow she must stop him, wake him, tell him who she was and why she was there.

"You're so beautiful, Ludmila . . . You know how much I love you . . ." His voice was caressing, saying the words she had always wanted to hear—if only they were addressed to her!

She could bear it no longer. "Valya, stop—wake up!" she said urgently, finding her voice at last. "It's not Ludmila. It's me, Alexia. I—I want to talk to you."

To her horror he chuckled and pulled her closer. "Alexia, by all that's wonderful! My little Polish wildcat: so you've come to me of your own accord. Did you guess I'd been thinking of you tonight—sitting alone in the library, drinking and thinking? Thinking and drinking. Trying to decide whether you wanted the same as I did. Well, I needn't have worried; you've made matters clear at last..."

"No, no! You're wrong," she cried, squirming in his embrace, dismayed to find that his only response to her struggles was to hold her in a grip of steel. "I want to talk. I only want to talk to you."

"Time enough to talk later, Lexi darling," he muttered indistinctly, his face buried in her hair. "Better things to do than talk now—I'll show you that. Don't push me away. This is what you want; you've been asking me for it every time you looked at me this whole long week."

"I haven't asked you for anything," she cried, pummelling uselessly at his chest, head, anything her fists could reach. "Let me go! Can't you understand a word I say?"

"Of course I understand." His mouth came down hard over hers and she jerked her head away sideways, panicking suddenly because this was not the Valerian she knew and loved. This was a stranger, stronger than she realized any man could be, smelling powerfully of brandy, intent on dragging her down some dark path of experience she was now very sure she did not wish to tread.

"You're drunk, Valya. Leave me alone. Let me go!" She struck him across the cheek as hard as she could, but he only laughed and held her more tightly.

"Oh no, Lexi darling! That's not the way to treat your lover. That's what the gypsies do. Have you changed your mind? Are you trying to say you don't want me for your lover after all?"

Oh, she did, she did! If Valerian was her lover nothing else in the world would matter. But why did love have to be like this? From the way he was treating her it seemed more as if he hated her and enjoyed her helpless struggles. The harsh stubble of his chin rasped her cheeks and her flesh shrank from the touch of his boldly exploring, infinitely experienced hands. She wished that he would lie still and hold her while she slept instead of feeling and prying, and touching her wherever she tried to protect herself.

"Don't, Valya... can't we go to sleep now?" she begged.

"I'm going to teach you to make love first..." he muttered. "Lie still now, darling."

Her soul rose in revolt. This—this struggle—couldn't be what he called making love? But then, what had she expected—moonlight and roses? Soft lights and sweet music leading up to *this*? From its hiding place far back in her memory, the image of Miss Louisa locked in Valerian's arms seemed suddenly to fill her whole vision.

"Don't, Valya," she gasped, frenziedly squirming. "Stop. I don't want to make love. I didn't know it would be like this..."

Too late. Drink had combined with his long abstinence from women to make it impossible for Valerian to obey her, even if he'd wanted to. She caught a jumble of confused phrases... "Lead a man on... teasing... all the same in the end... change your mind now..."

Alexia's head swam, and for a few frantic moments she was lost, unable to tell where she was, who she was, whether she felt pain or fear or even an inadmissible pleasure as she flung hereself to and fro, trying to escape the iron grip of his hands and the weight of his body that pinned her down. Her skull came in contact with the carved wooden bedhead, and she was pressed against it until she feared her neck would snap, pounded back against it again and again. Then the monster who was ill-treating her slumped over her with a sigh and became Valerian again. It was over.

She lay still, supporting his weight as long as she could bear it, afraid of making any movement that would confirm her hideous suspicion that she was no longer whole but torn into two separate pieces. She was aware of an overwhelming disappointment. Was this really *making love*? A sweaty, panicky grapple left an ache in her belly and her whole body throbbed from the pressure of his hands. The slumped, leaden weight across her had never figured in her romantic dreams.

Dared she move? What if she fell apart like a broken doll? Valerian solved her difficulty by sliding off her and rolling on to his side; at the same time he pulled her round to lie curled close against his chest and fell asleep. Gradually, as their bodies warmed the soft cocoon of rugs and blankets, Alexia's disappointment melted away to be replaced by an almost incredulous pride and delight. She had done it at last! After years of hopeless yearning she had achieved the impossible, captured the rainbow, made Valerian her own. Neither her physical aches and pains, nor the shock of discovering a man's violent way of loving mattered at all now that she was where she'd always wanted to be, safely sheltered from the world by Valerian's arms.

"Oh darling," she murmured, reaching a tentative hand to stroke his cheek, "I do love you so much."

"Wha—what's that?" Valerian jerked awake and groaned. "Just as I was—Oh, it's you, Lexi. Be a good girl: nip back to your room now and let me get some sleep. I'll have an early start, remember."

Alexia froze, while an icy chill spread through her body and soul. *Nip back to your room?* What did he mean? Was she to be dismissed like a child? Surely he must realise now that they belonged together and nothing could separate them?

She said in a small, shaking voice, "But, when are we going to be married, then?"

"Married?"

Beside her the bedclothes heaved and she heard the scrape of a match. Looking up she saw Valerian propped on an elbow, his lean torso stretched over her as his free hand groped for the candle. His dark eyes glinted at her, half exasperated, half amused. His voice was now quite sober. "My dear Lexi—what on earth's come over you? First you invade my bed—hardly the way a well-brought-up girl behaves, but never mind—and then you break all the rules by talking about marriage."

"Rules?" She was bewildered. "When you said you'd teach me to make love, I thought... I thought you meant..."

"That I wanted to marry you? Knowing *me*, you thought that? I find it difficult to believe. Who wants to get married?"

The dream of the past few minutes shattered into a thousand fragments. "I do!" she wailed. "I want you to take me away with you. I don't want to stay in this horrible place without you. I won't. I'll kill myself. Valya—you've *got* to marry me."

"Hush, little fool: do you want to wake the whole house?" His quick hug removed any sting from the words. "Now listen to me for a moment and stop crying. I haven't the smallest desire to marry you, my angel—I love you far too much to condemn you to such a fate, and if you'd even a grain of sense in that beautiful head of yours you'd never dream of marrying me either."

She stared at the handsome, determined face above her, and her heart seemed to swell until it threatened to burst her chest. He meant it. Nothing had changed. He was slipping away from her, treating her as an importunate child again. All her pain and panic had been for nothing and Valerian was as far from being hers as ever. Reckless with despair, she burst out: "I'll tell Mamma how you seduced me. I'll tell my father and he'll *make* you marry me."

He'll do nothing of the kind," said Valerian, quite unperturbed by this threat. "As for seducing you, don't you think I might fairly claim that the boot was on the other foot? I mean, when a weary soldier tumbles into his bed and finds a willing maiden warming it for him, what's he supposed to do? Kick her out on the floor? That'd hardly be the act of a gentleman."

"Did you behave like a gentleman? I didn't notice. Anyway, I wasn't willing," said Alexia furiously. "I tried to get away but you were so drunk you wouldn't listen to me."

"Then little girls should learn not to play with fire," said Valerian unmoved. "Are you going back to bed now, or do you want me to carry you?"

"It meant nothing to you, did it?" she said so forlornly that he stifled his urge to push her gently towards the door.

Valerian sighed. He wished that dear Alexia didn't take everything so much to heart. Why couldn't she realize that love was a game to be enjoyed, not agonized over? She was right in a way, of course. If he had come to bed stone cold sober, he'd have had the sense to send her back to her own room with a brotherly slap on the rump. But, her apparent availability combined with his own repressed desires regarding her must have temporarily anaestheticised his conscience. Now he smothered a growing sense of guilt and said briskly. "If you love me, the last thing you should do is tell me so. It takes all the excitement out of the chase. You've got a lot to learn about love, Lexi darling."

"You know *all* about it, of course."

He ignored the sarcasm. "More than you, at any rate. It's a

pity I haven't time to teach you..."

"You've taught me enough," she flashed.

"Just the beginning," said Valerian modestly. "Cheer up, Lexi. You may think you're in the grip of a grand passion, but I can assure you that the real thing's quite different. There's no comparison."

"How'd *you* know how *I* felt?" She was indignant now, and he grinned in the darkness, preferring any mood to Polish melancholy.

"All right," he countered, "tell me what you feel for me."

Alexia sought to describe her feelings, but the words slipped away like a shoal of fish before she could capture them. She'd never even tried to analyze her emotions. He was Valerian and she loved him because she always had. What more was there to say?"

"Well?" He was longing to end the conversation and snatch a few hours' sleep in the last comfortable bed he was likely to see for months.

"I—I feel happy when I'm with you," she faltered at last. "You make me feel... happy and safe." She was keenly aware how banal it sounded.

"'Happy and safe,'" he repeated disgustedly. "What a compliment! You must be the only woman in Russia who'd dream of saying that to me."

"You mean, it's not love?"

"Of course, it's not. Love's completely different—how can I explain it? It's fire and ice, Lexi; it's a living hell and the ecstasy of paradise. When you're in love you never feel safe for a single moment. Will she? Won't she? Do I? Don't I? Oh, there's a lot more to it than feeling happy. Today she loves me, tomorrow she'll hate me—or vice versa!" He shrugged, seeing her bewildered expression. "What's the use? I can't describe love. Don't worry—one day you'll recognize it for yourself. It's all in front of you, waiting for you..."

"But never with you?"

In the shadows she thought he smiled. "You never give up, do you? No, not with me. I've got a lot of loving behind me already, you see. I've too many other women to compare you with."

"Would you love me if I were beautiful?"

"You are beautiful—and you've got a one-track mind, Lexi. The trouble with you is that you've got nothing to think about except love, and no one to pin it on except me. You're obsessed by love. Women always are when they've nothing else to fill their minds."

She didn't agree, and she didn't at all like being lumped in his estimation with other foolish, moonstruck, lovesick women. Women like Varvara Danilova . . . A tiny spark of determination kindled in her heart: one day he'd take back those words. One day . . .

Valerian yawned again and pushed her gently off the bed. "You must go now, Lexi, and remember what I've told you . . ."

"I'll remember," she said. There was a new cool self-possession in her tone.

Tsar Nicholas II's sombre eyes gazed out of the window at the soldiers drilling in the Alexander Park, and he closed his mind against the droning voice of his Minister for War. There was too much bad news from the East—news he could not ignore—but he was determined not to listen to a word against his old friend Arkady Pavlovitch Kharkov.

What if the new blockhouses at Irkutsk *were* falling to pieces already? What if the soldiers there were filthy and undernourished, their feet wrapped in rags instead of boots and their rifles rusty? One could hardly expect Garde Equipage standards in Eastern Siberian, and no doubt Arkady Pavlovitch had more important things to occupy him than spit and polish.

With inward rage, General Kuropatkin recognised the closed, obdurate expression on his sovereign neat, bearded features, and knew he was getting nowhere. His voice trailed away into silence.

"Thank you for your valuable report, General," said the Tsar with distant courtesy, turning at last from the window. "I can assure you that I shall look into the matter personally. You have leave to go."

Kuropatkin knew that further argument would be useless. Nothing but the evidence of his own eyes would convince Nicholas that his old friend and playmate was a menace to the war effort. Once he made up his mind about something, there was only one person in Russia who could be more obstinate than the Tsar. The general bowed himself out and immediately sought an audience with the Tsarina.

She received him in her private apartments. As he entered the mauve-curtained room, she was reading aloud to the four young Grand Duchesses—Olga, Tatiana, Maria, and Anastasia—as they sat sewing by a window overlooking the park. He was struck by the charming domesticity of the tableau: five shining heads bent studiously over book and samplers.

Many courtiers accused the Tsarina of isolating her husband from the rest of the aristocracy, and it was true that she was on bad terms with most of the Romanov family. They considered her cold, remote, quarrelsome, and vindictive toward those who incurred her displeasure. But there could be no doubt that she was a devoted mother.

She was still a handsome woman, with finely drawn acquiline features beneath the upswept golden-chestnut hair that had brought her the nickname of "Sunny" at the English Court. But she lacked the grace or warmth of manner that would have made her truly attractive. Her complexion was bad, the blood rising in ugly blotches to her neck and cheeks whenever she was stirred by emotion.

She dismissed the children, who bobbed little curtsies and scampered away, then extended her hand for Kuropatkin to kiss.

"My dear General, how good to see you back from your travels. I trust they were not too tiresome? Tell me, did you deliver my letter to Countess Kharkova in Irkutsk? I have not received any communication from her in over a month, and I wonder how she is faring."

"Badly, I fear," said Kuropatkin bluntly. "When I visited, she was far too weak to write letters. In fact, she'd been so ill that her life was despaired of."

Briefly he recounted the details of Olga's sickness.

"Her husband absent and the house without servants," the Tsarina exclaimed indignantly. "How could such a situation arise without serious neglect on the part of Count Kharkov."

There's no harm in piling on the agony, thought Kuropatkin gleefully, and he began to provide full details of the misery to which the Kharkov household had been reduced at the time of his visit.

"She must leave that dreadful place at once!" exclaimed the Tsarina. "What fools men are! She has always suffered with her throat, and to make her spend the winter in Siberia was nothing short of lunacy."

"A second winter there would certainly be a death sentence," agreed Kuropatkin. He cleared his throat. "I mentioned the matter in my report to his Imperial Majesty, but I understand that he considers the work Count Kharkov is doing too important to allow a transfer."

The Empress compressed her thin lips. "Stuff and nonsense," she declared. She rose and began to pace the floor, kicking her trailing skirt aside at each turn. The general observed the telltale blotches that spoke of agitation already mottling her cheeks. "Count Kharkov—that frivolous nincompoop! Nothing he does could ever be important. It was only to get him away from his haunts of vice in Petersburg that—" She stopped abruptly. "Leave this to me, General," she ordered. "Please accept my thanks for bringing this to my notice. I'll see that Count Kharkov is transferred to a post where he can harm neither your Army nor my dear Olga. Perhpas a sunny, dry climate would benefit her health... perhaps the Crimea?... No, I have it!"

She stood for a moment with her head bent, then hurried across to a bureau. Drawing a list of posts from beneath the blotter, she scanned it intently, then turned a triumphant look on Kuropatkin.

"The very thing—Egypt! That will keep Count Kharkov out of mischief, and Olga will be so pleased to actually see those temples and monuments she's read so much about. Yes, I think that will solve our problems, General. We have a consul there already, of course, but that can easily be arranged..."

General Kuropatkin took his leave. As he was escorted down the stairs, he grinned as he heard her high, imperious voice calling out, "Nicky! Nicky, where are you? I wish to discuss an urgent matter with you. No, it won't wait. I tell you it's urgent!"

Chapter Eight

CAIRO, EGYPT 1906

The wailing chant of the oarsmen, as they rowed the great square-sailed *dahabeeyah* up the Nile, came faintly to Anastasia's ears. She sat beneath a canopy on the upper deck, watching the sun's low-slanting rays lend enchantment to the jumbled villages along the river banks, casting a rosy tinge over humble whitewashed walls and gilded minarets alike, and stretching long dark-blue shadows ahead of the trudging *fellahin* and their beasts of burden as they wound their way homeward across the patchwork of small irrigated fields.

The warmth, the glowing colors, seemed to belong to a different world from Siberia's white-and-gray monotony. But Anastasia, sunk in misery, felt no corresponding lift of the spirits. Every mile they traveled was taking her farther away from Valerian, and the painful memory of their parting brought her no comfort at all. If only he hadn't ridden away the very next morning! If only she could have had a chance to adequately explain before he left!

Remembering that awful, humiliating night, her cheeks still burned. Her whole spirit cringed with shame as she seemed to hear again his startled, furious voice:

"Why are you here, you fool, you crazy little fool? Don't you realize what you've done to yourself—and to me?"

Of course she realized. It wasn't so much the loss of her virginity she regretted, but the loss of her special relationship with Valerian. She'd been his little sister, the adopted waif to whom he'd always given his protection, even when he teased and provoked her. How she longed now for the brotherly affection that she'd always taken for granted. Why couldn't she have been content with that? How could she have been such a fool as to throw away that special relationship and bring herself down to the level of those Ludmilas and Malas and Anastasias who shared his bed but nothing else?

Sobbing, shivering, gathering up her torn dress as he watched scornfully, she had stumbled toward the door only to stop at his words:

"Oh, Stanya—why did you do it?"

"I didn't mean to!" Her tears had flowed anew. "I—I love you, Valya. I thought you were going away without saying good-bye to me and I couldn't bear it."

"You love me! What do *you* know about love?" he asked, his voice a whip. In a single quick movement he threw back the covers and strode to the door. Before she could recover from the shock of seeing him naked in the candlelight, he had scooped her up and dumped her back on the bed, pulling the bearskin rug around her.

"Let's have a talk about love, little Stanya," he said more gently. And she looked at him in wonder, for now his anger didn't seem to be directed at her. "What do you mean when you say you love me?"

Then she tried to describe her feelings, but the words slipped away like a shoal of startled fish before she could capture them. She'd never before tried to analyze her feelings. He was Valerian; she loved him because she always had. What more could she say?

"Well?" he demanded.

"I—I feel happy when I see you," she said, faltering. "I love you because you make me feel . . . happy and safe." She knew very well how banal she sounded.

"Happy and safe . . . hmmm. You must be the only woman in Russia who can say that," he replied. "What a child you are to mistake safety for love."

"I *do* love you and I'm not a child," she cried, furious. "You ought to know that by now."

Valerian grimaced. "Yes, and I regret my part in your . . . transformation more than I can say. However, I advise you to wait until you know what love really is before you force your way into another man's bed."

"You don't understand! I was trying to get *out* of your bed. I tried to creep away before you woke up, but you caught me and then you *wouldn't* listen."

"Ah, but why were you there in the first place?"

She had no answer to that. Instead she said, defensively, "But you enjoyed it—I know you did! You told me I was beautiful."

"I tell them all they're beautiful," said Valerian wearily. "Do you really think I'm such a monster of depravity that I enjoy deflowering a virgin?"

"You tell them *all*? How many mistresses do you have."

"That's no business of yours," he said. "Besides, they never last long. Ludmila, Mala, Irina, Natasha—yes, even Anastasia—I love them all... occasionally. Here today and gone tomorrow: that's the whole charm of it."

She couldn't understand. He was upsetting all her preconceived notions. Clinging to her childhood dream, she said, "When I love a man it will be forever. I'll live with him and bear his children, and we'll stay together till the end of time..." Before she had always cast Valerian in the role of her husband, but this was becoming increasingly difficult with every passing moment.

"How confoundedly dull," drawled Valerian. "Do you imagine he'll enjoy it, poor man, or doesn't that matter to you? That's not love, that's imprisonment. That's marriage—not my style at all."

"Then what do *you* call love?" she asked, her spirits in a great depression. "You'll know it all right when you find it. How can I explain? It's fire and ice, Anastasia. It's a living hell and the ecstasy of paradise. When you're in love, every day's an adventure and you never feel safe for a single moment. Will she? Won't she? Do I? Don't I? Oh, there's a lot more to love than just feeling happy!" He saw her bewildered expression. "Don't look like that, little one. One day you'll find out what love is. It's all ahead of you now, waiting for you..."

"But never with you," she said sadly.

In the shadows, she thought he smiled. "You never know when to give up, do you? No, not with me. I've got a lot of loving behind me already, you see. Too many other women to compare you with—beautiful, clever, sophisticated women."

"Would you love me if I was like that... clever and sophisticated?" she asked.

Valerian sighed. "You've got a one-track mind, Anastasia. The trouble is, in this godforsaken place, you've got nothing to think about except love—and no one but me to lavish it on.

You're obsessed by the idea of love. Women always are, when they've nothing else to fill their minds. Lovesickness, they call it."

She didn't agree and didn't at all like being lumped together with a lot of foolish, moonstruck women. A tiny spark of determination rekindled in her heart: one day she would make him eat those words.

Valerian yawned, stretching—and pushed her gently off the bed. "I'm tired and I've got an early start. You must go now, Stanya. But if you remember what I told you, perhaps tonight wasn't such a disaster after all..."

As she gazed into the blue waters of the Nile, the ignominy of that brusque dismissal was still a painful memory. But in spite of the way he'd humiliated and wounded her, she couldn't get him out of her thoughts. Throughout the long journey to Egypt she had been melancholy and abstracted. The Countess' sharp eyes, observing Anastasia's woebegone expression, drew their own conclusions. Fortunately, these stopped short of the truth. She'd been considering sending Anastasia back to Petersburg to attend the Smolny Institute and improve her mind when the news of Count Kharkov's unexpected transfer to Egypt disrupted this tentative plan.

Anastasia didn't want to leave Russia. "Can't I stay at home with Aunt Vera?" she begged yet again.

Her stepmother raised thin, plucked eyebrows. "You, my child, have no home except the one I give you," she said coldly. "I thought you understood that when I took you into the family. Of course, you'll go with me to Egypt—and make yourself more useful there than you have here, I trust."

Anastasia had bitten her lip and ceased to protest. The knowledge that she had no true home always created an empty, yawning ache in her heart. More than anything in the world—more even than Valerian's love—she wanted a home which belonged to her and to which she in turn belonged. Even as a small child, she'd been aware that the house in Poland belonged to Katya Gulyas, and not to her mother. And ever since leaving she'd been shuttled from one house to another, belonging in none of them. Of all the Kharkov family estates, Ostrovskoye in the Crimea seemed the most like home—mainly because it belonged to Valerian and not his stepfather.

Though Anastasia moped, the Countess was happier than she'd been for years. Her health had already improved, and although she ignored her doctor's instructions to stop smoking the fat oval Egyptian cigarettes she loved, the dry air and life-giving sunshine had combined to banish the last traces of her troublesome cough.

She had longed to visit Egypt ever since, at the age of nine, a French governess had fired her imagination with the story of how Jean-Francois Champollion, a young French Egyptologist, had solved the riddle of the hieroglyphic language used by the Ancient Egyptians to record their history.

As she grew up, she retained a profound—though necessarily distant—interest in the discovery and restoration of ancient monuments in Egypt, and even subscribed to learned journals in both French and English on the subject. This opportunity to visit the famous sites herself seemed a dream come true, and she looked forward with a passionate intensity to the next digging season.

Her collector's instinct was afire. Perhaps she would have the good fortune to uncover some lost archeological treasure that would carve the name of Kharkova among those of the immortals of Egyptology: Mariette, Drovetti, and the towering Italian, Giovanni Belzoni, once a circus strongman, who had done so much to inspire the modern world's interest in Ancient Egypt. Perhaps she'd be able to send rare vessels and tablets to the Imperial Museum in St. Petersburg, in token of gratitude to her kind sovereign who had answered an unspoken prayer by sending her here.

Admittedly she was no expert, but perhaps, she thought, before the weather cooled sufficiently to permit excavations to begin again, she could become one. After that it was surely just a question of exploring where no one else had yet explored. With a keen eye and bottomless purse, who knew what treasures she might not unveil from the sand, where it had covered all, preserved all . . . ?

Egypt in 1906 was a land of promise, a land of many faces—rich in opportunity for playboys like Count Kharkov, full of challenge for his ambitious wife. True, the interfering British were everywhere, making nuisances of themselves by rooting out corruption and suppressing ancient injustices, insisting on tiresome, impossible virtues like honesty in both public and private life. But even the British could not greatly influence the wily, raddled old courtesan that was Cairo. She was too skilled in intrigue, too well versed in human frailty, too full of the joy of life and the menace of silent, unheralded death for polished British boots to leave more than a faint imprint in her dusty streets, easily erased by the vascillating winds. The British might have caged the Khedive and trimmed his claws, but eventually even they would fall under the spell of Cairo's polyglot gaiety and Alexandria's opulence. In the end their energy would flag and their chilly sensibility melt like wax under Egypt's sun. Until they did, the land of the Pharaohs would exhibit a smiling face and wait.

The Kharkovs arrived in Cairo during the worst of the hot weather, when it was intolerable to go outdoors between eight in the morning and nightfall. Nevertheless, Kadya plunged happily into the whirlpool of Cairene social life, instantly locating kindred spirits among the well-bred, worldly diplomats and their languid, bejeweled wives, who directed their enormous households with a casual extravagance which made Kadya feel perfectly at home.

It didn't much worry him that Olga preferred her books and professors to the round of balls and soirees. For years they had led almost separate lives. Conscientious as ever on his behalf, she did her duty as a diplomatic hostess, carefully concealing her contempt for the brilliant cosmopolitan butterflies who gravitated toward her husband as naturally in Cairo as they had in far-off Petersburg.

About Anastasia, however, she was at first somewhat concerned. The girl was not officially out, so the part she could properly take in Cairene social life was necessarily rather limited. Miss Catherine Lonsdale, who had accompanied the Kharkov retinue from Russia, soon succumbed to the heat and had to be sent home, while gallant old Mademoiselle Froissart was hardly up to the strain of chaperoning an attractive, headstrong girl about the bazaars.

Casting around for some useful yet diverting way to direct Anastasia's energies, Olga's interest came to rest on Mr. Augustus Findlay, a tall, thin English artist of indeterminate age, eccentric yet unquestionably a gentleman, who was introduced to her by Lady Harding during a reception at the Caliph's palace.

"Mr. Findlay has such an eye for color!" gushed Lady Harding. "His pictures simply vibrate with life. He has that rare gift of being able to communicate his vision to his pupils. So few artists are capable of teaching, you know."

Mr. Findlay bowed and smiled deprecatingly. "You're altogether too kind, Lady Harding," he murmured. "As for teaching your daughter, I can claim very little credit for that, for she has great natural talent. All I did was give her some purely technical advice—what one might call the distillation of long experience."

"Don't listen to a word he says, my dear Countess," insisted Lady Harding playfully. "He's far too modest. As far as I can see, Emily's watercolors have improved out of all recognition since Mr. Findlay undertook to give her lessons." She added slyly, "Painting is all the fashion here and Mr. Findlay's tuition is greatly sought after."

It seemed to the Countess a relatively painless way of keeping in the social swim, and she made up her mind that Anastasia should take lessons from Mr. Findlay too. A succession of governesses, more or less artistically inclined, had taught the girl to draw restrained still lifes and watercolor landscapes. Now she should have the benefit of instruction from a real artist. Listlessly Anastasia agreed to be instructed, and Mr. Findlay was engaged to teach her for two hours, two mornings a week. Soon, to her surprise, she found herself enjoying her lessons.

In his quiet way, Mr. Findlay was a fanatic. No inconvenience was too great, no position too undignified for him to adopt if by so doing he could achieve a result that satisfied him. At first the Countess was reluctant to give her permission for Anastasia to go with him into the bazaars and coffee-houses, although he insisted that this was necessary to her artistic development.

"My dear lady, she will be perfectly safe, I assure you. As you see, I am always attended by my dragoman, Philippe, and in all the years I've lived here, I have never encountered anything but courtesy, even in the meanest quarters of the city. You have nothing to fear."

"But it would not be suitable, Mr. Findlay."

The artist raised his eyes to heaven. "I cannot teach the young lady to paint cooped up in a schoolroom with drawn blinds. The light, the color, the noise, even the smell of Egypt are essential to our work. Believe me, Miss Anastasia's talent deserves every opportunity to develop."

The Countess tightened her mouth. In her experience, a schoolroom or—possibly—a studio was the proper place for young ladies to learn to paint.

"I am afraid, Mr. Findlay, that it is out of the question. My daughter cannot tramp the streets even in your company. Allowing her to set up her easel in a public place, where every passerby could see her work, would be wholly incompatible with the dignity of our position."

"Then I regret, madam, that I cannot teach your daughter," said Mr. Findlay firmly, and took his leave.

Olga was incensed. How dare this impecunious artist refuse her patronage? It could never happen in Russia. She was sensible enough to remind herself, however, that she was not in Russia here. Living in a British protectorate, she could hardly order her servants to horsewhip Mr. Findlay for his impudence.

Seething, she consulted Lady Harding, who calmly assured her that her daughter Emily had been allowed to roam the streets freely, in the interests of Art.

"Mr. Findlay insisted, and to start with I was extremely worried that she might be insulted, or knocked down, or suffer some other accident. But nothing of the kind befell her. I believe I can reassure you that in Mr. Findlay's company your daughter will come to no harm."

With an effort, the Countess swallowed her pride and sent a note to Mr. Findlay's lodgings, informing the artist that she had changed her mind. She would be obliged if he would continue to instruct her daughter as he thought fit. This capitulation opened a whole new world for Anastasia.

Twice a week, early in the morning, Mr. Findlay would call at the Russian consulate. Anastasia, sedately dressed in slate-colored Indian cotton and strong shoes, would follow as her art master stalked through the crowded streets like an elegant, panama-hatted heron, his gold-knobbed cane in hand, his beaky nose and alert gray eyes questing eagerly from side to side in search of a suitable subject to illustrate a point of technique or perspective which he wished his pupil to grasp.

"Color, shadow, movement," he intoned, pausing to allow Anastasia to catch up. "That is the key to the mystery of Egyptian light. Movement, shadow, color. Never make use of an umbrella to shade your eyes while you paint, Miss Anastasia. So many artists employ them nowadays, but in my view it is a self-defeating measure since artificial shade alters all the light values you are observing. Sit in a coffee-house to sketch by all means, if the proprietor will allow it, but do not set up an umbrella in the street." A reminiscent smile creased his long jaws. "For one thing, it will prove too great a temptation to passing camels."

"Make way, make way for the English lords!" the burly dragoman would shout, banging energetically on a brass gong. Cropheaded urchins would gather to stare as the small procession continued its stately progress: the dragoman, the artists, the servants carrying easels and paints, canvases and stools.

Arrived at their objective, easels set up, Mr. Findlay would continue to lecture, with a magnificent disregard for the bustle around them as the street went about its daily business. Traffic eddied and flowed past their small island. Lordly camels padded by, casting covetous eyes at the paint-daubed canvases. Pattering donkeys brushed their loaded sacks of high-piled clover against the easels, and once Anastasia saw a runaway mule charge straight through a promising picture of Mr. Findlay's. The unlikely animal careered down the street, the easel hanging around his neck like a garland, while the artist himself smiled tolerantly, flat on his back in the gutter.

Willing hands picked him up and dusted him off.

"Are you hurt, Mr. Findlay?" Anastasia asked anxiously.

"Not in the least, my dear. Such trifling accidents add spice to our labors. Thank you, my good man—I'm much obliged to you," he added, as the easel was set up once more and the ruined picture placed reverently upside down upon it.

He was, Anastasia soon discovered, devoid of all inhibitions in pursuit of his objectives. He positively welcomed the comments of the crowd which invariably gathered behind their easels, and saw nothing odd in accepting cups of strong coffee and sticky sweetmeats which small boys brought out to them from nearby coffee-houses.

His Arabic was fluent, though she could not tell how correctly he spoke. The Countess would have been horrified to hear him talking and laughing with the most unsavory-looking natives, but even she would have been obliged to admit that they accorded him perfect respect. Even the most persistent beggar's whine of: *"Raboona khalik ya hawaga ana maskin!"* would be silenced by his murmured blessing: *"Al Allah."*

As the weather cooled, they began to make more ambitious expeditions outside the city. Although Mr. Findlay admitted that the peaceful, almost biblical countryside was less stimulating to him than the colorful bustle of the bazaars, Anastasia preferred it. Some deep Russian instinct in her nature yearned for far horizons. On the edge of the desert, where the bowl of the sky touched the ground without a break, she could find them . . . and remember Valerian.

Countess Kharkova, meanwhile, was far from idle. She explored the museums, cross-questioned the curators, and bent her mind to the study of the hieroglyphic language in preparation for her first expedition up the Nile.

Resting on a bench outside the Cairo museum one morning, her maid surreptitiously wriggling her sore toes in their buttoned boots, the Countess fell into conversation with an ingratiating Frenchman who introduced himself as Francois Soulier; he claimed to have made her acquaintance at a French consulate reception. The Countess didn't recall the meeting, but although M. Soulier's looks were unprepossessing—he was small, sallow, and bearded, with sharp black eyes close-set beside a twitching, inquisitive nose—her initial reserve soon melted when she discovered that he, too, was deeply interested in Egyptology.

Before long they were engrossed in conversation, and M. Soulier's free use of the names of archeologists of his acquaintance, and his obvious familiarity with the whole archeological scene, convinced the Countess that here was just the man she needed to guide her first steps in that field.

She mentioned the expedition she was planning.

"Alone, dear madame? Is that well-advised?"

"I shall be taking my daughter, of course, and my servants. My husband, alas, is too occupied with business to accompany us," said the Countess with dignity.

"Naturally," agreed M. Soulier smoothly. "Excuse my curiosity, but do you intend to hire a sailing-boat—a *dahabeeyah?* They are, without doubt, a most convenient way to travel, but their captains can be troublesome. They are inclined to dictate to their passengers in order to demonstrate their own independence."

"No one dictates to me," declared the Countess. She rose and took her leave.

Nevertheless, thinking over what the Frenchman had said, she felt a trifle uneasy. As their acquaintance progressed—and it was surprising how frequently they met in the museum gardens—she began to ask his advice on many aspects of the expedition.

"I do not wish merely to gape at the discoveries of others," she confessed naively. "My ambition is to find a site of my own, then to excavate it at my own expense. We Russians have been backward in the field of Egyptology. I feel it my duty to make some restitution."

Monsieur Soulier looked thoughtful. "In that case, perhaps..." he began, and stopped.

"Yes, Monsieur?"

There was a long pause. The Countess' maid shifted uncomfortably on the hard bench. She wished the mistress would dismiss this oily little rat of a Frenchman. Jabber, jabber, jabber! What did they find to talk about every morning in this godforsaken park? His eyes gave her the shivers, never mind the heat.

"You must understand, dear lady, that the information I'm about to give you is confidential," said M. Soulier at last. "I would not impart it to anyone until I was convinced that he—or she—had a sincere desire to uncover the past glories of this great country, with no thought of personal gain."

"I understand," said the Countess. Her heart beat faster. She felt that she stood on the brink of some important revelation; it would be unwise to mention her hope of filling the Petersburg museums at this point.

"I have told you already that I spent last season digging in the company of two Englishmen. They were vandals!" declared M. Soulier in outraged tones. "They did not deserve the title of archeologists. They wanted only to extract everything possible from their site, leaving desolution behind. Never again do I wish to be associated with such creatures."

The Countess longed to ask how he came to be associated with them in the first place, but fear of interrupting him stilled her tongue.

"In the course of our excavations," he continued, "I had occasion to explore a nearby valley—alone, you understand? And there I found—"

He paused impressively.

"What did you find?" the Countess was beside herself with excitement.

"A temple! A temple of the Twelfth Dynasty—perfect and untouched. Totally covered with sand, *bien entendu*, but no one of my experience could mistake the signs."

"Did you tell your colleagues?" she inquired breathlessly.

M. Soulier snorted. "Colleagues? They were vandals! No, I said nothing to them. They did not deserve to be associated with a discovery of such importance. I left them at the end of the season. Ever since I have been waiting to find someone with the right spirit, the right approach to antiquity, with whom to share my secret."

Olga tried hard not to sound too eager, too grasping. "If you will confide your secret to me, *cher monsieur*, you will not regret it, I can assure you."

He was silent, observing her sharply with shoe-button eyes. Recklessly, she plunged on. "My *dahabeeyah* and all my servants would be at your disposal. Together we could accomplish great things. With your experience and my—" she was about to say "money," but changed the term to the less specific... "resources, we could have a most happy partnership."

For a moment M. Soulier affected to consider, then he rose and bowed. "My dear Countess, it shall be as you suggest. I feel convinced that I am doing the right thing, and that this will be the beginning of a glorious and profitable association."

Luxuriously, Anastasia stretched, holding both arms high over her head in a Spanish dancer's pose as she pirouetted slowly in front of the mirror.

"Olé!" she cried softly, and snapped her fingers like castanets. Faster she whirled and still faster, until the walls were spinning before her eyes. She kicked one leg immodestly high and then knelt down on her heels to perform a vigorous Cossack dance. The cabin floor rattled and shook in protest, but the skirt of her dress remained demurely in place and showed no glimpse of leg.

"It is not entirely unbecoming," admitted the Countess, surveying her foster daughter's tall, slim figure as they breakfasted on the upper deck. "I believe it will prove a practical garment." She had given much thought to the problem of suitable clothes for this expedition, and had finally commanded her dressmaker to construct loose-fitting cotton dresses with divided skirts for herself and Anastasia. They were about to land near the village of Ankh-Rator, between the towns of Guergeh and el-Baliana, and the time had come to try out their work clothes.

Their floating palace, the *dahabeeyah*, was among the largest of the Nile's river barges, and the Countess liked to imagine it little changed from the ones that had borne Cleopatra and Nefertiti along the unchanging river. Naturally there were certain modern improvements of a purely practical nature: it was unlikely that Cleopatra would have found a grand piano necessary to her travels. And perhaps Nefertiti would merely have laughed at the complexities of the water-closet. The barge boasted a spacious saloon with yellow satin upholstery and a semicircle of windows affording an excellent view; a separate dining room richly furnished in red plush and mahogany; and a comfortable reading room, besides the well-appointed cabins and bathrooms. Their food was prepared in a kitchen quite apart from the crew's more primitive quarters, and was served by white-coated stewards. Best of all, Anastasia enjoyed the warm evenings when she and her foster-mother reclined in deep-cushioned hammocks on the upper deck, watching the dark water sliding by, when the glow of the Countess' eternal cigarette was imitated countless times by fireflies along the banks. Then she could really imagine herself back in the days of the Pharoahs.

The journey over, the *dahabeeyah* was now at rest, her graceful sails furled. Later in the morning, the crew lined up to watch them land. The captain, a short, independent Egyptian with twinkling little eyes in a walnut-colored face, salaamed respectfully as the ladies were ushered ashore by M. Soulier, resplendent for the occasion in a white suit and broad-brimmed Panama hat. A gold chain looped across his narrow chest made him look, for once, quite distinguished.

Mounting the donkeys he had hired, the little procession set off across country to the village of Ankh-Rator. Though they all began the overland journey in excellent spirits, laughing and joking as the donkeys pattered along, the sun became hot before they reached the village and the ladies' parasols were proving but poor protection against its burning rays.

Tired and dusty, longing to enjoy a cool drink in the shade, Olga was pleased to observe that the village headman—a tall, bearded figure of imposing mien—had the civility to emerge from the gates to meet them. But as she listened to the quick, unsmiling exchange between the headman and Monsieur Soulier, Anastasia sensed that something was wrong.

"What does he say, monsieur?" she asked softly.

A dusky flush of anger mottled M. Soulier's sallow complexion. "The insolent dog!" he exclaimed. "He's demanding to see our firman—our permission to excavate in his territory."

"Have we a—a firman?" It was the first time the Countess had heard such a thing mentioned.

"Of course not. It is completely unnecessary—just a device of those vile English to squeeze more money from bonafide archeologists. Milord Cromer seeks to conserve all Egypt's treasures for his own country by such means, but he shall soon discover his mistake."

The Countess' eyes flashed. She was not accustomed to being thwarted. "Tell him we have left the firman on the boat," she said haughtily.

After M. Soulier translated this explanation, the headman had the effrontery to spit in the dust near his feet. He growled four words, then folded his arms and continued to bar their way.

"What does he say?"

M. Soulier was now bristling with rage. "He says—he dares to say—that we will have to get it. We cannot pass until he sees the firman."

"This is intolerable!" declared the Countess. "How dare that insolent serf defy us? Tell our servants to push him out of the way."

She waved the donkey-boys forward. But when he saw her intention, the headman gave a shout which brought villagers running to join him, armed with cudgels and curving daggers.

"It's an outrage! I shall report this incident to Lord Cromer myself," said the Countess, trembling with fury. "I shall see this impertinent dog's feet beaten with the bastinado until he never walks again."

"All the same, Madame la Comtesse, I believe we'd be wise to retire and reconsider our position," said Monsieur Soulier in a low voice. "I may be able to write out a firman myself that will satisfy this blockhead, for I doubt he is able to read."

Disappointed and angry, the Countess allowed her servants to turn the donkeys back toward the river, though the triumphant shouts of the villagers as they saw the discomfited Europeans retreat were gall and wormwood to her pride.

The crew of the *dahabeeyah* was lounging about the river bank, washing their clothes and bargaining for food. They were astonished to see their passengers returning so soon, and sprang into action to bring them cool drinks and help them to the shade. The Countess retired to her cabin with a nervous headache, while M. Soulier went into an earnest conference with the boat's captain, and then disappeared on some mysterious errand of his own.

Anastasia and her stepmother ate their dinner in silence, each thinking industriously of how they might outwit the obdurate headman. The thought of the buried temple, so near and yet so far, was a torment to the Countess; she scarcely tasted the excellent meal their cooks had prepared. Up to this moment, the voyage had been perfect: they could not allow one officious native to wreck their high hopes.

"Play to me a little, child," said the Countess in a faint, pained voice, as they rose from dinner in the handsome saloon, with its yellow silk curtains and clean white paneling. Anastasia folded back the lid of the satinwood boudoir grand piano, which had taken ten men to carry aboard. With a small sigh the Countess sank down on the curved divan beside the windows.

"Bach, I think," she murmured. "Something calm and orderly to soothe my headache."

Barely had the first notes of a Bach *Invention* rippled from the pianoforte when they heard a knock at the door; Monsieur Soulier begged leave to enter. With him was a seedy-looking native in the usual dirty striped pyjamas, his shifty eyes scanning the handsomely appointed salon rapidly, as if setting a price on every piece of furniture it contained.

"This gentleman's name is Abdullah, Madame la Comtesse," said M. Soulier with an ingratiating smile. "I believe he may be of assistance to us."

With her haughtiest stare, the Countess looked him up and down. She was displeased with M. Soulier's earlier performance, and in no mood for agreeing to any request he might make.

"In what way, monsieur?" she said coldly. "The only thing

that can help us now is the firman which you failed to mention might be required before we began to excavate. Your blundering has wasted our time. Now, I suppose, we must return to Cairo and obtain this permit from the British authorities. Which will cost us three weeks of the digging season—not to mention the considerable expense of this vessel and crew."

Monsieur Soulier squared his narrow shoulders. "We have no need of a scrap of paper," he said boldly. "That is nothing but a ruse of the *sales Anglais* who wish to preserve this magnificent temple for themselves. Listen, madame, to what Abdullah here has told me. The headman who denied us access to the site this morning is nothing but an agent of the British *canaille* with whom it was my misfortune to work last year."

"You mean *they* are here?" cried the Countess in dismay. "They have started work before us?"

"Yes—and no," said the Frenchman portentously.

"Don't speak to me in riddles, man!"

"My apologies, madame la Comtesse. According to Abdullah, the facts are these: the Englishmen have indeed started work in the neighborhood of our temple, but a week ago the old man fell ill with a fever after an accident on the site, and they were obliged to abandon their work in order to have him treated. They attempted to protect the site in their absence by bribing the village headman to deny entry to anyone else—hence this ridiculous business of demanding to see our permit."

"They bribed him? Two can play that game," said the Countess with grim satisfaction. "Offer the headman twice as much to let us pass."

"With respect, madame, Abdullah here has a better idea. There is no need for us to trouble that officious peasant again. If we voyage upstream to the village of al-Katira, where Abdullah lives, we can approach the temple from another direction, and save ourselves the cost of the bribe."

"What if the Englishmen return?" asked Anastasia from her seat on the piano stool.

M. Soulier shrugged. "A remote danger only, mademoiselle. Abdullah says that the old man was *very* ill. A stone fell and crushed his leg. Then the fever set in. He will not return this season."

"And the others?" said Anastasia.

"We will just have to take that chance," said the Countess

briskly, her good humor quite restored and her headache forgotten. "Monsieur, you have done well. Tell me, how far away is this village you speak of?"

"About ten kilometers upstream. If we make haste, we can be there before morning."

"Excellent. Please inform the *reis*—the Captain—that I wish to speak to him immediately."

Slipping quietly along the palm-fronded banks, the *dahabeeyah* glided upstream to the village of al-Katira. There the party disembarked once more and, guided by Abdullah, set out again for the hidden valley where the temple lay.

No one hindered them. The sun blazed down from a cloudless cobalt sky onto sand which shimmered in the haze. The donkeys' black-edged ears moved gently back and forth as they trotted demurely across the great burning wastes. As they approached a line of cliffs rising starkly from the desert floor, even the cheerful donkey-boys grew silent, oppressed by some nameless awe.

Anastasia stared around uneasily. She felt the same sense of brooding suspense, as though they were in the presence of some watchful god looking down on the infidel humans come to ravish the shrine he had guarded for fifty centuries.

Monsieur Soulier cleared his throat. He alone of the party seemed unimpressed by the overpowering silence. After all, thought Anastiasia, that was natural: he had been here before. He knew there was nothing to fear from the spirits who had once inhabited this sacred place. All that was past. In the first decade of the twentieth century, it was absurd to tremble at the empty threats of long-forgotten pagan gods. But her fear and unease persisted, and she wished that the Frenchman would lower his voice.

"Here is where we made our excavation last winter," said M. Soulier, pointing to a neat crisscross of trenches and tunnels shored up with rough planks. "We found nothing but a few tombs—nothing of value. Just pottery and Roman mummies, all of late date, you understand."

The Countess dismissed a season's work by the Englishmen with a cursory glance. She would not be satisfied with such banal discoveries. She was after gold.

"Then where is your temple, monsieur?"

He pointed toward the cliffs. "About a mile farther on, madame, we will come to a fissure in the rock-face—a natural hiding place. Ah, they knew how to hide their treasure, those ancients! There you will see the temple."

But when, an hour later, they dismounted stiffly from their donkeys in a hidden valley that branched off from the main line of cliffs, neither Anastasia nor the Countess could conceal their disappointment. Hills of sand, a steeply angled slope, a few flat rocks jumbled together, a fallen column half submerged in rubble—this did not portend an exciting archeological discovery. Worst of all, three parallel trenches near the fallen column showed that they were not first on the spot.

"Nom d'un chien!" Sniffing and frowning, Monsieur Soulier examined the trenches. To Anastasia, he looked like a sly Siberian fox investigating the evidence that rivals had invaded his preserves. He scratched here and there with his stick, then spat on his handkerchief and rubbed dust from one of the flat stones that punctuated the area.

"It is the same Englishmen—I recognize their style," he said slowly. "Fortunately, they have not had time to do any damage. On the contrary, they have assisted us by clearing the ground and delineating the probable outlines of the temple itself. We must make haste to put their labor to good use."

The Countess' lips were pursed. "I see no temple," she stated.

"Ah *madame*, that is natural," said M. Soulier, baring his yellow teeth in a smile. "Have patience. Soon it will be revealed to you. Regard this only . . ." He scratched away industriously at the sand, soon disclosing a plain round plinth of grayish stone. To Anastasia's surprise, the more he dug, the taller the plinth appeared to be . . . Slowly the truth dawned on her. They were standing on top of a sand-drift which had piled up against the cliff just as a snowdrift might have. What she had taken for the base of a column was in fact its top—the rest was hidden beneath them, deep in the sand.

With new excitement she looked again at the trenches dug by the English archeologists. Yes, there were more columns, going down to a depth of about eight feet, and the sand below the shifting surface was quite firm enough to dig. The size of the enterprise—the tons of sand and soil that would have to be moved before the temple could be revealed, made her catch her breath.

"How can we ever dig deep enough to uncover it all?" she said, almost to herself.

"*Ne vous inquietez pas, mademoiselle*. We need not dig so deep to discover whether there is treasure here or not," said the Frenchman. His eyes gleamed. "We will sink a shaft and run exploratory tunnels off from it. That way we can soon unearth anything of value."

"But surely you don't mean to steal—I mean, to remove—any treasures, do you?" said Anastasia, confused. "I thought you wanted to *preserve* this temple, not rob it." She bent to rub again at the polished stone he had uncovered. "It's beautiful. I can imagine the people coming here to worship, bringing their offerings, thousands of years ago..."

Over her head, M. Soulier and the Countess exchanged a look of perfect understanding. Not for them any abstract fantasizing over the glories of a vanished civilization. If the temple held anything valuable, they meant to have it.

"Time enough to worry about that when we find something," said the Countess. "I for one, don't intend to leave treasures behind for the first robbers to find. Now, let's make ourselves comfortable before we start exploring. Where are we going to sleep? Those are tombs in the cliff over there, are they not? I've been told that rock-tombs make very tolerable quarters when engaging in excavation work."

"Tombs?" said Anastasia, startled.

"Certainly. That is to say, in the upper chambers where the Egyptians used to feed their ancestors with offerings—not in the sepulcher itself. They are cut from the solid rock and therefore well insulated against heat and cold," agreed M. Soulier. "I will instruct your servants to prepare your quarters in adjoining tombs. Then we must acquire a work-force without delay. Abdullah should be able to assist us there."

By nightfall the ladies were comfortably installed in two of the rock-tombs, and M. Soulier's own tent was pitched a little distance away, where, he explained, he could survey the approach to the secret valley.

The tombs were cool and airy, each with a large rectangular rock that served as a table. Furnished with canvas stools, a folding bed and her favorite icon with its little lamp glowing in one corner, Anastasia surveyed her troglodytic bedroom with pleasure. As a final touch, she took a framed photograph of

Valerian in his full-dress Preobrazhensky Guards uniform from her dressing-case and propped it up on a niche above the camp bed.

"Look, Valya," she said to his photograph. "I'm filling my mind with knowledge, as you told me to. I'm learning to paint and play the piano as well. But still I love you as much as ever. Why won't you love me . . . ?"

Chapter Nine

The work-force arrived with the dawn—a long line of men, women and children from Abdullah's village. Monsieur Soulier set them to work digging pits and carrying away the soil in cone-shaped baskets. They were a cheerful crew, singing as they worked, and the thin wail of their voices echoing from side to side of the narrow valley filled Anastasia's ears for the next three weeks.

Gradually the temple's outline took shape. A series of pits dug at one edge of the site served to show how far the ruins extended. Once that was established, the workmen began, under the Frenchman's directions, to enlarge the trench which the Englishmen had begun.

Almost at once, man-made objects of obvious antiquity began to emerge from the ruins: a number of pots, a stele with hieroglyphic inscriptions, an alabaster urn, and a small black basalt vase adorned with a picture of a hippopotamus. Each worker kept his day's findings separate from those of his colleagues, and in the evening everything was gathered for the inspection of Monsieur Soulier and the Countess, seated side by side at a rough table under an awning. The men were paid the market price for their discoveries. Monsieur Soulier argued that this was an unnecessary expense but he was overruled by the Countess, who insisted that paying the men would prevent pilfering. As the money was hers anyway, the Frenchman was reluctantly obliged to concede her this point.

Day by day the piles of pottery, ancient tools and scraps of papyrus grew. Anastasia assumed the task of sorting and cataloguing all their finds. She made careful sketches of the rarer objects, and copied the wall painting uncovered by the workmen on one side of what Monsieur Soulier referred to grandly as "la Salle Hippostyle." As she became more involved in the work she could not help but remember Valerian had been right: though she still yearned for him with all her heart, it was better to fill her mind with an absorbing new interest than to brood endlessly over what could never be.

"Where are you now, Valya?" she asked the photograph in her cool rock-tomb when she flung herself down to rest in the heat of the day. "What beautiful, clever, sophisticated women have you found to stir your love in far-off Manchuria? Do you ever think of me?"

Valerian's dark, amused eyes with their slight upward tilt seemed to glow in the cool dimness, and his mouth smiled its endless mocking smile, which burned behind her eyelids as she dropped off to sleep.

By the third week of their work, the exploratory shaft extended deep into the heart of the temple, and the Countess became impatient to transport the fruits of their excavations back to the river. Most of the smaller treasures had already been packed in stout crates; there remained only the problem of the lion-headed goddess.

Olga had the true Russian's passion for sheer size. She was determined to crown the expedition by taking back to Cairo the enormous statue carved from black granite which they found lying face up in the sand, as if guarding the entrance to the temple.

"It is too big, madame la Comtesse," protested M. Soulier. He seemed suddenly nervous and anxious to be gone, now that the treasures were safely on their way to the river bank. "You cannot transport so heavy a statue. Physically, it is not possible."

Olga frowned. "Cannot" was a word with no place in the vocabulary of a Russian aristocrat. Instantly she decided that she would find a way of transporting the goddess all the way to Petersburg—with or without the help of Monsieur Soulier. Remembering the story of a gigantic statue which the famous Egyptologist Belzoni had succeeded in carrying back to Alexandria nearly a hundred years before, she determined to copy his method. She commanded her workmen to construct a vast platform with rollers beneath it, and ropes fastened to their projecting ends. As the hundred and fifty men, women, and children took their places along the ropes to tow this huge platform-carriage from the river bank—where it had been built—back to the temple, Monsieur Soulier watched sardonically.

The Countess' voice was hoarse from shouting at the *fellahin*, and the sun had reached its height, before the platform was at last on the move. Once started, it traveled smoothly enough—though slowly—over the uneven terrain. They had traversed half the distance to the valley before nightfall halted their progress. But Olga had overexerted herself getting the platform built before the falling water-level of the Nile made transportation by river impossible. In camp that night she complained of a sore throat, and Anastasia recognized the warning signs.

"It is essential that you rest tomorrow, Mama," she said as firmly as she dared. "Or, you know as well as I do, you'll become too sick to see that the statue is properly loaded, and all our work will be in vain. You remember what happened at Nicholasgrad? Let me go on ahead with the platform, then tomorrow or the next day you can follow at your leisure. You mustn't make yourself ill now, because there isn't a doctor for miles—as those poor Englishmen discovered to their cost."

The Countess saw the force of this argument: indeed, her throat was too sore to argue. She nodded agreement and patted Anastasia's hand. "Just for a day or so, then," she whispered. "Mathilde can look after me here until you return with the statue."

At this unexpected sign of trust, Anastasia's heart swelled with pride. At last the Countess had consented to treat her as an adult, capable of doing an exacting job without supervision. She had expected to have to wait in the valley until her stepmother arrived. To be entrusted instead with the business of actually loading the statue was more than she had anticipated, and she was determined to prove that she could do it alone.

Early the next morning, while it was still cool, she got the platform moving once more, and before noon they stood again in the secret valley.

All was quiet. Everything looked exactly as they had left it, the shutters still closed across the windows of the rock-tombs they had occupied, and the outline of M. Soulier's tent still on the sand near the excavation shaft. But once again an uneasy sense of foreboding, a premonition of impending catastrophe, hung over the desert, stilling the *fellahin's* chatter and filling Anastasia with a vague dread. More than ever, she felt reluctant to carry away the statue representing the goddess of the place, and all her confidence of yesterday evaporated like dew in the desert sun.

She looked around. The workmen were eyeing her uneasily, waiting for orders. She must not hesitate, for they were already unsettled by the recent changes of command. First M. Soulier had directed them, and then the Countess. If Anastasia was indecisive, they might refuse to obey her, throw down their ropes and leave her to struggle with the great statue alone.

The thought of being alone in that silent valley was like an icy premonition of fear. Anastasia called M. Soulier over for consultation. She knew that he resented the fact that the Countess had put her in charge of transporting the statue. He considered the Countess both greedy and ill-advised to insist on removing the statue at all. In her heart, Anastasia agreed with him, but this was not the time to tell him so.

Face up in the sand, the great statue lay where it had fallen thousands of years ago, its calm eyes gazing blankly at the heavens.

To Monsieur Soulier, Anastasia said briskly, "Direct the workmen to place levers under one side of the statue. That way the platform can be slipped beneath it."

"You'll have to dig away the sand first, mademoiselle," he replied, a gleam of malice in his small black eyes.

"I don't think that will be necessary. However, we will see."

He was right, and this small return of his authority roused him from his lethargy and he began to direct the operation with more of his old energy. The men, too, worked with a will, as if eager to finish a job that had become distasteful. In a remarkably short time they managed to maneuver the platform beneath the statue, and then reinsert the rollers underneath. They had brought extra ropes of palm fiber with which to lash the goddess onto her chariot. When they finished, she lay there like a helpless captive bound with chains to be dragged away by a victorious conqueror. Once again a shiver of apprehension ran through Anastasia's body.

The workers took up the strain on the ropes.

"One... two... three... *pull!*" shouted M. Soulier.

"... Pull!" echoed the Egyptians.

They threw their weight against the ropes and slowly, reluctantly, the statue began to move. The *fellahin* shouted in triumph and redoubled their efforts, chanting as they strained.

The chariot moved faster, achieving a slow walking pace down the avenue of tall columns that led to the temple. Anastasia's heart lightened. They had done it! The seemingly impossible had been accomplished. There were still problems, of course. They might have to break the base of a column in order to drag the chariot through...

She turned to take a last look at the spot where the statue had rested so long. At the mouth of the excavation shaft something—she couldn't tell what—seemed to flash in the sun.

A moment later a great voice boomed out across the valley, reverberating from rock to rock and cliff to cliff, freezing the toiling *fellahin* dead in their tracks.

"Stop!" it thundered. "Despoilers of the sacred place—stop, I say!"

Screaming in terror, the *fellahin* flung down their ropes and fled, scurrying into the sand dunes like a colony of panic-stricken ants.

"Come back!" called Anastasia, almost clutching at the fleeing white-robed figures as they sprinted past. "Don't be afraid. Oh, stop them, Monsieur Soulier!"

But the angular form of the Frenchman, his tailcoat flying out behind him, was running as fast as any of his workmen. In a few seconds they had all vanished into the heat-haze, leaving Anastasia quite alone.

She stood there, rooted to the spot, like a tiny human offering sacrificed to the vast, prone statue on its makeshift chariot. The chill certainty crept over her that the goddess of the temple which her stepmother had pillaged had risen in her wrath to smite the ravishers. So great was Anastasia's fear that for one long moment she could move neither hand nor foot. Very slowly she turned and looked back up at the temple. After the sudden turmoil, the silence was so intense it seemed to ring in her ears.

Terror pressed in on her. Her instincts were demanding that she flee as far from this terrible place as she could, but the last vestige of sanity left in her mind warned that to do so would be even more dangerous than facing the wrath of an angry goddess. Knowing nothing of how to survive in the desert in the heat of noon, she couldn't be certain of finding her way back to her stepmother's camp, though it lay a bare two miles away. Her only hope of survival was to wait here in the temple valley until the Countess, alerted perhaps by the *fellahin*, who had run in that direction, sent a search party to her rescue.

Alone in the shattered temple, dwarfed by the mighty columns, stunned by heat and deafened by silence, no fantasy seemed too extravagant. That huge voice that had boomed across the valley, rumbling like thunder as it bounced sound waves off the cliffs—surely it wasn't human?

She crouched down in the shadow cast by the lion-headed goddess, trying to be calm, to think, trying to fight off the impulse to run blindly into the shimmering heat-haze that hovered above the sand. That way lay madness and certain death.

She heard quick footsteps on the stone slabs of temple floor which the *fellahin* had painstakingly uncovered. Anastasia looked up and tried to speak, but the words stuck in her throat.

A tall, broad-shouldered apparition—dust thick on his curly hair and once-blue shirt, the rest of his clothes festooned in cobwebs—strode toward her, a thunderous frown on his deeply bronzed face and a ship's megaphone tucked under one arm. He reached the goddess' chariot and stopped abruptly, staring down at the crouching girl in great amazement.

"Anastasia! What the—what the *devil* are you doing here?"

The sudden relief after the fear and tension of the past few moments was too much for Anastasia. A black mist swam in front of her eyes.

"Anthony Mills!" she whispered and keeled quietly over sideways into the sand.

"You've got some explaining to do, young lady," said Anthony sternly, half an hour later, as they sat in the relative cool of an abandoned rock-tomb sipping mint tea produced by Ibrahim, Anthony's servant.

"So have you," she replied with spirit. "Shouting at us through your megaphone like that. I've never been so scared in my life. We'll never get our workmen near the place again."

"A good thing, too, judging by the mess they've made

already. I've never seen a site so wretchedly vandalized by unskilled excavators."

Anastasia stared at him indignantly. "Vandalized? What do you mean? We took the *greatest* care to do everything right. We keep records of everything we found. If it hadn't been for my stepmother—and Monsieur Soulier, of course—these treasures would never have seen the light of day. You and your father were searching in quite the wrong place."

"Soulier?" thundered Anthony. "You don't mean to tell me that little rat of a Frenchman's been at work here? Oh, no, that's too much to bear!"

She flinched before his anger. "Wh—why, Anthony? What has he done?"

"What *hasn't* he done! Oh, yes, that explains a lot. I might have guessed that that misbegotten halfbreed would creep back and try to steal what he could, if only to revenge himself on my father. He sacked that Frenchman without a reference when he found that Soulier had been bribing our laborers to filch valuables for himself when our backs were turned. It's a thousand pities he was here with us when my father discovered this temple. No one but he could have destroyed so much in a few short weeks."

"He told us that *he* discovered the temple, and that you knew nothing about it," said Anastasia uncertainly. "He said he was an experienced archeologist who'd been trained by a member of the Egypt Exploration Fund."

"Trained monkey is more like it," said Anthony contemptuously. She was relieved to find that his anger was no longer directed at her. Anthony seemed far more formidable here in these empty sunbaked wastes than he had on the Trans-Siberian Express, and she was very conscious of how completely she was in his power. "Soulier was trained by my father, more's the pity, for a man like he will never have the patience or the conscience to make a true antiquarian. With him it's grab what you can and run—before anyone catches you. If I lay my hands on him, Monsieur Auguste Soulier will get such a hiding that he'll never dare to steal from a rival's site again."

Anastasia eyed his powerful hands and trembled on M. Soulier's behalf. "I think that's why he ran away so quickly. I think he must have recognized your voice, even through that machine." Then she remembered why Anthony had been obliged to leave his precious site unguarded. "Tell me, how is your father? We heard that an Englishman's leg had been injured in a rock fall, and I am so sorry."

He smiled—and was instantly transformed from an angry, formidable stranger into the good companion of her days aboard the train. "The doctors say he should make a full recovery, though there'll be no more digging for him this season. I'll have to carry on alone. Luckily he's a pretty tough old bird. Otherwise he'd have been killed when one of the exploratory pits caved in on top of him. We had to dig him out with our bare hands, and it was touch and go for a while if we'd get him out alive. If it hadn't been for that mischance, Soulier would never have had a chance to do any damage on this scale."

"Did we destroy so much? We took photographs and made sketches. We wrote long lists of all we found..."

"Yet everything portable has vanished. Your respect for antiquity did not quite extend to leaving the treasures in place to be properly catalogued," he said dryly. "That beautiful painted pavement you uncovered has been left to take its chances with dust and sunlight, and there are fragments of crushed papyrus all over the site. Who knows what they might have added to our knowledge of the Ancient Egyptians who worshipped here? Ah well..." he relented suddenly, remembering that she was very young and by no means the real culprit. "I mustn't vent my anger on you merely because you're here and Soulier isn't."

"No," agreed Anastasia fervently. "That would not be British justice."

Anthony laughed, his teeth startlingly white in his tanned face. Despite the deplorable state of his clothes, which had suffered during his hasty exit from the excavation shaft, she thought he looked very handsome. His good looks were of a very different type from Valerian's, of course. They were very English, she thought. After all, she had seen pictures of Englishmen in the Countess' old photograph albums and in Miss Catherine's books. She was sure that Anthony was just like them—a sportsman, devoted to dogs and horses, perhaps even a player of that mysterious game called cricket. He hadn't Valya's quick, graceful movements, and she doubted if Anthony would shine in the ballroom as Valya did, but all the same he was certainly attractive. Remembering her lonely situation, she sat up straight as Miss Catherine had taught her to, ankles primly crossed and hands folded. Just because her heart longed for Valya, she mustn't weave fantasies around every good-looking man she met, like that dreadful Varvara...

"What does a Russian autocrat like you know of British justice?" he said.

"I know that people must be presumed innocent until they are proven guilty," she said to his surprise. He looked at her with new respect. "We didn't mean to hurt your temple, Mr. Mills, and you mustn't judge us until you've heard the whole story of what we've done here."

"All right, I won't. It's obvious that Soulier is to blame for this—this destruction. If you've really taken some photographs, there may be something I can save here after all."

"My mother and I will help you," said Anastasia happily. "Since your father isn't here, you'll need our help."

She was so eager to make amends that Anthony hadn't the heart to tell her that the most helpful thing she could do would be to escort her stepmother straight back to Cairo. Instead he instructed Ibrahim to go at once to the Countess Kharkova's camp near al-Katira with a letter to tell her that Anastasia was safe with Mr. Mills in the temple valley, and would await her there.

"Don't move a muscle," whispered Anthony, a few days later. "Here they come!"

Behind him, in the makeshift blind constructed of dry reeds on the edge of the lake, Anastasia froze. She heard the crisp *snick* in the still dawn air as he pushed forward the safety catch.

"Got your camera ready?"

"There's not enough light."

"Pity... Shh!"

She glanced up, hearing the first whistle of wings overhead. A second later the lightening sky was almost blotted out by a cloud of flying ducks. Anthony swung the gun smoothly to his shoulder and fired twice.

"You got one!" cried Anastasia. "No—two!" She had forgotten the need for silence. "Shall I go get them?"

He looked down at her, his blue eyes alight with excitement. "Hush!" he scolded. "Two pintails won't feed us all. We'll have to do better than that. Don't worry, Hassan and Shafi will pick them up in a moment. Watch out, here come some more."

Eight Egyptian geese, grunting like pigs, flew away before he could reload, while Anastasia danced with impatience. Next came teal, whistling like high-powered bullets.

"That should do nicely," said Anthony as the tenth bird splashed into the shallow water. "Have you ever seen such a wonderful place for waterbirds?"

Besides pintails and shovellers, there were mallards, widgeons, spoonbills and tall white egrets, but Anastasia surveyed the scene with the eye of a gourmet rather than an ornithologist. The dead birds floated in the water and the Arab boys had already begun to collect them, with much splashing and shouting, when a gray torpedo plummeted out of the clear blue sky.

"Look, Mr. Mills!" exclaimed Anastasia indignantly. "That eagle—or whatever it is—has stolen your duck. Shoot it!"

"Good lord, no. That's a peregrine, the finest pirate of them all. *Bon appetit* to him!" He watched admiringly as the marauder rose unsteadily into the sky, the bundle of feathers clasped in its talons. Anastasia climbed into the punt and counted the bag.

"Nine," she announced. "I think that's all of them. At least we'll have fresh meat for a change."

"Don't tell me you're tired of bully-beef *already*?"

They grinned companionably. The ducks had gone, planing down into the shimmering blue water a mile away, and the sun was warm on their backs as the Arab boys began to row them to the other shore.

"Now, when the light is good enough to take photographs, you've driven all the birds away," she complained.

"We'll probably see a few pelicans on the way back. They often sit on that little island with the palm trees."

"Look . . . look!" She clutched his arm. "Those are flamingoes, yes?" Entranced, she watched as the pink and white clouds rose slowly on wavering wings and floated away. "They're beautiful . . . so beautiful!"

And you are, too, thought Anthony, with a sidelong glance at the vivid, rapt profile with its high cheekbones and delicate, cleancut jawline. Far too beautiful for my peace of mind. What *would* Mother say if she knew I was bewitched by a Russian girl? Poor Mother! He chuckled inwardly.

Lady Mills' unflagging efforts to marry him off to the

daughter of her old friend Matilda Dunwoody—"Such a nice girl, my dear boy, and you know she adores you!"—had done more harm than good to her own cause. Left to himself, Anthony might well have proposed marriage to Sybil Dunwoody years ago. She was attractive, forthright, intelligent. They shared the same interest in music and archeology. She was both a good sport and a good organizer. She would undoubtedly make a splendid wife. It was the pressure—the idea that he was being driven when he'd rather lead—that had made Anthony Mills so obstinate.

"There's plenty of time yet, Mother," he had said gently when she last brought up the subject. "Don't try to tie me down before I'm ready."

"It's not a question of tying you down, Anthony, as you very well know," his mother replied with dignity. Small but indomitable, crippled with rheumatism, she sat with her feet up on the chaise longue—the position from which she'd always tried to organize the lives of her entire family. "Sybil's a pretty girl with plenty of admirers. Don't think you're the only man available just because she happens to like you—heaven alone knows why."

"My fatal charm." He grinned.

"Please be serious, Anthony. I'm trying to help you and this is a serious matter." She paused, and then said: "Don't think that I'm trying to influence you in any way, but you must be aware of how your father longs for grandchildren..."

"He's already got three!"

"None bearing his own name, dear. He's very fond of dear little Charlie, and Benjamin, and Isabel, but it's not *quite* the same as grandchildren of his own *line*, who'll inherit his own *property*..."

Anthony laughed aloud. "Mother, I believe that's the damnedest reason ever for trying to make me marry Sybil."

Lady Mills' delicate eyebrows rose. "Don't swear at me, Anthony. I don't know what's come over you lately. You never used to be so difficult. So... so intransigeant. Once and for all, I am *not* trying to make you marry Sybil. Heaven forbid. I am merely pointing out the advantages of such a match."

"You're ruining the chances of there being one," he said quietly. After a glance at his withdrawn face, his mother had compressed her lips and said no more. He was well aware that she'd return to the attack the moment she found another opening.

Remembering that conversation, he gazed again at Anastasia. Her long blonde hair blew forward across her face in the light breeze. Her boots and skirt were covered with mud from splashing about in the blind, and there was a long rip in the sleeve of her jacket where she'd caught it on a thorn. By conventional standards, she looked dirty and disreputable, yet she seemed to glow with color and vitality in this wild setting. He couldn't help comparing her vivid, windblown beauty with Sybil's tidy, well-ordered features—and personality.

"Why are you staring at me?" demanded Anastasia, turning suddenly. She didn't wait for an answer but went on impulsively: "You know, Anthony, if only I had a gun, we could shoot twice as many ducks and never have to eat that horrible meat from a can any more."

"Do you know how to shoot?"

"Certainly," she said proudly. "Valerian taught me long ago."

"Well done, Valerian, whoever he may be. In that case you can borrow my little twenty-bore if you've a mind to. It's one I had as a boy. I hardly ever use it now. Who is Valerian? I'm sure you've mentioned him before."

"He's my stepbrother. That is, he's the son of my adopted mother by her first marriage to General Radek. He's not my real brother at all," she explained carefully, suddenly very busy counting the wing-feathers of a dead pintail.

Anthony noted her heightened color.

"Ah, I remember now. Didn't he come to see you off at the station that night you left St. Petersburg?" He envisioned the brightly lighted private carriage; the two figures springing apart as Countess Kharkova joined them.

Anastasia nodded as her blush deepened.

"Of course!" He snapped his fingers. "That's the handsome puppy in regimental clothes whose picture you keep by your bed."

"Puppy! Valerian a puppy?" Anastasia's eyes were blazing. For a moment he was afraid she would spring at him like the wildcat she suddenly resembled.

"Oh lord," he said ruefully, "don't take it like that. "The word 'puppy' is only a slang term for a very young man. I didn't mean to be rude." But he was altogether aware that he *had* used the word in a pejorative sense, and that the handsome young officer smiling from the photograph had made him feel immediately antagonistic.

"You must never speak of Valerian like that. It isn't respectful. Valya is an important officer who is fighting for the Tsar in Manchuria."

And, thought Anthony, you're in love with him, damn his soul.

"Why were you spying in my bedroom?" she demanded.

"I wanted to find out who'd been living there while I was away. I looked in Soulier's tent as well, if it's any comfort to you."

She glowered but said no more. In disagreeable silence they made their way back to camp.

It was not in Anastasia's nature to sulk for long, however, and when Anthony produced a well-balanced little shotgun and allowed her to take a few practice shots at a target, they were soon on good terms again and decided to hunt for ducks.

"Shoot anything you like—except pigeons," he instructed her, as they set out across mudflats toward the lake. "You can even hit a *fellah* by mistake—not that I'd recommend it—and he'll forgive you for twenty piastres. But if you shoot his pigeons he'll never forgive you."

Anastasia wasn't paying attention. Light as the gun had seemed when she first held it, it was growing heavy now.

"Can't Hassan carry my gun?" she asked.

"No. I thought you said it wasn't heavy."

"It isn't, but it's awkward. It digs into my shoulder. Why can't Hassan carry it for me?"

"Because I don't want the barrels filled with mud every time he hops across a ditch," said Anthony shortly. He was determined not to offer to carry the gun himself. "If you want to shoot, you'll have to take the rough with the smooth, Anastasia."

Behind his back, she made a face, shifting the gun so that it lay more comfortably across her shoulder. Hassan and Shafi whistled in alarm and moved out of the line of fire.

Anthony turned sharply. "Hey! Watch out where your barrels are pointing."

Anastasia smiled. "Valerian always lets me carry my gun like this. Don't worry, it's not loaded."

"Are you sure of that?"

"Of course I'm sure. Oh!" she said in surprise, when she checked to be certain. "How strange. I don't remember loading it."

"I suggest you check your gun in the future to see if it's loaded—before pointing it at one of my servants," said Anthony between his teeth.

She sighed. All these rules! This wasn't nearly as much fun as she'd expected. She wanted an opportunity to impress him with her brilliant shooting. She was bored with trudging across these wretched mudflats toward a lake that never drew any nearer.

Matters did not improve when they finally reached the lake. A party of Arab fishermen, smacking the water with their oars and beating drums to drive the fish into their traps, had already chased all the ducks away. After a fruitless hour of waiting for the ducks to return, Anthony joined Anastasia in her blind.

"We're wasting our time. Let's walk along the edge of that cultivated strip and see if we can't pick up a few snipe on our way back to the road."

"All right," said Anastasia. She was bored enough to welcome any new activity, even carrying her gun again. Perhaps now she could show him what a good shot she was. But unfortunately, most of the snipe they stirred up provided good shots for Anthony. She was offered only two chances, both of which she missed.

She didn't even hesitate when a flock of gray birds flew up from a nearby bean patch, but swung the stock to her shoulder and fired both barrels. Two birds fell, but almost before they touched the ground, a burly Egyptian rose from behind the wall of the irrigation ditch and began to jabber and gesticulate furiously.

What on earth did he want? Ignoring him as best she could, she walked forward and picked up the birds. Only then did she realize that they were pigeons. Dimly, she recalled Anthony's warning. It was too late now to regret her hasty shots. The birds were dead; she couldn't bring them back to life. Anastasia reached in her pocket and brought out a handful of coins, but when she offered them to the Egyptian he knocked them out of her hand with a torrent of invective. Then he began to shout.

Immediately, other men in dirty flapping robes materialized from the earthwork. Within seconds she was surrounded.

Wildly she looked around for Anthony, but he was nowhere to be seen. The Egyptians pressed closer to her, waving their sticks in a threatening manner. Suddenly, she was very scared.

"I'm sorry. I didn't mean to shoot your birds. I'm *very* sorry." She tried it in English and French and German, but the angry dark faces showed no sign of comprehension. Oh, why couldn't she remember even a few words of Arabic?

"I'm sorry!" she said again, in mounting despair. "I'll pay for the pigeons. Please let me by!"

Suddenly her prayers were answered and Anthony appeared on the other side of the irrigation ditch. "What's all the fuss about?" he called out, wading across. Anastasia felt dizzy with relief.

As one, the enraged *fellahin* turned toward him, reporting her crime, clamoring for justice.

"I shot these pigeons by mistake," began Anastasia. "I've said I'm sorry and offered them money, but they won't let me go..." Her voice trailed away as she noticed the grim expression on Anthony's face.

"You trigger-happy little fool! Didn't I warn you? Didn't you hear me when I told you not to touch the pigeons? Now you've really done it," he said, and handed his gun to Shafi. Hearing the commotion, more villagers had arrived. Their words had a menacing undertone.

"Tell them I'll pay them well..." she said in a trembling voice.

"That won't help. They're out for blood now." He seized her by the shoulder. "I'm going to thrash you within an inch of your life—and maybe we'll get out of this alive."

She backed away, her eyes wide with dismay. "You wouldn't dare..."

He grabbed her unceremoniously and bent her across his knee. With outraged astonishment she felt the sting of his hand through her thin cotton skirt, and began to kick and scream at the top of her voice.

The crowd grunted its approval. This was the way to deal with an evil woman. Beat her until her sins departed, until she cried out in repentance and vowed never to return to her evil ways. Mills Bey should not have allowed the yellow-haired devil-woman to carry a gun and shoot at the pigeons whose precious manure gave life to a man's fields, but now he was teaching her the error of her ways. *Aiee*, but it was hard to beat the sin out. See how she screamed and kicked and tried to bite at Mills Bey's hand! Now, surely, he would cut her head off and be done with it.

When Anthony's arm ached, he judged that the punishment was sufficient in the onlookers' eyes; he allowed Anastasia to slide into a crumpled heap on the ground. On hands and knees she glared up at him, her face blotched with tears of fury and her breath coming in gasps. Nobody had ever beaten her as hard as that, and the presence of a grinning crowd of natives made it a hundred times worse.

"You—you fiend! You vicious sadistic beast! How dare you treat me like that! I'll never forgive you, never in my life," she shouted at him in Russian.

He answered coldly in the same language: "That doesn't worry me in the least. By your folly and disobedience you endangered all our lives. The sooner you leave here the better. Two of our subalterns were stoned to death near this village for doing exactly what you did. If I hadn't punished you myself we might all have suffered the same fate."

"Killed . . . ?" she whispered.

"Yes, killed. Now pray that I can get you out of this. Get up and follow me."

He took his gun from Shafi again and shouted a ribald joke to the staring villagers. To his relief their angry faces relaxed into smiles. "Wah, Mills Bey!" they chorused, and opened their ranks to allow him to pass.

"Keep up the wailing and gnashing of teeth," he said, "at least till we're clear of the village." After a startled silence, Anastasia allowed her rage full rein again. She had no need to act; her soul was as sore as her rump, and that burned like fire after Anthony Mills uninhibited spanking. Worst of all, her humiliation had been watched in approval by every idle native in the village. How could she ever face the workmen again?

"We should be all right now," Anthony said, a few minutes later. "No one has followed us. You can stop that silly crying and pull yourself together. I don't suppose you'll believe me when I say that hurt me much more than you."

Anastasia glowered at him. "I don't want your nasty jokes. I hate you. I don't want to talk to you any more."

"As you like," he said indifferently, "but I hope you realize *why* I had to punish you at once."

"You had no right to punish me at all," she said. "Why didn't you only pretend? Why did you hurt me so much? I know it's because you like hurting me!"

"Don't talk nonsense. I didn't want them asking why I didn't use a stick to beat you," said Anthony cooly. "If I'd used a stick, you might have had something to complain about! Don't you realize that in this country a girl who disobeys and dishonors her family has her head cut off by her own brothers? That's how highly they regard their women."

"I think you agree with them," muttered Anastasia. For half a mile, she slouched along behind, deliberately keeping out of earshot as they crossed the mudflats. But when they came in sight of their camp in the hidden valley, Anthony heard her shout and turned to find her running to catch up with him.

"Wait!" she gasped. "Don't walk so fast. I must talk to you."

"What is it?" He was tired of her sulks and tantrums, and longing to get back to camp and wash off the memory of this disastrous morning.

To his surprise, she had already recovered her temper and even made an effort to smile at him.

"Please, Anthony. Don't mention this to Mama."

"I'll leave that up to you."

"She must not know. She'd be angry to learn that you beat me. She'd—" her voice trembled—"she would take me back to Cairo and not let me come here again."

Anthony only wished that would happen. The immediate removal of this beautiful, infuriating girl would allow the digging to proceed reasonably smoothly.

Softening a little before the pleading in her eyes, he said, "Don't you want to go back to Cairo? You're missing all the best parties, you know, stuck way out here in the desert."

"Parties!" Anastasia regarded him scornfully. "Of course I don't want to go away and leave you alone to dig. It's my temple now, as well as yours."

"Despite the fact that you haven't got a license and I have?" He grinned. Slowly, reluctantly, the corners of her mouth turned up in an answering smile.

"You *will* share it with me, Anthony? Please? And say nothing to Mama?"

"Oh . . . all right," he said reluctantly. "But only on the condition that you obey my orders implicitly from now on."

"Of course. *Implicitly*," she agreed with fervor. But he saw the naughty sideways glance she gave him through her eyelashes, and doubted very much that his troubles were yet over.

Chapter Ten

MANCHURIA 1905

The flimsy bedroom wall made of bamboo matting and rice paper bulged and shook. From within came the carefully simulated moans of a woman at the height of sexual climax.

Sergei moved hastily away from his post—guarding the door of the Chinese prostitute's room—and signaled to Ah Kee, the messenger boy.

"He doesn't like them noisy," he muttered, winking. "He'll be out of there in a moment now, mark my words. Hang on a minute, and I'll see that you get to speak to him."

Scarcely had he spoken when Valerian emerged from the bedroom, a cloying whiff of oriental scent surrounding him. He was frowning, his eyes narrowed. His dark hair was tousled and he pulled on his tunic as he walked.

"Get rid of *that*," he said quietly, jerking a thumb back toward the room he'd just left. "Pay her well, but make sure she's gone by the time I return. God! They all smell alike. I need a bath. Well, Ah Kee, what is it?"

While the boy delivered the general's summons, Sergei prepared his master's bath and laid out fresh clothes. He wasn't surprised by the abrupt order to get rid of May Wong. In his opinion she was a scheming little bitch and none too clean, either. She'd lasted a day longer than her predecessor in Valerian's household, but none of these Manchurian tarts were able to hold him for long. Sergei sighed for the good old days in St. Petersburg, before this hellish war began when the master lived in his own house and was content with a single mistress for months at a time.

Now there seemed to be a devil driving him on. It was weeks

since his household had heard him laugh, or received the least word of praise or thanks. Sergei was not much given to speculation, but sometimes he couldn't help wondering what had happened during the week that the master had spent at his mother's bedside way back in the first winter of the war. Something had changed him then, and none of them could guess at the reason.

Admittedly the war was enough to try a man's temper, and Sergei knew very well that the enforced inactivity at Headquarters, dancing attendance on his general when he wanted to be at the front, was one cause of Valerian's temper. His own company had been cut to ribbons at the battle of the Yalu River, and Valerian felt disgraced because he hadn't been there with his men. But that, thought Sergei, was only half the story. He wished he knew what else brought that terrible look of guilt and despair to his master's face.

Had he known the true reason for Valerian's malaise, however, he wouldn't have understood it. Among Sergei's friends it was no disgrace to sleep with your sister, or your daughter either, if she was willing and the nights were cold enough. The idea that his master was eating his heart out because he'd unwittingly deflowered his stepsister would have seemed to him absurd.

Nevertheless, it was the truth. The specter of what he had done to Anastasia had come between Valerian and his sleep ever since that fateful night. Even when he coupled with Chinese whores, he couldn't erase the image of Anastasia's shocked face and trembling mouth when she realized her mistake: having aroused the violence of his passion, she could do nothing to avoid the consequences.

How could I have done it? Over and over again, he asked himself the same question. Each time, the answer stared him brutally in the face. He had ravished her—not because he was drunk but because he desired her. Anastasia's, fresh young body had the power to tempt him that night because, deep down, he had wanted it ever since she kissed him when she left St. Petersburg.

He tried to throw himself into his work, but there was little except bad news coming into Headquarters—constant orders to retreat when they should have dug in, and to dig in when they should retreat. Knowing that a once-proud brigade or division had waged yet another unsuccessful battle drove him into a state of helpless fury that bordered on madness.

Ever since the war started, one disaster had followed another, and still the Russian high command could do nothing to stop the relentless advance of the Japanese.

On New Year's Day, 1905, Port Arthur—the great white elephant that had trapped the Russian warships ever since the fighting began—had surrendered to the Japanese, and a week later the prisoners had been marched out. Over fifteen thousand sick and wounded had been among the thirty-two thousand survivors of General Stössel's gallant, hard-pressed garrison, and who knew what would become of them in the hands of those devil-eyed yellow monkeys?

Hardly had Valerian's war-weary mind adjusted to this defeat when more bad news arrived—this time from Petersburg itself. Troops had fired on peacefully marching workers led by a socialist priest named Father Gapon, who were on their way to the Winter Palace to present a petition to the Tsar. Arms locked, chanting hymns, the workers had surged through the icy, windswept streets until confronted by infantry backed by Cossacks and Hussars, who fired point blank into the crowd of marchers. Too tightly packed to scatter, the unarmed workers bore the brunt of repeated Cossack charges which left the snowy streets red with blood. The subsequent manifesto issued by the Tsar, condemning the "evil-minded leaders of the revolutionary movement," had been greeted with cynicism both at home and abroad.

Then, in March, toward the end of this terrible winter, after a series of blunders which gave the Japanese the opportunity to cut the railway—their vital supply line—north of Mukden, General Kuropatkin had been relieved of supreme command and succeeded by General Linevitch, bald as an egg, with ears sticking out like wings and a snow-white walrus mustache above his scrubby beard. Kuropatkin was given command of the First Manchurian Army, but it soon became plain to Valerian that these changes in leadership were only a last desperate gamble that might save a fraction of Russia's Far Eastern possessions.

In the eyes of the world, the plucky and successful fight that little Japan had waged against her huge adversary had usurped all of Russia's prestige. Nothing remained to hearten her generals but the fabled endurance of the Russian fighting man, and that, too, was now overstrained. Badly trained, badly equipped, badly led, the Russian soldiers hung on tenaciously in the face of disaster and refused to admit defeat while a single breath remained in their bodies. If they ever realize how lightly their leaders treat their valor, thought Valerian with helpless rage, those same men will turn on the generals who have betrayed them, and who will blame them for it?

He pulled his fur hat closer about his ears as he set off for Kuropatkin's headquarters. The icy wind from the north cut through his heavy greatcoat and tried to carve the skin from his face. He was glad to sit and thaw his frozen fingers by the pot-bellied stove while the orderly went to announce his arrival.

General Kuropatkin was finishing a substantial breakfast in the well-appointed railway carriage that served as a mobile HQ.

"Captain Count Radek, sir," announced the orderly, ushering Valerian through the sliding door with ceremony better suited to showing an ambassador into the Imperial presence.

"Ah, there you are, my boy. Come in, come in," exclaimed Kuropatkin, patting his mustache with a snow-white napkin. "Take a seat and listen. I've got a job for you. A dispatch has just come in from Colonel von Lidenburg of the Eastern Siberian Rifles. The wires are down again. Apparently, they can't keep communications open for more than a few hours at a time, and the situation appears confused."

Here we go again, thought Valerian wearily. He won't trust the dispatch to tell him the truth. He'll have to send me all the way to Nantung to confirm it.

"You know that von Lidenburg's still holding the old Chinese fort at Nantung," continued the general. "He's been facing two Japanese divisions and an independent artillery brigade, but he's well dug in and has managed to dominate the situation so far. But now, it seems, General Oku is moving up reinforcements. Von Lidenburg thinks he can hold them a few miles farther north where there's a range of hills." He pointed them out on the map. "They call it the Ricebowl Mountain. He's requested permission to retire on Ricebowl and asked for the support of the First Orenburg Cossacks to cover his retreat. I'm sending you up the line with orders to that effect for Major Grassevitch, and I'd like your report on the situation at Nantung, as well."

Another withdrawal, just when they should stand firm. Another brigade uselessly sacrificed. "We can't retreat again, sir!" Valerian said. "If General von Lidenburg abandons Nantung, the Japanese will break through our line and occupy Mukden!"

"Are you questioning my orders, boy?" The general's eyes snapped open in surprise.

"No. Yes. Yes, I am." Valerian could bear it no longer. After the frustration of the past months, he no longer cared what he said. "I wish to protest, sir, against the way this campaign is being conducted. A single regiment of sharpshooters should be able to cover General von Lidenburg's retreat, instead of throwing away Cossacks who are unsuited to the country or the job. Why have we no marksmen who can pick off the Japanese scouts before they cut our wires and site their guns where they can blow us to pieces? I'll tell you, sir. Because our soldiers are the worst shots in the world. They get no target practice except firing in volleys, at the speed of the slowest man among them, and that's worse than no practice at all. It's a disgrace, sir! The Russian Army is the laughingstock of the world! Every day, thousands of our troops are slaughtered because they are neither trained nor equipped as a modern army should be."

"Captain Radek, you have said quite enough," snapped Kuropatkin angrily. "You are entitled to your views, but I will not tolerate insubordination, even from the son of an old friend. Your father would turn in his grave if he heard his son speak in such terms to his commanding officer. I may have lost the supreme command, but you are mistaken if you think I have lost my mind as well. Be so good as to report to me when you have carried out your mission."

He paused, and peered closely at the younger man. Then he said in a quite different tone, "I think it's time you applied for leave, Valerian. Clearly you are feeling the strain of boredom here at Headquarters, when your regiment is so heavily engaged. Believe me, I sympathize. That's why I'm prepared to overlook your remarks."

"In that case, may I request permission to rejoin my regiment?" said Valerian stiffly. He knew that Kuropatkin was trying to make excuses for him—for his mother's sake, no doubt—but still he couldn't bring himself to apologize for his outburst.

Looking every year of his age, Kuropatkin sighed. "I'm sorry, my boy. I can't spare you."

You promised my mother you'd keep her darling son away from the fighting, thought Valerian savagely. That's what you mean. Every man in my regiment knows it. They sneer at me behind my back.

"Then do you want me to ride to Nantung with Major Grassevitch?"

Kuropatkin permitted himself a small smile—a mere twitch of the mustache in his careworn face. "If you can keep up with those wild devils of Cossacks—yes. Take the train to Sinhaio and join up with Grassevitch at his winter quarters at Telayama. I want to know everything that's going on at Nantung, and especially why the supplies of ammunition haven't been getting through to von Lidenburg. Every detail, now..."

Valerian was glad to escape. He knew he had made a fool of himself and gained nothing. Indeed, by voicing his discontent he had put himself even farther from the fighting which was now what he craved. He was obsessed with a desire to come face to face with those Japanese devils who had stripped Russia of her self-respect. He knew that, given the chance, he could lead his own men to victory. But when would he get the chance? Officers more junior than himself had been promoted in the field, while he wrote reports and lists, pandering to his general's love of detail. He grimaced, remembering Kuropatkin's parting words. Of course, *detail* was what he could never escape. Kuropatkin was fascinated by minutiae, but the administrative talent which had made him an excellent Chief of Staff was no asset—indeed, it was a serious drawback—in a Commander-in-chief. Kuropatkin was incapable of seeing the wood for the trees, and his strategy was always blurred by an obscuring mass of foliage. Valerian was certain that all the defeats Russia had suffered in this nightmare war could have been victories had even one commander of genius emerged from the Russian High Command. The thought of so much wasted heroism, of those thousands of simple *moujiks*, filled him with savage, helpless rage.

During these last months, frustration and self-disgust had been his constant companions, his moods swinging between recklessness and black depression. As he boarded the small, crowded troop train that would carry him to Sinhaio, sandwiched between a young artillery captain and a huge, bearded Cossack, he looked around the compartment and wondered if anyone else shared his disillusionment with the army he had once been so proud to serve. Death before dishonor, he thought bitterly. If that were truly our motto we should all be dead by now. As for me—doubly dishonored—I should be dead twice over. He closed his eyes. Immediately, Anastasia's beautiful green eyes seemed to stare at him in silent accusation. "You never loved me," they seemed to say: "You took all I had to give and then left me."

Valerian groaned. The fresh-faced reservist opposite, who was going south to join his regiment, looked at him in surprise.

"I beg your pardon, sir?"

"I wish I was dead," mumbled Valerian. Above his bent head the young captain and the Cossack exchanged indulgent smiles. The handsome staff captain must be talking in his sleep.

Six hours later, before it was fully light, Valerian was awakened by a tremendous crash which shattered the windows into fragments and flung the men to the floor. The train shuddered violently, tilted and came to a halt. Struggling up in the sudden confusion, points of light stabbing behind his eyes, Valerian groped his way to the door and jumped down onto the track. He didn't think; he simply reacted.

Just as his feet landed, a second explosion ripped the dawn stillness, blowing the leading cars of the train sky high. Burning sticks and chunks of metal rained down. Waking soldiers screamed, trying to fight their way out. Crouching and stumbling, Valerian half ran, half fell down the steep embankment. He cradled his head in his arms and fell to the ground as a third, even bigger, explosion reduced the rest of the train to rubble. This blast hurled him fifty yards and a piece of flying debris hit him on the head and knocked him unconscious.

Doctor Susanna Macdonald packed the surgical instruments into her large black bag and stood for a moment, head bent, looking sadly at the mortal remains of her late patients. The black-haired young mother and her baby lay side by side behind the partition of matting that divided the peasant hut. Blue-lipped, waxen-faced, their limbs were already setting in the stiffness of death. The family had called her too late. There was little any doctor could have done to save either one, but all the same Susanna felt the familiar sense of exasperation. She possessed only the most basic of medicines, and had pitifully little experience to combat what disease, war, and accident inflicted on these poor Manchurian peasants. But there were other, older ways of treating sick bodies and minds—ways unrecognized by Western science. She had seen how effective these ancient drugs and skills could be when used by the right hands, and she longed to master their mysteries. She had watched a Chinese physician, bent and wizened but with marvelous dexterity, practice acupuncture, removing a cataract from the eye of a fully-conscious patient after first inserting needles to release the harmful vapors from the afflicted part of the body. The patient, who hadn't even appeared to suffer, submitted stoically to the surgeon's knife although Susanna could hardly bear to watch the operation.

She was fascinated, too, by hypnosis—the waking sleep which a strong will could impose on a weaker one. She had experimented among her patients and knew the extent of her own power, but the Buddhist priest who had guided her first tentative efforts at hypnosis had recently been arrested by the Japanese. He was suspected of conveying intelligence to the Russian Army. Like a vampire deprived of blood, Susanna thirsted for more knowledge of his dark art.

Few people would have guessed, on first meeting Susanna, that her neat, freckled features and hazel eyes concealed a fiercely acquisitive soul. Good-looking in a sturdy Scottish way, she was only twenty-five, the youngest daughter of a Free Kirk minister who'd had to fight the rest of his large brood from the nursery onward. Throughout her childhood, "I want," were the most frequent words on Susanna's lips. Though she was aware that such a nature did not endear her to other people, she couldn't change it.

She had reveled in the fight that greeted her when she tried to gain entry to medical school in Edinburgh. And she triumphed. Now, as a fully accredited missionary doctor, she sought to minimize the effect of her youth and beauty by wearing the plainest, dullest, most practical clothes, and scraping back her thick red-gold hair—which often struck superstitious terror into the hearts of her Chinese patients—into a tight, unbecoming bun at the nape of her neck.

"Manchuria? You can't be serious!" the handsome young ship's purser had exclaimed on hearing her destination. "I cannot understand why you lovely Scots lassies insist on burying yourselves in these impossible places. Why can't you stay at home for travel-weary sailors like me to come back to?"

He had eyed her in hunger. He'd been a well-built fellow, with broad shoulders and bold black eyes, but ever since Willie Carmichael had jilted Susanna three years ago, sneaking off to Glasgow to marry sly Meg McIntyre, she had resolved never again to succumb to the blandishments of bold black eyes and broad shoulders. No man was ever going to deceive her again. She replied curtly that the heathen Chinese had far more need of her than any travel-weary sailor, and sent him away puzzled that such an attractive girl should dislike men so cordially.

Her sisters and brothers had sympathized and told her it was too bad of Willie, but she sensed a degree of gloating behind their sympathy. Deep down, they were, somewhat pleased that clever little Susanna had fallen into the oldest pitfall known to woman. Her father agreed that she was better off not marrying a man who could behave so deceitfully. But even he didn't know the shame and rage that burned in her heart, because Willie was not solely to blame...

She had been too certain of her own power over him to refuse his entreaties in the warm soft dark of an August night when he walked her home from the *ceilidh*. But her calculations had failed to include one vital factor: to Willie, the chase was much more exciting than the conquest. After that night, she never saw him again. It was a chilling blow to her pride to realize that he preferred a posturing little nincompoop like Meg McIntyre to her.

She tried to forget him, but her sexual awakening had been long overdue, and however hard she concentrated on other things, the memory of Willie continued to haunt her during the hot Manchurian summer nights, when the nightingales sang and the soft breeze sighed through the waving *kaoliung*. Her whole body seemed to cry out for his embrace in a way that would have been shameful in any woman, but was positively shocking in a doctor. An intellectual, she thought, should be above that kind of human weakness. She took to blunting her cravings with the opium which was readily available to her, and found it gave her a measure of serenity.

Sighing, she picked up her bag and went to tell the Chinese family the bad but not unexpected news that the Number Two wife and her baby were no more. She left the house as their ritual wailing began, and mounted the shaggy Mongolian pony which her servant Lin Tong had sheltered in a cowstall during her visit to the family.

The wind had been rising steadily all afternoon. Now, at four o'clock, the sky had an ominous yellow tinge that spoke of the heavy snow to come. The long hairs on the pony's back and quarters were already lightly dusted with white.

"We'll go home by the iron road," said Susanna, and Lin Tong nodded agreement. He glanced at the sky.

"Much snow coming. Go home quick now." He knew all too well her habit of calling on other patients in lonely homesteads, often doubling the length of their journey home.

"Very well." She nudged her heels into the pony's sides and he began the curious shuffling amble peculiar to ponies from Mongolian caravans.

When Valerian recovered his senses it was broad daylight. He was colder than he had ever been in his life. His head and every muscle were aching and frozen blood had made a mask of his face. Trying to roll over in order to sit up, he realized that both feet and both hands were numb. If he lay there any longer he would certainly freeze to death.

It was agony to restore the circulation to his limbs, and several times he was tempted to give up and let the numbness creep through his body until it extinguished the spark of life itself. Only the possibility that there might be other survivors of the wreck made him persevere, tearing off his gloves with his teeth and rubbing his hands in the snow until at last they were strong enough to unlace his boots and let his feet receive the same treatment. He listened for any sound from the train on the embankment above him, but nothing reached his ears except the wail of the wind and his own gasping breath.

When he finally got to what was left of the train, he realized that his efforts had been in vain. Small flakes of snow were falling on the twisted metal and jumbled bodies, turning the whole wreck into a scene of vast desolation. Some of the bodies were naked, the uniforms blown off by the blast, while others—though equally dead—were still fully clothed. Packs, rolls, and suitcases were recognizable in the debris, but there was no sign of whoever had planted the mines.

They will come back, thought Valerian. Soon they will come

back to see what they've caught in their trap. Then it will be worse for me than if I had died in the explosion. Nonetheless a certain perversity made him pick his way carefully through the mounds of wreckage for over an hour, hoping to find a flicker of life in even one of the silent bodies.

At last he gave up. No one else had reacted quickly enough: they were all quite dead. Then, as he turned over a broken packing-case, he heard a faint whine. It was not human, certainly, but any living sound was companionable in this vast empty silence.

Finally, he managed to pry the case open. Bending down, he peered inside and found a dog's cold nose pressed against his. It was a half-grown puppy of uncertain breed, pale yellow in color, with a long silky coat, a sharp nose, and an extravagantly curled tail which was now pressed miserably between its hindlegs.

Whimpering, she crawled out. Valerian spoke to her. The tail slowly rose as her confidence returned, and he concluded that she was badly frightened but uninjured.

What shall I do now?, he wondered. What *can* I do?

General Kuropatkin's orders were still tucked in his wallet. It was his duty to deliver them. A treacherous devil at the back of his mind wished that the blast had destroyed the orders and himself with them. He had no way of knowing how far from Sinhaio the engine had struck the mines. And his watch had stopped. The train had been due to arrive at nine that morning, but he didn't know if it was behind or ahead of schedule.

The bitter north wind cut through his clothes. He would have to endure that wind if he marched across country, and although reason told him that his enemies would return sooner or later, he couldn't bring himself to leave the narrow silver track that was now his only link with civilization.

He looked around him at the snowy desolation of fields where the *kaoliung* had waved so luxuriantly before the harvest. Then, head down, shoulders hunched, boots sliding, he began to stumble down the track. A bag, stuffed with rice and canned meat which he'd salvaged from the wreck, banged against his kidneys at each uneven step. Behind him, following her savior as he was following the tracks, trotted the dog.

It was hard going to begin with, and it rapidly became harder. The wind rose to a piercing scream and the stinging snow flakes whipped his face viciously. Valerian turned to look back at the wreck of the train, but it had already been covered by the white fury of snow. On and on, he trudged. Concentrating only on setting one boot in front of the other, left, right, left, right, he lost all sense of time.

The falling snow was strangely mesmerizing. He could no longer tell whether he was walking uphill or down. His head began to swim. Suddenly he became aware that he was lying in a snowdrift—with no recollection of having fallen.

This can't go on, he thought hazily. I must find some shelter until the storm is over. But where could he find any refuge from the screaming whiteness? He tried to get up but the muscles of his legs appeared to have atrophied. He swayed for a moment, trying to regain his balance, and fell over again. Lying down, the fury of the storm seemed less fierce. It was even warm in the space which his body had pressed in the snow.

Valerian knew how dangerous it was even to contemplate resting in the snow, but the strain of the previous months had sapped his will power. The prospect of lying down out of the wind seemed overpoweringly seductive. He lay there without moving. Then the yellow dog began to whine. It rubbed up against him. Feebly, Valerian tried to push it away.

"Leave me alone, damn you. I want to lay down..."

Clearly the dog wanted something else. Its whimpering became so insistent that Valerian made the effort to get up once more. He managed to stand and stumble forward a few more yards before collapsing. The dog repeated its performance, nosing his face as it became bolder, tugging at his collar. He couldn't tell whether the growls of the dog were threatening or merely playful. Either way they disturbed the delicious drowsiness that was overcoming him. More and more he longed to sink into the soft, thick whiteness forever, to let oblivion wash over him like a wave—sweeping away his guilt and remorse over Anastasia, burying the disgrace of his country's defeats under an everlasting blanket of peace.

It would be so easy... if only that damn dog would leave him alone. Why had he ever released the pestilential creature from its prison? *Yap, yap, yap!* There it went again. Valerian flinched as the needle-sharp teeth tugged first at his collar and then his ear. Painfully, slowly, he dragged himself upright again, determined to end this nuisance once and for all. He pulled out his revolver with clumsy fingers from beneath layers of clothes, pointed it at the yellow dog's heart and tried to fire, but his frozen fingers couldn't flex to pull the trigger. He cursed, weakly. Tears ran down his cheeks, freezing before they fell from his chin. He took a swipe at the dog's skull with the butt of the gun. Delighted with this new game, the dog darted nimbly out of reach, and the force of his blow caused Valerian to topple over again.

Disappointed by this sudden end to its sport, the dog whined and pawed. Valerian, growing cunning, lay quiet until the dog came within reach, then suddenly clamped both arms round the small body. The dog struggled, then seemed to become resigned to captivity. It shoved its head into the opening of Valerian's heavy coat and lay still.

Peace at last, he thought thankfully, closing his eyes. He didn't feel cold any longer, just very tired, incapable of moving again. I'll lie here for a few minutes, he thought—not long, just a few minutes while I get my strength back. Then I'll be on my way . . .

In the distance, a wolf howled, and the snow drifted softly down to cover both Valerian and the dog as they lay on the railroad track.

Susanna's small home was in the compound belonging to a missionary couple, the Reverend Elias and Martha Armstrong, who were old friends of her parents' and treated her as a favorite daughter. They, indeed had influenced her choice of Manchuria as a missionary field. In their cheerful company, she could feel that, far from wasting the best years of her life—as the young purser had implied—she was doing something worthwhile and making her contribution to the powers of Good in their battle against Evil. She usually shared the Armstrongs' evening meal in the handsome brick farmhouse with its cozy tile roof. Seated on the *kong*—the raised dais under which the flue from the kitchen fire guided its warmth—she was happy to hear their homely Scots brogue after a long day's struggle to comprehend the high-pitched voices of her Chinese patients.

As the bitter wind drove needles of ice through her cloak, she was looking forward to meeting the two new nurses and the chaplain from Sinhaio who'd been invited to the Armstrongs' for supper. Martha was one of Nature's matchmakers, and it worried her to see Susanna leading such a solitary existence, cut off from friends of her own age. She was doing all she could to remedy this situation.

The pony's pace quickened as they came to the railway. He avoided the rails with the ease of long practice, as Lin Tong hurried to keep pace with him. Susanna sat loosely in the saddle, longing to be home and out of the wind. When the pony stopped suddenly she nearly fell off.

"What's the matter, boy?" she exclaimed sharply, recovering her seat. Lin Tong gave her steed a hearty thwack on his snow-covered quarters, but he wouldn't budge. Neck extended he sniffed at an uneven snowdrift rising from the track.

"Wait a minute," said Susanna. Stiffly, she dismounted and followed the pony's head. The drift was covering a bundle of some kind. There was something horribly familiar about the size and shape of the bundle. Even covered in snow and wrapped in layers of cloth there was no mistaking its human origin. She brushed off more snow, then started back with a cry.

"Lin Tong—come quickly! It's a soldier—a Russian officer, I think, and a dog. I'm afraid he's frozen to death, poor fellow."

She pulled off her heavy gloves and burrowed until she could thrust a hand beneath Valerian's coat. She felt for a heartbeat. Her fingers seemed to detect the faintest warmth lingering in his skin—a lessening of coldness rather than warmth. It was enough, however, to make her hastily withdraw her hand and turn to Lin Tong with an air of decision.

"We will take him home with us," she said.

The officer's stiff arms were locked around the equally rigid figure of the dog, and all their pulling could not separate man from beast.

"We must be quick," said Susanna breathlessly. "We can't leave him here where the next train will crush him, and there's no time to fetch help. I think he's alive—just—but he won't last long."

"Put on pony?" suggested Lin Tong, and she blessed his placid readiness to cope with any problem.

"Yes. Yes, that's what we'll do. Perhaps . . . if you can raise him up, while I steady his legs . . ."

Together they managed to hoist the unwieldy bundle across the back of her pony, who had recovered from his first surprise and stood patiently waiting to resume their journey home.

Fortunately they had only a short distance to go. Martha

Armstrong came running out in her apron on hearing their shouts for assistance, and between the three of them they dragged the stiff bodies into the kitchen.

"Off with his clothes," ordered Martha immediately. "Snow's the only cure we have for frostbite. He's alive, all right, and so's the wee dog, but he'll lose all his toes and fingers if we dinna look sharp. It's a right shame that Elias isna home, for yon's a big lad and we'll have our work cut out to handle him. But never mind, we'll save him."

Briskly, she began to unbutton Valerian's tunic and unwind his puttees. Then, somewhat pink-cheeked and flustered, she glanced up at Susanna.

"Better leave this to me, lassie. It's no job for a young girl. You go and get some soup heated up for when he comes to himself."

"Heavens, Martha! I'm not a young girl—I'm a doctor," said Susanna sharply. "I've seen naked men before, so don't worry about my blushes. The cook can see to the soup while I help you."

Martha compressed her lips in disapproval but said no more. They stripped off the last of Valerian's clothes and he lay naked and defenseless on the kitchen table.

"A right bonny lad he is, too," said Martha. "What a terrible war it is, to bring a man to such a death."

Susanna said nothing, trying not to stare. It was true that she had seen naked men before, but they were usually old or sick, their wasted bodies mere living frameworks on which lecturers and surgeons could demonstrate their skills. Sheets were draped here and there to render their anatomy impersonal. She was quite unprepared for the sight of an outstandingly handsome young man, in the flower of his strength, lying before her as naked as the day he was born.

Silky dark hair fell across his forehead. The winged eyebrows on either side of his high-bridged, acquiline nose, the nostrils slightly flared, gave him a look of a hawk—a look contradicted by the gentle, relaxed curves of his mouth and the closed eyelids. He looked, she thought, like a proud young pagan god—or a fallen angel still dreaming of Paradise. Swiftly she reproached herself for so whimsical—and indeed unchristian—a thought. Encased in his long gray overcoat and boots, he had been nothing but a lump of suffering humanity who needed her professional skill. But now that she saw him stripped she could hardly bring herself to lay rough hands on those strong, well-shaped limbs, hard-muscled and very white in contrast to his weather-bronzed face and hands, or rub handfuls of snow—as Martha was doing—over the broad chest that tapered into a narrow waist and the sinewy legs of an athlete.

"Dinna gape at him, lassie. Time enough for that later," snapped Martha, her reddening face a sure indication of embarrassment. "The poor lad must have walked all the way from Shenfeng, and that's a fair step even in good conditions."

"Shenfeng? How do you know?" Susanna steeled herself to pick up a handful of the snow that Lin Tong had shoveled into a big tin tub, to scrub it over Valerian's shoulders, kneading and pinching, knuckling and slapping as she tried to stir his sluggish circulation.

"You haven't heard about the train crash? The Japanese mined a Russian troop train. Turn him over now, that's right. We'll need more snow, Lin Tong, if you please. Yes, that's where this lad's come from, I've no doubt. Ten miles he'll have walked in the blizzard, him and his dog. How is the wee beastie?"

"The animal lives," said Lin Tong with satisfaction, for he enjoyed the taste of dog meat and liked to butcher it himself.

Martha spared the time to give him a sharp look. "Don't be thinking of adding him to your family's stew yet awhile, or you'll have his master to answer to," she warned. "See, he's beginning to stir the noo. Keep on rubbing, lassie. I think we've saved him."

Valerian groaned and opened his eyes the smallest slit.

"Wake up, laddie. Wake up!" said Martha urgently. She pulled him into a sitting position and slapped him back and forth across the cheek. Helplessly, his head rocked from side to side.

"Leave him alone! Don't hurt him like that," said Susanna. She tried to stop Martha's hands.

Martha turned a grim, flushed face to her. "It's the only way. You're a doctor, lass—you should know. Once the snow-sleep sets in they're awful hard to rouse. You've got to be cruel to make them want to live again. Come on now, man! On your feet and march!"

With Lin Tong's assistance they hoisted Valerian to a standing position and forced him to stumble outside into the snow. He groaned and tried feebly to push them away, but his eyes stayed open for longer and longer intervals and at last his legs began to move like an automaton's. Martha was relentless. When Lin Tong was exhausted, Susanna took his place, her shoulder propped under Valerian's armpit, his arm draped across her back as they marched him up and down the courtyard, around and around the courtyard, to the gate and back again. As it grew dark they fetched torches and shone them in his eyes. "Wake up!" Martha kept urging. "I won't let you go back to sleep. Use the muscles God gave you and march, man, *march*!"

Valerian saw his rescuers through a fog of pain. Why wouldn't they leave him alone? He was unable to resist these determined female demons who wouldn't let him slip back into the snow-sleep he craved. He was tired, and they forced him to open his eyes. He was naked and cold, and they made him stumble to and fro, back and forth, until the first painful tingling in his arms and legs became a torment, an agonizing throbbing of reopened blood vessels that stretched his flesh so tight he felt it would split like the skin of a grape.

"It . . . it hurts," he whispered, in Russian.

"What's that? What did he say?"

Susanna had worked among the Russian settlers before the victorious Japanese Army drove them away to the north. "He says it hurts him," she replied.

"It'll hurt a deal more before we're out of the wood. All right, lass. We'll take him within and get some clothes on him. He's maybe able to take a dram the noo."

The circulation returning to his limbs made Valerian scream with pain. As it spread through his fingers the agony became so acute, and his screams so piercing, that Susanna had to muffle her ears. Despite all Martha's efforts, the toes on one foot remained obstinately numb and she shook her head.

"I'm thinking he'll lose those toes, and there's nothing more we can do to save them."

"Oh, no!"

"Look at them. The blood's been gone from them too long. Once gangrene sets in they'll turn black and drop off. I've seen it happen so many times."

Shouts outside now heralded the arrival of the Reverend Elias—a big, boisterous Presbyterian Scot with a bushy black beard—and his companions, the two young nurses from Sinhaio and the new chaplain. Suddenly the brick farmhouse seemed full to overflowing as they crowded in with their servants, their loud, cheerful voices raised in greeting. The smell of wet sheepskin rose steaming to the rafters.

"Ye've done a grand job, the pair of ye," said Elias approvingly, when he took a close look at the half-conscious Russian. "He may lose those toes, there's no saying for sure, and he's had a terrible crack on the head somewhere along the way, but he'll live for all that. Did you get him to take any soup? Good, good. Now let's see who he is—where did you put his clothes? Ah, yes . . . a Russian, indeed, and a noble one too, by the looks of it. Captain Count Radek, no less," he said, carefully spelling out the Cyrillic lettering, "of His Imperial Majesty's Preobrazhensky Guards. Well, well, well! What a prize he will be for our little Japanese friends if they march this way."

"They mustn't catch him," said Susanna quickly. She felt a strongly protective—almost proprietary—instinct toward the young man she had saved.

Elias raised his bushy eyebrows. "They are our allies, lass. You mustna forget that. It may be our duty to report the finding of Count Radek to them."

"I won't allow it," insisted Susanna. "I found him and he's my patient. He's far too sick to hand over to those cruel little Asiatics. I hate the way their coolies stare and poke their fingers at European prisoners—as if they were wild beasts in a cage. I won't give him up to them."

Elias frowned, as he always did when she spoke slightingly of Asiatics. "They are all God's children, lassie."

Soothingly, Martha said, "Now, Susanna, dinna fash yersel'. There's no hurry yet to decide what we do with the puir laddie. All he needs now is a good long sleep . . ."

"Then we'll take him over to my hut," said the girl, determined at all costs to keep him away from Elias, who sometimes had strange ideas of where his duty lay. "It's warm and quiet in there by the stove, and I can keep my eye on him if he becomes feverish."

Martha and Elias, doubtful about the propriety of this arrangement, exchanged troubled glances, but Susanna overrode them and instructed the coolies to carry Valerian to her hut on the other side of the courtyard.

And so it was that late that night Valerian awoke from a

sweating, monster-ridden dream to find, bending over him, not the female demon with tightly screwed-back hair that he remembered through the mists of pain, but a beautiful goddess whose long red-gold tresses streamed over her shoulders like a cloak. Her eyes were wide and anxious, staring at him above the flame of the candle.

With a stifled scream, Valerian half raised himself on the pillows. When he spoke, his voice was a croaking, horror-stricken whisper that made Susanna's flesh creep.

"Stanya—for God's sake, tell me—what are you doing here? Go away! Leave me alone. Can I never escape from you?"

With a dry sob, he flung himself back down on the bed and clasped both hands over his eyes as if desperate to shut out the sight of her.

Chapter Eleven

Susanna's heart gave a sudden lurch when Valerian spoke and tallow from the candle she held splashed onto his blankets. How could he know her name? What was he afraid of? A moment later reason informed her that he was hallucinating: he had said "Stanya", not "Zanna." He had mistaken her for someone else—someone he apparently feared.

Slowly and plainly, she said in her soft Lowland voice, "I am not Stanya. My name is Susanna Macdonald and I am a doctor. I found you in the snow. Can you understand what I am saying?"

He was silent so long, eyes closed, that she feared he must be deaf, or else unconscious. Then his eyes opened and she saw with relief that they were rational.

"Yes, I speak . . . a little English. Where am I? How did I get here?"

"You are in my hut, about ten miles from Sinhaio. You were nearly dead when I found you on the railroad, but your dog was keeping you warm. Do you remember who you are?"

He shook his head wearily, and she saw that it was too soon to bother him with questions. "Go to sleep now, Count Radek. In the morning you will feel stronger."

Hesitantly, as though reaching far back into his memory, he said, "My name is Valerian. Valerian Vassilevitch Radek."

"Yes . . . yes. Don't try to think any more. Just drink this medicine and go back to sleep."

He took the cup obediently. "Sleep, yes. I was asleep in the snow. It was warm and peaceful and I wanted to die. Why didn't you let me die?"

"Go to sleep," said Susanna. She watched over him until his

eyes closed, then took the clothes he had been wearing over to her bedroom, divided from the living area by a heavy curtain of dyed leather.

Searching every pocket, systematically, every seam, she tried to find additional clues to his identity. Why had he come so close to the enemy lines? She knew full well the danger and difficulty that harboring a Russian officer in Japanese-held territory would present, but she was determined not to let him go. Lin Tong wouldn't betray the Russian's presence, but other Chinese might unless she took steps to prevent it.

Her questing fingers felt the stiff bundle of official papers which Valerian had been carrying. Without hesitation she broke the ornate seals. Kuropatkin's flowing signature was all she could read with certainty, but she immediately resolved that neither the Reverend Elias nor the Japanese intelligence officers should have the chance to translate the papers fully. Deliberately Susanna dropped them into the stove and watched them burn. She had known as soon as she gazed at the stripped and helpless Russian lying on Martha's kitchen table, his limbs half frozen and his handsome face caked with dried blood, that this was the man she wanted. She felt a deep reluctance to let anybody else care for him. For the moment he was totally hers, and she would do everything in her power to prolong her period of possession.

Valerian slept off and on for three days. The fever that Susanna anticipated soon gripped him and his temperature soared so high that she neglected her other patients to sit with him day and night, bathing his burning body and face, holding his hot, dry hand in her cool one as he tossed and turned on the bed.

"Stanya! Stanya! Don't go away. Help me!" he cried in despair.

Again and again she assured him that all was well, that he was quite safe. "I'm here. I'll take care of you."

To her infatuated eyes, the fever heightened his striking good looks. His over-bright eyes and flushed cheeks gave him a wild, untamed expression, utterly different from the stolid Scots boys and shy medical students she had known at home. He was infinitely exciting, irresistibly attractive—and completely within her power. She smoothed back the silky dark hair that fell across his forehead. For the first time since leaving Scotland, she forgot all about Willie Carmichael and the wrong he had done her.

The fever broke, leaving Valerian exhausted and fretful. It worried him that he couldn't remember anything that had happened before the mines exploded, though he was convinced that he'd been on an important mission.

"What does it matter now?" asked Susanna. "The Japanese are advancing all along the front and any orders you may have had are outdated now. You'll be captured if you set foot outside this compound, for Japanese patrols are everywhere. Don't even think of leaving yet. Wait till they've gone on their way and you're strong again."

"Orders!" exclaimed Valerian, fastening eagerly on the word. A tiny chink of light seemed to open in the darkness of his brain. "I was carrying orders to . . . to Major Grassevitch. Where are they? What's happened to them?"

"We found no orders," lied Susanna brazenly. "You must have lost them when the train crashed."

"No, no . . ." He grew so agitated that she fetched his uniform and overcoat and showed him the pockets were empty. "You have nothing to worry about," she assured him. "All you must do is get well and strong again." She laid her cool hand on his forehead. At her touch the worried lines smoothed from his face and he slowly relaxed again.

"You are so good to me, Zanna." He carried her hand to his lips. She made no effort to pull it away.

Gradually he grew stronger, but his war-weary mind had been unbalanced by the explosion, followed by his long walk through the snow, and it healed more slowly than his body. His dependence on Susanna deepened with every day that passed. For her part, she took care to foster this relationship, inventing Japanese patrols where there were none, and pretending to be more worried about his health than she actually was.

Martha and Elias were busy attending the souls of their parishioners, but Martha observed with disapproval the growing intimacy between Valerian and Susanna. As soon as he was able to leave his bed, she insisted, for propriety's sake, that he move back into the farmhouse.

"It's no' right for a man and woman to share the same room outside of holy matrimony," she declared roundly. "You're a bonnie lass, for all you're a doctor, and that young Russki has a look in his eye that tells me he's well aware of the fact."

"You're imagining it, Martha," laughed Susanna. "It's no more than the gratitude any patient has for his doctor." But she knew that Martha was right, and rejoiced. She sensed the admiration in Valerian's dark eyes as she moved about his bedroom. She noted the way his glance rested on her deep bosom whenever she bent over him, fussing with his blankets, bringing him small, tempting meals from the Armstrongs' kitchen, or dressing the blackened toes that still might be saved from falling off. It was easy to interpret his physical desires, but less simple to guess what was going on in his mind. He had terrifying nightmares that left him limp with exhaustion. Every battlefield horror he had ever seen haunted his dreams. Mutilated comrades with blood-spattered faces fought on and on with slant-eyed orientals in Japanese uniforms. And always, Anastasia was there in the thick of the fighting. Menaced on every side, she kept crying to him for help but he could never reach her.

One night he woke up screaming, his face running with sweat as he wrestled with his horrible visions. Susanna hurried to calm him.

"Wake up, Valerian. It's all right, you're safe in your bed at home, and I'm here with you."

Trustingly, like a child, he took her hand and held it tightly until the terror ebbed away. "Stanya," he murmured.

"Who is this Stanya you're always shouting for in your sleep?" she asked jealously. He was hers; no other woman could have him.

"My young sister," said Valerian, but his eyes would not meet hers.

"Why do you keep dreaming of her?"

"I cannot tell you that."

Though she sensed a mystery, Susanna didn't press. A sister was hardly a rival. She bent to soothe his brow. As if drawn by a magnet, his hand reached up to caress a lock of her loosened hair.

"You are beautiful, Zanna . . . so very beautiful," he said dreamily. "Why are you so cruel to this lovely hair, hiding it in an ugly knot . . ."

She laughed. "A fine sight I'd be if I left it streaming down my back like a schoolgirl! The Chinese are scared of it, you know.

They think only devils have red hair. I have to keep it hidden when I go to their homes."

"But alone with me, you can leave it loose," persisted Valerian.

"Not in the daytime. What would Martha and Elias think?"

"I don't care what peasants think," said Valerian. Susanna had to hide her smile at his unconscious arrogance. Coaxingly, he said, "Don't go away, Zanna. Lie beside me for a moment and chase away my dreams."

Ears alert for the sound of Martha's approach, Susanna allowed him to pull her down beside him. Very gently he drew her closer, his long, sensitive fingers caressing her cheeks, her neck, traveling downward with practiced ease to open the fastening of her warm dressing gown, and fondling her breasts which tingled suddenly with desire. Firmly she pushed him away and sat up again.

"Don't do that!" she exclaimed, trying not to betray by her quickened breathing how his touch had aroused her.

"Why? You enjoy it. I enjoy it..."

Susanna feigned indignation. "In my country such pleasures are reserved for marriage." She observed him closely as she spoke, and saw a wary expression cross his face.

"Who spoke of marriage? Pleasure has nothing to do with marriage, Zanna." With a strength and dexterity surprising in so recent a sufferer, he caught her wrist and pulled her close to him again. "Now I've caught you, little doctor with the golden hair," he said smiling. "I will keep you here until you give me a kiss."

"Why should I kiss you?"

"Because I love you, of course," said Valerian, surprised.

"You *love* me?"

"Certainly. That's why I want to kiss you."

As his lips met hers, Susanna closed her eyes, afraid he would see the triumph in them. She must not appear too eager. She must lure him further on, tease and tantalize him until he did her bidding. She must never give in to him until he met the conditions she demanded.

"Then I shall love you, too, Valerian," she whispered, and drew quickly away from his grasp.

Neither of them knew how widely different were their interpretations of the word "love." For Valerian, love was a delightful, frivolous, spur-of-the-moment affair, here today and gone tomorrow, the highest of all physical pleasures—and the most fleeting. For Susanna, love meant marriage. The bitter lesson she learned from Willie Carmichael was not easily forgotten and she was determined not to repeat her mistake. Before this handsome Russian nobleman possessed her body, she meant to possess his name.

She knew little about the after-effects of concussion and less of battle shock, but it was clear to her that his recent experiences had left him extremely suggestible, with a mind too tired to oppose for long a will as strong as hers. This time, Susanna resolved, the man she loved wouldn't get away.

Her methods were as simple as they were effective, and Valerian was clay in her hands. Shamelessly she invited his kisses, then pretended modesty and puritanical outrage when he tried to take things farther. Valerian, whose good looks and easy charm had always combined with his wealth to insure the eager cooperation of any woman he chose, was alternately puzzled and frustrated. As his physical strength returned, his craving for Susanna's inviting curves, so near yet so far from his grasp, became the purest torment.

At times she was warm and loving. At others she scolded him like a naughty schoolboy if he so much as brushed against her.

"You men are all the same," she snapped at him one day late in spring, when the fresh young shoots of beans and *kaoliung* were beginning to show green against the freshly turned earth. They were standing in the orchard where falling plum blossoms covered the grass like confetti. "You imagine that saying you love a woman entitles you to take any liberty you like. Well, for once you're mistaken. You've picked the wrong girl. I don't believe in that kind of behavior."

Valerian, who had only placed an affectionate arm around her shoulders as they strolled, looked at her in affected surprise.

"How can you say you love me when you won't let me touch you?" he asked.

"There are other kinds of loving, Valerian."

"If that is true, I do not know them," he said simply. "Tell me, what must I do before you allow me to touch you?"

It was a rhetorical question, for he knew the answer only too well. Wherever he looked it stared him in the face. *Marriage.*

If he wanted Susanna—and by now she so dominated his thoughts that he wanted no one else—he would have to marry her. She alone had the power to soothe his fears and lift him from the trough of self-disgust and despondency. She alone was strong enough to chart his way through the demons that beset him when he was alone. His mental breakdown had produced a strange state of apathy. Valerian, who had scarcely known a day's illness in his life, and had never needed the support of any other human to help him reach a decision, now found himself devoid of willpower and so completely dependent on Susanna that the idea of life without her filled him with blind, unreasoning terror.

"Will you marry me, Susanna?" he asked hesitantly. When she nodded in a satisfied way—like a teacher whose pupil has at last, after much prompting, produced the right answer—a great burden seemed to slip from his shoulders, leaving him light and free as a bird.

There, beneath the flowering plum tree, oblivious of the interested stares of the coolies working in the orchard, he took her in his arms and kissed her with passionate gratitude. Susanna drew his head to her breast and stroked his hair as if he were a small boy again.

"Now you can never leave me," she said, so softly that he hardly heard.

Valerian panted hard as he climbed the conical hill behind the missionaries' farmstead. But although sweat poured down his face and his shirt clung clammily to the furrow of his spine, he didn't slacken his pace until he was out of sight of the house. Then, gasping for breath, he sat down on a rock. Heart beating with excitement and exertion, he observed with a kind of guilty triumph the neat patchwork of the cultivated plain below.

It was now six weeks since the Reverend Elias Armstrong, his voice harsh with disapproval, had pronounced Valerian and Susanna man and wife. Today was the very first time the bridegroom had managed to elude his wife's determined supervision and escape up the hill with a gun and a dog, free at last of human company.

He carried Elias' gun for, unexpectedly, the minister had not only aided his escape, he had suggested it. The thrifty, downright Scotsman considered it high time that his young Russian guest contributed more than a hungry mouth to the homestead's frugal larder. Elias had a shrewd idea that Susanna had, for her own purposes, forced the poor lad into marriage before he had fully recovered his wits. Although neither he nor Martha had been able to sway her from her resolution, the minister decided to rouse the bridegroom from his apathy with a little discreet needling of his own.

"You're putting on weight, my boy," he exclaimed after dinner one night, while Martha and Susanna were sewing by the fire.

Valerian shrugged indifferently. "I have no exercise and much food. Zanna doesn't allow me to go beyond the orchard, lest the Japanese soldiers see me."

"She's like a hen with a single chick where you're concerned," snorted Elias, pleased to see by the quick jerk of Valerian's head that he resented this description. "There hasn't been a Japanese patrol around here for a month. But since you mention it, what I'm thinking of is food. You're a soldier: I assume you can use a shotgun?"

Valerian nodded. A tiny flicker of interest replaced the apathy in his eyes.

"Then why don't you take my gun up the hill tomorrow and see what you can find? We need fresh meat. I don't have time to bag a brace of pheasants myself, but there's nothing to stop you from getting them."

"But, Zanna wouldn't like—" began Valerian.

The minister's sharp blue eyes regarded the Russian intently. "Get awa' wi' ye, man. You canna be tied to your wife's apronstrings in the daytime." He laughed. "At night's a different matter. It's no concern of mine who wears the trousers between the sheets, if you take my meaning. But whether Susanna likes it or not, you'll have to earn your keep if you're going to live with us much longer."

Valerian flushed darkly. Until that moment it had never occurred to him that he might be overstaying his welcome. In Russia it was common for unexpected guests to stay whole months and years without a murmur of protest from their hosts, and Susanna had repeatedly assured him that the Armstrongs were as glad to have him there as she was. It was therefore a shock to learn from another man's lips that he was nothing but a parasite in the house he had looked on as a refuge.

"I'll go tomorrow, if you wish, and take Susanna with me," he said stiffly, "I'm sorry to have imposed on your hospitality for so long."

"Ye've learned to speak good English, at least," chuckled Elias. "Wheesht, man! Trust a Russki to catch hold of the wrong end of the stick. I wasna' suggesting you leave us—quite the reverse. All I ask is a mite of assistance in keeping the wolf from the door, and if you're handy with a gun there's any amount of game here for the shooting." He winked. "There's no need to mention your wee foray to Susanna, if you think she'll be against it. What the eye doesna' see, the heart willna' grieve over, as we say."

Valerian thought it a most convenient philosophy. The very next day, when Susanna had departed on her shaggy pony to visit her outlying patients, he took the gun from the rack, whistled to the yellow dog, Lucky, who was dozing in the sun-warmed courtyard, and started uphill at his best pace.

Elias' words had unsettled him. He felt restless, and unsure of anything. The warm cocoon of Susanna's love and solicitude seemed suddenly smothering—a prison instead of a refuge. He's right, she treats me like a child, he thought, and instead of feeling grateful a tiny spark of resentment flared up within him.

Full spring had come at last to Manchuria. Above the neatly ridged and furrowed plain, the pointed hills were carpeted with daisies, dandelions and buttercups against a background of emerald velvet. The woods were bright with wild flowers in dramatic masses amid clumps of dark firs and oaks with the palest golden foliage. Mellow-voiced orioles sang in the sunny glades, and the blue flash of a kingfisher caught the edge of his vision as he approached a swift-flowing stream, sparkling over pebbles gilded by sunlight. He looked with curiosity at the village as he passed it by.

Lucky's silky yellow tail was wagging as she nosed the alluring scents on either side of the winding path. Martha had adopted her, giving her the same warm-hearted welcome she extended to all strays, human or animal, who crossed her path. When fully grown she would be a formidable watchdog. Already the good food and shelter of the Armstrongs' roof had changed her from a gangling puppy into a handsome, streamlined hunter. She flushed a few small birds from the undergrowth, but of pheasants there was no sign.

Getting his second wind, Valerian scrambled down the first hill and began to trudge up the second. He was aware that with every step he was getting farther away from home and increasing the risk that Susanna would return to discover his absence, but he felt strangely unmoved by the knowledge. It was as if the strong bond of dependency which she had fostered was being subtly loosened by distance. Away from her he became a man again, capable of planning his life without her approval, and capable of knowing, too, when to go home.

Odd that he should think of it as home, he reflected. A hut in another man's compound was hardly the sort of home that the Valerian Radek of a year ago would have envisioned. It was only because the hut was home to Susanna that he had adopted it too. Now, for the first time since his illness, he began to think of his real home, remembering the splendor of the Radek palace on the Morskaia, and the crenelated facade of his great country house surrounded by woods and lakes, mountains and rivers, that had sheltered his forebears for so many years. With a shock, he realized that Susanna would never fit in there. He should have married a girl of his own people, not a Scottish missionary doctor who had never learned how to direct a great household, with its armies of servants and its rigid protocol. Of course, he should never have married Susanna. Now, that was only too apparent. But how could I help it?, he thought. She stole my mind and I had to do what she wanted.

His head seemed to be clearing today of the cottonwool that had fogged it for so long. Here in the clear air he felt free to question his own docile acceptance of Susanna's judgment. Was he actually in such danger? Was it really necessary to hide in the house all day in fear of Japanese patrols? Was it right that she—and she alone—should dictate the pattern of their lovemaking? Did he, in fact, love her?

So much unaccustomed thinking made his head spin. Nonetheless, he had a feeling that the solitary walk had restored his good sense. He had eaten the lotus for long enough. Now it was time to go back out into the hard, cruel world and make what he could of it.

The decision both frightened and exhilarated him. He tried to gauge in advance Susanna's reaction to the news that he wanted to leave this Manchurian refuge. Would she agree to go with him, or would she exert that formidable, almost hypnotic willpower of hers and sap his strength of mind until he did as she wanted again?

Valerian shivered. It would undoubtedly be much easier to go away without telling her, just as he had today. But that was hardly an honorable course. After all, he owed her a great deal. Without her help, he and Lucky would have slowly thawed out only to provide an unexpected hors d'oeuvre for hungry wolves. He sighed. Why was a man so surrounded with conventions that compelled him always to take the hard road instead of the easy one?

When the sun was slanting low, he reluctantly called the dog and turned back toward the farmstead. He had shot nothing. Elias would be disappointed, but Valerian had come to terms with himself and that was far more important.

Valerian was stumbling with fatigue when he reached the village. He saw that a crowd had gathered in the village square. He knew it was safer to make a detour along the edge of the field and avoid being seen, but a sudden longing for fresh company, any company, made him ignore the warning in his mind and continue toward the village. After propping the gun against a building, he told Lucky to guard it and walked toward the square. Chattering coolies, their pigtails toward him, blocked his way. Valerian stood on tiptoes to see what was going on.

In the center of the square was a stout Chinese farmer, dressed in the ubiquitous blue cotton—a man of substance judging by his girth and air of consequence. He was carefully appraising half a dozen husky young mules, who twitched their ears and swished their tails as he poked and prodded them, feeling their legs and examining their mouths.

At last he made his choice and waved away all but two of the animals. The mules made a magnificent pair, one brown and the other nearly black, with mealy muzzles and bellies. Their white-rimmed eyes rolled nervously as they awaited the farmer's next move.

He gave an order. Soon each mule was attached to a stout plowline with a wooden handle tied to their ends. The farmer turned to the onlooking crowd and spoke a few short words, whereupon an excited cheer went up. Somewhat puzzled, Valerian decided that he was asking for volunteers. The coolies were shoving and nudging one another, as excited as schoolboys. They were all far too interested to notice Valerian, who gradually moved forward, curious to understand exactly what was going on.

When each mule was separately harnessed, the prospective purchaser pointed to two of the sturdiest coolies, who were shoved forward by their companions. The two coolies rolled up their sleeves to display brawny forearms and tucked up their tunics to free their bulging thighs. Then they walked to the center of the square, where each man grasped a wooden handle.

The mules were faced in different directions. At a given signal, they were ordered to start, as each coolie, hanging on to his handle for dear life, tried with all his might to prevent his mule from moving.

The result of this contest was not long in doubt. After a brief struggle, the mules triumphed and both coolies were dragged after them across the square.

The farmer nodded and frowned. He tossed a few coins contemptuously at the defeated coolies but he still couldn't decide which of the two mules was the stronger. After running an eye over the front ranks of the crowd, he suddenly caught sight of Valerian, whose head rose above the others.

Come, he gestured, hollering. You look like a strong man. Let's see if you can hold one of these mules.

It was easy enough to understand what the man wanted, and Valerian was tempted to accept the challenge. His neighbors were already pushing him forward, with much laughter and advice, when, to his horror, he saw a Japanese cavalry patrol, mounted on tough little ponies, ride into the square from the opposite direction.

Seeing the crowd, they halted, smiling and pointing, eager to watch the unexpected sideshow.

Valerian stood stock-still, his heart racing. He cursed himself for walking into a trap he could so easily have avoided. Three courses seemed open to him, but all had drawbacks. If he ran away he would certainly draw even more attention to himself, and he couldn't outrun the Japanese ponies. If he refused to take part in the absurd pantomine of testing the strength of the mules, he would alert the entire gathering to the fact that he was a Russian. To go through with the test seemed the height of folly, but it was the best choice he had.

Already the fat farmer, who had chosen another husky coolie to match Valerian, was waiting for him to take his place behind the mule. There was no help for it. Valerian hunched his shoulders both to make himself smaller and to hide the fact that no pigtail protruded from beneath his peasant's conical hat. He grabbed the wooden handle, which was smooth and warm with use, and stepped back to take up the slack in the plowline.

Once more the mules were faced in opposite directions. Once more the farmer's whip cracked and the hopeful owners urged their animals forward. The mules strained into their collars. Valerian braced himself against the pull and found to his surprise that he could withstand it easily. Either the animal was tired from its first effort, he thought, or else it had better things to do than drag a man across the village square.

His co-driver, however, was not faring so well. Valerian glanced over his shoulder to see the luckless coolie digging his bare heels into the dust in a futile effort to stop his mule. His body was bent like a half-open penknife as he was dragged inexorably forward, inch by inch. Suddenly he capitulated, running forward without resistance, and the mule broke into a canter. It charged head down at the crowd, knocking some of them over as their companions roared with jovial laughter.

"Banzai!" shouted the Japanese soldiers approvingly. They concentrated their attention on Valerian as he continued to hold the second mule. Valerian could see them watching, and wondered fleetingly if it would be diplomatic to give up the struggle, but an odd, irrational pride forbade him to do so.

The farmer shook his head decisively. He tossed the rejected animal's lead-rope back to its owner who led the mule away, giving Valerian an unfriendly look as he did so.

Only then did it occur to Valerian that perhaps the first two coolies had been shamming, bribed by the mules' owners to behave as if the animals were stronger than they actually were. The same thought had apparently entered the farmer's mind, for his next move was to place Valerian at the handle attached to the plowline of the final, remaining mule.

Let's see what you can do with this one, he appeared to be saying.

Valerian nodded. From the corner of his eye, he saw that the Japanese troopers were growing impatient; they were glancing at their watches, preparing to ride on. He blessed the military discipline that made them conduct their patrol to a rigid timetable. Our men would have stayed here all day, he thought, never mind reporting late to their commanding officer. That was a close shave, all right. I must not let it happen again.

He braced his muscles for the final test of strength. His narrow escape had sent the adrenalin flowing through his veins.

Suddenly he felt that he could outpull half a dozen mules, and was pleased to discover that his long convalescence hadn't left him as out of condition as he'd feared.

He signaled that he was ready, but a shout and the yelping of a dog distracted his attention.

Riding out of the square, the Japanese corporal had spotted Elias' shotgun propped against the building, the dog lying patiently beside it, her yellow coat shining like a beacon in the late afternoon light. Dismounting, the corporal tried to pick up the weapon. Lucky, outraged by this cavalier attempt to make off with what she was guarding, bit him sharply in the calf. The corporal yelled and struck out at Lucky with the butt of the shotgun, whereupon Lucky circled behind him to nip again before the other Japanese soldier could drive her away. Yelping, running on three legs, she threaded her way between the legs of the watching coolies, dodging the hands stretched out to catch her, and arrived at Valerian's side just as the farmer's cracking whip set the mule plunging forward into its collar.

Lucky's sudden appearance startled the mule, which laid back its long ears and bolted, catching Valerian off balance. He fell to his knees and lost his grip on the wooden handle. Off went the mule like a runaway express, while Valerian struggled in the dust, trying to recover his hat and fend off the importunate Lucky, who was barking in his ear and licking his face as Chinese coolies and Japanese soldiers stared at them both in astonishment.

The soldiers were the first to recover their wits. Before Valerian could jump to his feet and run, he was surrounded. His hands were lashed together behind his back. Cursing himself and the dog, he was dragged away, as Lucky whined and yelped at his heels.

Zanna!, he thought in desperation, help me! He was suddenly filled with terror. "Go home!" he shouted in English to the dog, kicking at it as best he could while jogging to keep up with the ponies' pace. "Go home to Zanna!"

Lucky knew the word "home" all too well. Elias often used it when she followed him to the hamlet. Her tail dropped between her legs and she stood stock-still, puzzled and dejected, watching the little procession as it trotted out of sight.

* * *

"Where can he be?" cried Susanna. Darkness had long since fallen and Valerian had still not returned.

"Dinna fash, lassie. He'll be back directly," Elias assured her comfortably. "He'll have gone a wee step up the hill, I'm thinking."

She turned blazing eyes on him. "So it was your doing! You sent him out by himself without a word to me. Tell me where he's gone this minute or I'll never speak to you again."

"Such a fuss," grumbled Elias. "Canna the poor lad be more than an hour or two out of your sight without working you into a fit? He's a grown man, you know."

"Where is he? What's happened to him? I know something terrible has happened. He'd never stay out this late without telling me. What time did he leave the farm?"

Neither Elias nor Martha had seen him go, but Lin Tong, when consulted, volunteered the information that the sun had still been high when the Russian officer had climbed the hill, the yellow dog at his heels.

"He taking Reverend's gun," Lin Tong added.

"Then he's been gone six hours or more! He must have had an accident." Susanna's voice was tight with fear.

"Hush, child, calm yourself," said Martha from her chair beside the lamp. She, too, was worried. "I'm sure he'll be back soon. For one thing, the dog won't forget her dinner, even if he does." She looked toward the plate of scraps which would be Lucky's evening meal. There was nothing they could do but wait.

Another hour passed before they heard a soft whine outside, followed by scratching at the door. Susanna opened it. A bedraggled yellow dog limped in and flopped down by the stove, too tired to lick herself dry. They waited, straining their ears, but there was no sound of footsteps outside.

"Valerian!" called Susanna, pushing the door even wider. Mockingly, the courtyard walls echoed ". . . erian . . .!"

"He's gone! I knew it—he's been caught. The Japanese have captured him!" she whispered. Ashen-faced, she sank into a chair, clasping her arms across her stomach and moaning like an animal in pain.

"What—what ails you, lass?" cried Martha in alarm, hurrying to her side.

"He said he'd never leave me, but now he's gone," whispered

Susanna. "He's left me, just as Willie left me. And I—I'm going to have his baby."

She bowed her head. Martha and Elias stared at each other in dismay. This was terrible news!

A moment later Susanna spoke again—in a flat, hard voice they'd never heard her use before. "But he won't escape me. I am his wife. One day I'll find him again—though it takes me the rest of my life..."

Part Two

Chapter Twelve

EGYPT 1913

"Who is that appalling creature with the henna'd hair dancing with Papa?"

Anthony Mills had no need to glance over his shoulder at Count Kharkov's flamboyant companion. Only one person present could possibly fit that description. "Do you want her to hear you, Anastasia?" he said. "I'd advise you to lower your voice, or you'll make a bad enemy. Fatima is quite a power in society—at a certain level."

"A very low level. That's probably why I don't know her," said Anastasia scathingly, not bothering in the least to lower her voice. She frowned, leaning over the flower-decked balustrade of the ballroom in the Gezira Sporting Club, watching the dancers below. The Italian consul had been recalled and his farewell ball was a lavish affair. With distaste—and something more, a kind of fear—Anastasia observed the redhead's voluptuous body tightly molded against her father's, as his hand pressed the curve of her bosom in its indecently low-cut dress. In a tight, disapproving voice, she said "She seems very friendly with Papa. Really, he shouldn't hold her so tight. It isn't at all *comme il faut*."

Anthony sighed. Was Anastasia really so blind? Didn't she know by this time what her father was like? Everyone else did, including Olga, whose long sallow face was turned away from the dancers as she discussed archeology with gray-bearded Professor Hartmann.

"Perhaps she's holding *him*, and the poor man can't get away," he suggested. "Perhaps he's toiling selflessly for the good of his Tsar and country, allowing his partner's face powder to ruin his coat simply in order to hear the State secrets she's whispering in his ear."

"Oh—*you*! Why must you joke about everything? It's nothing to joke about."

"I prefer to joke rather than make a drama out of everything. It's much less wearing, you'll find, in the long run. *'Aequam mementum, rebus in arduis servare mentem,'* to quote Horace's useful piece of advice."

"I don't know what you're talking about."

"I'm simply saying that there's no point in worrying about what you can't change."

"You mean I can't change my father's nature?" she said in a small voice.

"That's what I mean. Madame Tabbouleh's relationship with your father is his own affair. It has nothing to do with you. Why not just accept it?"

"Even when his disgraceful behavior wounds Mama?" she exclaimed.

Anthony sighed. "Countess Kharkova is a woman of the world. She's no fool. She knows when to accept the inevitable."

"Are you saying that I am a fool?"

"Only that you are foolish to let it worry you. Come on, Anastasia, cheer up. None of us are perfect, after all. Let's dance again if you've finished your drink, or had you rather walk in the garden?" He observed the elegant figure of Captain Mohammed Aly of the Royal Bodyguard advancing closer with the obvious intention of claiming Anastasia.

"No, I've promised Aly this dance. Perhaps later," she answered abstractedly, still watching her father. Anthony surrendered her to the smiling Egyptian and went to the bar in search of gossip and companionship.

Cairo had always seethed with intrigue and rumor, and these days there were more serious matters to discuss than the latest diplomatic scandal or Count Kharkov's affairs of the heart. Anthony wondered why the sight of her father in the arms of a paramour still aroused such indignation in his daughter.

Superficially, Anastasia had changed a lot from the headstrong, impulsive girl he'd met in the temple valley. She had lost all of her puppy-fat. Her taste in clothes was faultless, and at twenty-two years old she was a lovely, apparently assured and sophisticated woman. Below the smooth surface of cosmopolitan polish, however, Anthony sensed a deep insecurity, which showed itself in unexpected ways—such as this ridiculous outrage at her father's attachment to Madame Tabbouleh, and her own reluctance to form anything but the most superficial relationships with the handsome young men who clamored for her favors. Anthony wondered why she distrusted men so much. No doubt that wretched Valerian was at the root of the trouble. She carried his photograph everywhere. She used Valerian as a kind of shield to prevent other men from getting near her, yet she hadn't seen him for years.

The bar was crowded and for an hour or so Anthony talked and gossiped with his colleagues, swapping information.

"The Germans are certainly feeling their oats tonight," said George Chetwode, assistant to the police commandant.

"They're always feeling their oats," said Anthony. "Why tonight?"

"We've rounded up a dozen of them fighting drunk outside the Parisiana, upsetting the natives' stalls and proclaiming that they'll be the masters here soon. They're becoming a damn nuisance, and complaining to the German consul is like bashing your head against a brick wall. I gather there are lots of them in Constantinople these days, too." He cocked an inquiring eyebrow at Anthony.

"Yes," said Anthony. "Enver Pasha's given them far too free a hand to run his show for him in Turkey. One day he's going to wake up and realize he can't get rid of them, however much he wants to."

Chetwode nodded, his round, freckled face unusually solemn. "Where's it all leading, that's what I'd like to know? Germans everywhere in the Near East, bragging and swaggering, behaving as if they ruled the roost. Wherever they go it means trouble. Where's it going to end?"

"There's only one way it *can* end. You know that as well as I do."

"War. Yes . . . I suppose we all know it, deep down. But when? That's the question."

"Your guess is as good as mine," said Anthony, but Chetwode shook his head.

"It isn't, you know. I often wonder just how many dark secrets you've got hidden away behind that innocent smile of yours."

"Dark secrets? My dear chap, you coppers live in a fantasy world! If you could only see the humdrum routine in the Diplomatic Corps! I wouldn't know a dark secret if it came up and shook my hand. We do the *Times* crossword puzzle. We check to see if the Comte de Chatellerault takes precedence over the Comte de Chateaubriand, or vice versa. We try to find a fresh gardenia for the chef de protocol's buttonhole... That's what keeps us busy from dawn to dusk. How we envy you your exciting life!"

Chetwode gave him a very straight look. "All the same, you won't deny that you have your exciting moments, will you? I've been meaning to ask you for days exactly what happened to the mummy and other things from that tomb that Auguste Soulier and the fat Dutchman Van der Plug were excavating near Luxor. You wouldn't know anything about that, I suppose? Come on, I promise you it's off the record. There's not a scrap of evidence to connect you with their disappearance, but I know you, and I'm perfectly certain you spirited them all away while poor old Soulier was asleep."

"And people say that policemen have no imaginations!" said Anthony, in deeply admiring tones. "George, you amaze me. Still, since it's off the record, I'll tell you this much: Soulier's a rogue and Van der Plug's a fool. They make a bad combination. Don't worry, they'll get it all back in time, as soon as proper records have been made of everything they've found. As you know, it's always a pleasure to pay off an old score and put the record straight at the same time."

"An old score with Soulier, I suppose. He was the one who brought the Department of Antiquities thundering down on us like a ton of bricks," said Chetwode. "They seemed to think our native policemen have nothing better to do than guard their wretched digs while the diggers are celebrating in Alexandria. So it was your doing, then? You're a clever devil, Anthony, but let me give you a friendly word of warning: one day your playing at Robin Hood will get you into trouble, and I doubt if I'll be able to help you then. So just watch your step."

"I'll watch it," promised Anthony.

"Good," said Chetwode. He added casually, "Anyway, you won't bother us much longer—if what I hear is true."

Anthony groaned. "Oh, no! What do you hear?"

"That you're leaving us. Joining the embassy in Constantinople, isn't that right? Getting a step up on the way?"

"I knew they shouldn't have sent that dispatch in English," said Anthony, shrugging, and Chetwode burst out laughing.

"You knew nothing of the kind. You asked them to send it in English so you wouldn't have the bother of telling everyone yourself!"

"Just because your own methods are as devious and convoluted as a whore's lower . . ." began Anthony. But the sight of Anastasia leaving the dance floor on the arm of a portly bemedaled admiral reminded him suddenly that she, as yet, knew nothing of his new appointment. It would be best to tell her himself before some garbled backstairs version reached her ears.

"There's one other little matter I've been longing to discuss with you," Chetwode was saying to empty air, as Anthony slid off his stool and melted into the crowd. He reached Anastasia's side just as another Egyptian officer was about to claim her, and she turned toward him with relief. The admiral's notions of dancing had been firmly based on the hornpipe, and her feet had suffered as a consequence.

"How about that stroll in the garden?" said Anthony. "I'm told the roses are fine just now." Gratefully she tucked her hand in his arm and they went out into the warm, sweet-scented night. Other couples were strolling arm in arm around the smooth lawns, or stretched out in deck chairs to gaze up at the star-bright heavens. For a while they walked in silence, enjoying the peace after the ballroom's clamor. "When will you be going down to work at the temple again, Anthony?" asked Anastasia at last.

"Not for a while, I'm afraid . . . Something's just come up. I wanted to tell you about it myself . . ."

"Something nice?" The pale blur of her face swung quickly toward him, but it was too dark to read her expression.

"Yes and no. You see, I've been transferred to the embassy in Constantinople. We had the confirmation of my posting this morning. I'll be leaving here early next month, and there won't be time to go down to the temple before then."

He hadn't expected her to greet this news with much enthusiasm, but all the same he was unprepared for her reaction. The slender fingers resting on his arm seemed suddenly tranformed into hooks, digging into his skin, and there was a note of suppressed hysteria in her voice as she exclaimed: "No—oh no! You can't, you mustn't go away. I can't bear it if you leave me . . . leave the temple unfinished. You must tell your Foreign Office that you refuse to go."

"Be your age, Anastasia," he said brusquely. "Do you think I want to lose my job?"

"Who cares about your silly job?" she said scornfully. "What does that matter? You're always telling me you're paid for doing nothing, and that the only thing you've learned to do here is waste time. Why must you go to Constantinople and waste time there?"

"Perhaps there'll be more to do in Constantinople."

"Of course there won't. Embassies and consulates are the same all over the world. I know because my father told me."

"And he's an expert, of course."

"I forbid you to mock my father," she cried angrily.

"Then stop talking about matters of which you're entirely ignorant," he said so sharply that she gasped, as if he'd slapped her in the face. Not for years had Anthony used that tone to her, and the layers of sophistication seemed to peel away, leaving her naked and vulnerable.

She cried, "I don't want you to go!"

Anthony gripped her by the shoulders and looked into her face. "What you want has nothing to do with it, Anastasia. Stop behaving like a child and listen to me. If I've misled you a little in the past about the nature of my work, it was for your own protection."

"My protection?"

"Certainly. I had no wish to see my colleagues in the pay of less than friendly powers trying to extract information from you which they couldn't obtain from me, simply because of our special relationship."

Anastasia stared at him, her heart beating with hammer-like strokes as she grasped his meaning. "*Misled* . . . ? You mean you lied to me? Ah, I understand now. You're a British intelligence agent and you didn't tell me. You let me think that all you did was answer invitations and translate documents for Lord Cromer."

"I did that, too," he murmured.

"You tricked me because you didn't trust me!"

"Don't talk so loud, Anastasia. Do you want the whole wide

world to hear you? I'm obliged to trust no one. Believe me, I trust you more than most."

"If you think that will make me happy again," she said, "you're wrong—Mr. Lying Cheating Intelligence Agent! I see now what a blind fool I've been. I'll never believe anything you say again. Oh, yes, you were always very interested in what I had to tell you about what was going on in the Russian consulate. I must have been very useful to you. That's what you mean by our *special relationship*! Not... not all the work we've done together in the desert, and the picnics and parties..." She choked on a sob. "But now that's all over. I'm no more use to you so you throw me away like a... a worn-out glove. Now you can make other 'special relationships' with more interesting ladies in Constantinople. You're nothing but a..." she searched her vocabulary for the most humiliating word she knew—"an opportunist. I hate you."

Anthony was shaking with suppressed laughter. "Anastasia, you're the prettiest worn-out glove I've ever seen. Don't try to hit me. Now you've got all that off your chest, pull yourself together and listen to me."

Her eyes widened as she recognized the sudden note of authority in Anthony's voice—the note that meant she had gone too far—and she tried to back away. She wouldn't listen to him. She would refuse to let him talk his way out of this situation and persuade her she had not been wronged. But his hands still gripped her shoulders firmly, holding her prisoner, and try as she might she couldn't break away. As he towered over her in the moonlight, she was very conscious of both his physical strength and something more—an electric current of excitement which seemed to stream from his body into hers. In the space of a second he had changed from the easygoing friend and companion she'd known for years into someone more formidable and mysterious—a hunter who could enjoy tracking his prey through all the hidden alleys of international intrigue—a dangerous animal who reveled in danger.

"Let me—let me go!" she whispered.

"When I'm ready to. Come over here where it's quieter, and I'll explain just why I have to go to work in Constantinople."

He drew her into a little arbor lit dimly by Chinese lanterns and heavy with the scent of jasmine. They were about to seat themselves at the rustic table near the entrance when a movement at the back of the arbor caught Anthony's eye. With a muffled exclamation he moved to block Anastasia's view, but he was too late.

"What's wrong?" she said. "Oh . . . !" She recoiled with a cry of dismay.

Lying on a pile of cushions at the back of the arbor was an all too familiar figure in a low-cut green dress. On top of her, in a state of considerable dishevelment, lay the unmistakable form of the Russian consul.

It was the last straw for Anastasia. She burst into noisy tears, picked up her trailing skirt and ran blindly away toward the lights of the ballroom. Cursing, Anthony followed. He caught her before she'd gone twenty yards and drew her close to him, putting his arms tightly around her. "Don't cry . . . Don't worry . . . What does it matter? Come on, that's better . . ." He could feel her whole body shaking as she cried out her grief upon his shoulder. When her sobs seemed to be subsiding he offered her a handkerchief and led her to another table at the edge of an ornamental pond.

"Why?" he asked at last.

"Why what?" Anastasia sniffed. "I'm sorry. I've ruined your nice handkerchief."

"I want you to tell me why you mind so much."

"He was *kissing* her!" Her voice rose. "Kissing that vulgar, horrible creature . . ."

"I know," said Anthony with a touch of impatience. "But that doesn't answer my question. Why does it matter so much to you?"

She was silent for so long he thought she wasn't going to answer. But at last she said, "Because he did the same . . . he must have done the same . . . thing to my mother."

"But I thought you agreed with me that Countess Kharkova is a woman of the world . . ." he began, but she cut him short with a hiss like that of an angry cat.

"Fool! Not the Countess—my real mother."

"Your *real* mother!" Anthony was deeply interested. She'd never mentioned her mother to him before and he'd assumed she'd never known her. This, he sensed, might be the key to much of Anastasia's behavior. "You can remember your real mother, then?" he asked cautiously.

"Of course I remember her. Sometimes I remember her too

much..." She shivered. Faintly, she could still hear Tamara's cold, embittered voice: "You are the last of the Galzinskis. You must avenge me." She had tried to bury the memory, but the sight of that woman locked in her father's arms had revived her old doubts. Which of them had told her the truth: her father, or her dying mother? Was the taint of insanity in her blood, as her father had implied. Or was her mother right and Kadya Kharkov the monster who had ruined the Galzinskis?

"Why too much? Who was your mother?" Anthony's voice was insistent.

Reluctantly Anastasia said, "She was Polish. A Polish Princess whom my father seduced when he was in the garrison at Casimirvek. Her family name was Galzinski. That's all I know for sure. But when she was dying she told me that my father, Count Kharkov, had brought ruin and destruction to the house of Galzinski, and that I was the only one left to avenge them. She sent me to Russia so my father would know how he wronged her."

Anthony hid his surprise. "And Countess Kharkova took you in. Does she know of your origins?"

Wearily, Anastasia shook her head, but he heard a slight lift in her voice as she replied: "She took me in because Valerian begged her to. Valerian can always get people to do what he wants."

And that's where Valerian acquired his hold over you, thought Anthony. Feeling his way, he said, "You must have hated your father at first."

"No, I didn't hate him. I was scared of him. My mother told me he had killed my grandfather and my uncle Stepan, and burned their palace to the ground. After that, my grandmother was so sad she killed herself."

"It's a...strange story," he said slowly. "Have you never asked your father if what your mother said is true? Galzinski... if you've got that name right there should be some way of finding out what happened to them."

Anastasia looked up in sudden hope. "Do you think so? Do you think you could find something out? My father won't talk about it. He says my mother was mad, and that the ruin of the Galzinski family was all their own fault. I don't know what to believe. Was my mother... mad?" Her voice shook a little as she forced out into the open the fear that had haunted her for years.

Behind the words Anthony caught a sudden glimpse of the long loneliness of her childhood.

"The best way to find out," he said firmly, "is to demand the full story from your father. He won't like telling you—I can see that—but you must tell him it's your right to know."

"My *right*," echoed Anastasia, heartened by this brisk, confident approach to the mystery which had lurked like a fearsome monster in her subconscious, setting her apart, branding her from birth with the double stain of illegitimacy and insanity.

"That's it. Make him tell you everything. It's the only way to put your mind at rest. You might even try blackmail if he seems reluctant to . . . to spill the beans. Threaten to tell the Countess about his scandalous behavior. If that doesn't work, I'll dig around and see what I can learn about the Galzinski family myself. It shouldn't be too difficult. Perhaps both versions of the story are true—seen through different eyes."

"That would mean that my mother *was* mad and that I am a—"

"Don't cross your bridges till you come to them. Comfort yourself with the thought that genius and insanity are only a hairbreadth apart. And remember: throughout history all the best people have been illegitimate."

In the dim light, he thought he saw the beginnings of a smile. "Oh, Anthony, how can you say that?"

"It's perfectly true. Common knowledge. All the best people—from William the Conqueror onwards."

Her smile widened. That's done the trick, he thought thankfully. That's stopped her worrying—for the moment, at least. He put his hand beneath her chin and tilted her face to the light. The green eyes met his steadily, trustingly. Moved by a sudden uncontrollable impulse he bent and kissed her. As their lips met she sighed deeply, surrendering herself with an instinctive hunger that set his pulses racing. Her lips parted beneath his. Deaf to the far-off music of the orchestra, oblivious of their surroundings, their bodies clung together. Time seemed to hang suspended and the rest of the world was forgotten.

Finally, Anthony drew back, gazing in wonder at the beautiful, passionate face so close to his. Her long lashes made shadowed half-moons on her cheeks, veiling the green brilliance of her eyes.

"You're so . . . beautiful," he murmured.

As he spoke, her eyes flashed open and something sparkled in their depths, as if she was listening to the same words in another voice, another language. *"I tell them all they're beautiful."*

With the speed of a striking snake, Anastasia's hand flashed up and slapped Anthony hard across the face with a force that snapped his head back. Then she jerked herself from his embrace.

"Damn you—is that all you can say?" she hissed. Pulling up her long skirt she fled across the lawn.

Anthony made no move to follow. He watched the pale blur of her dress in the starlight until it vanished among the rose bushes, thoughtfully rubbing his cheek. Anastasia, he said to himself, you never cease to amaze me! What in the devil provoked that? Slowly he made his way back to the ballroom.

Valerian had returned to Russia after his brief captivity in Japanese hands with a profound distaste for rice and an equally deep admiration for the well-organized Japanese army. His experiences in Manchuria had changed him in many ways. He no longer regarded his late adversaries as yellow devils: General Kuroki's men had treated him well, and Japanese Army doctors had done their best to treat the severe headaches he still suffered as a result of the railway explosion. But they could no nothing to alleviate his strange feeling of rootlessness, of apartness, which almost corresponded to a loss of identity. Sometimes when in this state, he was plunged into a pit of black depression. He felt as if he had made a violent effort to wrench himself free of a guiding hand which had become oppressive, but escape had left him drifting as aimlessly as a straw in the wind. Susanna's experiments in hypnosis—her attempts to gain a hold over his mind while he was too weak to resist her—had not been entirely successful, but they had the effect of reducing his power of decision. Now he groped helplessly for a new sense of purpose, a mission that would give some point to his life again. A vestige of Susanna's power remained with him, but with each day the memory of his life with her had faded until it seemed no more than an errant dream.

Barely four months after his capture, the Peace Conference in New Hampshire had ended in complete agreement between Russia and Japan, and the victorious Japanese politely waived all claim to war indemnity from their late enemies. The repatriation of prisoners had begun at once, and before the year was out Valerian Radek, thinner, paler, and more serious than before, was home once more in St. Petersburg, watching snow fall on the broad streets, and it was while he brooded on the humiliation of Russia's defeat at Japanese hands that the first tiny spark of a new ambition began to burn in his heart.

Never again, he vowed, should a Russian Army be so shamed. The key to military success lay in transforming the huge, unwieldly war machine into a streamlined, efficient and modern army on the Japanese model. The topheavy hierarchy of senile senior officers must be swept away and the whole Russian Army reorganized from top to bottom.

Once lit, the spark blazed like dry tinder, and Valerian, fired with new enthusiasm, began to study military historians and strategists and draw up proposals for sweeping reforms. Soon he became totally absorbed in his work, and the idea of military reform dominated his waking thoughts.

With mingled amusement and surprise his friends watched Valerian, who had never taken anything seriously except women and horses, immerse himself in his self-appointed task. They invited him to parties, they challenged him to races: he refused them all. Neither the laughter of his friends nor the furious opposition of 'Old Guard' officers, who saw their comfortable careers threatened by this fanatical young captain, could deflect him from his purpose.

But when, after years of work, he tried to get support for his reforms among senior officers, he met a total lack of interest. No one, from the Grand Duke Nicholas to the Minister for War, from the Tsar to the Colonel of his own regiment, would take him seriously.

"Linevitch practically patted me on the head and told me to run away and play," he raged to his crippled half-brother, Andrei, who shared Valerian's town-house on the Sadrowskaya. "He wouldn't even read the memorandum I'd written—let alone my treatise. He thanked me for bringing the matter to his attention and said he'd get a clerk in the Ministry to make a note of the salient points. A note! After all my years of work!"

From his wheelchair, Andrei observed his dark, handsome half-brother with cynical amusement. The accident that had twisted his body had deeply embittered his soul, and it gave him much secret pleasure to see Valerian disenchanted and at odds with his superiors. Such a situation, Andrei reflected, might even prove valuable.

"I hear you've been making yourself unpopular in certain circles, my dear Valya," he said softly. "If you're determined to stir up a hornet's nest, you ought to wear protective clothing—or at least be prepared to run."

"By 'certain circles' I suppose you mean at Court," said Valerian in disgust. "Well, I simply don't care. I'm through with trying to persuade a lot of mummified stuffed shirts to look at the dangers they're staring in the face. Nobody listens to me. They'll talk about worker unrest and strikes crippling the economy, but they won't recognize that reforming the army is far more urgent than any constitutional changes."

"At least we've got an elected Duma at last. His Imperial Majesty had to give in on that. Perhaps he'll come round to your army reforms later on."

Valerian snorted. "Electing a Duma was like squeezing blood from a turnip. Nowadays the only adviser the Tsar listens to is that filthy Siberian *starets*, Rasputin. If I only had one-tenth of the pull that rascal has with the Imperial Family, my reforms would be effected tomorrow, whatever stupid old buffers like Linevitch said."

"'That filthy Siberian *starets*! You *are* laying your head on the block," mocked Andrei, shaking his head. His pale blue eyes sparkled with malice. "You could end up in the salt mines for saying that about the Empress' pet? She won't hear a word against him. She simply adores her *dear* Father Grigori, and it isn't merely spiritual adoration either. I'm told he sleeps with her—and the Grand Duchesses as well—and the Tsar does nothing to stop him. It's a scandal."

"You and your scandals," grunted Valerian. He flung himself down on a brocade sofa, his long, booted legs stretched out on the parquet floor, and gazed moodily at the magnificent ceiling of Italian plasterwork installed by his great-grandfather. "I once had the chance to break Rasputin's neck," he said reflectively. "The world would have been a better place if I'd done it. It makes me sick, the way they all bow and scrape to that foul-mouthed peasant. He has only to snap his fingers to get what he wants, but no one else can persuade the Tsar to change anything from the way it was in his grandfather's time. My God, Andrei, this is the twentieth century! Every other country in the world is changing fast, but not Russia. Oh no. Sometimes I think I'd be happier if I resigned my commission and went to live at Ostrovskoye. At least the Crimean climate's bearable, unlike this pest-ridden swamp."

"Before you depart," said Andrei, watching him through narrowed eyes, "you really ought to meet some friends of mine."

Valerian stretched indolently. "Why?" he inquired without much interest. He'd often thought it might be pleasant to retire to the Crimea and watch his vines grow, to idle away the sunny days with some pretty girl... someone like little Anastasia... He tried to push the thought of her away, but she wouldn't be pushed. She smiled at him with that teasing, provocative smile, her long green eyes tilting up at the corners. Strange how well he remembered her smile, after all these years...

Andrei was saying, "These friends of mine think it's time for a change. Not just the army but other things as well. I think you might have a lot in common."

"Oh, I know your friends," said Valerian, hardly troubling to hide his contempt. "Anarchists, Nihilists, Social Democrats, Social Revolutionaries... No, thanks! I doubt that I'd find their conversation enlightening."

"You're behind the times, Valya," said his stepbrother smoothly. If Andrei resented Valerian's contemptuous tone he gave no sign of it. "I used to see a lot of young hotheads a few years ago, but they don't have the answers to any of our problems. These friends are very different. Serious people—professional men, most of them: journalists, doctors, lawyers. There are even a few officers among them, and they're all dedicated to bringing about the changes our country needs so much."

"Bolsheviks and Mensheviks, I suppose you mean. Don't you know that most of them are double agents for the Tsar's police?" In spite of his world-weary pose, Valerian couldn't entirely conceal his interest. "What are the names?" he asked casually.

"Never mind their names." Andrei smiled thinly. "But you won't find them in the police files."

Valerian nodded. He fitted a cigarette into a long amber holder, lit it and blew thoughtful clouds of smoke at the Italian plasterwork. "Do you know, Andrei, you might be right. I might enjoy talking to your friends. Why not invite them after supper one night, and I'll see what they have to say for themselves."

Andrei's shoulders, over-developed from maneuvering his wheelchair, shook with silent laughter as he rocked the chair back and forth.

"What is so amusing?"

"You're still the complete aristocrat, aren't you, Valerian? Bring them along; I'd like to inspect them," Andrei mimicked. "Again you've quite misunderstood. My friends are too shy to enter this noble palace. If you want to meet them you'll have to come with me to their weekly meeting. It's at a little place called the Red Basilisk—not the kind of place you're used to. And if you come, I'd advise you to leave your uniform at home. They're not fond of uniforms at the Red Basilisk . . . Now, do you still want to meet my friends?"

Valerian stubbed out the half-smoked cigarette and leaned forward to stare directly into Andrei's face. He nodded.

"I think I'd find it very interesting," he said.

Chapter Thirteen

TURKEY
1914

Clouds of sulphurous steam rolled like a sea fog around the domed and vaulted hall of the Turkish public baths, and the high-pitched chatter of female voices reverberated throughout. A double tier of balconies, divided into cubicles, lined the sides of the hall, and within these curtained recesses were ladies dressed and undressed. Here, mysterious rites were performed by numerous maidservants, each washing and drying her mistress' hair, painting her face with rouge and white lead, and rubbing her body with the powerful cloying perfumes, oil of violet and attar of roses, so beloved of Turkish women.

Anastasia, arrayed in a long white bathgown, emerged apprehensively from the curtained cubicle where the servants were busy unpacking the food hampers, dressing-cases, towels and other impedimenta which her hostess considered essential to the enjoyment of a bath. As she walked across the heated floor to the bathing hall, the pandemonium struck her like a physical blow.

"Oh, Halide—I can't stay in long. I shall be boiled alive!" she cried faintly, recoiling from the steamy inferno.

Halide Kisladi's round, cheerful face had already lost its customary creamy pallor and shone with perspiration, but she laughed merrily and took Anastasia's arm, propelling her forward.

"In a minute you'll get used to it, and then you will love it," she promised. "The bath will make you so beautiful that every man at the ball tonight will want to add you to his harem."

An ancient bath attendant, her skin stretched tight as parchment over her skull and hanging in pendulous folds around her dewlap, came forward to guide them to a stream of near-boiling water.

"It hasn't made her so beautiful!" whispered Anastasia, as the old crone turned away to fetch a basin full of water.

"That's because she's worked here so long," said Halide seriously. "Almost forty years. Too much of the steam makes the skin tired. When she walks outside, she finds the fresh air too cold to bear."

"But why does she—" began Anastasia, then gasped with shock as the scalding water was flung over her, drenching her from head to foot. The important business of bathing had begun and there was no further opportunity for conversation. Anastasia's will to resist was evaporating in the noise and heat. Certainly the crowds of naked children, shouting and laughing as they flung water over one another, seemed to be having the time of their lives, although small babies screamed their furious disapproval of the ablutions forced upon them.

It was the last Wednesday of Anastasia's visit to Constantinople, and Anthony's friend Halide Kisladi, a vivacious young woman married for two years to a portly bureaucrat twice her age, had been persuaded to introduce her to the delights of the Turkish bath. Gazing through the steam at the frenetic scene, Anastasia was thankful that her foster-mother, who detested noise and commotion unless she was causing it, and whose health was somewhat precarious, had decided not to join the bathing party. Anastasia was also glad that the Countess had at last agreed to leave Egypt as the summer heat laid its stifling blanket over the dusty land, and the Nile dwindled to a muddy trickle.

Every doctor in Cairo and Alexandria had tried and failed to cure the Countess' constantly aching throat and dry, hacking cough. Her face was now prematurely seamed with wrinkles and her hands shook continually, but still she refused to give up smoking, and Anastasia believed that nothing less than a miracle would cure her.

Indeed a miracle was what the Empress Alexandra had promised—even guaranteed—her friend, in her last letter.

> ... Have no fear, the Lord will hear your prayers as He has so often heard mine through the Divine Intercession of Our Friend ...

she had declared in her flowing, spidery scrawl.

> Have Faith only, dearest Olga, for all Evils of the Flesh bow to his Command. He is a true Man of God, sent by Heaven to Aid us in our Time of Trial...

"Stuff and nonsense," the Countess had croaked, reaching out a shaking hand for another cigarette after reading this missive. "Alexandra needn't imagine she can whistle *me* home for her latest miracle-man to practice on. That kind of rubbish doesn't cut any ice with *me*. Have faith, indeed!"

"There may be something in it, Mama," argued Anastasia. "Surely it will do no harm just to see the man? Besides, now that the treasures from the temple are all crated and ready to leave for Petersburg, don't you think you ought to be there in person when they arrive? Do the museum officials know enough about them to display them properly? It would be a thousand pities if they ended up in some dusty storeroom, after all the trouble you've taken to collect them..."

"It most certainly would." The old frosty spark kindled briefly in Olga's sunken eyes. "That curator of Egyptology at the Imperial Museum is an ignorant fool. I can't imagine why he was appointed, except that he's Spassky's brother. Unless he's supervised, he'll put everything in the wrong light and in the wrong place. You're sure the crates are ready? Well, then...perhaps we should consider going home—for a brief visit. You'll have to come with me, of course. You can spend your time better with me than idling around Alexandria staring at pyramids. We'll break our journey in Constantinople, as your friend Mr. Mills is always asking us to." She added tartly, "I can't understand why you don't make up your mind to marry that young Englishman. He's got a good head on his shoulders—which is more than I can say about most of your admirers."

Anastasia blushed scarlet. The Countess was rarely so outspoken. "Mama!" she protested. "He's never even asked me to marry him. Anyway...anyway, I wouldn't want to. I shall marry a Russian and live in Russia."

She had a sudden, blindingly clear vision of herself and Valerian, standing in the orchard at Ōstrovskoye, looking at the blue V of sea through the cleft in the steep, rocky cliff, where they had so often picnicked and gone swimming. She felt sick with longing. The Countess' hooded eyes watched her intently.

"Romantic nonsense," she said witheringly. "You don't belong in Russia—or anywhere else for that matter. It should make no difference to you whom you marry."

With an effort, Anastasia suppressed the spasm of anger that often flashed through her nowadays when confronted with her foster-mother's casual cruelty. The Countess was a sick woman; she couldn't be held responsible for everything she said or did, though Anastasia suspected that she never spoke without careful consideration of the effect her words would have.

Now, when the girl turned away without answering, Olga snorted derisively and returned to the matter at hand. "I don't care a rap for the Empress' miracle-worker and all his holy mumbo-jumbo, but my Egyptian treasures are certainly not going to be treated like a load of rubbish by that ignorant curator. I'll go home if only to see justice done to them."

Preparations for their departure had been swift. Count Kharkov was more than delighted to be rid of his wife for a few months. He found her cough and her aging appearance depressing, a constant reminder that he, too was approaching middle-age, his apparent perpetual youth only an illusion.

Defiantly he planned an extravagant garden party followed by camel racing in the moonlight to celebrate his own birthday, assuring his wife blandly that Madame Tabbouleh was quite capable of dealing with all the arrangements. Anastasia and the Countess, accompanied by a wagonload of crates, had traveled to Turkey in late May.

"You've chosen the best time of year to visit Constantinople," said Anthony, greeting them with pleasure and whisking them aboard the British ambassador's yacht for a cruise around the Golden Horn. He stood at the rail with Anastasia while the sleek yacht threaded its way between cargo boats and transports, battered old hulks and others ferrying fruit and vegetables across the busy, crowded harbor. "I see you're returning home laden with plunder from your excavations," he remarked with a smile. "Why do Russians always want to carry off everything they dig up?"

"We're almost as bad as the English," she retorted. "I've been told that there are whole rooms of antiquities stolen from their sites and carted away to the British Museum. Egyptian,

Babylonian, Hittite, Etruscan... treasures from all the ancient civilizations, not to mention the Elgin marbles..."

Relaxing on her comfortable couch when at last the soaping and scrubbing was over, Anastasia smiled as she remembered that conversation. But her pleasure died away as she recalled Anthony's next remark:

"Well, I suppose if you've got to take them at all, you're wise to take your plunder home now before war breaks out. It won't be so easy to transport wagonloads of statues from one country to another when that happens."

"What are you talking about? Why should there be a war?"

"Take a good look around while you're here and you'll see what I mean. There's trouble brewing, and soon it will boil. The streets here are full of German officers. Although they look quite absurd in those fezzes they wear, I warn you it's not safe to laugh at them any more. There are Germans manning the guns along the Bosporus and the Dardanelles. Of course they pretend that they're soldiers in the Turkish Army, but I expect you've heard the joke about that?"

"Deutschland über Allah?"

"Exactly. It's far too true to be funny. We're being outmaneuvered here in Constantinople. The Germans are shoving us and the French out of position as fast as they can. Have you ever thought what it would mean to Russia if Germany—a hostile Germany—controlled the Dardanelles? Ninety percent of Russia's grain and easily half her exports go through that narrow channel to the outside world. The effect on your trade could be catastrophic."

He had never spoken to her of politics so seriously before, and despite the bright sunshine on the warm deck she felt a shiver run down her spine. In Egypt she'd been aware of uneasy undercurrents among the diplomatic personnel as German arrogance increased and rumors flew concerning the buildup of German military power. Yet the menace had remained vague and shadowy; no one had talked of war at the picnics and dances, receptions and races. Here the menace seemed more threatening—and more immediate. Suddenly she understood Anthony's haste to leave Cairo the previous spring, and get nearer to the theater of action.

"But we have an ambassador here! Can't he—can't all of you—do anything to stop these Germans?" she asked indignantly. "Why should they be allowed to push everyone else out of Turkey and spoil our trade?"

Anthony shrugged. "Believe me, we're doing all we can, but I don't think it's going to be enough." He smiled and took her cold hand in his strong brown one. "Cheer up. Don't look so worried. I didn't mean to spoil your visit, but I think it's important that you know what's going on."

"Yes." She gazed at the sparkling waves framed by the mosque-crowned hills. The vivid azure sea and sky stretched away into the misty distance. In the distance, the grim old forts guarding the Bosporus stood like crumbling sentinels to repel invaders. It was hard to imagine war dominating this land- and seascape.

Softly, glancing to where the Countess sat smoking within the saloon, she said, "If there—if there's a war, you and I will be on the same side, won't we? Not enemies, as we were in Manchuria?"

"Even then I found it difficult to regard you as my enemy," said Anthony, grinning. "Don't worry. This time, all the chessmen have been moved. We'll be on the same side, all right."

Anastasia found herself greatly comforted by this assurance.

"*Vous permettez, mademoiselle?*" Halide's dark-haired maid peeped shyly into the cubicle and Anastasia beckoned her in. She began to work on the damp mass of golden hair, combing out the tangles and polishing it dry, strand by strand. Another girl carried in a dressing-case full of creams and lotions which she began to massage into Anastasia's skin, starting at her throat and working down until every inch of skin glowed and tingled. Then she took the pot of henna paste and carefully tinged each toe- and fingertip with a rosy shine.

The girls chattered softly as they worked, eager to make her beautiful for the British ambassador's ball tonight. Anastasia lay in a delicious torpor, submitting to their gentle ministrations, drowsily aware of voices in other cubicles, the clatter of cutlery as Halide's maid prepared the luncheon to follow, the sleepy, contented gurgles of babies tucked up to rest as their mothers smoked and gossiped.

On one side of her cubicle, Anastasia could hear a pair of sharp-tongued matrons driving a hard bargain over a marriage they were arranging. They seemed to be evenly matched, one extolling the riches of the bride, the other the beauty of the bridegroom. On the other side a languid voice spoke slow, accurate French as if it were not her native tongue.

"Oh, I quite agree, dear madame, he has neglected you shamefully this week. But is it really his fault? Didn't you know that he's been saddled with that tiresome Russian girl? Yes, quite young and utterly naive. You'd hardly consider her a rival... She has a terrible old mother—a real Tartar if ever I saw one. That's the real reason he hasn't visited you; he's had no time for amusement. *Le pauvre Antoine!* From morning till night he's been obliged to look after them, escort them here and there, show them the sights of Constantinople... What a fate! You shouldn't blame him, you should be sorry for him."

They were talking about Anthony—and her! Anastasia stiffened and strained her ears to hear more. How dare this impertinent woman imply that Anthony was required to entertain them against his will! Whatever could she mean?

The languid voice continued: "He'll be there tonight, he told me so himself. The Russians are staying at the Pera Palace Hotel, and poor Anthony's been roped in to drive them all the way to the ball. He can't get out of it now. But he told me he'd escape later on and join you upstairs as soon as he's arranged enough dancing partners to keep *la petite Russe* occupied. You and he have better things to do than dance, *hein*? We'll time our arrival for midnight—he should be free of his obligations by then. Now, if you're ready, dear madame, perhaps we should go home. I've so many things to attend to, and you must rest in order to look your most beautiful..."

Who was she? How could she tell such lies—such horrible, hateful, unfounded lies? Anastasia's cheeks burned with rage and shame. So that was how Anthony spoke of her to his grand new friends in Constantinople—as a tiresome Russian girl with a terrible old mother, pretending it was his *duty* to show them the sights. And she, Anastasia, had been deceived into thinking he was glad to see them and enjoyed their company, the treacherous, two-faced dog! Well, she'd show him. She'd teach him not to speak that way about her. But first she must find out if...

Completely forgetting that she was naked, Anastasia swung her legs off the couch with the wild idea of rushing into the cubicle next door and confronting that vile, slandering woman! But a sharp tug at her hair and the shrill reproaches of the two maidservants recalled her to her senses. Mademoiselle must wait. They had not yet finished making Mademoiselle beautiful. If Mademoiselle would have the goodness to turn her body this way a little? Ah, that was better. In a short while Mademoiselle would be ready to be dressed...

But in a so short while it would be too late to discover the identity of the women next door. She wanted to know them when she saw them at the ball. Fully awake now, Anastasia fretted and fidgeted, making the job twice as difficult for the girl trying to pin up her long yellow hair. She could hear the next-door occupants preparing to depart. They scolded as crockery hit the floor, ordering the servants to pick up the damp towels. She heard curtains being drawn back, then footsteps on the marble floor.

They were going! Wrenching her head free at the cost of a dozen flying hairpins, Anastasia jumped up from her couch and put her eye to the crack between her own curtains. She was too late! All she could see was a little procession of servants carrying hampers and bundles, and over their heads two women walking arm in arm, their heads close together. One was tall and dark, but her shorter companion had nothing at all to distinguish herself except the floating cloak beneath which so many Turkish women hid their charms.

Unsatisfied, she returned to her couch and the gentle scolding of Halide's maids. What was Mademoiselle's hurry? Why must she spring up like a tiger and scatter pins and combs all over the floor? Now she, Edeh, must start again from the beginning to wind up Mademoiselle's hair, and she hoped that this time Mademoiselle would be good enough to remain seated until she had finished.

Dressing for the English ambassador's ball that night, Anastasia's mind was still in an angry turmoil. When he arrived to collect them, she could hardly bring herself to speak to Anthony.

He asked how she had enjoyed her visit to the Turkish baths.

"Oh, it was pleasant enough," she said shortly.

"Only pleasant?" Anthony was surprised at her lack of enthusiasm. He had gone to some trouble to persuade Halide to arrange this treat for Anastasia. He expected a word of thanks, at least.

"I thought it nothing unusual." With an effort Anastasia suppressed the torrent of angry abuse that threatened to spill from her. She knew only too well how easily he could make her appear foolish and childish for losing her temper, and she couldn't risk such a scene in front of her foster-mother. She should confront Anthony in private with what she had overheard in the baths. She resolved to freeze him with icy politeness until be begged to know what had offended her. That would be her opportunity to repeat to him the exact words of that horrible unseen female—and ask if he could deny their truth.

The Countess frowned as she overheard Anastasia's rudeness. She herself wore a high-collared evening gown embroidered with black jet, which made her look regal in spite of her emaciation, and she had bestirred herself to lessen her pallor with a touch of rouge. She thought that Anastasia had never looked lovelier than tonight, in her formal Court dress of sea-green silk, its low-cut neckline showing off her white shoulders and bosom, and the huge skirt billowing out from a close-fitting waist. Why, she wondered, was the silly child sulking and flouncing and being disagreeable to obliging Mr. Mills, who was so kindly escorting them to the ball?

She shot a warning look which said *Behave yourself* at Anastasia, and tried to cover up for her lack of grace by saying hastily, "It was so kind of you to ask your friend to take Anastasia. I only wish I could have gone myself. I have heard that a Turkish bath is a unique experience."

"Some people find them enervating. Naturally, they are hotbeds of malicious gossip, most of it mere fabrication," said Anthony, with a sharp look at Anastasia. Not for the first time, she wished he was less perceptive. Trust him to make a lucky guess at the cause of her mood! No doubt he would now do his best to persuade her that nothing ever heard in a Turkish bath approached the truth. Let him try!, she thought angrily.

But Anthony did nothing of the kind. He chatted easily with the Countess as the chauffeured embassy limousine drove smoothly through the steep streets of Pera, its horn blaring every few seconds to warn donkeys, horses, and pedestrians of their approach. The Englishman allowed Anastasia to smoulder in silence as they rattled along the bank of the Bosporus toward

Sir Louis Mallet's summer residence, where the coastline curved north before joining the Black Sea.

I might as well be a stuffed dummy for all the notice he takes of me, she thought resentfully. The way he's behaving only shows that what I heard was true. He regards me as a nuisance who's spoiling his fun. He's longing for us to go back to Russia so he'll be free to carry on his affair with that woman—whoever she is. What do I care, anyway? I'll show him tonight that I can enjoy myself without any help from Mr. Anthony Mills. Let him go upstairs to his *chere amie*, and good riddance to him. But when she remembered how much she'd been looking forward to this last ball of their visit, and how different everything would have seemed if she hadn't overheard that vicious gossiping tongue, her throat felt tight and the glittering ballroom suddenly blurred with tears she was too proud to shed.

The British ambassador greeted his Russian guests warmly, and complimented Anastasia on her dress.

"I'll ask you for a waltz later on in the evening," he promised, "but I can see I'd better not leave it too long. There'll be a score of young fellows queueing up to dance with you. We're always glad to see a new face—especially if it's a pretty one. Now let's see, who do you know already? Have you met young Fytton here? He's only just joined us, too." He clapped a pink-cheeked young man in very new regimentals on the shoulder. "Percy, you may be in time to ask Miss Kharkova for a dance."

Anthony and the Countess had vanished into the throng. Captain the Honorable Percival Fytton opened sleepy eyes very wide and set himself to make the most of this chance introduction to the prettiest girl he'd ever seen. Her Russian accent enchanted him. Her slanting green eyes were almost on a level with his as they danced, and he was very put out when the bustling two-step changed to a slow waltz and he was obliged to surrender his charming partner to a German military attaché who, he considered, had no business at this ball anyway. Damned, supercilious Hun, he thought.

"May I take you into supper, Miss Kharkova?" he asked, before releasing her. Anastasia, determined to avoid Anthony's company at all costs, turned her most radiant smile on him.

"That would be delightful, Percy. *À bientôt!*" She glided away in the arms of the German attaché, although she would have preferred to remain with the admiring young Englishman. Anastasia's German was a good deal less fluent than her English, and she disliked Heinrich von Stuckel's proprietorial air and stiff, forceful style of dancing. He propelled her around the ballroom as if he was pushing a wheelbarrow.

She saw from the corner of her eye that Anthony had managed to settle her foster-mother among a group of bemedaled graybeards and tightly corseted ladies who appeared to be exactly the right company for her. Anthony, standing by a pillar entwined with roses, seemed to be watching her intently. At once she began to laugh and chatter to her partner with such animation that Heinrich von Stuckel was encouraged to clasp her even closer to his gold-braided chest.

"Ach, so! You have never wisited my country?" he said. Inwardly she sighed. He was boring her to death already.

"I have not had that pleasure," she admitted, with a smile which showed nothing of the distaste she felt for being held so tightly and stared at so lasciviously by his prominent pale-blue eyes. Across the room, Anthony observed the smile and raised his eyebrows slightly.

"Germany is the most beautiful country in the world. You should wisit it soon."

"It sounds most interesting." Anastasia wriggled slightly, and the hand which had crept up toward her bosom retreated an inch or two. She saw that Anthony had turned away now to talk to a tall, dark-haired woman. Could this be the woman she had overheard! No. A glance at her watch told her that it was barely half past eleven, although she felt as though she'd been dancing for hours with this arrogant Prussian brute and his pomaded hair. Anthony was paying her no attention. She let her mask of enjoyment slip a little and told her partner that she was tired.

"A glass of lemonade, perhaps!" He had no intention of letting her go. The young Englishman had claimed her for supper, but perhaps before that he, Von Stuckel, would succeed in luring her into the garden. He had heard that Russian women were very passionate. It would be interesting to find out if that was true.

"I prefer champagne," said Anastasia recklessly. She needed champagne to get through this terrible evening. Von Stuckel gripped her arm possessively and steered her toward an empty table in the library. Instead of leaving, himself, he snapped his fingers at a passing waiter.

"Two glasses of champagne, immediately!"

"Very good, sir." The waiter departed as slowly as he dared and brought back a bottle, which he left on the table.

Etienne Labbaye, a friend of Anthony's seated at a nearby table, smiled at Anastasia and she waved gaily back. Perhaps he would rescue her from this overbearing German. But when Von Stuckel saw the exchange he turned and frowned so murderously that Etienne shrugged and stayed where he was, though he blew her a kiss.

Coward, thought Anastasia. Never had an evening seemed so long. As though they were lemonade, she drank three glasses of champagne. She began to feel more cheerful. Von Stuckel watched approvingly as a flush mounted to her cheeks.

"You like strong wine?" he inquired.

Anastasia shrugged. "Vodka is much stronger than champagne."

"Ach, so! Wodka—that is schnapps, yes? You say that Russian women drink schnapps?"

"Of course," said Anastasia airily. She felt a compulsion to shock him. Von Stuckel watched her closely and licked his lips: she was a wild one, all right. He thought again of ways to get her alone in the dark garden.

He said, "You must know that in Germany there is the best wine."

"Of course. And the tallest trees and the highest mountains and the prettiest women . . ."

"You know this already?"

"No; I merely guessed it."

Anastasia drank more champagne. She looked at him with new eyes. Why was she sitting here as if chained to her chair? Why hadn't she the simple courage to get up and leave this Prussian bore to drone away at someone else?

She rose abruptly. "You must excuse me, Heinrich, but I think my mother . . ."

She stopped as a hand touched her shoulder. "Ah, there you are at last, Anastasia," said Anthony's lazy, amused voice. "I was wondering where you'd managed to hide yourself. You promised me this dance, remember?"

She turned and saw that there was a girl with him,—a tall, dark English girl who held his arm as possessively as Von Stuckel had held hers. Anastasia caught a quick impression of chilly hazel eyes, dark hair and a very determined chin. "Sybil, my dear," said Anthony, "I don't believe you've met Miss Kharkova—Anastasia—or Captain Von Stuckel. Miss Sybil Dunwoody. Sybil visited your country last year, Captain, and found it most interesting, didn't you?"

He was offering Anastasia a means of escape, sacrificing the English Sybil to Von Stuckel instead. Neither Sybil nor the German looked pleased at the exchange.

Sybil inclined her head in a nod that was only just civil, and Von Stuckel bowed stiffly.

"Gnadige Fraulein."

The olive branch was there, within her grasp, and Anastasia longed to accept it. What did it matter if Anthony laughed at her in front of his friends? What if he *had* called her naive and the Countess a Tartar? Without his jokes and gossip, his half-teasing, half-flattering attention, this ball was proving as flat as yesterday's champagne and she wasn't enjoying it at all. Now was her chance to save the rest of the evening, at least...

Miss Sybil Dunwoody observed her with barely veiled dislike. She said: "Anthony tells me that you sampled the joys of the Turkish bath today, Miss Kharkova. Did you find it to your taste?"

Anastasia recognized the drawling nasal voice the instant Sybil spoke. Sybil Dunwoody had been in the cubicle next to hers that afternoon: Sybil—and who else? Was the English girl aware that Anastasia had heard what she'd said there?

"I found the noise somewhat overpowering. So many voices speaking so many languages. It made me think of a parrot-cage," she said carefully. Sybil smiled. Her teeth were very small and white and her canines extremely pointed.

"Yes," she said sweetly. "Sometimes one overhears the most *fascinating* conversations there."

"Come on, Anastasia, remember your promise," said Anthony impatiently.

It was their private code—the words he had used to rescue her from countless bores at countless diplomatic functions, but now she was too angry to acknowledge the signal. Sybil must have wanted her to know what Anthony had said about her, and the knowledge reawakened all Anastasia's wounded pride. Her chin went up and her eyes flashed green fire.

"I promised you nothing, Anthony. Nothing!"

"I must have misunderstood you, then. Still, it would be a mistake to miss the highlight of the evening, no matter how much you enjoy sitting here with Captain Von Stuckel. The British naval band has sailed all the way down from Pera especially to entertain us, and H.E. is very anxious that all his guests should show their appreciation. Now they're about to begin! From the verandah we should have an excellent view across the water."

"Ach, yes; I was told there would be band music," said Von Stuckel patronizingly. "I will escort you to the verandah, Fraulein. The English know little of music, but it would be *unhöflich* not to attend their performance. Come now."

Gripping her arm again, he propelled her past the puzzled Anthony toward the verandah, which was already crowded with laughing, chattering guests, watching the floodlit naval vessels and the white-uniformed band.

"Mmmm... I only hope she knows what she's doing," murmured Anthony.

Sybil took his hand. "The little Russian girl? I'm quite certain she does," she purred. "She looked rather overwrought. Perhaps she disliked having her tête-à-tête with the handsome Staboffizer interrupted."

"You consider that brute *handsome*, Syb?" Anthony stared at Von Stuckel's swaggering figure as it ploughed a ruthless furrow through the other guests.

"Hush, darling. You're not supposed to offend them. You know how touchy they are!" Sybil wagged a playful finger. "Of course, between ourselves I agree with you entirely. But the uniform has a—a certain distinction, you must admit. Just the kind of dazzle to steal the heart of a simple Russian maiden."

"Anastasia isn't my idea of a simple Russian maiden," said Anthony, and Sybil's eyes narrowed.

"Is she the other kind perhaps? One of those moody Slavs, all great emotional dramas... How have you managed to put up with it all this week? You've been wonderful, darling—absolutely wonderful."

All this week? All these years, thought Anthony. And has it made a single pennyworth of difference to Anastasia? I doubt it.

Maybe I'm a fool to keep hoping—to keep trying. Perhaps she'll never change. Perhaps she'll spend her life yearning for handsome fools in splendid uniforms like Von Stuckel—and Valerian Radek. Sometimes I think that Mother may be right, that I'd do better to cut my losses and settle down with Sybil. That's why Sybil's come here, of course. That story of escorting poor old Madame de St. Valery to visit her son is only an excuse. Syb's out to get me, but the damned thing is, I don't like being chased! I don't like it when she behaves as if she owns me. Heaven knows what she engineered this afternoon to put Anastasia in such a mood. Sybil must have been at the bottom of that, I know. But she's a good sort really, old Syb . . . if only she wouldn't try so hard to *organize* me.

"We ought to go and listen to the band, too." Sybil was becoming restive. "And you simply mustn't forget that poor old Madamoiselle De St. Valery is waiting upstairs for you. She's longing to see you—she's talked of nothing else all day. She wants a game of chess with you. '*Où est mon cher Antoine?* she says. 'He's neglected his old friend shamefully this week.' I told her you'd been busy, but when you're as old as she is, you can't help being rather demanding. Promise me you won't disappoint her, darling?"

Anthony suppressed a groan. He had never felt less like playing chess. "All right. I'll come up as soon as the band plays its party piece."

The strains of "Rule Britannia" floated over the floodlit water and the guests clapped and cheered.

"Dear Anthony," purred Sybil. "I knew I could depend on you."

Rely. Depend. Lean on. Trust you to be responsible . . . If she only knew how he loathed those words! But they were part of the image needed to cover up his less reputable activities—activities of which even the British ambassador was only vaguely aware. They involved secret meetings and close contacts with very unsavory characters, in the interests of keeping British military intelligence fully informed of developments in the Turkish capital.

No one—particularly Sybil—must ever connect the correct, reliable, dependable Mr. Mills, whose vaguely defined duties as cultural attaché gave him an excellent excuse to explore every corner of the city, with the bearded figure in dirty pyjamas who was sometimes to be found in cafés in the seedier quarters of Stamboul, talking softly with shabby men who shared a tendency to choose seats near doors with their backs to the wall, and who frequently exchanged crumpled scraps of paper for equally dirty banknotes...

For one crazy moment, Anthony had an urge to chuck it all and be himself again—to shake off Sybil's clinging hand and pursue the arrogant figure of Von Stuckel into the garden. To seize him by his braided collar and the seat of his too-tight pants and fling him bodily into the black waters of the Bosporus, then throw Anastasia across his shoulder and stride away with her into the darkness.

Picturing the scene, the black moment passed and Anthony grinned. One day his chance would come. Until then it was only a question of hanging on, maintaining his cover and keeping Sybil Dunwoody at arm's length...

"Can't I share the joke, darling?" she asked, but he shook his head.

"I doubt if you'd understand it, Syb. It's not much of a joke anyway."

Anastasia was not enjoying the band. Her head was beginning to ache from too much champagne, and the blare of the brass section, beamed directly toward the guests on the verandah of the Summer Residence, sent stabs of pain shooting through her temples at every crescendo. The swelling refrain of "Rule, Britannia," which the ebullient Miss Louisa had been fond of thumping out on the old schoolroom piano, reminded her all too sharply of the circumstances of that unscholarly governess' departure—and, by extension, of Valerian.

Thinking of him, she felt a kind of panic. Very soon she'd be back in Petersburg. Would Valya have changed? Would he think she had changed? Would all the efforts she'd made to acquire poise and sophistication—to become the kind of woman of the world he used to admire—prove enough to banish the memory of a naive, moonstruck fifteen year-old? A girl who hadn't known the difference between love and affection, who'd made the humiliating discovery of her ignorance in his bed?

Remembering that night still made her burn with shame, but her devotion to Valerian was not in the least diminished. Nor had she swayed in her determination that one day he would truly love her. She had been faithful to him, with no hope that he'd be faithful to her, because she recognized that in this respect their natures were different. And she loved him none the less.

He had laughed at her in those dim, distant Siberian days. He had called her lovesick and moonstruck because she adored him, and he had been right. It was inevitable that her schoolgirlish fantasies should have centered on him because, then, he had no rivals in her heart.

But now it was different—very different. In Egypt she'd met hundreds of men, attractive, attentive, cosmopolitan men who had courted and flattered her in ways that would have amused Valerian very much. Yet none of them had touched her heart. None of them? For an instant her thoughts toward Anthony wavered, but she pushed any hint of disloyalty to Valerian firmly aside. Anthony understood how she felt about Valerian. He was different from the other men with whom she'd danced, played tennis, laughed and flirted. He was a friend—but not a lover.

She knew that other women were attracted to Anthony. Many of them envied Anastasia the long winter weeks she'd spent each year with Anthony and her stepmother, excavating the temple. Cairene society had speculated feverishly on the possibilities for romance in such a situation. She and Anthony had laughed about it together, knowing it was a cover for her love for Valerian.

Anthony could be trusted to keep that secret; just as she could be trusted with the knowledge that his work at the embassy went beyond mere cultural duties. But that had been in the happy, carefree days in Egypt. Here in Constantinople he had changed. Despite all his attention during the past ten days, she felt that he was holding her at a distance, careful to prevent her seeing too much . . . Leaving Cairo had changed him, and she felt herself an interloper in his new world, as though he had left her behind. He was playing a game now in which she had no part. Of course, it was because of the threat of war. In war you had to turn to your countrymen—the only ones you really understood and trusted. Anthony had turned toward that cold-eyed, cold-hearted Sybil just as she would soon turn to Valerian. Nevertheless the loss of his easy friendship made her heart ache as much as her head, and she longed for the ball to be over.

The band was playing "God Save the King." Anastasia

stiffened to attention, then thought: Why should I? It isn't my King they're asking God to save. Captain Von Stuckel felt her fidget. He looked down, smiled, and imprisoned her hand within his warm, damp one, holding it too tight for her to free it without a struggle.

"So many English ceremonies are tiresome," he whispered in her ear. "Come. Now we'll walk in the garden until it is time for supper."

"I should go back to Mama," Anastasia began, but he cut her short.

"Later I take you to her. But first we walk. I have something to show you."

What was the matter with her? Why was she allowing this overbearing, over-dressed German staff officer to march her away into the lantern-lit grounds when she had no wish at all to accompany him? A strange lethargy possessed her, and she drifted along at his side as aimlessly as a sleepwalker, watching the dark sparkle of water running beside the garden. She knew it was time she went back to the house and found the Countess. It must be an hour since she last saw her playing cards in an anteroom, and although Olga would be happy to gamble and smoke until dawn, that was precisely what her doctors had forbidden. Somehow the Countess must be persuaded to leave.

Anastasia sighed; the task of persuasion was not an alluring one. The Countess usually brushed aside her foster-daughter's efforts to make her obey the doctors' orders, declaring that she wouldn't give up the last of her pleasures. Only Anthony was master of the precise blend of flattery and cajolery that would make her see reason. Would he undertake the delicate task tonight? But no. He would undoubtedly escape to the arms of Sybil... Now there was no one to help her get the Countess home to bed...

They had reached a patch of deep shadow, beneath the huge umbrella of a mulberry tree through whose branches a white rambling rose had been trained to climb. Beneath it was the shining dark surface of a lily pond. The warm fragrance of rose and syringa seemed trapped within the umbrella of branches, heavy and decadent...

Here Von Stuckel stopped, and Anastasia looked around her, wondering why. Her head still throbbed, but less savagely. She felt tired and depressed. "Is this what you wanted to show me?" she said. "It's very pretty, but I should go back to Mama. She may be anxious."

"I have something more to show you."

"No, Heinrich. I must go now." She was annoyed at his persistence—annoyed and a little uneasy. He was so strong and heavily built, and he showed none of the usual deference a gentleman should toward the wishes of a lady. Perhaps he wasn't a gentleman at all.

A moment later she was convinced. Von Stuckel pulled her suddenly into his arms and said in a guttural whisper, "First, *schöne Fraulein*, I shall show you how a German loves. Then you will not want to go back to your mother." He laughed in a way that made her shiver.

"You won't do anything of the kind," said Anastasia furiously, torn between fear and revulsion at the look in his pale eyes. His waxed mustache tickled her, and then his cold, determined mouth sought her lips. She struck out at him in a panic. Laughter rumbled in his chest, and he said:

"Ach, that is good. They tell me Russian women make love like wild tigers. Show me your claws now, little Russian, and I will cut them for you."

His wet lips fastened against her throat. She couldn't move, so tightly was she clasped to his gold-braided tunic, and her pride forbade her to cry out, for fear of being discovered in such a humiliating situation. Von Stuckel's hands, hot and damp, fumbled at the low neck of her ballgown, pulling it down from her shoulders. His breath rattled hoarsely in his throat.

He was like a wild beast. The thin veneer of propriety had cracked wide open to expose the naked brutality of the Hun whose ancestors had satisfied their lusts on women too weak to resist them.

With an enormous effort, Anastasia wrenched away from those groping, fumbling hands—and heard her dress rip as she broke free. Clutching it, she stumbled out of the dark umbrella of the mulberry tree and into the brilliant moonlight.

"Miss Kharkova!"

Anastasia almost collapsed with relief as she blundered into a man who was standing on the gravel path, staring into the water. Quick hands reached out to steady her. "Oh! I'm so sorry. I beg your pardon—" she gasped, then raised her eyes and saw who it was.

"I'm glad to be of assistance." His cool glance took in her wide, frightened eyes and the torn dress. Percy Fytton had no need to ask what had happened. He had seen Von Stuckel and Anastasia leave the verandah together and disappear in the direction of the lily pond. Because he was a persistent young man who had no intention of losing the promised supper-dance, he'd followed at a discreet distance.

"Was it that—that German?"

She nodded, and he flexed his hands, smiling, anticipating the joy of battle.

"Excuse me a moment, Miss Kharkova." Gently he detached himself and walked past her into the shadows.

"Von Stuckel? Are you there?"

The big German was standing with his back to the lily pond. He had heard an English voice speaking to that little Russian wildcat and decided it might be prudent to remain where he was until they withdrew. He realized now that he had allowed his feelings to carry him away. Perhaps he had handled the Russian girl more roughly than he should have. But wasn't that what Russian women were reputed to enjoy?

"I believe you owe Miss Kharkova an apology," said Fytton steadily.

"Gott im Himmel!" Von Stuckel's eyes bulged as he stared at the slim young Englishman, half a head shorter than himself and a fraction of his weight. Could he have heard right? Was it possible that this impudent bantam was demanding that he, Von Stuckel, apologize?

"Well," said Fytton into the silence, "are you going to apologize?"

The German's blistering reply made Anastasia clap her hands to her ears.

"Excellent," said Fytton pleasantly. "I hoped you'd say something of the kind." Rocking backwards slightly, he pivoted on the balls of his feet, and shot out his arm. His fist caught Von Stuckel on the point of the chin with admirable precision. It wasn't a particularly heavy blow, but Percy Fytton had been the most scientific boxer of his weight at Rugby. He might even have achieved an Oxford Blue if, his trainer told him, he could learn to put a little more aggression behind his punch.

Now science and aggression had blended with a harmony they had never known before. With a grunt of astonishment the tall German toppled backwards into the lily pond. The splash as he hit the water threw an arc of sparkling spray into the air.

"That should cool his ardor," said Percy Fytton with satisfaction, returning to Anastasia and rubbing his knuckles. "It may even teach him some manners. I wish I'd worn gloves. He's got a jaw like cast iron."

"Oh, pull him out! Pull him out before he drowns," cried Anastasia, shivering between tears and laughter.

"Don't worry, Miss Kharkova, he'll pull himself out. The water isn't deep."

The truth of this statement became only too clear as Von Stuckel lumbered to his feet and stood, bedraggled, knee-deep among the lily pads. His hair was plastered over his forehead. Mud and weeds festooned his epaulettes. His eyes were glittering with hatred.

"You will regret that blow, Englishman," he snarled. "Before this year is out, you and your friends will pay a thousand times over for striking a German..."

"Don't let him annoy you, Miss Kharkova," drawled Fytton. "Huns are infernally touchy, and they talk an awful lot of rot. Come along. Let's see if we can't find a maid to mend your dress. Then perhaps you'll allow me the pleasure of a dance."

Already the evening had gone on far too long for Anastasia. She felt dirty and defiled by the German, and was miserably conscious that she had only herself to blame. It would have been so easy to accept Anthony's offer of liberation from Von Stuckel hours ago. Now the thought of facing the ballroom again in a ruined dress, proclaiming her embarrassment to every curious eye, was altogether too much.

"No," she whispered. "I'm sorry, Percy. You've been very kind but you must forgive me. I—I feel tired. I want to go home."

Looking hard at her white face, Percy nodded. "My dear Anastasia—may I call you Anastasia?—I quite understand. You've had a nasty shock. Say no more. Go home you shall—and the sooner the better. I'll take you now."

"But I must tell my stepmother, Countess Kharkova..."

"I'll deal with her." He thought for a moment and said, "Let me run you back to the hotel in my car. You're staying at the Pera Palace? Suppose I drive you home—it won't take long—and then come back here to tell your mother you've left because you didn't feel well? How about that? Good! There's nothing I enjoy more than taking my motor for a spin in the night air. It's the most agreeable sensation in the world..."

Chapter Fourteen

"Don't you ever open your letters, darling? Not even the interesting foreign ones?" Princess Maria Beloselsky hovered like an inquisitive bird over Valerian's desk, her bright brown eyes glancing at postmarks and stamps while her busy hands riffled through the spreading pile of envelopes. "Look—here's one all the way from Egypt! Doesn't that make you curious?"

"Leave my mail alone, Maria—there's a good girl," said Valerian, yawning and slamming shut the photograph album he'd been looking at. "I know you've got enough natural curiosity for two, but all the same my private letters have nothing whatever to do with you. I've been busy. I haven't had time to read them yet."

"Then I'll do it for you," she offered at once, picking up a letter-opener. "Allow me to take over the duties of your social secretary, my dear Valerian."

"Certainly not."

"Can't I even open the one from Turkey?" said Maria, disappointed.

"That'll be from my mother, no doubt, containing a detailed description of every mosque and palace in Constantinople. I have to be strong to read that. Now I'm too busy.

Maria giggled. "You don't *look* busy, darling." Stretched out on a well-upholstered sofa in the library of his comfortable house in St. Petersburg, wearing a crimson silk dressing-gown and smoking a thin gold-tipped cigarette through a long amber holder, Valerian was the very picture of indolence. A new thought struck her. "Did you know that your mother is on her way home? You'd better read her letter before she arrives."

"On her way home?" Now she had his full attention. "Where did you pick up that rumor, my pretty little gossip-monger?"

"From an unimpeachable source," she said with dignity. "And it isn't a rumor."

"Oh, from the Empress? Well, well," said Valerian, with deep interest, "then I'll take back everything I've said about your natural curiosity. It can be extremely useful at times. Please hand me that letter, sweetheart. I need to bone up on my knowledge of Byzantine architecture before she gets here."

"I thought that would make you sit up," said Maria with satisfaction. "The Empress said your mother was ill. She wants Father Grigori to cure her."

"Father Grigori? Mama would have a fit..." said Valerian absently, skimming through his mother's letter as fast as he could. "She doesn't say anything about being sick."

Maria looked soulful. "If it wasn't for me, you'd probably never bother to read your correspondence. You need a wife to look after you, Valerian, darling. I feel terrible when I think of your poor mother, sick and neglected in a strange land, writing her fingers to the bone by the light of a guttering candle, trying to share her knowledge with a son who's too lazy even to open his letters..."

Valerian laughed and pulled her down on the sofa beside him. "Keep your sermons to yourself, little gossip-monger," he advised.

"And keep your hands to yourself, Valerian! It's true that you neglect your mother... When did you last write to her?"

"My dear Maria, you sound just like the Tsarina," he teased. "My mother neglected? You wouldn't say that if you ever saw servants scurrying around when she's in a mood. She doesn't *allow* neglect. Poor Anastasia usually bears the brunt of her temper."

"Anastasia!" Maria's nose twitched, scenting gossip. "I've always wanted to know more about her. Isn't she an orphan your mother adopted? What a noble, saintly act!"

"My enchanting foster-sister..." said Valerian, with a reminiscent smile. "Don't pretend you don't know that my stepfather begot her."

"Yet your mother took her in..."

"And never let Anastasia forget it, from that moment to

this," said Valerian dryly. "She's paid for her keep many times over, poor child."

"I believe you're in love with your foster-sister," said Maria triumphantly. "I think she's the dark secret you've been hiding all these years. Perhaps that's why you never married. Now admit it!"

"As I've told you before, I don't believe in marriage," said Valerian, quite unruffled. He unbuttoned the high lace collar of her blouse and kissed her firm white throat. "Why are women so determined on marriage? Isn't love enough?"

She nestled closer into his arms. "Can't you even pretend that you'd like to marry me?"

"No, I can't," said Valerian cheerfully. "Even if you were free—which, thank heaven and your good old husband, you aren't—I wouldn't marry you. By the way, can you persuade him to invite me for the partridge shooting? There's nothing I enjoy more."

"Of course—if you don't march off to war before then," said Maria. She wished Valerian were a little less outspoken about being so fickle. It would have been pleasant to maintain the illusion, at least, that he thought more of her than shooting partridges. Honesty was all very well in its place, thought Maria, but its place was not necessarily in the arms of your lover.

"Ah, yes—the war. The war will claim us all in time."

Valerian's voice was bleak. She wished she hadn't mentioned the war. Everyone knew it was coming, but only the Tsar's generals really wanted it. Trying to return to the subject that really interested her, she said, "If you don't believe in marriage, Valya, what *do* you believe in?"

Valerian's ears caught the creak of Andrei's wheelchair in the hall. Gently, he disengaged himself from Maria's clinging hands.

"I'll tell you some day," he promised. Andrei approved of Valerian's liaison with Maria, whose position as Lady-in-Waiting to the Empress gave her access to interesting Court gossip, which she happily reported to Valerian who, in turn, passed it on to his stepbrother to make what use of it he liked.

Even now, it still seemed strange to Valerian that Andrei, with his twisted body and bitter tongue, should be so highly regarded by the Bolsheviki, as they called themselves, the group of men and women dedicated to revolution to whom he had introduced Valerian. Initially suspicious, the Bolsheviki had finally accepted him, welcoming his military expertise as Andrei had predicted they would. But they still didn't trust him as they trusted Andrei, and probably never would. Was it because of his position, he wondered, his birth, his access to the Court? Or was it because they sensed that his interest sprang more from a desire to further his own crusade—the reform of the army—than a true commitment to the overthrow of the Tsar and all he stood for?

Their very coolness toward him intrigued Valerian. It was a new experience to be judged strictly on his merits, rather than as a member of his powerful family. Although he recognized that he would never become one of their leaders, he found the clandestine meetings and covert dissemination of propaganda—as well as the cautious recruitment of disaffected fellow officers in the army—curiously satisfying. He enjoyed the sense of playing a double game—a dangerous double game whose discovery would mean disgrace and imprisonment.

Maria had just asked him what he believed in. She would have been deeply shocked if he had told her the truth—that he, Valerian Radek, was beginning to believe that revolution was now the only answer to Russia's problems. The Duma—the body of elected representatives—had not been able to fulfill the high hopes of the liberals. The Duma had no real power. The reins of government were still in the hands of the Tsar alone, and Nicholas II was a complete autocrat, despite his shy and retiring manner. Backed by his imperious, high-handed wife, he would never surrender a shred of his power or privilege, or allow the business of government to have any truly democratic or constitutional base. Sooner or later the Tsar would have to go. War was coming, but Andrei and his friends were not yet ready to assume control.

News of the assassination of the Archduke Franz Ferdinand, heir to the crumbling Austrian Empire, had reached St. Petersburg on the last day of June. Ever since, Russia's armed forces had waited for the order for mobilization, while telegrams flew back and forth between the Tsar and his cousin Wilhelm, the German Kaiser. The army which Valerian had dreamed of remodeling into a streamlined modern force was still the same unwieldy, old-fashioned blunt instrument it had been in 1905. All that had changed was his dream. Before, he had wanted reform. Now he was ready for revolution.

He shook himself, smiling at Maria, who had gone to arrange

her hair in front of the long gilt mirror.

"Wouldn't you really like to marry me?" she asked, her romantic soul brimming from the depths of her moist brown eyes, but Valerian only laughed.

"My dear girl, Mama wouldn't allow it, even if I wanted to," he said solemnly. "You aren't grand enough, in her opinion."

"Grand enough!" Maria drew herself up, quivering with hauteur. "Isn't a Princess grand enough for your high and mighty mother?"

"Nothing but Imperial blood will do, I'm afraid. She wants me to marry a Grand Duchess."

"Oh, Valya, why must you always tease me? Who cares what your mama wants! What do *you* want?"

"I only want to have fun," said Valerian softly. "Don't go yet, Maria, darling. Andrei's gone into his study. He's about to compose one of his thundering editorials, no doubt. We have plenty of time now to have a little fun before he comes in to spoil it."

Maria hesitated. She looked longingly at the comfortable sofa, but then shook her head. "Sorry, darling, but I must go. I'm already late for Galina's séance. She's hoping that the old general will get in touch tonight, and I can't disappoint her. *À bientôt, mon amour!*"

She skewered her saucy little boater onto her glossy dark hair, waved an airy hand, and was gone.

Idly, Valerian picked up his mother's letter. He reread the final paragraph, frowning.

> We are returning to Petersburg next week to supervise the installation of my Egyptian collection in the Museum. We arrive on July 21st, and I trust you will be at the station to meet us. I have the highest hopes that by then I will be able to announce to you the news of Anastasia's forthcoming marriage. She has kept the estimable Mr. Mills dangling after her quite long enough, and I intend to see the matter settled before we leave Constantinople. He is a delightful young man of whom the British ambassador has an excellent opinion. Nothing could be more suitable...

Valerian stared at the paper for a long time before he finally tossed it on the fire. As the edges curled and darkened, a slow anger began to burn his heart. His mother's message could hardly be plainer. Keep away from Anastasia: she isn't for you, nor you for her. Her fate has already been decided.

Damn Mr. Mills, he thought. Damn all Englishmen, estimable or otherwise. Damn Mama and her meddlesome, high-handed matchmaking. The thought of Anastasia being helplessly married off to a man of his mother's choice filled him with angry revulsion, and his old affection for his stepsister was suddenly redoubled. Perhaps Maria's feminine instinct was right, he thought. Perhaps Anastasia *is* the girl I've been in love with subconsciously, all these years. The idea was absurd, yet as he acknowledged it he felt a curious elation. How deeply is she committed to this Englishman?, he wondered. Will I be able to win her away from him after all these years? The odds are against it...

The challenge—the prospect of a tug of war, with his delectable little Anastasia as the prize—appealed to him, as nothing else had for months. He could hardly wait for the Countess' special train to arrive in St. Petersburg...

Carefully wrapped and padded in layers of fine cotton, packed in stout wooden crates and strongly corded, even the most fragile of the Countess' Egyptian treasures—the delicate bowls and vases, the alabaster lamps and ivory miniatures—survived their trip north without loss or damage. But the human cargo on the special train found the long journey in the heat of summer a grueling experience.

The Countess' deadly disease bacteria had attacked in strength, reducing her rapidly to a semi-comatose condition from which she would rouse only for fresh doses of morphine and laudanum. She bore her suffering with a patient stoicism which, for Anastasia, who was doing everything in her power to alleviate her foster-mother's pain, was almost worse than her usual complaining.

At least while the Countess had the strength to find fault with the arrangements for her comfort, it showed that she was interested in putting up a fight for life. This new numb acceptance of her fate was so uncharacteristic that Anastasia was frightened. As the train chugged onward, only the thought that she might soon see Valerian again saved her from despair.

She counted the villages, the towns, the days, the hours, and finally the minutes left to travel. Whenever the Countess drifted into a drugged sleep, Anastasia stared out of the window and willed the train to make haste.

She wondered what to wear when she saw Valerian again. Thanks to the Countess' impeccable taste and her own slim, well-rounded figure, her wardrobe had been the envy of every lady in Cairo who had any pretensions to fashion. Too, she couldn't decide how to dress her hair and whether or not to paint her face. Her maid urged her to outline her eyes in the manner of Cairene women: "It makes you look older. Something different always catches the gentlemen's attention," she argued. But Anastasia thought the contrast between kohl-rimmed green eyes and fair hair was too striking for daytime. She didn't want any hint of vulgarity to mar Valerian's first impression.

Neither must he see any trace of the impetuous, unsophisticated schoolgirl he had left so abruptly in Siberia. She would be cool, elegant, poised—more cosmopolitan than any of those ladies of the Imperial Court she used to envy because Valerian so clearly admired them. During the years in Egypt, she had learned to hide her feelings and employ the kind of feminine tricks that could enslave a man . . . without committing herself. She resolved that she would never, ever again be foolish enough to throw her heart openly at Valerian's feet.

Nevertheless, as the train at last drew into St. Petersburg one stifling morning in July, a wild excitement gripped her—a primitive, nerve-tingling excitement neither cool nor cosmopolitan. After years of wandering she had come home again. In a moment she would feel her lover's arms around her . . .

Eagerly she scanned the crowded platform, searching the jostling throng for the tall, dark-haired figure whose proud bearing and military swagger made him a standout in any crowd. There were so many men in uniform!

"Where is he?" croaked the Countess, fully dressed and propped up on cushions. "Can you see him?"

"No," said Anastasia, searching frantically.

Gradually the noise and bustle died down and the throng dispersed. As it did Anastasia's hopes faded, too. Tears of disappointment trickled down her face and she drew a deep, shuddering breath.

"No one has come to meet us," she said at last.

"Impossible!" declared the Countess, struggling to rise. "Valya would have sent word if he couldn't come, or at least sent someone else."

Neither of them knew of the shots fired by a young Serb that had killed the Archduke Franz Ferdinand, heir to the Austro-Hungarian Empire. That assassination in far-off Sarajevo three weeks earlier had provoked such a flurry of diplomatic and military activity that Valerian had been obliged to hurry to his regiment which was on summer maneuvers. Russia, as protectress of Serbia, felt bound to support her small, reckless ally against the vengeful wrath of Austria. Already the Tsar's war-hungry generals and ministers were urging him to stand firm and reject Austria's demands for vengeance on the conspirators who had engineered the assassination.

Before leaving, Valerian had summoned his younger half-brother Petya from his medical school in Moscow, and asked him to complete the arrangements for their mother's homecoming. Even as she brushed away the disappointed tears, Anastasia noticed a familiar head and shoulders hurrying toward them, waving and calling as he approached.

"Mama! Here I am, late as usual. Welcome home—and welcome to you, Anastasia. How good to see you again! I'm sorry I wasn't here when you arrived. I meant to be waiting on the platform with bouquets of flowers to greet you, as Valerian told me to, but I stopped on the way to buy them, and then the car had a puncture and we got held up behind a crowd of strikers, all waving banners and blocking the road. And anyway, it's unheard of for trains to be on time..."

"Petya! My dearest boy," whispered the Countess. She put her thin hands on his shoulders as he stooped to kiss her, then held him at arm's length to gaze at his face before hugging him again. "My baby! How you've grown since we saw you last!"

"Surely you hadn't expected me to shrink?" he exclaimed, with a laughing glance at Anastasia. On his last visit to Cairo, three years before, he'd been all wrists and elbows. Now he was tall and handsome, the image of Kadya as a young man, with sleek dark hair and coal-black, laughing eyes.

His amusement faded as he took in his mother's altered appearance. "What's happened to your voice, Mama?" he asked.

"Just a touch of my old trouble, you know. I'm going to see a specialist about it—there's nothing to worry about." She had rallied her strength for the moment of homecoming, and she was determined to let nothing spoil the joy of reunion.

"Are you certain, Mama?" Petya asked.

"It's nothing serious," she insisted. "Please don't start fussing. I'm just a little tired after the journey, and longing to be home again. Give me your arm, Petya—and you, Anastasia. There, I can manage splendidly like that. Tell Mohammed to see that the crates are taken straight to the museum with my letter, and inform the curator that I shall call on him in the morning to discuss the way they're to be unpacked. Don't let him start until I get there. There: now we're ready to go. Where is the car, Petya, darling?"

"Over here, Mama." Between them they supported the Countess' tottering steps to the shiny black Delaunay-Belleville limousine, whose uniformed chauffeur was waiting in the blazing sunshine outside, enjoying the admiring glances of small boys and the drivers of humble, horse-drawn *izvoshchiki*, hoping for fares.

"There's no point in arguing with her, Petya," sighed Anastasia, when she and her stepbrother were alone at half past ten that night, sipping tea. The samovar hissed gently on its little spirit-stove. "I know she's sick, but she won't admit it. We've seen more doctors than I can count, and they've all said the same thing: "Give up smoking cigarettes immediately and you may live for a year or two." But Mama just laughs and calls them fools. 'How can I give up my only pleasure?' she says. And she's right: it *is* her only pleasure. She can hardly eat or drink and she doesn't seem to want to. Oh, Petya, it's nice to be able to share my worries with you! Papa just goes on pretending that everything's all right, though he must know as well as I do that—that..."

"She's dying," said Petya flatly. Frowning, he stared at the icon in its niche above the mantel, the small lamp flickering in the dark, warm shadows of the room. Faintly the sounds of Petersburg at night—rumbling wheels, faraway shouts and the laughter of late revelers—were borne in to them on the summer breeze. "What can we do? I've never seen anyone change so much."

"She hasn't really changed—not inside. She still thinks it's all just a passing inconvenience, and that the reason the doctors haven't done any good is because they're bad doctors. She won't acknowledge that they can't cure her because she's incurable. And she loathes any suggestion of fuss. She was even annoyed, at first, when the Empress insisted she must come home to consult Father Grigori—you know, the *starets* they call Rasputin?"

"I don't blame her," said Petya. "That charlatan won't please my mother at all."

"That's what she said. 'How dare Alexandra ask that dirty creature to make magic signs over *me*? I'm not one of her fawning Court ladies, who'll believe whatever she's told.' Later on, she began to think it was funny. 'I suppose I'll have to endure it out of loyalty to my Sovereign,' she said. 'But it will be a great temptation to expire as soon as he enters the room. *That* would shake poor Alexandra's faith.' But if you ask me," said Anastasia sadly, "I think that Father Grigori, may be our last hope, charlatan or not."

Petya looked at her strangely. "But haven't you heard?"

"Heard what?"

"Rasputin won't be performing any more miracles. It'll be a miracle if he survives at all," said Petya.

"Why? What's happened to him?"

"He is at death's door himself—and has been ever since he was stabbed in the belly by some half-crazed woman who claimed that he had seduced her. As if she was the only one! She followed him home to Tioumen and pulled a knife on him in the street, shouting out that she was killing the Anti-Christ. I heard all about it from a friend at medical school. He said that Rasputin's entrails spilled out on the pavement, and that it was only because he's as strong as a bull that he didn't die right there."

Anastasia's cheeks were paper-white. Rasputin had been her last, desperate hope, and the picture Petya painted was anything but reassuring.

"Hey!" said Petya in sudden alarm. He rushed to the sideboard and poured out some brandy. "I'm sorry, Stanya. I didn't mean to shock you. We see so many grisly sights in the course of our training that we forgot our manners. Here, drink this, it'll do you good."

Anastasia choked down the brandy, and a little color

returned to her face. Petya watched her closely, then nodded, reassured that she wasn't about to faint.

"That's better. Now, where was I? Yes, the 'holy devil' is in the hospital, where he'll probably be for a good long spell. And I have to tell you, Stanya, most people think it's good riddance."

"But maybe he could have cured Mama!"

Petya shook his dark head. "I doubt it. No one believes all those wonderful powers he's supposed to have. Because he helped the Tsarevitch Alexis several times, the Empress thinks he can do no wrong. Personally, I'm inclined to believe that he was lucky. Where a 'cure' took place, I think the worst was over before the holy man even arrived. Anyway, it's academic now. And I doubt if the Empress will have time to be interested in Ancient Egyptian relics, either, with both her son and her *starets* on the danger list, and with the threat of war staring us in the face."

"How can you be so heartless, Petya?" said Anastasia. "Don't you care at all whether poor Mama lives or dies?"

"Of course I care and I'm not being heartless either," said Petya, quite unruffled by the accusation.

Anastasia was again surprised by his new found maturity. Although he resembled his father physically, there was a suggestion of steel in his character which belonged more to the Countess than to the feckless Kadya.

He continued: "I'm trying to think constructively. What Mama needs is a good sanatorium, not a lot of magic and mysticism. And I know just the place down in the Crimea, not far from Livadia."

"How can we get her to go there?" said Anastasia.

"We'll pull out all the stops," said Petya cheerfully. "Between us, we should be able to convince her. But it's a pity Valerian isn't here. He can always persuade Mama to do what he wants—whenever he wants. Without him, we'll just have to do the best we can."

Anastasia went to bed late, comforted by Petya's sensible matter-of-factness. She had been alone with the problem too long to consider it rationally. That's why she'd begun to pin her hopes on miracles. Of course a sanatorium was the place where Mama might regain her strength, properly cared for by a well-trained staff. Tomorrow she would try to persuade her.

Tomorrow... Who knew what tomorrow might bring? News of Valerian, perhaps. His unexpected absence still cast a pall over her spirits, and the uncertainty of the future made her toss and turn restlessly in the hot, still bed.

Tired as she was, she couldn't sleep. Her head still hummed with the same fruitless tune: if only Valya were here; if only the train had arrived two days earlier; if only they hadn't lingered so long in Constantinople...

The bedroom was suffocating. Anastasia went to the open window and stepped out onto the balcony, leaning against its fretted woodwork, a pale, glimmering wraith in her loose white nightgown as she drank in the opalescent magic of the northern summer night. She noted the luminous gleam of the great silver river with its graceful span of bridges, and the silent mystery of the sleeping palaces along its banks...

Full darkness would never cloak St. Petersburg during the coming weeks. And like other city dwellers, the famous "White Nights" induced in Anastasia a strange restlessness—as if every moment of life was too precious to waste in sleeping even an hour. Instinctively, she knew that these last days of peace could never be recaptured. From what Petya had told her, she sensed that the world she knew was about to go up in flames.

Everything pointed to it. The brooding, oppressive heat that lay over the city was underscored by the sullen, silent groups of strikers, like those who had stared at the gleaming car with hate in their eyes as the chauffeur drove them home. Now there were more Cossacks than usual, warily patrolling the streets, and the few buses she'd seen were almost empty.

Anastasia shivered. More powerfully than ever in this atmosphere of impending doom, she longed for Valerian. If he were there, gloomy midnight fantasies such as these could never depress her spirit. Why had he been ordered away at the very moment of her homecoming...?

As she leaned on the rail half dreaming, she became aware of the dull, muffled *clop-clop* of horses' hoofs in the distance. Gradually the sound came closer. Then, through the night mists, came rank upon rank of mounted men, swaying in their saddles with fatigue, their eyes dark shadows in their pale faces. Like an army of ghosts, they looked neither to the right nor the left. But as they passed below her balcony, she heard a muttered command, and the column halted.

Suddenly conscious of her flimsy nightgown and the disordered hair streaming down her back, Anastasia shrank back against the balcony door. But although the smells of leather and horses' sweat rose to her nostrils, the men below were too tired to glance upward.

A single horseman detached himself from the front rank. Then the column moved forward again, ghostlike in the river mist. She watched until the last horse and rider had faded from sight, then stole back into her bedroom, shivering in spite of the night's humid warmth. Where had they come from, this regiment of shadows, riding so wearily through the darkness? Where were they going? She had recognized the splendid uniforms and handsome mounts of the Chevalier Gardes, but why were they returning to the capital when they should be at their summer quarters in Krassnoye? And who was the man who had stopped at this very house?

From the hallway below, she heard the muttering of a servant's voice. Then a man's long strides crossed the hall, his spurs jingling at every step. Without even waiting to snatch up her dressing-gown, Anastasia ran to the head of the stairs. A tall figure was standing alone in the great hallway, his back toward her as he unfastened the cloak from his shoulders. Her heart leapt up and then began to race. Was it—could it be . . .?

"Valerian!" she called, and he spun around on his heel. In no time he had crossed the hall. She pattered barefoot down the polished stairs, her nightgown billowing, her golden hair streaming loose down her back. He caught her in his arms and swung her off her feet.

"My darling! At last!"

He hugged her to his uniformed chest and his lips eagerly sought hers. Anastasia forgot all the cool, sophisticated things she had planned to say, and the elegant way she had meant to hold out her hand for him to kiss, in the manner of the Cairene ladies. Instead, she clung to his body, murmuring endearments and repeating his name over and over again. "Valerian! Oh, Valerian. It's been so long."

At first his kisses were gentle. Then, as his hands slipped under her thin nightgown and caressed the warm, voluptuous curves beneath, his lips grew more insistent. She swayed against him, drunk with happiness, aware once again of the passionate awakening of all her senses, vibrating now like tightly coiled springs, drawing her ever closer to him until at last they could fuse into a single being. The years of separation were wiped out as swiftly as if they had never been, and she felt again her body's hungry clamoring for total union with him, as she had that long-ago night in Irkutsk. The knowledge that his touch could arouse such a primitive response was at once a dream and a nightmare. Wildly happy, yet shaken by the intensity of her own feelings, she finally drew away from his encircling arms.

"My little Anastasia!" he said, laughing. "You haven't changed at all, and I'm so glad you haven't. I was afraid I'd find you dressed like a mannequin and smothered in Egyptian paint, like you were in that portrait Mama sent me last Christmas. You don't know how scared I was at the prospect! Instead, you come racing down to greet me in your nightgown . . . as you used to in the old days."

His warm, admiring gaze told her plainly that she was no longer a little girl in his eyes, but a desirable woman. Suddenly, Anastasia was keenly aware that she was standing in her filmy nightdress directly in front of the lamp; that the servant who had admitted Valerian might be watching from the shadows; and that the Countess would be appalled! This was not the way a sophisticated young lady should greet a handsome officer in the small hours of the morning.

She made a great effort to regain her self-possession. "If only you'd been at the station, you'd have seen me in all my finery. I wore it to show you just how much I *have* changed," she said lightly. "Where were you, Valya? All my effort was utterly wasted when you didn't show up."

He grinned. "You're just how I like you. Come and let me look at you."

She hurriedly backed away. "I—I'll get my wrap from upstairs. Mama's fast asleep already, but she'd be scandalized to see me like this. I was standing on my balcony when the Guards came riding past, and I wondered who would come here so late . . ."

"Would you hasten to kiss any soldier you saw in the hall?" he teased. He took his cloak from the chair where he'd dropped it and wrapped its thick folds around her. "There, now, you're decent enough. No need to run upstairs. I've got to talk to you, Stanya, and there isn't much time."

"Are you still in the same old hurry, Valya?"

It was as well that Anthony Mills wasn't present to envision the ruin of his hopes. Far from growing fat and flabby in the years since she'd seen him, Valerian looked more attractive than ever. There wasn't an ounce of spare flesh on his lean, muscular body, and his dark hair was as thick as she remembered, waving back from his forehead and curving onto his high cheekbones. But the mustache he'd worn had vanished, and the mouth thus revealed was downcast. In repose his face had a look of weariness, which she longed to banish by making him smile again.

Ruefully, he said, "I only wish I wasn't in such a hurry. My poor men have been riding all day and most of the night so I could get home in time to see you."

"What has happened?" she asked in quick alarm.

"The Guards Regiments have been ordered back to their barracks. At dawn we leave for the front. I had to see you before I left."

Anastasia caught her breath. "Not war... again?"

"We think so. There's a partial mobilization already. I should be spending the night in barracks myself, but I had to find out about Mama. I've heard all kinds of rumors from other people, but of course not a hint of anything wrong in her letters to me."

"She didn't want to alarm you," said Anastasia. Already the golden glow of reunion had turned to dust. "Petya thinks she should enter a sanatorium. She's failed a lot since Constantinople. She could hardly talk to Andrei when he came to see her tonight."

"I'll get Petya to speak to Dr. Botkin in the morning," said Valerian decisively. "She must have the best care available. How typical of my stepfather to do nothing until it's almost too late! My poor Anastasia, you've had all the responsibility for looking after her—it must have been hell on earth. Don't worry. We'll take charge of her now."

"But if you're leaving for the front...?"

"Petya will look after her. He's going to be the best doctor in Russia before very long. If a doctor can cure Mama, Petya will find him. But before I wake Mama, tell me all about you." His voice was deep and caressing, his face very near hers as he drew her down beside him on the window seat. You've grown very beautiful, Anastasia..."

"Do you still say that to every woman you meet?" She tried to speak lightly, but to her own ears the question sounded tense and over-anxious. He hadn't changed. Even to herself she dared not admit how much she had wanted him to. She mustn't let him know how much she still longed for his love. She must never give herself away again, although at his touch the old spell threatened to creep over her, crumbling the careful defenses she had built up over the long years.

Valerian was frowning. "So you remember that night?"

"How could I ever forget it?"

"What a fool I was," said Valerian, and there was a bitterness in his voice that she had never heard there before. Could this be Valerian speaking—fickle, carefree Valerian? "What an arrogant, ignorant fool to abuse your love and then try to indoctrinate you with my own cynical philosophy because I was too blind to recognize real love when I saw it. Well, I've been punished for it. You'll never trust me again, and who could blame you? All these years I've tried to get you out of my head, but, I couldn't. Now, when I've got a chance to tell you, it's too late."

"Too late?" She was bemused by what he was saying, overcoming all her defenses in spite of her resolution. Did he regret what he'd said to her that night? Is that what he meant? That he hadn't wanted to shoo her away from his bed like an importunate puppy? With an effort she controlled the trembling that threatened to overtake her, and asked cooly: "Why is it too late, Valya?"

"It's years too late, my sweet," he said wearily. "I've changed and so have you. If I'd had the courage to defy Mama then—to insist that I loved you, things might have been different. But now—" he shrugged—"it's too late. I'm off to the war, and you're going to marry some damned Englishman . . ."

"Who told you that?" Anastasia wondered if she was dreaming. Only in a dream would Valerian say that he loved her, and it was equally dreamlike that he should utter some nonsense about marrying an Englishman. It wasn't—it couldn't be—real, but Anastasia knew she must say nothing, admit nothing, do nothing that would banish the dream, or Valerian would disappear again, and all the sweet words she longed to hear would fade away into the misty night like the ghostly regiment seen from her balcony.

"Mama" he said. "Who else? Her last letter reported the news about you and Mr. Mills—such a brilliant young diplomat, such a suitable match for you, just what she'd always hoped for..."

"It's a lie, Valya," she said quietly. "Mama is too sick now to know the difference between lying and the truth. She's always tried to keep us apart. Don't you realize that? She only wants to marry me off because she's afraid that you and I might—might fall in love. That's why she's made me stay so long in Egypt, and never asked you to visit."

"I could have gone to Egypt any time I wanted."

"Yes, of course. But if you had, I would have been packed off to stay with the French consul's daughter, or sent to study ruins until you were safely out of the way."

They stared at one another, each filled with inexpressible longing. "Yet you don't seem to mind," said Valerian with a kind of wonder. "You've changed. You've grown up, of course, but it's more than that."

Because I'm not trying to smother you with my love?, she thought. I may have grown up, but I haven't stopped loving you. I know better than to tell you so, that's all. Ah, Valya darling, you don't realize how carefully I listened to the advice you gave me that long-ago night in Siberia. You showed me the way to your heart then; now you're surprised to find I know it.

As if following her thoughts, he said: "Have *you* ever been in love?"

She nodded. Why deny it? "Fire and ice—ecstasy and despair. Wasn't that how you described it?"

Valerian smiled. "Your memory is much too good... Yes, that's what I mean by love. Have you ever felt my kind of love?"

"Only once," said Anastasia sadly, "but it wasn't like that at all. Afterwards I was rather... discouraged. I decided I'd try not to fall in love again."

"Then this Englishman means nothing to you?" Valerian felt a momentary disappointment. It was proving too easy. A tug of war was no sport if your opponent walked toward you of her own free will. He wanted to wrestle Anastasia away from the Englishman by his superior powers of seduction, to reawaken her love with some extravagant gesture which would win her to him body and soul. Anastasia hesitated so long before replying that he began to wonder if she'd heard his question.

What did Anthony mean to her? she wondered. Certainly not

nothing: Clearly she remembered her own jealous anger against the woman in the Turkish bath, the woman whose company Anthony apparently preferred to hers. Yet she had never thought of him as a lover, for in her heart there was room for one man, one lover, only—Valerian.

"Well?" he said impatiently. "This Englishman, what does he mean to you? Do you love him?"

"N—no," she said in confusion. "But I like him a lot."

"Then I needn't lose hope yet."

"Hope?"

He took her face between his hands and looked deep into her green eyes. Then very slowly, very gently, he brushed her lips with his. "Don't pretend you don't understand me, little Stanya," he whispered. "It's taken me a long time to come to my senses, but I've recovered them at last. It's you I love, and you I want . . . Will you give me hope that when this war is over I'll find you waiting for me?"

How could she refuse him, when it was the very thing she had always wanted to hear him say? Yet, this time the fleeting touch of his lips had awakened no response in her heart. No joyful bells had rung. Her breath didn't quicken, her heart didn't palpitate. She felt drained of emotion, as indifferent as a fisherman who, having assembled every lure his skill can devise, finds the fish content to nibble at a bare hook.

"Will you promise?" whispered Valerian. His eyes were brilliant—glowing, admiring. Why should she suddenly feel resentful of their easy charm, the confidence they showed in their own power to seduce? Why did her thoughts turn to all the other women who had so willingly succumbed to Valerian's blandishments? Hadn't she always wanted to be one of them?

His arms tightened possessively around her. "Little Stanya, little darling, there'll be a new world waiting for us when the war is over—a wonderful new world where all men will be equal. I want you to help build it with me. What are another two or three years, after we've waited so long?"

Her throat felt dry. She knew he meant his words to be affectionate, but still she found it irritating to be addressed in diminutives, as if she was ten years old again. And this "wonderful new world" of his sounded more like a child's dream than the sober expectation of a grown man. Valerian had seen plenty of war, and what did it ever leave except blood and destruction, widows and orphans? Why should this war be different?

Valerian watched her approvingly. He liked women who were hard to get, and despised those who dropped like ripe plums into his arms. That was the trouble with Maria and most of his ex-mistresses. They were only too ready to give in to his demands, however outrageous. Anastasia's resistance fascinated and challenged him. Now he was determined to overcome any rivals for her love.

As she hesitated, he slid the gold signet ring with the snarling wolf's-head crest from his little finger.

"Do you remember this? Will you wear it again—for me this time—until I come home to claim you?"

Mesmerized, she stared at it, reliving old memories. "No," she said at last, "I can't."

"Please, darling. Please take it," he said urgently. "I want you to wear something of mine, something that will remind you of me when I'm far away, fighting for my country. That will bring me luck. It's only a small thing to ask..."

He imprisoned her hand and slipped the ring on her third finger, where it hung loosely.

"No, Valya," she said again. "I can't wear your ring. What if Mama should see it?"

"Then you don't love me after all?" he said, with such a look of hurt pride that she regretted her refusal.

"Of course I love you. I don't need to wear a ring to prove it, that's all. Please take it back..."

"Not till you swear you'll wait for me." He caught her to him passionately, stifling her protests, pressing her body against his while a heady triumph sang in his veins. He had done it! In a bare ten minutes he'd won her back, bound her to him, and banished that estimable Englishman to the loveless limbo Englishmen deserved to inhabit. Experimentally, he tried to slip his fingers beneath her cloak, but instantly her hand checked their advance.

"No, Valerian. Mama..."

A sudden sharp clatter on the marble floor made them both look up. It was the Countess' ebony cane, fallen from her hand as she stood, ashen-faced, her eyes blazing with fury, at the top of the stairs.

"Anastasia!" she croaked. "Have you lost your senses, girl? What is the meaning of this disgraceful behavior?"

Anastasia flinched before the cutting, scornful voice, which seemed to take her back instantly to the unhappy, insecure days of her childhood, when those cold gray eyes would condemn every detail of her appearance and deportment, while that acid tongue carefully pronounced sentence on her for each small misdemeanor: "You will have to be thrashed for such behavior, Anastasia. You must learn how a lady behaves." "Write out fifty verses from the Book of Ecclesiastes and let me see them tonight." "Go to your room at once, Anastasia, and tell Miss Stevens she is not to bring you any supper tonight."

Instinctively she drew closer to Valerian, who had protected her then and would protect her now, but the small gesture roused the Countess to fresh fury.

"Devil's spawn!" she went on in that cracked, painful whisper, and it was plain that the drugs she had taken to ease her pain had removed all the usual guards from her tongue. "Are you trying to steal my son's heart now, just because I swore he was the one man who should never succumb to your wiles? Can't you ever be satisfied, you Polish halfbreed? Have you learned nothing from my efforts to teach you manners? All these years I've given you the best of everything, just as if you were my own child, and this is how you repay me."

"Don't blame Anastasia, Mama," said Valerian, with the smile that always softened his mother's heart. "It's not her fault—it's mine. I was so glad to see her that I persuaded her to stay and talk to me..."

"Don't try to protect her, Valerian," broke in the Countess. "She's not worth it. I should have recognized that long ago. She's bad—as bad as her mother before her—and any child of hers will carry the same taint. I was a fool to believe I could beat the wildness out of her nature and make a lady of her. Instead, I should have dispatched her to the kitchens where she belongs. You can't tame a wildcat, but you can stop it from mixing its blood with your own, and that's what I'm going to do, whether you like it or not."

"Don't talk like that, Mama," said Valerian, and now the conciliatory note in his voice was replaced by a much firmer tone. "Come back to bed: you're overwrought. I promise you that things will look very different in the morning light."

"Leaving you to make love to that treacherous little slut?" sneered his mother. "Oh, no. She's going to bed before I do—and alone. Come here, Anastasia."

Reluctantly Anastasia moved toward the stairs, but Valerian's arm tightened about her shoulders and restrained her.

"I refuse to let you speak like that about the woman I love," he said boldly. "Anastasia is of age now and you have no further power over her. We are going to be married before my regiment leaves for Galicia and you can do nothing to stop us."

As she listened, the Countess swayed, then turned blazing eyes on her son. "No, no, no! You shall not marry. Any union between brother and sister is accursed in the eyes of God and the world—and you *are* brother and sister. I shall call on the Tsarina herself to prevent it. You shall never receive my blessing, or a single kopeck of my fortune. Consider that well before you defy me, my son."

Gently Anastasia detached herself from his encircling arm. She couldn't stand by and see him quarrel with his mother over her, risking his inheritance for her sake. "I must go now, Valya," she said in a low voice.

After a moment he nodded. "I'll see you in the morning. Don't worry—I'll look after you," he said softly, squeezing her hand in farewell.

"Bring me my stick, Anastasia," ordered the cracked voice above, and now there was a distinct note of triumph in it. The dogs had dared to defy her, but a crack of the whip had brought them to heel, just as it always did.

Slowly the girl mounted the wide stairs and handed over the dropped ebony cane. As she did so, the Countess raised it and struck at Anastasia's head with all her strength. The heavy stick missed by a hair's breadth, but the force of it swung the Countess off balance at the very top of the gleaming, polished stairs.

"Mama!" shouted Valerian and Anastasia in unison, but the warning came too late. The Countess staggered, clutched at the rail, missed her footing and sprawled headlong down the stairs, her body rolling and bouncing from step to step like an evil, overturned totem.

Valerian caught her as she reached the half-landing, but her head lolled halplessly as he lifted her and her eyes were closed.

"Wake up the servants! Get Petya! Call a doctor," he said

urgently to Anastasia, who bent over the limp figure in horror-struck disbelief. He listened intently for a moment, then nodded in relief. "She's breathing. We may save her."

The girl fled down the hall to awaken the servants. As she hastened away, Valerian heard a single word issue from his mother's bloodless lips:

"Accursed!"

Then her jaw dropped and her eyes rolled sightlessly up to the beautiful Italian plaster ceiling. And still the gasping, wheezing breath continued to force its way in and out of her lungs with a noise like that of a broken-winded horse who has galloped too far and too fast—and still her heart continued to beat...

Chapter Fifteen

Flames licked hungrily at the little mission hospital's thatched roof. Showers of sparks from a collapsing beam flew upward toward the cold, starlit sky, and Susanna, helpless, furious, tears streaming down her face, watched the wanton destruction of all she had striven to build in twelve long years.

"My notes!" she screamed, twisting and struggling in the Reverend Elias Armstrong's bony grip. In the lurid glare of the flames, her face had a wild, crazed look. For a moment Elias feared that the shock of seeing her life's work go up in the blaze had tipped her over the edge of sanity.

"No, Lassie, no!" he exclaimed, wrestling with her. "Dinna despair. We'll soon build it up for you again."

"Let me go," she wailed. "My notes—I may be able to save them." She would have darted into the blazing holocaust if Valentin, her dark-eyed son, hadn't caught at her other arm to restrain her.

"Mother, don't!" he cried. "You'll be burned up alive if you go in there. It's too late."

"Too late," she echoed dully, and suddenly the fight went out of her body.

"Come away now," urged Elias. "Yon bandits may turn their attention to the mission house next, though why in heaven's name they should want revenge on us, the Lord alone knows."

"Revenge for Yuan Chen's son," said Susanna, as she let the old man lead her away. She knew only too well what had provoked the attack on the hospital, and blamed herself bitterly. A week earlier, Yuan Chen, a local bandit chief, had brought his ailing baby son to the hospital and begged her to cure him of the demons who were causing him to waste away. He promised her a great sum of gold—all the money needed for building a new wing to the hospital—if the baby were healed. Tempted by this offer, Susanna broke her own rule never to accept hopeless cases, and agreed to do her best.

She kept her side of the bargain, but to no avail. The child died. When he heard of it, Yuan Chen flew into a murderous rage. Then he and his men had set fire to the foreign devils' temple where his son had died, destroying all the notes describing Susanna's experiments in Eastern medicine.

It was the final blow to her ambitions.

Later, when Elias spoke optimistically about rebuilding the hospital, she stared at him blankly, causing him to wonder again if her loss had temporarily affected her reason. He knew it was her fascination with the medical lore of the Orient, far more than a desire to save either souls or bodies, that had kept her so long in Manchuria. Now her book, which was to have been the distillation of all those years of labor, had been destroyed.

When she finally answered, however, it was with a kind of weary bitterness that was rational enough.

"What's the use, Elias? My work here is over. Tonight's disaster had made that much clear to me, at least. I should have listened to you and Martha and gone home long ago. I was a fool to believe that the East would ever allow an outsider to steal her secrets. She has mocked me—taken my youth, my strength and my dreams—and left me nothing."

She has certainly stolen your looks, poor bairn, thought Martha, eyeing her sadly. The thin, yellow-complexioned woman with rusty red hair and burning eyes set deep in their sockets, was a far cry from the bonny fresh-faced Scots lassie who had captivated that handsome young Russian officer these many years past.

"Nothing is left to me now," went on Susanna, "nothing except my son. The East shall not enslave him and drain out his life as she did mine. I shall take Valentin to Russia to claim his inheritance—as I should have done years ago."

"To Russia!" Valentin regarded his mother with narrowed eyes. Did she mean it, or was the opium speaking through her mouth as it so often did nowadays?

Martha nodded briskly, though the same thought had occurred to her. "Aye, it's right that the bairn should know his father," she agreed. "But it's no' a decision to take lightly, Susanna. Yon's a long and hard journey, and who knows what you may find at the end of it? You have your husband's address in St. Petersburg. You should write and warn him of your plans, or you may find you've traveled in search of a will-o'-the-wisp."

It was the voice of reason, but Susanna shook her head. She knew why Valerian had run away from her before; this time she meant to arrive on his doorstep unannounced and demand that he acknowledge his son. Over the years her own acquisitiveness had turned into a compulsion to provide for her son—the one person who truly belonged to her. Nothing but the best was good enough for Valentin, and she drove herself too hard trying to be father and mother, homemaker and provider rolled into one. She wanted him to become a doctor, and have all the secrets of Eastern medicine at his command—thanks to her experiments and notes. The mission hospital had been the symbol of her achievement, the notes her insurance for Valentin's future. Losing them both had brought her—as Elias had suspected—to the brink of madness. Now, in desperation, she caught at the memory of Valerian Radek's riches, his vast estates and uncountable treasures. Since fate had robbed her of all she possessed, there was only one course open to her: she must see that Count Radek provided for his son and heir. He might have married again . . . but remembering his resistance to the very idea of marriage, she doubted it. Once bitten, twice shy, she thought grimly, but he won't escape his obligations, for all that . . .

With a practiced gesture, turning her head aside, Susanna slipped a rolled gray pellet beneath her tongue and began to chew gently. The opium had never let her down yet; it would give her strength to surmount all her difficulties.

"Go to bed, Valentin," she ordered, as the thickness in her head dissolved and she began to drift into ecstasy. "Tomorrow we will plan our journey."

For four months the Countess hovered between life and death, while summer turned into a golden autumn and the mighty war machine of the Russian armed forces rolled into ponderous, irreversible motion. There could be no turning back now. Once the Tsar's tentative order for partial mobilization was made, the whole nation was committed to the struggle, a conflict which had begun as a purely local feud and now threatened to engulf the civilized world.

After a painful period of hesitation, Britain and France in their turn had honored their alliances with Russia and declared war on Germany. The assassin's bullets in far-off Sarajevo had set in motion a pendulum which swung in ever-widening circles and brought the flower of youth of a dozen proud armies into the grim orbit of war. Husbands, sons, lovers, fathers—all were hastening to defend their homelands. Trains hour after hour, carrying troops to the front rumbled out of St. Petersburg, leaving the platforms thronged with weeping women.

Every man she knew seemed to be in uniform, and every woman had enrolled for training as a nurse. But Anastasia could do nothing, chained as she was to the bedside of her dying stepmother.

Most of the time Olga was conscious, although since her fall she had lost the powers of speech and movement. Her expression never changed, but without warning her glittering, diamond-shaped eyes would flash open and fix on Anastasia a look of vindictive triumph. See, I am still alive, they seemed to say, and while I live you cannot marry my son. Every day that I cling to life, the war is carrying Valerian farther away from your clutches. And who knows how long it will take me to die?

Then an awful sense of her own helplessness would envelope Anastasia. Dispatched to East Galicia, where the fighting was fierce and casualties already heavy, Valerian had been one of the first to leave the capital. Petya, too, was serving with a hospital unit on the western front. Of Olga's family, only Andrei, with his crippled leg and bitter, twisted smile, had returned to live in the Countess' house on the Sadovskaya, overlooking the Catherine Canal. Andrei quickly filled it with his unwashed, down-at-heel friends. High-pitched voices argued politics into the small hours, while the smoke from countless cigarettes rose in a blue haze to obscure the Italian plaster ceilings of the enormous rooms.

Anastasia suspected that Andrei's friends were dangerous to know: anarchists and agitators who fermented strikes in the munitions factories, sleazy journalists preaching sedition against the Tsar and his Court. Most of them were young—in their late teens and early twenties, and came and went as the spirit, or their political commitments, moved them. These earnest, bearded boys and dowdy, bespectacled girls were far too deep in their own dreams of revolution to trouble with Andrei's half-sister, whom they dismissed—after a few futile efforts to recruit her to their own ranks—as a typical product of the Tsarist regime, frivolous, extravagant, and politically unaware. She was no threat to them and hardly worth converting.

Boris Miliukoff, however, thought differently.

The moment she first set eyes on Boris, Anastasia felt an instinctive fear of him. He was older than Andrei's other friends, a broad-faced, broad-shouldered bear of a man, only one generation removed from serfdom. He had a bear's long, mean snout above a thick, cruel mouth, and small, slanting eyes set high in his head. Unlike the peripatetic students, Boris lived—more or less permanently, though quite unofficially—in the Countess' town-house. Every day it was he who maneuvered Andrei's wheelchair from his bedroom to the study, and thence to the chauffeur-driven limousine. Together they drove to the office of the newspaper which published Andrei's weekly review of the political scene—a review which was suppressed by the Okhrana as invariably as it appeared on the streets. Most of the inflammatory statements which brought police trouble for Andrei had come from Boris' pen. Frequently, for safety's sake, the author of these tirades was obliged to remain at home while Andrei went alone to the office.

Anastasia grew to dread these days when Boris was in hiding. After spending hours alone in his room, muttering incoherently, guzzling vodka, Boris would emerge glassy-eyed and spoiling for a fight with anyone who dared to argue with him.

One hot and sultry August afternoon, he cornered Anastasia on the stairs as she left the Countess' room. Longing for a quiet hour, strolling in the park to clear her nostrils of the clinging sickroom smell, she wore only a thin summer walking-dress of pale green muslin, with a wide, floating skirt and close-fitting bodice, which she had opened at the neck against the heat. Avidly, Boris' small eyes fastened on the full curve of her breasts, outlined by the clinging material as she ran lightly down the polished stairs.

"Where are you going in such a hurry, Anastasia?" growled

Boris, stepping out of the shadows as she reached the half-landing.

Startled, she halted abruptly. When she realized who it was she shook her head and tried to brush past. "Oh, Boris! I didn't see you standing there. I'm not going anywhere..."

He continued to block her way, licking his thick, rubbery lips as he stared up and down at her body. Against her will, Anastasia could feel herself blushing beneath that bold, insolent scrutiny. "Then no doubt you'll allow me to go with you. After spending the whole day in this hothouse of Andrei's, I could do with some fresh air myself. We'll go as far as the park and I'll let you buy me a glass of vodka."

It was the last thing Anastasia wanted. "I think you've had more than enough vodka already," she said sharply. "Anyway, I don't have time to go to the park—Mama might wake up and need me." She attempted to pass him, but he reached out a hand and grabbed her wrist, pulling her so close to him that she smelled his bad breath.

"Let the old hellcat find someone else," he said thickly. "The house is crawling with servants; why should a pretty girl like you be chained to that bitch's bedside when you could be entertaining me?"

Anastasia had often asked herself the first part of the same question, but to hear it so crudely expressed by Boris, for whom she felt a mixture of contempt and revulsion, shocked her profoundly. "How dare you speak of Mama that way!" she said. "Let me go at once! I don't have time to waste here with you, and I advise you not to let Andrei hear you insult his mother.

"Andrei won't mind," sneered Boris. "Little Andrei depends on me. He can admit what an arrogant bitch like you won't acknowledge until you're made to. One day you'll crawl to lick my boots. Then you'll be sorry you didn't make a friend of Boris Ivanovitch when you had the chance."

Angry as she was with this presumptuous lout, who both frightened and repelled her, Anastasia had to suppress a smile. What an absurd idea! How could she, daughter of the proud Count Kharkov, ever stoop so low as to beg the son of a serf to be her friend?

As Boris read the amusement on her face, his grip tightened savagely. "You may laugh now, but you won't laugh when you see what the Revolution achieves," he said, his voice menacing.

Her temper rose, making her reckless. "Let me by, Boris," she said. "And if you ever dare to lay hands on me again I'll tell my brothers to drive you out of the house like the drunken dog you are. If you had even the smallest spark of patriotism, you wouldn't be talking about revolution when there's a war to be won. Why aren't you in uniform? Is your life too precious to risk for Russia's sake?"

Boris looked down at her, a mocking smile on his face. "I'm an only son, didn't you know? I'm exempt from the fighting. You won't find *me* feeding the cannons of the Tsar. I'm saving my ammunition for the day when his gives out."

"Your ammunition! I suppose that means those articles you're always scribbling. Do you consider that trash more important than driving the enemy from your homeland?"

"Listen to the Tsar's little propagandist!" he jeered. "So you read my lowly articles, do you? Come to my room and give me your opinion of what they preach. It should be most instructive!"

She tried to get away, but he twisted her arm behind her back and jerked it painfully upwards. "Don't make a fuss, Anastasia," he warned. "No one but the servants will hear you, and they know better than to cross my path. They've learned the hard way, damn them."

"There is Mama," said Anastasia, more boldly than she felt. Her heart sank as she realized that what he said was probably true. The servants were frightened of Boris; they would turn a deaf ear to any shouts for help she might give. Oh, why wasn't Valerian here to swoop down on the ugly brute and knock him senseless? Then, with a sudden gleam of hope she remembered that Andrei would be home at any minute. He wasn't overly fond of his stepsister, but he would hardly allow her to be mauled by the son of a serf in broad daylight. At all cost, she must not allow Boris to drag her upstairs to his room.

She twisted and squirmed in his grip, but her struggle was futile. Boris held her easily, and pressed her closely against his chest as he slipped his free hand suddenly through the open collar of her dress. She felt his thick, hot fingers against her breast. At the same moment, to her inexpressible relief, the great front door swung open and a shaft of dusty sunlight lit up the hall's dim interior, as the uniformed chauffeur wheeled Andrei's chair across the marble floor.

"Andrei, Andrei! Help me," she shouted. The two men below raised startled eyes toward the landing. But instead of letting her go, as she had expected, Boris bent his pockmarked face down to nuzzle at her neck, his fingers tightening painfully on her breast. She kicked at his shins, but he only laughed.

"Look who I've got here, Andrei!" he shouted triumphantly. "The ice maiden herself! You didn't expect me to win our bet so soon, did you?"

"You haven't won yet, my friend," said Andrei calmly, staring up at his struggling stepsister with no more emotion than he would have displayed at the sight of a fly's frenzied efforts to free itself from a spider's web. "You said you'd have her in bed before the month was out. You'll have to do a lot better before you see my money."

"I'll do better, don't worry," promised Boris. Despite her desperate struggles, he swung Anastasia off her feet. The shock of finding that, far from coming to her rescue, Andrei was actually encouraging Boris to ravish her, had taken her breath away.

"Igor—help me, stop him! Don't just stand there, help!" she pleaded, but the chauffeur merely shrugged and turned up his palms. He wasn't going to risk losing his job by interfering in his master's amusements.

Boris was now pulling her up the stairs toward his room, ignoring her struggles. In a moment of paralyzing fear, she tried to picture the next few minutes: the clothes stripped from her body by those brutal, powerful hands, her screams smothered as Boris drove deep into her shrinking, quivering flesh, laughing at her pain as Andrei listened, perhaps even watched, enjoying the degradation of the girl he had hated and envied ever since she had been adopted by his mother usurping the daughter-substitute that Andrei himself yearned to be.

Anastasia nearly gave up then, knowing that the coming ordeal was inevitable—and might even hurt less if she stopped fighting. But suddenly there was a commotion in the courtyard outside. Bells were ringing through the vastness of the hall, dogs were barking furiously, and then a deep voice thundered: "Open in the name of the Tsar!"

Boris froze. The blood drained from his pocked face, leaving it white. He dropped Anastasia's body and sprang for the top of the stairs. Lying there in a crumpled heap, thankful, she heard the rapid tattoo of his feet on the landing, heard him raise the window, heard his grunt as he leaped down to the flower bed below. A moment later, faintly and from far away, she heard the muffled splash of his body entering the warm, oily waters of the Catherine Canal.

I hope the brute drowns in it, she thought in outrage, sitting up at last and testing her body for bruises. The carved newel post against which Boris had flung her had left patterns in bas-relief on her buttocks and thighs, she was certain, and her arms were sore. Worse than her bodily aches, however, were the blow to her self-esteem, the knowledge of Andrei's treachery, and the deadly fear that when Boris returned—as he almost certainly would unless they caught and arrested him, he would do everything in his power to win the prizes of which the unexpected arrival of the Tsar's police had cheated him. Furthermore, she could expect no help from anyone, especially not her stepbrother.

She could understand Andrei's feeling; she herself was still burdened with a deep sense of guilt. She couldn't honestly blame him for hating her. Not only had she usurped his place in his mother's affection, she had also contributed to the cause of his crippled legs. After all, if she hadn't provoked him into climbing that crumbling tower, whose collapse had left him semiparalyzed, he might have grown up as handsome and open-hearted as his brother Petya, instead of becoming a warped, bitter misogamist as he was now.

In the days following Boris' attack, she avoided Andrei's company and that of his friends. She devoted herself to caring for the Countess during the daytime, and worrying about the future at night.

There was plenty in the future to worry her. What, she wondered during the long hours of pearly gloaming as August stretched into September, was she going to do when the Countess died? Olga was growing weaker with every passing day. The end could not be far off, and still Kadya had not come home. Anastasia had no money, no training for any profession, no talents beyond a certain gift for languages and a facility with paintbrush and canvas. She had nothing that would enable her to survive in this grim new world that was rapidly replacing the old carefree one.

She had the feeling that, for her at least, time was running out. Yet, paradoxically, every hot summer's day seemed endless in its monotony, mocking her forced inactivity.

Desperate though she felt for news of Valerian, as the first war reports began to filter through, it was to Anthony Mills that she poured out her worries and frustrations in a series of long letters. She knew from past experience that writing to Valerian was unlikely to bring any response from him. He hated writing letters. He lived in the moment, for the moment, and was always totally immersed in what he happened to be doing. Any recital of her anxieties would do nothing but bore and depress him since, at this distance, there was nothing he could do to help. Besides she thought, how do you tell any man—particularly your lover—that you're counting the minutes until his mother dies?

So she wrote to Anthony instead, and the mere act of putting her troubles down on paper served to lighten them.

You would hardly recognize St. Petersburg if you saw it now, she wrote him. *The buildings and bridges are the same, of course, but they are mostly deserted. Everywhere there is this strange sense of oppression and unease. I cannot go about much, since Mama requires constant attention, but already it seems to me that the food lines have doubled in length, and Petya tells me there are constant complaints of shortages at the front—both of arms and ammunition. He was home for a few days last week. He says that we are still advancing in Galicia, but doesn't seem confident that our armies will prove so successful when they come face to face with German soldiers, instead of the Austrians they have met so far.*

Anastasia hesitated, chewing her pen. That was as far as she dared go—not for fear of censorship but because it would surely be disloyal even to hint to an Englishman that Russia wasn't invincible. Anastasia had seen British soldiers in Egypt, and knew a number of British, French and German officers, and she couldn't help being aware that the simple, illiterate peasants now being drafted into the Russian Army were men of a very different caliber—no less brave, but slower, lacking in initiative and, above all, woefully short of modern weapons.

She sighed and abandoned the treacherous ground of military power. It was better to live from day to day, and not attempt to look too far into the future. Turkey and Egypt—and Anthony himself—seemed very remote now, yet she clung to the memory of them as the only brightness in a fast-gathering gloom.

I can hardly believe it is only five months since we stood together on the Balata Bridge and watched the ships at anchor in the Golden Horn." she wrote in November. *Do you remember it, too?*

Her lips curved in a smile as she relived that summer morning in Constantinople. The turquoise waves with their sparkling white crests had chopped and danced beneath the wide span of bridge, where the Sweet Waters of Europe met and mingled with the Sweet Waters of Asia. Anthony had watched the ships, she remembered. She herself had been more interested in the cluster of domes and pavilions, walls and towers, that formed the mass of the old Seraglio Palace, once the harem home of the beauties of the Sultan's Court. For centuries it had been the scene of intrigue and mystery, but that day it stood lifeless and empty beneath the wide blue arc of sky.

"Is it really true that the heir to the throne was always imprisoned up there, with no one but deaf-mutes for his attendants?" she had asked with a delicious shudder. "Halide told me that if one of his wives displeased the Sultan, he had her put in a sack and dropped into the Bosporus."

"I expect she knows all about it," agreed Anthony, smiling, but she thought his attention was elsewhere. He glanced briefly at the elaborate structure above them, then back at the slender arm of water called the Golden Horn. "Have you noticed how many ships—even warships—are docked here?" he said. "The German Naval Mission will soon be putting poor Admiral Limpus out of a job, it seems to me."

Anastasia shook her head. She hadn't wanted to discuss the prospects for the Turkish Navy during these few precious moments of freedom from her stepmother's constant surveillance. Halide Kisladi, a cheerful young matron whose aunt owned the house where the Countess sometimes stayed, had invited Anastasia to accompany her that morning to the Spice Bazaar near the bridge. It was while they were weaving their way briskly along the pavements crowded with load-carrying *hamals*, donkeys balancing heaps of charcoal faggots, bootblacks, coffee vendors, veiled women on their way to buy food, and their unveiled, liberated sisters teetering over the uneven footpaths in ridiculously high heels, that Anthony joined them and offered his escort on their expedition. Halide had vanished inside a dress shop selling the latest French fashions, while Anthony and Anastasia refreshed themselves with tiny cups of sweet, thick coffee and watched the world cross the Galata Bridge.

"Let's walk across the bridge and buy *simit* from that vendor on the Pera side," she suggested. "Halide will take an hour to buy her clothes, I know. Did you go to the dance at the Jockey Club last night?"

"Why weren't you there? You missed a good party. Bertha Balfour engaged a Hungarian gypsy band, and there were Spanish dancers as well, I believe, but unfortunately I had to leave early and wait on H.E., who is being plagued out of his mind with dispatches. Villancourt and Gilles de Speville had breakfast with me, though, and told me the fun went on until broad daylight..."

"Don't tell me!" Anastasia clapped her hands to her ears to shut out his voice. "You know how I wanted to go. Mama didn't feel well enough, though, and Halide wasn't invited, so I had to stay home after all. I had a beautiful new dress specially made for the party. I wish Mama would let me go around on my own. It's not as if I was sixteen years old any longer, and had never left Russia before..."

This was a recurring complaint. The Countess seemed to grow more possessive of her adopted daughter when they visited Turkey. Although Anastasia enjoyed much more freedom than most of her Turkish contemporaries, by English standards she was chaperoned with positively Victorian rigor.

"Never mind," said Anthony, who was still watching the slim silhouettes of the battleships at anchor in the Golden Horn. "Things will be different after the war. You may even sigh then for the old days, when you weren't allowed to go anywhere unchaperoned..."

"You told me there was going to be a war," she wrote, *"but I didn't really believe you. If I had, I don't think I would have*

returned to Russia to see it start. Now there seems to be no escape for me... What can I do but sit here and watch Mama fade away under my eyes...?"

Toward the middle of December, Olga slipped gently into a coma from which she couldn't be roused. Suddenly time, which had appeared to stand still, began to move with breakneck speed. Kadya arrived home in time for the funeral, and immediately altered all the simple, dignified arrangements which Andrei had organized in favor of a ceremony both ostentatious and vulgar.

How Mama would have hated this!, Anastasia reflected, as the slow-moving procession of chanting priests and acolytes bearing banners and wreaths moved into the church. In her open coffin amid bowers of heavy-scented lilies and other forced blossoms, surrounded by friends and relations as she had never been during her lifetime, Olga's long sallow face with its customary sardonic expression appeared to Anastasia to be waiting still for a chance to scold or find fault. When her turn came to go forward and kiss the waxen cheek of the woman who had dominated her life for so long, she felt a childish fear of seeing the sunken eyelids snap open once more as the Countess repeated her benediction: "Your union will be accursed. Do you understand me? Accursed."

Andrei saw his stepsister hesitate, and his thin lips curved in a smile that was a replica of his mother's. "Why are you frightened?" he whispered. "Are you afraid that Mama will haunt you for causing her death?"

Anastasia's cheeks flamed. She shot him an angry look and stepped boldly up to the coffin. Bending down, she brushed the air with her lips an inch away from that cold, unnaturally smooth flesh smelling of myrrh and the other unguents used by the Court embalmers. Why did it have to be Andrei, whose sharp, unsympathetic eyes monitored every move she made? Where was Petya? Why hadn't Valerian been able to be present to see his mother laid to rest? Yet, as she knelt and stood and murmured the responses during the remainder of that interminable ceremony, an excitement, a wild elation, grew inside her body until she could hardly stop herself from shouting out loud.

She was free! Her stepmother's death had released her from

the silken bondage she had endured ever since Vanya had brought her to Kharkov when she was a child. The last obstacle had miraculously vanished! Now there was nothing to prevent her from marrying Valerian. Her father might object, but who cared about Kadya? Valerian was bound to him neither by affection nor financial dependence, as he had been to his mother, and Kadya's disapproval would probably make Valya all the more determined to carry Anastasia away from all contact with Count Kharkov's dissolute household and friends. If only Valerian were here, she thought. The heady taste of freedom was in her heart, and it was hard to behave with the solemnity and decorum which the funeral demanded.

At last it was over, and the carriage drove them home to the great house on the Sadovskaya. Scarcely had Kadya flung off his heavy fur coat when the butler was at his side, holding a salver toward him with trembling hands. At the sight of the envelope Anastasia's heart skipped a beat.

"A telegram," said Kadya, frowning. "Why is it addressed to the Countess? Who on earth—?" He ripped it open, then handed the message to Anastasia without saying another word. It was from Colonel Gagarin, an old friend of the Countess now second-in-command to General Samsonov in East Galicia. The message was stark:

> Deeply regret to inform your son missing since last night's attack on Podgaytsy stop making every effort to ascertain his whereabouts stop will keep you informed
>
> Gagarin

Valerian was missing in action! Anastasia felt cold with horror. Her knees buckled, and she sank into the nearest chair, shaking. Surely it wasn't possible! Her mind refused to accept the possibility that God could be so cruel. How could He snatch Valerian away at the very moment when her dreams had come true and she was free to marry him.

"No," she murmured. "No, no, no!"

Kadya took the telegram from her trembling hand and briskly patted her shoulder. His face wore a strange expression: with a shock she identified it as relief. "Now then, my pet—pull yourself together" he said. "Don't believe that fool Gagarin. Ten to one he doesn't know what he's talking about. Night attacks are always misleading when it comes to counting your casualties. He was afraid that his daughter was going to faint. She looked alarmingly pale. He called for a maid to attend her. "Missing in action doesn't mean dead, you know," he went on reassuringly. "Besides, all the Radeks have nine lives, just like cats. Trust old Gagarin to scare my poor wife to death. Of course he doesn't yet realize that Olga's beyond scaring now, God rest her soul."

He smiled reassuringly at his daughter and she stared back at him, her green eyes enormous in her dead-white face. "The general must be wrong," she murmured mechanically. "Valerian can't be missing. I would have known if anything had happened to him."

Kadya offered her his hipflask. In spite of his long trip home and the interminable ceremony, he looked as fresh and carefree as if he had just awakened from a good night's sleep. His neatly parted dark hair shone like patent leather; his skin was clear and his eyes were bright. It was difficult to realize that he was husband to the prematurely aged and wrinkled woman whose corpse they had just laid to rest. He seemed to belong to another generation, another world, thought Anastasia, not for the first time. How unfair it was that Kadya, who thought of no one's pleasure but his own and had never done a day's work in his life, should enjoy perfect health and the best of luck in everything he did. Whereas Olga, who had tried so hard to be virtuous herself and instill virtue into others, had died from bad health and ended her days without even the comfort of a grieving husband at her deathbed.

Already Kadya appeared to have put his wife out of his thoughts, closing his mind to her memory as he might have closed the door behind a departing guest. She was gone, finished, of no further use to him, and now he was busy with plans for the future.

"We'll go back to Alexandria when we get things here settled," he chatted, trying to coax Anastasia out of the apathy that had gripped her the moment she read the telegram. "It won't take long. I'll send for the lawyers and stewards tomorrow morning and we'll get everything laid out and see where we stand. The sooner we leave the better. Petersburg is no place to be in wartime, I can see that already. There won't be much in the way of entertainment here for a while."

He grinned. "Of course, that suits the Empress. She hates to see people enjoying themselves. She's even worse than poor Olga. Why, she won't even let her pretty daughters go about in Society to parties and balls. She'll have a pack of old maids on her hands if she doesn't watch out. Poor Nicky is completely under her thumb . . . So we'll take ourselves off to Egypt in a few days' time—and no regrets. Andrei can keep an eye on the house while we're gone and the war will probably be over very soon, anyway."

"You may be going, Papa," Anastasia said in a dazed, faraway voice, "but I'm not going with you. My place is here in Russia. I don't want to leave before—" Her voice cracked, and she found herself struggling with tears.

"Before what?" said Kadya, his smile fading.

"Before we find out what's happened to Valya . . ."

"Why should that matter to you? He's only your stepbrother, when all is said and done. I don't want to leave you behind merely because your stepbrother is reported missing. It would be a great inconvenience to me not to have you as hostess at the big reception we're planning for Easter . . ."

Could she have heard him correctly? Anastasia looked at her father and saw with astonishment that he was serious. He regarded a stepson missing in action as a minor inconvenience which should never interfere with his plans for pleasure—parties, receptions, races, moonlight picnics by the pyramids . . . The fact that Valerian might be mutilated or even dead meant nothing at all to him.

"How can you say such a thing?" She tried hard to control her voice but found it rising. "How can you imagine that a reception is important when Valya may be wounded or—or dead?"

Kadya frowned. "I told you, I don't think he's dead. Anyway, try to be reasonable. How will your presence in Russia help if he is? Not at all. You'll be nothing but a nuisance if you moon about here, when your duty clearly lies in taking your poor Mama's place in Egypt. Have you no gratitude, Anastasia? After all, we've cared for you all your life."

"Not *all* my life," said Anastasia, a mutinous light in her eyes.

Kadya paid no attention. "How can I manage without a

hostess to help me in my work?" he demanded. "Have you considered that? Has that aspect of the situation entered your selfish head?"

"I'm sure that Madame Tabbouleh would be only too pleased to lend you her assistance," said Anastasia.

Kadya was not amused. "Don't be impertinent. I've been much too indulgent with you—indeed, all of us have. And if you imagine that you're at liberty now to exercise your wit at my expense, you're very much mistaken. Madame Tabbouleh is a charming and delightful person, but it would be quite inappropriate for her to act as hostess for the Russian consul. That is a duty which you must now undertake."

"I'm afraid that will be impossible, Papa," said Anastasia, whose obstinance was equal to his own. "I've decided that I'm going to remain here and train to be a Red Cross nurse. Don't try to stop me. I'm grown up now. I can make my own decisions."

"Then you'll make them without a kopeck from me," said Kadya, and her heart sank. He couldn't be so cruel as to cut off her small allowance.

But this was precisely what Kadya intended to do. "Not a kopeck," he repeated with satisfaction. "What's more, you won't be able to touch the money your mother left you either, unless you do as I say. We discussed the terms of her will before she left Egypt. For the time being, I have complete control over your legacy."

"Complete control?" echoed Anastasia in dismay. "I don't believe you."

Kadya's eyebrows rose. "Would you prefer to hear it from a lawyer?" he said. "Until you marry, you'll be dependent on me for money—just as you've always been, although your expenses will be met from your mother's estate instead of from mine."

Although she still didn't entirely believe him, she heard the magic words: *until you marry.*

"Then I'll marry as soon as I find a man who sees the advantage of Mama's legacy," she told him defiantly. "Do I have to submit my prospective husband for your approval, Papa, or may I marry whom I wish to?"

Kadya shrugged and lit a cigarette. "Choose whom you like," he said, "—except Valerian, of course, although there's little danger now of that. But I warn you, if you insist on staying in Petersburg, you'll be living entirely on Andrei's charity. We'll have to find out how *he* feels about feeding an extra mouth during the austere months ahead. There are shortages enough already. A country at war can't afford the luxuries it takes for granted in peacetime, you know. Before long, all Petersburg will be living on *kasha* gruel.

"Come now, Anastasia," he continued, trying to be diplomatic. "You've had a tiring day and a terrible shock. Don't make your decisions now. Things will look better in the morning. I know you're fond of Valya—all of us are. But don't let this bad news ruin your life. What future is there for you here, alone in this barracks of a house with only Andrei and his friends for company? They're not your friends, you know it as well as I do. You're not interested in politics."

He gave a short bark of laughter. "Andrei! I've warned him over and over again that he's playing with fire. Sooner or later the Tsar's police will clamp down on his clandestine activities, and then exile to Siberia will be the best poor Andrei can hope for. He's my son, all right. He doesn't listen to me any more than I listened to my own father; but if Andrei is arrested, what will happen to you?"

She thought chillingly of Boris. If Andrei was arrested, put in prison or exiled to Siberia, she'd be at the complete mercy of Boris. Was there no one else she could turn to? What of the uncles, aunts, cousins, and friends who used to throng to Kadya's parties in the old days? Surely there was someone among them who'd agree to feed and shelter her while she trained at a hospital? Then she realized how the Countess had allowed friendships and family ties to lapse. Anastasia could see no alternative to remaining in the same house with Andrei—and Boris.

Unless . . .

Uncertainly, she said feeling her way, "I could move to Valerian's house. Somebody ought to look after it until—until he comes back."

"Valerian left his steward in charge, as you very well know," said Kadya. "He won't want you interfering." He blew a smoke ring at the ceiling.

She hated her father's air of superiority, his refusal to take her seriously. Anastasia lost all caution. "He would so! He's going to marry me."

"Marry you!" Kadya's laughter was like a whip. "My dear

girl, don't tell me you've fallen for the oldest trick in the world? Like mother, like daughter . . . Valerian will promise anything to get what he wants—any man will. By now, you should have too much sense to believe him. Valerian can't marry you—any more than I could marry your mother."

"Why couldn't you marry my mother?" she demanded, and the intensity of her voice made Kadya's smile fade. "Why do you say, 'Like mother, like daughter'? *Who am I?*"

Kadya remained silent.

"Tell me, Papa," she pleaded. "You promised you'd tell me sometime, but you never have. I have a right to know."

"A right to know? You sound like one of those insufferable Americans. You have no rights, my dear. Your mother and all the rest of her vicious, treacherous breed are dead and gone. What's the point in opening old wounds and raking up ancient history?"

"But can't you see?" she said desperately. "I'm part of that ancient history. I've got to know about my family. You're good at closing your mind to things you don't care to remember, Papa, but this time it's my right to know the truth about my mother—and you. Why couldn't you marry her?"

"Because I was already married, of course," said Kadya smoothly.

"Was that the only reason?"

"Yes. No. You have no right to pester me with such questions at the end of a long, tiring day."

Anastasia summoned a servant, and asked him to bring a bottle of cognac. She sensed that her father was weakening. "Very well, Papa," she said coldly, "if you won't tell me I'll find out some other way. Anthony Mills has friends who can look up the Polish records and find out what became of the whole Galzinski family."

Kadya stared at his daughter's white, determined face. She wasn't going to give up. Perhaps it was better, after all, that she hear the story from him . . .

"Tell me now, Papa," she begged. "Tell me!"

His eyes seemed to turn inward, remembering the past, and that far-off summer in a vanished century. Clearly, a single image metamorphosed in the jumble of his memories: the white, shocked face of Frau Sturmer as she stared at the two bodies lying naked in the sun beside the mountain stream.

"It was all the fault of the governess," he said. "If she hadn't fallen asleep, it would never have happened. *You* would never have happened, Anastasia."

He drained his glass. Silently she refilled it.

"I suppose in a way that Miesko was to blame as well," he continued. "And your grandmother, Princess Galzinski, who could freeze a man with a single look, and of course, Colonel Solokov..."

"But not you, Papa...?"

"Certainly not. I was their victim. I was too young, and far too much in love, to see where it was leading. If you'll stop interrupting, I'll tell you the whole story. Then you can judge for yourself. It began in the guardroom at Casimirvek, a small town near Lvov, way back then..."

Chapter Sixteen

"We were playing cards in the guardroom when I saw her first," said Kadya. "I was bored stiff. We had been confined to barracks because of a riot in town and all leaves were canceled. We had hanged half a dozen rebels. The rebels were giving us a lot of trouble, as I remember...

"Anyway, I was sitting there facing the window overlooking the courtyard when the door of the Galzinski Palace opened and Princess Tamara came running out. She never walked anywhere. She always seemed to be running or skipping, with poor old Frau Sturmer bustling along behind, trying to keep up. God, she was lovely! I remember... she was wearing white furs."

Across the gulf of years he saw once again the slim figure flying down the snow-covered steps. Her hood had slipped back and sunlight glinted on her golden hair. Her long, slightly tilted green eyes glanced up at the guardroom window and he was certain she smiled at him. As she did so, the brightly painted *troika*, a sleigh with gilded runners drawn by three chestnut horses harnessed abreast, whirled into the square, bells tinkling and manes flying. It pulled up with a flourish in front of the palace steps. Almost before it stopped the girl had swung herself aboard, visibly impatient as the coachman heaped furs over her until only her laughing face could be seen above a cocoon of rugs.

Then the whip cracked and the horses plunged forward.

"I threw down my cards and prepared to follow," said Kadya. "They shouted at me, telling me to come back, but I knew that the general had ridden into Lvov and wouldn't know the difference, and I didn't give a damn about anyone else. I wasn't going to miss this chance of catching Princess Tamara alone, without her governess *or* her mother. She was just like a snow tigress, the old Princess. She could freeze your blood with one of her icy stares. Even Solokov was careful not to offend her.

"I took Caspar from the stable and galloped after the *troika*, keeping my distance at first, of course. I didn't think she'd be going far that time of day. I guessed she might be going to see her aunt, Baroness Blixheim, who lived at the edge of the forest. But the sleigh went straight past the Blixheim castle and into the woods.

"That puzzled me, I can tell you. I wondered if I should give up and return to the barracks. It was against orders for Russian officers to ride out of town unaccompanied. There was a lot of support for Miesko in those parts and he had a dozen different hideouts in the forest. I didn't want to blunder into one of them. Then I thought, What kind of game is that dumb ox of a coachman playing?

He ought to know better than to take the Princess into the forest so late in the day. It'll be dark in a couple of hours, I thought. What if he loses his way in a snowstorm? What if he meets a gang of wolves? I'd better catch up and order him to take the Princess home.

"The trouble was, he knew the forest roads better than I did, and he had a good start. Pretty soon, all I could do was follow his tracks in the snow.

"We came to a frozen river. The way across was marked by a line of great blocks of ice, two meters high or more, spaced out from bank to bank. I wondered who had taken the trouble to put them there because it must have been quite a job. I rode up close to the first pillar and got a terrible shock . . . Miesko was a vicious devil, and inside each block of ice was the body of a Russian soldier he'd captured. They were *our* soldiers. It must have taken them several hours to die. They'd been trussed up like chickens as water was poured over them, again and again. When they were frozen solid, he had them propped upright on the ice as a warning to us. It was his idea of a joke. One of them was my own brother-in-law, poor Constantin Feodorovitch, twin to your foster-mother. He had been missing for weeks."

Kadya poured himself more brandy. Anastasia sat as if she, too, were encased in ice. Mama's twin brother, murdered by the Poles! No wonder she had hated them.

"I knew I should report what I'd seen," Kadya went on, "but first I'd have to stop the troika. That fool of a coachman was heading straight for trouble, if I was any judge. I rode after them for all I was worth. When I was close enough to shout, the coachman whipped up his horses and drove as if the devil himself was pursuing. I was certain the troika would overturn.

"We reached a clearing where I gained on them and nearly caught up. Suddenly the coachman pulled up his haunches. Then he jumped out, the cowardly dog, and ran into the trees, leaving his young mistress to face the dangers of the forest alone."

"Leaving her?" Anastasia was startled from her trance.

"I was shocked, too. I rode up beside the troika to tell the Princess she had nothing to fear, that I would escort her home..."

From her nest in the pile of white rugs, the emerald eyes of Princess Tamara had blazed at him, he remembered, like the eyes of an angry kitten. "Fool," she had hissed. "Why have you followed us? Don't you know that it's certain death to venture so deep in the forest? Ride back to your barracks as fast as you can, or you'll pay for your boldness with your life. Go!"

"I was surprised, I don't mind admitting," continued Kadya. "I thought she had taken leave of her senses. I introduced myself and said I was glad to be of service to her, that I'd be happy to escort her back to Casimirvek, and all the time she was glancing over her shoulder into the forest. She wouldn't even listen to what I was saying. She cut me short and told me *I* was the one in danger!

"I said, 'My dear Princess, I'm a Russian officer. I'm not scared of wolves. I'm not going to ride away and leave you stranded by your fool coachman. Allow me to drive you home.' I meant to tie Caspar behind the troika and take the reins—and possibly her hand as well—but she wouldn't let me. She called me a fool—me!—and said she had nothing to fear, but that if I persisted Miesko's men would kill me—as they'd killed those poor Russian prisoners out on the river. That gave me a shock, I can tell you.

"'Why are you certain they won't harm you, Princess?' I asked. She gave me an odd kind of look, as if she didn't want to tell me but knew I wouldn't leave till I had the answer.

"'Why?' I asked again.

"'Because Miesko is my uncle,' she whispered. And then, of course, I saw it all. She was acting as the rebels' messenger. They were using little Princess Tamara as their go-between, to carry information and food between Miesko's hideout in the forest and his supporters in Casimirvek. Obviously old Princess Galzinski, Tamara's mother, was in it up to her aristocratic neck. But the daughter was different. I could tell—even then—that her heart wasn't really in it. I knew from the way she spoke of those poor frozen prisoners. Now she was urging me to save myself instead of allowing her uncle's men to catch me, too. I knew I hadn't much time to spare, but I bent down and kissed her little gloved hand, and saw her blush...

" 'Go away! Go quickly,' she begged, pulling her hand away. And this time I obeyed her. Men were running toward us already, stumbling through the snowdrifts like a lot of clumsy bears. I heard one rifle shot, and knew it was time to go...

"'*À bientôt*, my snow princess,' I said, and she smiled. Then I caught Caspar up short by the head and charged through the circle of rebels closing in on us, sending a couple of them sprawling before they could fire.

"When I got back to the barracks I made my report at once. Later on that night Colonel Solokov had a long talk with me..."

Kadya shifted in his chair. In the lamplight his face looked younger, more animated, his jawline clearcut, and the slight puffiness beneath his eyes invisible now as he relived a part of his youth. Anastasia sensed that he was tailoring his story to show himself in the most advantageous light. How much he had been to blame for what followed, she must judge for herself.

"The very next day we had an invitation from Princess Galzinski," continued Kadya. "It was full of the usual stuff: regreting the recent events which had led to an estrangement between our peoples; suggesting that the leaders of the two communities be the first to reestablish amicable relations; and an invitation to Colonel Solokov to bring some of his young officers to a *soirée musicale* in honor of her daughter's birthday...

"Of course Solokov was delighted to accept. He was a good chess player as well as a soldier, and he thought the old hellcat was playing straight into his hands. He gave us a lot of instructions on how to behave—Polish men are very jealous—but I didn't bother to listen. I'd cut my teeth at the Imperial

Court, and I didn't need advice on etiquette from Solokov, even if he was my Colonel. Besides, he'd already told me where *my* duty lay: I'd been detailed to bring a little glamour and pleasure into the life of Princess Tamara—and find out all she knew about her Uncle Miesko's activities at the same time. If I enjoyed myself in the process, so much the better."

"You were *ordered* to make love to my mother?" cried Anastasia, unable to contain herself. "How could you agree to such a suggestion? To discover her secrets . . .?"

"Don't be absurd," snapped Kadya. "You don't understand at all. In those days a well-bred Polish girl was chaperoned every minute—or should have been. There was no question of seduction—at least there wouldn't have been if her duenna had been conscientious. That's why the whole thing was Frau Sturmer's fault. I was young, hotheaded, far from home. Your mother, Princess Tamara, was wild, headstrong, and passionate . . . One summer day when we went to pick wild strawberries by a mountain stream, Frau Sturmer drank too much wine and fell asleep. What do you expect?" He shrugged. "She was entirely to blame for what happened."

"And—and afterwards?" Anastasia's voice shook from her effort to speak calmly, dispassionately. If she betrayed her indignation now, her father would never finish his story. And she must know the ending . . . she must. She could imagine the scene by the mountain stream all too clearly: her father's flushed face; his complete self-absorption as he satisfied his lust; the wild young Polish girl suddenly—brutally—tamed . . .

"Afterwards that nest of treacherous vipers did their level best to kill me! Tamara either told her mother or—more likely—Princess Galzinski woke up to the fact that Frau Sturmer had neglected her duty. The next time I saw Tamara she told me that the old hag had been dismissed, packed off home to Berlin without a word of farewell. I didn't think much of it at the time—German governesses were everywhere in those days—but later I saw what it might mean.

"Anyway, there we were, Tamara and I, going off for a picnic at the cottage in the woods, with only a kitchen maid to act as chaperone. Before we left the palace, Tamara told me her brother, young Stepan, had warned her not to go to that part of the woods . . ."

"'Why?' she asked him.

He told her he'd be hunting bears and it might be dangerous. Bears! Now I ask you! Tamara told me that she'd laughed at him, of course. Nobody hunted bears in June. She said he probably had a rendezvous there, and didn't want our company, but I had another idea. I sent Vanya, my orderly, back to the barracks with a message for Colonel Solokov, telling him just where we were going. Then we set out.

"It seemed a long drive to the forester's hut. The weather was humid, thundery, and the flies were terrible. Tamara was wearing a veil and she was very quiet—not her usual self at all."

Kadya paused, looking uncertain and puzzled. "Did she know what they planned to do to me? I've often wondered. Sometimes I think she must have, and sometimes I'm not so sure. If she knew, why did she warn me? If she didn't, why did her mother allow her to drive into the ambush at my side? Even a cold-blooded bitch like Princess Galzinski would hardly do that to her daughter.

"I had a sword, but that wasn't much use, and I can tell you I was glad to hear the sound of hoofs coming up behind us. Solokov had received my message and turned out his cavalry. Tamara didn't seem to hear them. She was looking ahead, playing with the ring I'd given her . . . I think she knew—but you can never trust a Pole, especially a woman. We had reached a narrow place in the road, where the trees grew close on either side, when suddenly they rode out and surrounded us. Old Prince Marek, Tamara's father, was there—the crazy fool—and her brother Stepan. Best of all there was the devil Miesko himself, come to join in the fun.

"I was ready for them, though. I knew I'd have to delay them a minute or two to give Solokov time to catch up, so I grabbed Tamara around the waist and held her against my chest. Then I dared them to shoot at me.

"Miesko tried to pull us both out of the carriage—I can still see that wolfish grin on his face. While we were struggling, the cavalry galloped up, and old Prince Marek got a ball through the head. I let go of Tamara, and the next thing I knew she was scrambling onto her brother's horse, clinging for dear life as they galloped away. She left me to fight it out alone. I'm sure she'd been expecting the ambush and knew just what to do. She was no more than another treacherous Pole, like all the rest of them, leading me into the trap her uncle had prepared. I didn't know then that it was the last time I'd see her..."

"But how...?Why...?"

"Solokov had the last laugh," said Kadya resentfully. "He didn't want me attached to his staff in the first place, and now he saw a chance to get rid of me. I told you he was a chess player. He should have been grateful, but life isn't like that—as you'll learn to your cost one day. I'd helped him capture the leader of the rebels and clear out a whole hornets' nest at considerable risk to myself, but did he recognize the fact? Never! He ordered me back to Petersburg. Not a word of thanks, no recognition whatsoever of outstanding gallantry and devotion to duty. I was simply ordered to report to headquarters without delay. He even had the impudence to ask me to convey his warmest regards to my wife!" Kadya was still fuming with indignation.

"What happened to my mother?"

"I told you. I never saw her again," said Kadya brusquely. "I had thought of bringing her to Petersburg with me, finding her a little house, perhaps, where I could be with her. You're old enough now to understand these things. But after the ambush I knew it would never work. She was too wild—too untamed. I could never trust her again. Naturally, I did my best for her. I left my orderly, old Vanya, with instructions to keep an eye on her till things settled down. Solokov's men sacked the Galzinski Palace. I believe your grandmother, Princess Galzinski, blew her own brains out, but that happened after I left. The servants looked after Tamara until her nurse, an old woman with her wits very much about her, took her away to live in Lvov. My orderly went with them."

The candles were guttering low in their sconces and the brandy bottle was nearly empty. Kadya poured the last of the brandy into his snifter and said, "And you arrived in Russia, looking like a scarecrow, that was the last I knew of your mother. Well, now you have the full story. Now you can understand why I don't feel in the least responsible for the downfall of the Galzinski family. My conscience is clear: I was only doing my duty..."

Anastasia regarded her father with silent wonder. He meant it. He really believed what he said. Her father's capacity for self-deception was complete: in his own opinion, he had acted according to the strictest rules of patriotism, chivalry, and honor throughout his sojourn in Poland.

Suddenly she could no longer bear his smug self-satisfaction.

"You're wrong," she said. "It *was* your fault, Papa. I see that even if you don't. So much suffering, and it all goes back to you. Why did you have to make love to that poor girl? Why can't you admit that you seduced her because you wanted to, and for no other reason? Why did you tell me she was mad?"

"All Poles are mad," Kadya assured her blandly.

"They aren't—you know that as well as I do. If my mother went mad, you were to blame. No wonder her family tried to kill you—I wish they had. And then you ran away; leaving her to face the uncertain future alone. Now I can understand why she hated you..."

She had gone too far. Kadya raised pained and uncomprehending eyebrows. "That will do," he said. "Be silent at once, Anastasia. Your behavior is most unreasonable. First you pester me for an account of your origins, then, when I comply with your request—against my better judgment—you bombard me with hysterical accusations. I know you're upset and that you've had a trying day, and I've made every possible allowance for your behavior, but I refuse to put up with your censure. Don't you realize how fortunate you are? You've been brought up in the lap of luxury, and enjoyed every advantage. But that doesn't give you the right to bite the hand that feeds you."

It was useless to argue with him. Kadya was capable of seeing one point of view only—his own. From that lofty vantage point his actions were always above reproach. And at least his recital had laid one ghost for Anastasia: it was plain that her mother had not been mad.

"Well?" Kadya observed her closely. "Are you prepared to go with me to Egypt?"

Egypt... Into her mind, unbidden, came a picture of the moonlit temple in the secret valley, timelessly peaceful, a refuge far removed from the grim reality of wartime Petrograd. Without Valerian, Russia seemed suddenly, a bleak and hopeless place. She couldn't stay there alone. She would go back to Egypt and carry on the work in the temple—the work that Anthony and her foster-mother had been forced to leave unfinished.

Slowly she nodded. "Yes, Papa. I will go with you," she said.

On the day before their departure, when all the Countess' furniture and valuables had been stored for the duration of the war, Anastasia and her father drove out to Tsarskoye Selo to take formal leave of their Sovereigns.

She had not seen Nicholas II since she was a child, and as she curtsied to the small, erect figure—whose haunted, uncertain eyes contrasted so strangely with his fierce mustache and stiff military bearing—he seemed to have shrunk in stature, while his wife had grown even more commanding. Wearing frilly white dresses and long gloves, the two elder Grand Dutchesses Olga and Tatiana, smiled encouragingly at her.

"Your dear mother," murmured the Empress. "Such a sad loss to us all." Graciously, she embraced Anastasia. "We know how hard she worked for Russia and how great her sacrifices were. We are happy to know that you are prepared to take her place at your father's side. He has great need of your support, and all our prayers go with you to Egypt, dear child."

As she looked searchingly at Anastasia, her meaning was plain: I am relying on you to use your influence with your father and prevent him from disgracing us in the eyes of our allies.

"I will help him in every way I can, Your Majesty," she replied with a sinking heart. Surely, where the Countess had failed, she, Anastasia, was not likely to succeed. The Empress smiled, however, and appeared to be satisfied.

"May God go with you, my child."

"What was the old German *hausfrau* saying to you?" demanded Kadya suspiciously, as they drove home through the snowy streets.

"She told me to be a good influence on you and keep you out of trouble," said Anastasia cooly.

"What supreme impudence!" exclaimed her father. "So she imagines that you'll do her spying, and watch every move I make! Now I'm tempted to leave you in Petersburg after all."

But it was only a token threat. In the bitter cold of January 1915, only three weeks after the Countess' funeral, Count Kharkov's special train steamed south again, carrying the consul and his daughter on the first stage of their long journey back to Egypt . . .

Chapter Seventeen

The Alexandria Harbor was thronged with ships when their boat docked on a day of sparkling late-winter day in March. Emerging from her cabin, her arms full of parcels, Anastasia stared in amazement at the change in the town she remembered.

Gone were the stately *dhows* with their high-raked bows, the crowded ferryboats and graceful lateen-sailed skiffs that had skimmed like low-flying birds across the water. They were pushed out of sight by the gunboats, naval transports, mule boats, ammunition carriers and hospital ships now jostling for cargo space on the wharves. Sweating sailors in English and French uniforms shouted orders to the dockyard *fellahin*, whose donkeys teetered unsteadily under their loads.

"They are reloading their transports for war," commented Kadya thoughtfully, as he leaned on the rail at her side and watched the busy scene through binoculars. "I must call on the British Commander-in-Chief at once. I believe that Britain is preparing an attack on the Dardanelles, just as the newspapers have been telling us. Strange that they should make no secret of their plans..."

The Dardanelles—the slender passage of water linking the Mediterranean Sea to the Black Sea—had been blocked the previous autumn, as Anthony Mills had predicted. Baron von Wangenheim, the wily German ambassador to Constantinople, had by this one stroke isolated Russia from her allies in the west, and insured Turkey's entry into the war on the German side. Already Russia, who relied heavily on her grain exports to earn the money to buy arms, was feeling the pinch severely, for her merchant ships, laden with corn and timber, lay helplessly bottled up in the Black Sea, unable to reach their markets. If Britain and France together could force the Turks to reopen this vital thoroughfare between East and West, Russia would be in a much stronger position to continue the fight.

The morning after their arrival, Kadya and his daughter waited on General Sir Ian Hamilton, the British Commander-in-Chief, at his headquarters on the rue el Caied Gohar. At her father's insistence Anastasia was dressed in an elaborate afternoon dress of floating green chiffon, and wore a large picture hat adorned with paler green roses. Kadya had chosen his glittering blue-and-gold full-dress uniform. They found the British general, who was soberly attired in khaki, about to leave on a tour of inspection.

"Perhaps you'd like to accompany me, Count Kharkov," he suggested, politely allowing no flicker of amusement at their clothes to cross his sensitive face. "We can talk things over as we go along. I'm very glad to have you here. By jove, Miss Kharkova, you look fine enough for a garden party! It'll do the boys in hospital the world of good just to see you."

Anastasia smiled at the lanky Scottish general, whose courtly manners and dreamy Highland eyes seemed to belong more to a poet than a soldier. "Thank you, Sir Ian," she responded. In her heart, she realized that they were absurdly overdressed, that they must look like two frivolous butterflies who had strayed by accident into this new world of dusty uniforms and marching feet, so different from the Cairo they used to know.

"You go now to visit a hospital, *mon general*?" Kadya frowned. He had an instinctive distaste for the sickroom, and would have preferred to inspect the fighting troops. He was longing to see for himself the newly arrived Australians and New Zealanders, those bronzed, sinewy giants of men from the Antipodes, with their own very special approach to military life. It was said that Cairo trembled when they rode in, whooping and yelling, for an evening's entertainment.

"I plan to stop by the hospital on my way to the Anzac lines," explained Sir Ian. "One of my family—my staff, you know—smashed himself up yesterday in an accident. I don't wish to know the details. Apparently a wheel came off when his vehicle was subjected to unusual stress. Anyway, I want to see the young rascal and read him the riot act. Can't have the men killing themselves before the battle, you know."

"We'll be delighted to accompany you, *mon general*," said Kadya graciously, and allowed Sir Ian to hand Anastasia into the gleaming staff car.

The hospital had been set up in the cool and airy rooms of a former palace belonging to the Khedive. Anastasia remembered how the walls had been hung with embroidered silk. Black servants had once waved fans where now stood a neat double row of utilitarian iron beds, their gray blankets folded underneath the domed mosaic ceiling. Only a few of the beds were occupied. Nurses bustled efficiently to and fro, their trays full of mysterious, gleaming instruments. The matron, in a snowy white apron and veil, came forward to greet the little party.

"Good morning, Sir Ian. Everything is going very well, and the girls are settling down nicely. We've had a few more cases of sunstroke and food poisoning—nothing serious. And an Irishman had a nasty kick from a camel yesterday. It broke his leg in two places..."

The men in the beds behind her were winking and blowing kisses at Anastasia. When she looked away, embarrassed, her eyes met those of a tall, dark-haired nurse standing at the end of the ward. Something about the nurse was oddly familiar—the tilt of her head, the firm set of the squarish jaw, familiar but also hostile. In a flash, Anastasia remembered where she had seen her before. Seen and heard her. It was the woman from the Turkish bath, the tall English girl who'd held Anthony's arm so possessively at that terrible ball in Constantinople. Sybil Dunwoody... strange that she could so easily remember her name. The English girl had looked at Anastasia then just as she did now, with a cold dislike that seemed to contain a hint of challenge. *Keep off*, she seemed to be saying. We don't want you here. Her contemptuous expression, as she eyed the picture hat, intensified Anastasia's feeling that she was unsuitably dressed for a visit to a hospital.

Instinctively she moved closer to her father, using him as a buffer between herself and the openly admiring soldiers in the beds. She wished that Sir Ian would hurry up and finish his visit.

But the general had halted in front of another bed. The head and half the face of the occupant was swathed in bandages.

"Well, my lad," he said with mock severity, "when will you stop driving a car as if you were riding a horse? They tell me you were lucky to escape with a few burns and a broken leg. I'm very sorry about poor d'Erlanger. That's a sad blow. Now you must hurry and get well again. Next time you go out on the town with your French friends, try to take better care of yourself."

"Sorry, sir," said the man in the bed. "It's good of you to visit me." At the sound of his voice Anastasia had moved forward: it was none other than Anthony Mills. "I'll be up and about in a day or two," he was saying. She pushed past General Hamilton and seized the patient's hand.

"Anthony!" she exclaimed. "Oh, this is terrible! Oh, you poor man! Sir Ian, why didn't you tell me that Anthony had been wounded?"

The General looked amused, and Anthony embarrassed. He drew his hand away from her grasp and replaced it beneath the bedclothes.

"I didn't know that you were acquainted with Captain Mills, Miss Kharkova, although I shouldn't be surprised. Anthony seems to know everyone. Perhaps you'd like to remain here and comfort his solitude while I finish my tour? See that you're in better shape before my next visit, Anthony—that's an order!"

With a cheerful wave he moved away, leaving Anastasia standing beside Anthony's bed, very conscious of Sybil Dunwoody's hostile gaze.

"Just a few minutes," said the matron kindly, following Sir Ian. "Captain Mills will enjoy talking to an old friend."

But what little Anastasia could see of Anthony's face didn't appear the least pleased, and she felt the hot blood rise to her cheeks. She had done the wrong thing again. She should have shown more reserve.

"Well, go on . . . sit down," said Anthony. "I suppose I should have expected you to turn up here sooner or later. Wartime conditions in Russia would hardly appeal to Count Kharkov—or his daughter."

"What do you mean? Besides, what do you know of wartime conditions in Russia?" She was as baffled by his cool, indifferent tone as by the impliplication that she'd returned to Egypt for its pleasures. The fact that the implication also applied to her father didn't make it more palatable.

"You don't seem very pleased to see me, Anthony?" she said in a low voice.

"I'm sorry you don't find me quite at my best, but there are a thousand things I'd rather be doing than lying in bed. Well, why don't you sit down? The nurses won't let you stay very long. Tell me, how is Countess Kharkova?"

"She died just before Christmas."

"I'm sorry to hear that," said Anthony, and his regret sounded genuine. "I hope she had the pleasure of seeing her Egyptian collection properly displayed and admired before she died."

"No, the collection is still in crates. No one has even unpacked it yet."

"What a shame."

Was Anthony blaming her? What could she have done? The crates had been delivered to the museum: she herself could hardly have forced the curator to unpack them. She sat uncomfortably on the small hard chair beside his bed, aware that every word they spoke could be heard the length of the quiet ward. Some of the patients were reading, but most merely dozed or stared at the ceiling. She tried to find some neutral topic with which to while away the visit, but all she could think of was his cool reception and the unfriendly looks of Sybil Dunwoody as she went about her duties. Anthony's one visible eye surveyed her dispassionately and he gave her no help.

"How did it happen—the accident, I mean?" she asked with an effort. Surely it was all right to ask such a harmless question?

"I'd rather not discuss it, if you don't mind. One of my best friends was killed."

Silence fell between them again. At last, in desperation, she said, "Perhaps you'd like to visit the temple with me when you're better? I want to carry on with Mama's work . . ."

"My dear Anastasia, don't you realize there's a war on? All excavation has been suspended—along with a lot of other enjoyable activities. No more dances, no more picnics by the pyramids. You won't be able to carry on the kind of social life you're used to. I'm afraid you'll find Egypt very dull these days."

Beneath the absurd picture hat, her green eyes suddenly blazed. "Is that why you think I've come back? Is that all you think I'm good for?"

"Isn't it?" he asked quietly. "If you were prepared to do anything else you'd have stayed in Russia, and tried to help your country win this war she's dragged us all into, instead of flaunting around your former playgrounds in the kind of clothes you'd wear to a Royal garden party."

Color flamed in her cheeks at the gross unfairness of the attack. "I wanted to stay in Russia," she said, "but Papa wouldn't let me—just as he won't let me become a nurse..."

"And you, a grown woman, take orders from Papa as if you were still a child? Sorry, Anastasia," he said, watching her closely, "but if there's one thing I can't stand in a woman it's a pretense of helplessness. If you really wanted to work, nothing would stop you. I can therefore conclude that you don't really want to. And now, if you'll excuse me, I'm feeling a bit tired. I didn't get much sleep last night."

He rolled onto his side, away from her. At once Sybil Dunwoody left her instrument trolley and walked toward the bed.

"Can you find your own way out, Miss Kharkova? I'm afraid I'm rather busy just now." The words were civil enough, but the look of triumph on Sybil's face was enough to stiffen Anastasia's spine.

"Perfectly well, thank you, nurse. Please don't let me disturb your important work."

She swept out with her head high, oblivious of the grins and winks her appearance occasioned. I *will* be a nurse and help win the war, she thought angrily, whatever Papa says. I'll show Anthony I'm not the idle social butterfly he thinks I am. And I'll wipe that patronizing smile off Sybil Dunwoody's face!

Buoyed up by her indignation, she went straight to the cubbyhole which served as an office. Much to the surprise of the temporary registrar, she asked to be enrolled in the next training course.

Kadya was waiting for the evening samovar to be brought into the drawing room when she told him of her decision. Predictably, he was surprised and annoyed, and did his best to dissuade her, but fresh from her clash with Anthony, Anastasia refused to be cowed.

"You? Dressing the wounds of naked men? Slaving in the filth of a field hospital? Anastasia, you must have taken leave of your senses. I won't let you do it."

"You can't stop me, Papa," she said calmly, pouring tea. "I've already enrolled at the British hospital. I start my training on Monday. You may as well accept it. For once in my life I'm going to do what I want."

"For once!" shouted Kadya. He raised his eyes to heaven. "As God is my witness, you're a vain, ungrateful child. You've been given your own way as long as I can remember, and this is the way you show your gratitude! I forbid you to become a . . . a nurse, do you hear? It's completely incompatible with the dignity of my position."

"Be reasonable, Papa. Don't you know that the Empress, and the Grand Duchesses too, are proud to wear nurses' uniforms and help Russia win the war?"

"You won't help Russia by working in a British hospital."

"They are our allies, Papa. You're being absurd. Your ideas are fifty years out of date," said Anastasia firmly. "This isn't the Crimean War, you know. I refuse to listen to you any longer."

"Thank God my poor Olga isn't alive to hear such disrespect," grumbled Kadya, but Anastasia knew she had won. "You'll regret it. Nursing isn't the glamorous, exciting business you silly females imagine. There's more to it than walking around in a starched uniform laying your hand on the fevered brows of heroes—as you'll soon discover if you persist with this foolishness."

For once in his life he was right, as Anastasia found out during the week that followed. Time and again she was tempted to give the whole thing up. Only the thought of Anthony's contempt and her father's doubts made her stick to the grinding, exacting routine.

One day, she could no longer restrain her longing to tell Anthony what she had done. When she came off duty she hurried across to his ward.

Sybil met her at the door. "May I help—? Oh, it's Miss Kharkova, isn't it? I hardly recognized you without your hat. The patients talked of nothing else for days. How strange to see you wearing our uniform. Don't tell me you've taken up nursing?"

Anastasia bit her lip and kept her temper. If only another nurse were on duty! "I came to visit Captain Mills," she explained. "How is he getting along?"

"You're in for a disappointment, I'm afraid. Captain Mills has returned to duty," said Sybil with satisfaction. "So your trip is wasted."

"But his leg—wasn't it broken? How could it mend so soon?"

"It was only a fracture, and he insisted on being discharged, even though Matron cautioned against it," said Sybil loftily. "Was that all you wanted?"

Anastasia tried to collect her thoughts before being hustled out of the ward. "Could you perhaps tell me where he is staying?"

"I'm afraid not. It isn't our policy to disclose the patients' addresses," said Sybil.

"But you know where he's living, don't you?" persisted Anastasia.

"If I do, it's no concern of yours, Miss Kharkova," snapped Sybil. "Excuse me, please. I'm very busy."

She turned away and began to remove the dressing from a patient's leg with unnecessary speed.

"Slow down, nurse, there's a duck," complained the owner of the leg. "What's all the bloomin' rush, anyway?"

Anastasia sighed and went to the office, where the registrar gave her Anthony's address. Soon she was on her way to his house in the tree-lined rue des Pyramides.

General Hamilton had been allowed only three weeks to prepare his multi-national force for the invasion of the Gallipoli Peninsula, and his staff worked around the clock. Exhausted from his first day back in harness, Anthony was half sitting, half lying in an armchair, his injured leg propped up on a stool and a strong whisky-and-water in his hand when Perkins, his manservant, announced: "Miss Kharkova to see you, sir."

Damn, thought Anthony. He wasn't in the mood for feminine dramas. But when she burst into the room, the white veil billowing round her charmingly flushed face and her apron flying, he couldn't help smiling.

"You see? I did it! I told Papa I didn't care what he said. I'm a nurse now. I took your advice. Can't we be friends again?" She looked at his face, where the bandages had been removed. "Oh, your face is burned. You shouldn't have left the hospital so soon."

"Don't start fussing over me, please. I get quite enough of

that from Perkins. Well, so you took the great step? Congratulations! Of course I'm pleased. Sit down and tell me all about it. Perkins, get Miss Kharkova some tea."

"Very good, sir."

Anastasia sat down and pulled off her cap with a weary gesture. Golden hair cascaded down her back. In spite of her elation, Anthony thought she looked very tired.

"How do you find the work?" he asked, smiling.

"Exhausting. I'm not used to such hard work. Then when I get home, Papa makes me entertain his guests for dinner when all I want to do is sleep. Sister Price—do you know Sister Price?"

"I don't think so."

"She's a devil—a Welsh devil. All day she chases the nurses who are training: " 'Hurry up! Go here—go there! Get this! Scrub that! Why haven't you washed your hands?' How I hate her! She makes me wash out dirty bowls and pans, and even when I do them twice she says they aren't clean enough.

"Poor Anastasia. It sounds like a nightmare."

"Flies, dirt, groaning men, and all in this terrible heat! Sometimes I think I can't bear it any more. But if I give up Papa will laugh, and you will look down your English nose and say: 'These Russian girls, they have no stamina. No moral fiber. I knew it all the time.' She flashed him a mischievous glance. "So you see why I can't give it up."

"All the trainees say the same thing," he reassured her. "But they say it gets easier as you go on."

Anastasia looked thoughtful. "What does Miss Sybil Dunwoody say? She is *very* efficient, and a *very* good nurse. Sister Price tells me how clean Miss Dunwoody gets her hands, how perfectly she puts on a bandage, how she's never late, never untidy, never *in-so-lent*..."

"You must remember that Syb's been doing it longer than you," said Anthony hastily. "She's bound to be better. She's always been rather efficient."

"Do you know her well?"

"Oh, yes. I've known Sybil all my life. Our families are neighbors. Sybil's determined to cover herself with glory, that's why she's working so hard for her diploma. She wants to be sent out to Lemnos—that's the island where the wounded will be disembarked from the hospital ships."

"How do you know?"

"Well, for one thing, her brother shares this apartment with me."

"And for another she told you herself." Anastasia rose from her chair. "Now I must go. Papa has invited someone very important to dinner—a banker, I think. Thank you for the tea."

"Come again and tell me more about Sister Price."

"Oh, that terrible woman! No, after this week I go to work with the surgeons in the operating theater. That will be better, I think."

"Come again, anyway."

From the window, he watched her walk down the darkening street, wondering yet again why this rootless, beguiling girl held such a powerful attraction for him. She was beautiful, of course, but he knew many other beautiful women and none of them exercised Anastasia's fascination. She was headstrong, exasperating, willfull; as quick to tears or laughter as a child. As the wife of a diplomat, she would be a disaster. But then again, would she? There was a strange directness about Anastasia which seemed to allay criticism, a lonely gallantry about the way she tackled her problems head-on without asking for anyone's help, and an unswerving honesty about how she told the truth, no matter how inconvenient the truth might be. This might make her more of an asset in diplomatic life than Sybil's everlasting tact...

He shook himself. It was impossible to compare them. Sybil had every virtue a wife should possess; Anastasia had few of them. Yet the spell she had cast over him long ago on the Trans-Siberian Express had only grown ever more powerful...

"A very nice young lady," said Perkins, coming in to draw the curtains. "A real charmer, as you might say. Now, Mr. Anthony, it's time you gave that leg a rest. Standing by the window is not what the doctor ordered..."

She did come again. Soon, Anastasia became a familiar sight in the house on the rue des Pyramides. She adopted the habit of calling for tea when she came off duty and regaling Anthony with the news of the day. Sybil Dunwoody was not at all pleased.

"I'm surprised that her father allows her to visit you alone," she said disapprovingly one night, after passing Anastasia, who was on her way out.

"You come to see me alone, Syb," Anthony pointed out.

She laughed. "It's rather different for me. *I* come to see my brother."

"What a pity he's hardly ever here," said Anthony, and she gave him a sharp glance.

"It's no good this way, Anthony," she said.

"What do you mean?"

"We can't go on like this. I've been very patient, waiting for you to come to your senses, but now I'm going to speak my mind. You're making a fool of yourself over that Russian girl—and a fool of me, too. You even took her to watch General d'Amade's parade at the Victoria College, when she had no business there at all. It's not very pleasant for me to hear these things from other people, you must realize that. Everyone knows about our—our understanding, and when they see you chasing after this wretched little Russian, whom everyone knows is no better than she should be..."

"Everyone, Syb?"

She should have recognized the warning note in his voice, but she was too full of her own grievance to heed the danger signal.

"Of course they do. You remember that business at Sir Louis' ball in Constantinople, when Percy Fytton knocked Captain Von Stuckel into the lily pond? Your precious Anastasia was at the bottom of that unfortunate episode. I know Percy refused to talk about it, but Von Stuckel wasn't so reticent. He said that she dragged him into the garden and then simply flung herself into his arms."

"He would say that," murmured Anthony.

Sybil ignored the interruption. "That's the trouble with those Russians. Scratch a Russian and you'll find a Tartar. They're simply not civilized. They don't know how to behave decently."

Grimly, Anthony said, "I don't want to hear any more of your stories, Sybil. I may as well tell you that I don't believe a word of them."

"My dear Anthony, I've hardly begun. I came here tonight to tell you that I won't put up with it any longer. Either you give up seeing Miss Kharkova, or—"

"Or?"

"Or you must consider our . . . understanding at an end," said Sybil recklessly.

There was a long silence. Then Anthony said: "I'm sorry, Sybil. I really am."

Sybil smiled triumphantly. "I accept your apology. We won't say any more about it."

"I'm afraid you don't understand. I mean I'm sorry because I can't do what you ask. You see, I'm in love with Anastasia. I think I have been for a long time."

"You're in love with that—that little slut? I never heard such nonsense in my life," cried Sybil angrily. "You're not in love, Anthony. You're infatuated."

"Call it what you like," said Anthony calmly. "We've known each other a long time, Syb—as you're fond of pointing out. But that doesn't give you the right to dictate to me—or to slander the girl I hope to marry."

"*Marry!*" The blood drained from Sybil's face, leaving it bone-white. In a low, trembling voice, she said, "If you do, I swear you'll regret it. She'll take everything you offer and give nothing back. She's a man-eater, I warn you. Although she looks so pretty and helpless, she's nothing of the kind."

"You know nothing at all about her," said Anthony sharply. "Anastasia hasn't had an easy life. She needs my help, far more than you ever will."

"You were always fond of helping lame dogs over stiles," jeered Sybil vindictively. "When this lame dog—this bitch, I should say—bites your hand, you'll remember what I said." She pulled on her gloves with quick, angry jerks. "And there's one other thing you should bear in mind before you commit yourself to something you may regret."

"What's that?" asked Anthony politely.

"I don't give up easily," said Sybil, and swept past him to the door.

"Come in, my dear. Come in!" cried Kadya genially, waving away his secretary as Anastasia entered the study. The sun shone brightly through the uncurtained windows. Faintly, from across the garden, came the cries of street vendors.

"I came to say good night," said Anastasia, smiling.

"Are you actually going to bed at ten o'clock in the morning?

This nursing is terrible! It turns the day upside down and leaves you no energy for amusement," grumbled Kadya. Then his expression brightened. "Before you go to your bed, you might care to read Andrei's letter. It came this morning. He has some interesting news about Valerian."

Anastasia's heart began to race. Although she still told herself that Valerian was alive, she had nearly given up hope. "Oh, Papa," she said breathlessly, "tell me quickly—is he . . . alive?"

"As I predicted, the black sheep has returned to the fold," said Kadya blandly. "What's more, he appears to have brought a ewe and a lamb with him."

"What do you mean?"

"I mean that he is married, my dear. He has apparently been married for a number of years, though he had the good sense to conceal the fact while my wife was alive. She wouldn't have taken kindly to the appearance of a Scottish daughter-in-law with no breeding and no fortune either, according to Andrei."

Anastasia's hands were shaking. She clasped them tightly together. "I don't understand," she whispered, almost to herself. A Scotswoman? But when . . . and how? "He can't be married. The girl must be an impostor."

"I'm afraid there's no doubt on that score." Kadya couldn't conceal his pleasure at reporting the full extent of his stepson's folly. "The woman—Susanna is her name—has documents that prove her story. A marriage certificate dating back to the time when Valerian was in Manchuria. All perfectly valid and legal, Andrei tells me."

"Manchuria, so long ago!" The room seemed to swim in front of Anastasia's eyes, and she sat down on the nearest chair. Valerian had always considered marriage a prison, a trap. He'd told her so himself. The chilly certainty crept over her that he'd used those metaphors because he was speaking from his own experience. Manchuria was where the Japanese had held him prisoner, yet he had never seemed to bear them ill will. Had they perhaps rescued him from the far worse prison of his marriage?

Her mind was twisting and turning, trying to find a satisfactory explanation, but she knew there wasn't one. He had cold-bloodedly deceived her.

"You look shocked, my dear, and shaken . . . Perhaps I

should have broken the news to you more gently." Kadya was playing the role of a solicitous parent. "I'll call Galina to attend you."

"No, don't do that," she said, then added in a whisper, "He told me to wait for him. He said he was going to marry me."

"As I said, that's the oldest trick in the world," noted Kadya, enjoying his moment of power. "Now aren't you glad I made you come back to Egypt? Suppose you'd been the first to greet Valerian's wife?"

"Don't Papa . . ." She couldn't bear her father's gloating complacency, his satisfaction at Valerian's downfall. But she had to know more: "Where had this—this *wife* been living all these years? Why has she suddenly appeared?"

"Andrei explains everything. You can judge for yourself how little credit the story reflects on Valerian. Apparently he married Susanna in Manchuria, but they were separated when a Japanese patrol took him prisoner. When he was released, he decided to abandon his wife, even though she had sheltered him and nursed him back to health at considerable risk to herself before he was captured. Susanna, who is a doctor, subsequently gave birth to a son. A few months ago, her mission hospital was destroyed and she was left destitute. She went to St. Petersburg with her son to search for her husband. In late February, they arrived at Valerian's house. Andrei took them in.

"And—and Valerian?"

"Of course, that was while he was still missing in action. The Austrians took him prisoner during their offensive, but Valerian was later rescued by our troops. He returned to Petersburg to discover his wife and son living with Andrei. That must have been some surprise! To think that Valerian has such a lurid past! Are you certain you don't want me to call Galina, Anastasia? You look somewhat pale."

"No . . . please. I'll go upstairs and lie down. I want to be alone."

How she got out of the stifling study and escaped upstairs, Anastasia never knew. A sick ache was numbing all her senses. She felt that the whole structure of life, her world, had been brutally swept away, leaving her tottering on the brink of an abyss. She knew that any moment the shock of Valerian's betrayal would turn to grief. And when the tears came, she wanted to be alone. No one, not even her maid, must witness the mourning for her lost love, her lost ideal, the death of a hope to which she had clung through the years, the hope that someday Valerian would be hers.

She flung herself across her bed and wept until she had no more tears, then stared at the window with hot, swollen eyes as the hours dragged by, struggling to come to terms with her sense of loss. If only Valerian had told her the truth himself! If only she hadn't heard the bitter news thirdhand, relayed first through Andrei, who rejoiced in the misfortunes of others, and her father, whose jealous dislike of his handsome stepson had never wavered.

But Valerian would never have told her himself, she realized with dull pain. He never met trouble head-on: he, too, shied away from restrictive, uncomfortable facts. His was the skill of the juggler, keeping half a dozen hoops spinning, simultaneously, half a dozen girls happy, without apparent conflict. If two hoops accidentally collided, he simply threw them away. Anastasia had seen him disengage himself adroitly from many finished love affairs. She should have known better than to cling to her hope that his affection for her—however much he professed to despise it—would outlast them all. So long as he remained unattached, her hope could endure, but Andrei's letter had killed it stone dead. Valerian was married already.

Slowly, then, anger began to deaden the disappointment and replace the grief. How cheaply he valued her love! Her father called it the oldest trick in the world. But until today, however clear the evidence, she had resolutely refused to believe that Valerian would deceive her. She tried to remember every word of their last conversation, every inflection. Had he given her any hint that he was married? No, on the contrary, his greatest anxiety had been to extract from her a promise that she'd wait for him. To win her from the Englishman, he'd painted his glowing picture of a new world after the war—a world which they would share. He'd given her his ring.

Dog in the manger, she thought bitterly. You didn't want me yourself until you thought I was going to marry Anthony Mills. Then you were determined to win me back. You didn't care how many lies you told, or how much suffering you caused, so long as you knew you still reigned supreme in my heart...

She looked at the clock; it was almost time to return to the hospital for the night shift. For once she welcomed the prospect of work—hard, demanding labor that would drug her mind and blunt her misery. Anything, even the taunts of Sister Price, was better than grappling with bitter memories that never stopped haunting her. As if in a dream, she washed her swollen eyes and put on a clean uniform, ignoring the tray of food which a tactful Galina had placed temptingly outside her bedroom door. Although she had hardly eaten for the past twenty-four hours, she had no appetite. She felt strangely light-headed, as if her mind and body were miles apart, her body automatically following the evening routine while her mind looked on from a distance.

Off-duty soldiers laughed and jostled in the narrow streets as she passed through the bazaar. They haggled with coppersmiths and lemonade sellers. Some were riding donkeys, awkwardly, unused to the special gait. Everywhere she looked there were uniforms. Not for the first time Anastasia was glad of the protection of her nurse's cap and veil. An uncapped young woman walking alone through the bazaar after sundown might have risked insult or even injury, but as a nurse she was privileged and protected. Where the crowd was thickest, the soldiers stood politely aside to let her pass.

She scarcely noticed where her feet were taking her until she stood before the house on the rue des Pyramides. Perkins answered her knock.

Chapter Eighteen

"Good evening, Miss, it's close tonight, isn't it? Come in. I'm afraid you find us disorganized. The captain's upstairs, if you'll follow me."

Anastasia stared uncertainly at the trunks and boxes that filled the hall. What did they mean? Surely Anthony wasn't leaving?

Perkins, his neat black coat half hidden by a long striped apron, said apologetically, "You'll have to excuse the state of the study, miss. The captain's going through all his papers, every blessed one, and there are a lot after all these years. He won't ever throw them away—says they might come in useful. Though how a lot of heathen smudges and scribbles could ever be useful, I don't know..."

As he opened the door of Anthony's study the draught created a minor windstorm among the loose letters and documents piled on every available surface. Bookshelves, desk, the mantelpiece, and the chairs were stacked high with dusty manuscripts, cuttings from yellowed newspapers, bulging manilla envelopes and dog-eared notebooks. The floor was a sea of maps and sketches, among which Anastasia immediately recognized examples of her own work on the temple.

Amid this chaos sat Anthony, wearing a blue silk dressing gown over gray flannels, contentedly puffing a pipe as he leafed through a large folder containing yet more close-written scraps of paper, one long leg slung across the arm of his chair.

"Be careful where you tread, Perkins," he said, without

looking up, "or you may disturb the only evidence that Queen Hatshepsut ever married—"

"Miss Kharkova to see you, sir," cut in Perkins smoothly.

"Anastasia!" exclaimed Anthony, springing up from the chair and snatching the pipe from his mouth. "I'm so sorry—I didn't expect you for half an hour at least. As you see, I'm just tidying up my papers and putting them in order while Perkins finishes the packing."

"What does this mean?" she asked. "Why are you going away?"

"Hadn't you heard?" he said, and an icy chill seemed to settle on her heart. "The G.S. had been ordered to Lemnos, and we sail in a few days' time. I think the battle's about to begin—and high time too. While we've been building up our forces here, the Turk and his German bosses have had plenty of opportunity to dig themselves in on the peninsula, and if we wait any longer we'll find them a hard nut to crack." He waved a hand at the cluttered room. "Perkins is going back to England, taking everything I won't need on active service. We've been having a grand time clearing the decks for action."

Anastasia seemed to hear his voice from a great distance. The room darkened about her and the old familiar sense of desolation caught her in its iron grip. She was being left behind again. It wasn't enough that Valerian had betrayed and left her; now Anthony was going too.

He looked down at her ashen face with swift concern. "What's the matter? Don't you feel well? Sit down for a minute." His arm was warm and comforting as he guided her to the chair he had just left, and she leaned against him, trying to control the shuddering that shook her whole body.

"It—it's a shock to hear that you're going," she whispered. "I thought you'd be here for a long time..."

"Order, counter-order, disorder," he said absently, observing her face, which wore an expression of frozen misery. "There *is* something wrong," he said. "Come on, out with it. What has happened to upset you so much? Is it Sister Price again?"

"No... It's Valerian," she said, slowly and painfully, as if the words were being forced out. "Papa had a letter from Andrei today... about Valerian."

She stopped. A primitive spark of hope flicked through

Anthony's heart and was sternly suppressed. What right had he to wish another man dead? But Valerian had been missing for so long . . .

"But what is wrong?" he asked, his voice carefully neutral.

"Valerian is married."

"Married!" It was the last thing he'd expected.

"He's been married a long time—ever since the war in Manchuria." Anastasia began to cry. "He—didn't—tell—me. All this time he's been married, and he let me think—let me hope—"

"That one day he'd marry you?" said Anthony in a hard, tight voice.

"Yes! He lied to me. He told me that after the war we would be together, and make a new world where everyone is equal, but it was all lies. All that time he had a wife in Manchuria. Now she has gone to Petersburg to claim him and brought Valerian's son with her." Her voice rose hysterically. "Oh, Anthony, what shall I do? You must tell me what to do. My world is shattered!"

"Then it's up to you to put it together again."

"I can't!" she wailed.

"You must," he said, with quiet deliberation. Rage against Valerian Radek was beating at his temples, but outwardly his face was calm. Commiseration, he realized instinctively, would only encourage this distraught, overwrought girl to go entirely to pieces and cry her heart out all night on his shoulder—as she'd clearly been doing all day on her pillow. At all costs he must prevent that and make her pull herself together.

"Cheer up, Anastasia," he said. "Where's your pride? Where's your fighting spirit? Surely you're not going to weep and wail like a forsaken mermaid because some worthless man has jilted you? You're not the first girl it's happened to, and you certainly won't be the last, but beating your breast in front of all the world isn't going to help matters."

It worked. Anastasia's sobs stopped abruptly and her green eyes flashed ominously. She had expected sympathy, not crude taunts. "I am *not* beating my breast." she said angrily. "I see I was wrong to tell you my trouble, even though you asked me. You are a hard, cold, cruel and heartless English beast. You don't know what it is to feel sorrow."

At least she had stopped crying. "That's not sorrow," said

Anthony brutally. "That's self-pity. Your pride has been hurt and you're feeling sorry for yourself, that's all. The trouble with you, Anastasia, is that you expect too much of people. Then, when they let you down, you make a great commotion because they haven't lived up to your expectations. It's yourself you ought to blame, not Valerian. He didn't deceive you—you simply deceived yourself."

"That isn't true!" she cried. "You don't know anything about Valerian. He did deceive me. He said he loved me and wanted to marry me."

"Are you sure you didn't imagine it? How could he love you when you'd hardly seen each other twice in a dozen years? I tried to warn you not to imagine yourself in love with someone like Valerian Radek, but you wouldn't listen. You had to find out for yourself—the hard way. Well, are you going to open your eyes now and see the world as it is, or are you going to go on living in a childish dream? It's your choice."

"Don't you dare tell me what to do," said Anastasia venomously. "I hate you, Anthony Mills! I wish I'd never told you about Valerian at all."

"You asked my advice, didn't you?"

"I don't want that kind of advice, you English . . . pig!"

"That's much better—now you sound more like yourself," he said approvingly. "The next thing you must consider is the question of revenge."

"Revenge?"

"Certainly. You don't want your ex-lover—who's treated you so shamefully—to know that you're eating your heart out, do you?"

Anastasia stared at him. Was he—could he possibly be—laughing at her? Why were the English so complicated? She felt confused and lightheaded. One half of her was still mourning Valerian's betrayal, but the other was clamoring for vengeance. After a short struggle, vengeance won. "No," she said bitterly. "Eating my heart out does no good. He wouldn't care how much I suffer. He'd only care if I married another man." Even as she spoke, she knew she had found the perfect revenge. Valerian would be furous if he knew that she had broken her promise to wait for him. But why not? What claim did he have on her now?

"Splendid!" said Anthony warmly. "Marriage on the

rebound—the classic jilted reaction. That's undoubtedly what you must do. Forget all about Valerian and marry someone else."

"But I don't want to marry someone else. I don't love anyone else."

"You might learn to, if you forgot Valerian. You've never given anyone else a chance. You've never given *me* a chance." His voice was suddenly serious, all trace of laughter and mockery gone as if they'd never existed. "Look at me, Anastasia," he said quietly, "and tell me again that you don't love anybody else."

Shyly she looked up to meet his eyes. "I—I can't," she said at last.

He took her cold hands in a warm, strong clasp. "That's what I wanted you to say. Will you marry me, Anastasia?"

Everything was happening too fast. A moment ago she'd told him she hated him. Now the touch of his hands was more than a comfort; it sent a tingling thrill through her. She must answer him, but how? It wasn't possible that Anthony should want to marry her. His proposal was just a gesture, a chivalrous English gesture designed to patch up her shattered self-respect.

"Will you?"

"No," she whispered. "You only asked me because you feel sorry for me."

To her great surprise he laughed. "Sorry for you? What kind of a fool do you take me for, Anastasia? I'm not in the least sorry for you—I thought you'd have gathered that by now. If anything, my sympathies are for Valerian Radek, not you, What kind of hell has he been going through, keeping his guilty secret from you all these years?"

Anastasia put a hand to her aching head. "Then why ask me to marry you? What is your reason?"

"The simplest reason in the world. Can't you get it through your head that I love you? That's the best and only possible reason I could have for asking you to marry me at this highly inconvenient moment."

"But you can't love me—"

"Why can't I?"

"Well..." she faltered, "...the things you say to me. You always scold and tease me..."

"Do I? Ask yourself whether I'd bother to do that to someone I don't love?"

Her mouth had opened in soundless surprise.

"Would I?"

"I don't know. But, Anthony, I never knew. I never guessed—"

"Not even with all the hints your stepmother kept dropping?"

"Oh, those!" said Anastasia, blushing. "You know what Mama was like. She wanted to marry me off so Valerian would be safe from me. It didn't matter to her who I married."

"Yet I often had the distinct impression that she'd set her sights on me," said Anthony thoughtfully. "It used to scare the living daylights out of me. I figured that if anyone was going to prejudice you against me, it would be Countess Kharkova. She had a certain way of telling you to do something—"

'Which made you want to do the very opposite?"

"That's it, in a nutshell. So when she was practically ordering me to propose—"

"And ordering me to accept if you did—"

"I refused to do anything of the kind. But that doesn't mean I didn't want to."

Anastasia felt a little dizzy. It was hard to grasp what Anthony was saying. "Then you didn't propose just on the spur of the moment?"

"Oh, by no means! Good lord, no—I've loved you for years. I'm asking you now because I've seen my chance at last, and I don't mean to let it slip through my fingers."

"Is it because of what I told you—about Valerian?"

He nodded. "He's always been between us, Anastasia."

"I think he always will be," she said sadly. Again the empty ache of losing him threatened to overwhelm her, and she stared out at the starry sky, blinking away her tears. Anthony longed to embrace her and kiss away her misery, but he sensed that her grief was too fresh for any physical solace. The wound was too deep and too recent: any rapid healing might leave a permanent scar or, worse, a festering sore that would erupt again to destroy any fragile happiness they might have attained. Anthony knew that Valerian would remain between them until he managed to supplant the Russian completely. And he would have to face up to the grim possibility that he might never succeed in doing so.

"I'm prepared to take that risk, Anastasia," he said. "Are you?"

She was silent for a long time. She yearned to say yes, and commit herself to his care, laying down at last the burden of loneliness she had shouldered so long. But the habits of a lifetime couldn't be easily broken.

"I don't know," she said at last. "Please don't make me answer you yet. I must have time—to think. To decide."

"All right. But remember: there isn't much time before I leave for Lemnos. I must have your answer before then."

He knew he was hurrying her into a decision, but he felt no compunctions. Left to herself she might vacillate for weeks and finally refuse him, because some trifling coincidence had reawakened her longing for Valerian all over again. If she thought about it long enough, she was certain to discover an excuse for his treachery, perhaps persuading herself that he hadn't meant to deceive her, or that he'd been forced into marriage against his will. It was amazing what a woman could believe if she wanted to. He must strike while the iron of her anger was still hot, and trust that thereafter he could win and secure her love for himself.

He looked her in the eyes. "Before I leave, then?"

Slowly she nodded, and moved toward the door. "I must go now or I'll be late for duty. But I promise I'll give you my answer tomorrow."

The Welsh Dragon had plenty to complain of in Nurse Kharkova's behavior that night, but even her most vitriolic rebukes went unheeded. Anastasia arrived for duty late, and moved about the ward in a daze, lightheaded with lack of food and sleep, attending to the patients' needs with the slow, dreamy movements of a somnambulist.

She dropped thermometers and mixed the wrong dosages of medicine for the wrong patients. She left Corporal Ackroyd, who was suffering from sunstroke, with a bright light shining into his eyes as he slept, and failed to remove the bottle of Scotch which misguided friends had smuggled in to Sergeant Pearce. As a result, his drunken baritone awakened the ward and he had to be removed hurriedly to an empty room.

"You're more trouble than you're worth, girl," snapped

Sister Price as the ward settled down at last. "I don't know why I bother with you. You'll never make a nurse, that's plain to see."

Anastasia looked at her vaguely.

"Can't you even apologize for the fuss you've caused?"

"I'm sorry, Sister."

"So you should be. I'd find it easier to believe if you pulled yourself together, Nurse."

Anastasia scarcely heard her. Her concentration was turned inward, trying to decide whether to accept Anthony's offer of marriage. Should she or shouldn't she? She had lost Valerian: why shouldn't she clutch at the chance of happiness with Anthony? He was handsome, intelligent, rich, good company—all the things her foster-mother had considered important in a husband—and he claimed to love her. What possible reason could she have for turning him down?

Her reservations were strange enough. Although she had been friends with him for many years now, worked beside him in the desert excavations and joined with him in every aspect of Egyptian social life, Anastasia felt a kind of panic at the thought of marrying a man she knew so little about. His work was a mystery to her, and so were all but the most superficial of his likes and dislikes. She knew practically nothing of his background. What would be his parents' reaction to the news, if their eldest son married not the suitable Sybil Dunwoody but an unknown Russian girl? How could she live in England, that strange island of mists and myths and stiff upper lips? Would she ever learn to fit into that mysterious, carefully structured society? Would Anthony ever replace Valerian in her heart?

When the ward was quiet, she sat with her head in her hands by the little green-shaded desk lamp, remembering landmarks in her love for Valerian: the childish infatuation which had ended so abruptly that night in Siberia; the long struggle to grow into the kind of woman he admired, her strange sense of anticlimax when she knew she'd succeeded. The old, impulsive Anastasia had changed into the cool, sophisticated woman of the world, and Valerian had begun to pay court to her. Was the woman of the world the one Anthony loved, too? Would he feel cheated when he discovered that the old Anastasia was still the real one, that the woman of the world was nothing but a careful facade?

She glanced at her watch. Only another hour on duty and

then she could go home to her father, who would probably want to continue talking about Valerian, gloating over his stepson's extraordinary misalliance, congratulating himself on removing his daughter from the deceiver's clutches. She didn't think she could bear it. She would creep in softly through the garden gate and tiptoe upstairs...

If only she could sleep forever, and never have to face her father again. But however long she slept, she knew there would always be the moment of waking—and deciding what to tell Anthony...

Yes or no?

Perhaps, she thought, she would say no. She need give no reason: a gentleman would not question her decision. Then, at the long prospect of the months and years stretching ahead, she realized that a future without Anthony looked ever bleaker than the future with him. At that moment she knew that her decision was made.

Sitting at the little marble-topped desk and its shaded lamp, with nothing but soft snores and an occasional groan from the ward to break the silence, she pulled out a sheet of paper and wrote:

> Anthony-
> Yes, I will marry you.
> Anastasia

She folded the note, addressed it and gave it to the messenger. She felt no joy, no excitement, nothing but complete exhaustion, both mental and physical. Dazed with weariness, she walked home, and fell into a deep sleep the moment her head touched the pillow.

The wedding was a very subdued affair, overshadowed by news of the death of Rupert Brooke, the handsome young English poet who'd joined the Gallipoli volunteers only to die of sunstroke on the eve of battle. His death cast a gloom over his friends, but the imminence of the invasion made Anthony insist on an immediate wedding.

"I'm not going to risk having you change your mind," he said, only half jokingly. Anastasia didn't smile.

"Don't worry. I won't change my mind."

She was glad that wartime conditions prevented her father from indulging his love of ostentation. Although the two quiet religious ceremonies were followed by a reception, where Count Kharkov's champagne flowed like water, the gaiety seemed forced. General Hamilton was already aboard his command ship, and the bridegroom and many of his guests wore uniforms, which emphasized the closeness of battle.

When Anastasia went upstairs to change into her traveling dress, her father followed.

"Can you spare me a moment, my dear?"

"Of course, Papa." She waved her maid away.

"Because we've all been so busy, there hasn't been time to discuss financial matters with you," he said, sounding unusually apologetic.

She put down her hairbrush with some surprise. "Financial matters?"

"Uh, yes. The matter of your mother's legacy. As I think you know, it comes to you on the day of your marriage. I've prepared the necessary order to my bankers here . . . All you have to do is sign. Then you can draw on this account."

"Thank you, Papa." She signed quickly with his pen, and wondered why he lingered.

"These are yours, too," he said. With no hint of embarrassment he thrust two letters into her hand. With a shock, she recognized Valerian's bold handwriting on the envelopes.

"I thought it wise to keep them until after your marriage to Anthony," explained Kadya blandly, "in case you felt compelled to do anything foolish—like running back to Russia."

Anastasia stared at the two envelopes. Her heart was pounding and she suddenly felt sick. "You hid my letters? How could you be so cruel?"

"Now don't start making a fuss. You made a sensible choice, my child, and I didn't want a silly infatuation to put that choice in jeopardy. It was your foster-mother's wish that you never marry Valerian, and the wishes of the dead should be respected."

He laid a fatherly hand on her shoulder, but she shook it off with an angry movement. Kadya shrugged and left the room.

Her hands were shaking. It was several seconds before she regained enough control to open the letters. She gazed at them through a blur. The first one was dated February 21, 1915—only six weeks after she had left St. Petersburg.

My darling,

I'm not a great letter writer, as you know, and at the front they worked us so hard that even Madame de Sevigné might have fallen behind with her correspondence. First we advanced, then we retreated, then we advanced again in a sea of mud, just like the tides on the seashore and about as well armed . . . At times, my fellows had only one rifle to share between six or seven men, and there was a terrible shortage of ammunition. The guns could only fire two shells a day. Sometimes our soldiers had to kill the Germans with their bare hands. You can't imagine what it was like. No other army could have fought as we did.

All that seems long ago now. As you must have been told, I was captured before the battle of Tannenberg, but the Austrians left me behind when they in turn retreated, and I was picked up by one of the hospital units we call *Letuchkas*. The nurses were wonderful—patient and brave, although few of them had done any nursing before the war.

They set my broken arm, and fixed me up as well as they could before putting me on a train bound for home. I shall always be grateful to them.

Now I come to the part I find hardest to tell you, my darling . . .

As if to reinforce this statement, the color of the ink now changed abruptly, as if the latter part of the letter had been written some time after the beginning:

When I arrived at our house on the Sadovskaya, I found the windows boarded up and thought the building was deserted. I knocked at the door, and old Igor Petrovitch let me in. He was astonished to see me. Then Andrei appeared with that hulking brute Boris pushing his wheelchair. Boris seems firmly installed in the house, though I can't understand or share Andrei's liking for him. After our greetings, Andrei said he had a surprise for me and called a child into the room. It's hard to explain this, but suddenly I seemed to be staring at a portrait of myself as a boy. Stanya, the child is my son. I knew it even before Andrei told me.

How he came to be is a strange story which you will find difficult to forgive and forget, yet I beg you to do both.

As you know, during the winter campaign in Manchuria, I was blown up by an explosion in a troop train. Some months later I was captured by the Japanese. My memories of those missing months are still hazy, since I suffered a severe concussion in the explosion, but it now seems plain that I was nursed back to health by a Scottish missionary doctor, Susanna Macdonald, and in gratitude for her care I committed the supreme folly of marrying her. Valentin is the child of my marriage. The days of my infatuation with Susanna now seem like a dream, and she, poor woman, has not been kindly treated by the passing years. She is of unsound mind and addicted to drugs, and it will not be difficult, when the war is over, to commit her to an asylum. Meantime, I am thinking of sending the boy and his mother to our old *dacha* at Ostrovskoye in the Crimea. They will be safe there until matters improve in St. Petersburg, and I will visit them when I can.

I will write again, my darling, when the situation becomes clearer. Until then, remember that my heart belongs to you forever—

Valerian

It was the first love letter she had ever received from him. With trembling hands, Anastasia clutched the crumpled paper and pressed it to her lips. He still loved her—that was all that mattered. His wife meant nothing to him. As soon as the war was over, Valerian would put her aside so that he and Anastasia could build their new world together.

Drawing a long, steadying breath, she read the second letter:

My darling—

Still no word from you, although nearly a month has passed since I wrote to tell you of my return home and my wife's reappearance. I pray that you are not angry with me, Anastasia, my darling. Your silence fills me with foreboding. Please write and tell me that you love me as much as I love you.

your Valerian

There was a scrawled postscript:

I go tomorrow to join the Commander-in-Chief in Galicia, where prospects for crossing the Carpathians look rosy. Susanna and Valentin, escorted by Boris, have reached Ostorvskoye in safety.

V.

Downstairs they were waiting for her. *Anthony* was waiting—her husband. For the next two days she would be alone with him on the brief honeymoon which was all that wartime conditions would allow. Her father had made them a present of a cruise upriver in a *dahabeeyah*, and until a moment ago the stately, gliding craft had seemed an ideal way to begin the marriage, safe from the rest of the world. Now the thought of those two long days filled her with panic and revulsion. *Valerian loved her.* How could she get through all those weary hours without revealing to Anthony her triumphant secret?

Valerian loved her. She'd been wrong to doubt him for a moment. His wife must have snared him in a moment of weakness. His child . . . Anastasia pushed away the thought of his child. If Valerian wanted a child, *she* would give him one, only—her thoughts raced full circle and came back abruptly to reality—only *now* she could do nothing of the kind. She was married to another man. Anthony had played skilfully on her emotions when she was too tired, angry, and bewildered to know what she was doing. Now she, too, was trapped.

Helpless rage washed over her, blotting out all other feelings. Rage against her father, who had deliberately withheld from her those vital letters; rage against Anthony, who had hurried her into marrying him while she was still dazed and shocked—in no condition to look calmly at anything; rage against the war, which made it impossible for her to quit this stifling, decaying, intrigue-ridden land of Egypt where she'd been duped and manipulated like a puppet, and hasten home to Russia and Valerian's waiting arms.

"Anastasia!"

She didn't care if she kept them waiting. The mirror reflected her unbecomingly flushed cheeks and stormy eyes, but she didn't care about that, either. Let Anthony's friends gossip as much as they liked. They'd never guess what had transformed her from the meek, suggestible bride, who'd gone upstairs to change from her wedding dress, into an angry, determined young woman who was never again going to trust anything but her own judgment. If she must go through with this sham of a marriage and its ritual honeymoon, she would do so on her own terms.

Head high, she swept downstairs to the flower-decked hall where the guests waited to speed her departure. Her father was the last in line to kiss her. "You're as beautiful as an angel, my dear. I wish you every happiness," he murmured, but his eyes shifted uneasily. He could read only too clearly the message conveyed by her heightened color and her eyes, which now resembled splinters of green glass above her set jaw.

"I shall never forgive you, Papa. Never!" said Anastasia, averting her cheek from his kiss.

Poor Anthony, he thought. Thank God it's not my duty to take that angry little hellcat to bed tonight. There were, after all, occasional compensations to belonging to the older generation. He cleared his throat.

"Please raise our glasses to the happy couple!" he called. Amid showers of confetti, the gleaming, open-topped Bugatti bearing the bride and bridegroom rolled slowly away from the curb.

The river-barge which Kadya had insisted on hiring was the most luxurious on the Nile, complete with staterooms and bathrooms, dressing rooms and a dining room paneled from floor to ceiling. The finest mahogany. In addition to the master bedroom, with its massive silk-hung fourposter, there were three other bedrooms—all unoccupied since Perkins was leaving for England and Anastasia's maid had remained in Cairo.

Early after dinner that evening, Anastasia excused herself. When Anthony emerged from the bathroom in pajamas, his hair still damp, he found his wife fully dressed, sitting on a chaise longue with a book in her hands.

"Hullo," he said in some surprise. "I though you'd gone to bed."

Anastasia stretched elaborately and swung her feet to the floor. "No," she said vaguely, "I'm not tired yet. It think I'll go up on deck and watch the stars for a while."

"I'll go with you. Wait while I get my dressing gown. God knows where that useless steward has hidden it."

She watched him search fruitlessly in cupboards and drawers, then said lightly, "I think I'd rather be alone, if you don't mind."

"But I do mind. Damn it, Anastasia, we've only got two days together. Inviting though that bed looks, I don't propose to lie there alone while you wander about on the decks, like Lady Macbeth." She was silent. He added gently, "Come on, let's go to bed. The stars won't run away. You'll have plenty of time to observe them when I go off to Gallipoli."

Anastasia said clearly, "I am not going to sleep in that bed with you."

"Now what's possessed you?" Anthony wanted to be patient, though there was a warning edge to his voice. "Where else can you sleep?"

"There are other rooms."

"The beds are probably not made up, since we're the only passengers."

"Then I'll sleep on deck in that hammock."

"And freeze to death? Don't be absurd." He took her by the shoulders, shaking her gently. "What's the matter with you, all of a sudden? We're married now. You can't start behaving like some hysterical Victorian maiden at the prospect of sleeping with your husband." He remembered her lack of a mother, and the Countess' frigid fastidiousness. Was it possible that Olga had never explained the physical side of marriage to her adopted daughter?

Curbing his impatience, Anthony said, "Don't be frightened, darling. There's nothing difficult about making love. Come on, I'll help you off with your clothes."

He began to unbutton her blouse with firm, quick fingers, but she pulled away from him so violently that she tripped over a footstool and fell across the bed. In an instant he was beside her, cradling her face between his hands, his mouth coming down hard and insistent on hers as his weight pressed her onto the bed. "Gently, darling," he murmured. "You don't have to fight me every inch of the way."

"No, no!" she gasped, striking out at him with clenched fists. "Let me go. Take your hands off me. You don't understand—I've . . . I've got a headache."

He didn't move. "This is the best cure I know for headaches."

"I mean, I'm indisposed!"

"How *very* inconvenient, darling." Reluctantly he released her and stood, rebuttoning the top of his pajamas. "Or should I say, how very convenient for you?"

"I don't understand what you mean," she said. Curled on the bed, she tried to feign innocence, tried not to notice how, perversely, her body felt cheated of its rough contact with his.

"I'm sorry," she added. "I should have mentioned it sooner."

"Only you didn't think of it sooner, did you? You only remembered this . . . inconvenience when your other excuses failed. What is the matter? I have a right to know. What happened between the time you went upstairs to change your dress and the time you came back down?"

He had pinpointed the time frame exactly. Those deceptively lazy blue eyes had noted the change after she had read Valerian's letters, the change she thought she'd concealed from him so well.

"Nothing," she said, not meeting his eyes.

"Don't lie to me." He caught her arm roughly. "I want the truth, and I'm going to have it if I have to beat it out of you."

"Spoken like a true English gentleman!"

"Don't push me too far, Anastasia. I find your headaches and indispositions somewhat improbable. And if you can lie about one thing, you can lie about another."

"All right! If you want the truth so much you can have it," cried Anastasia angrily. "The truth is, I wish to God I hadn't married you, and I refuse to sleep with you tonight, or any other night."

"And what, may I ask, has prompted this sudden disinclination to my company? Let me guess. Has it something to do with Valerian Radek?"

Anastasia found herself unable to reply, but her hot blush betrayed her.

"I would assume that Valerian Radek has managed to persuade you that he didn't mean to jilt you. Tell me, am I on the right track? Now, I wonder how he managed to convey that intelligence to you on our wedding day?"

She remained silent.

"Are you going to tell me," said Anthony in a dangerously quiet voice, "or shall I make another attempt to claim my conjugal rights?"

She shrank back from him. "You're an uncivilized caveman!" she spat at him. "All right, I'll tell you. Valerian wrote to me, two letters. Papa didn't give them to me until after the wedding." Her voice caught on a sob. "Papa hid them. He didn't want me to read them . . ."

"Damn Papa and his interfering half-measures! You Russians are all alike. You start something—like this war—and then regret it and try to undo what you've done. Your father kept Valerian's letters, but he didn't have the moral courage to burn them—oh, no! He gave them to you just when they'd do the most damage—when you, having decided to marry me, could still change your mind about making me a decent wife."

"Why did you marry a Russian if you think so little of us?" said Anastasia coldly. "If you wanted a good wife, a 'decent' wife, you should have married Sybil."

"You may very well be right." Anthony shrugged and turned away.

"Where are you going now?"

"To bed," he said shortly. "You're apparently determined to keep yourself pure for your precious Valerian, and I have no wish to force myself upon you."

"But where will you sleep?"

"I'll find a bed, have no fear. Uncivilized cavemen are skillful at camping out. I wish you pleasant dreams, Anastasia."

The door closed behind him. He was gone. Slowly she undressed and lay down on the bed, but the cool sheets seemed to offer no welcome. Her dreams, when at long last they came, were far from pleasant. Tossing and turning, she tried to convince herself that she'd done the right thing in refusing to share Anthony's bed. She tried to believe she was glad he hadn't carried out his threat to take her by force, but her victory seemed hollow. The thought of Anthony sleeping alone on his wedding night was strangely disturbing.

"Valerian . . . " she whispered into the dark, "I'm still yours, my darling. I still belong to you. I'll come to you someday." But no matter how hard she tried to conjure up his face behind her closed eyelids, all she saw was Anthony's astonished disappointment when she refused him. All she could hear was his bitter admission that Sybil Dunwoody would have made him a better wife . . .

Chapter Nineteen

General Sir Ian Hamilton, Commander-in-chief of the Allied Forces, launched his attack on the bleak, inhospitable cliffs of the Gallipoli Peninsula at dawn on April 25, 1915.

His aim was to silence the German-manned guns in the old Turkish forts along the narrow length of the Dardanelles, and wrest from the Germans the mastery of Constantinople. Since the Gallipoli Peninsula was shaped rather like a long pointed slipper, the Australian and New Zealand Army Corps—under General Birdwood's command—planned to strike at Gaba Tepe, the point corresponding to the front of the ankle, while the British seized the toe at Cape Helles. At the same time a French force, commanded by General D'Amade, was sailing for the Asiatic coast of the Dardanelles, in order to prevent the Turkish gunners in the old fortress of Kum Kale, near Homer's Troy, from shelling the British fleet across the straits.

From the general's command ship, the warship *Queen Elizabeth,* Anthony and his brother staff officers, uncomfortably crammed into steel towers and six-inch batteries, watched the first boatloads of fighting men head for land through the early dawn mist. Unable to communicate with the troops, the Staff officers watched them swarming across the rocky shore just north of Gaba Tepe like an army of reckless ants, straight into the hail of bullets and shrapnel from Turkish entrenchments.

The thin, stony soil was covered with tough roots of brushwood, but wave after wave of Australians and New Zealanders hacked improvised trenches and finally disappeared from the sight of the anxious onlookers aboard the *Queen Elizabeth.*

When four thousand men were fairly ashore at Gaba Tepe, the general's command ship steamed south to discover how the British troops were faring on the toe of the peninsula at Sedd-el-Bahr. Here, in the vicinity of Cape Helles, five beaches were under simultaneous attack. "Y" Beach, in the north, had offered no initial resistance to the men of the King's Own Scottish Borderers and South Wales Borderers. But further south, beneath the toe at Sedd-el-Bahr, it was a very different story. Here the narrow little bay code-named "V" Beach, barely a quarter of a mile long, was overlooked by one of the most powerful of the Turkish entrance forts, surrounded by a heavy barbed-wire entanglement. Within the fortress' shattered walls, which had been blasted by Admiral Carden's naval attack on March 18, snipers and machine guns now lay concealed.

A company of the 1st Dublin Fusiliers, the 1st Munster Fusiliers and half the Second Hampshire Regiment disembarked from the *River Clyde* into a line of small boats towed by launches, then set off against the current for the silent shore. But just as the first boat grounded, the Turks concealed within the fortress began to fire, and within minutes the attacking force was cut to pieces. Only the few who managed to jump from their boats into the water survivied long enough to take cover beneath a low parapet of sand, above which they dared not raise their heads, while the rest of the troops aboard the *River Clyde* waited helplessly for a chance to get ashore. The thin line of survivors clung to their small refuge, while the tows from which they had landed, manned only by the dead, drifted aimlessly away in the blood-reddened waters of the bay.

Throughout that long, hot afternoon, the mighty guns of the *Queen Elizabeth,* the *Cornwallis, the Albion,* and other ships pounded the Turkish fort above the beach. Their efforts prevented a counter-attack that would have thrown that thin line of survivors back into the sea. After dark the remainder of the landing party braved a furious fire from the fort and joined their comrades on the moonlit shore.

Meanwhile, the quiet landing on "Y" Beach had suffered an unexpected reverse. The attacking troops climbed the precipitous cliffs flanking the beach unhindered, although one of the conducting ships, the *Goliath,* ill-advisedly shelled the summit and raised a hornet's nest of Turkish snipers in response. But there was no organized counter-attack, and for eleven hours the British soldiers were left in peace to dig shallow entrenchments in the stony ground. That night, however, the Turks attacked in force, and by dawn there were over seven hundred casualties, including one of the colonels in charge of the landing.

Hand-to-hand fighting under a barrage of shrapnel and machine-gun fire continued all night. At daybreak the Scottish Borderers' trenches were rushed by fanatically yelling Turks, who directed a devastating fire down onto the beach as the navy attempted to take off the wounded—which amounted to more than half the officers and nearly half their men. The remaining colonel realized that his position was hopeless, and gave the order to withdraw. The "Y" Beach landing had failed.

More successful was the French assault on the fortress of Kum Kale, on the Asiatic side of the Dardanelles. There, by nightfall, the men of the 6th Colonial Regiment, the Senegalese wearing their dark blue greatcoats and red *chechias* covered with blue cotton, were masters of the "Tomb of Achilles" and the Kum Kale fortress on the Scamander River, the fabled anchorage for Agamemnon's thousand ships.

As General Hamilton wrote in his diary aboard the *Queen Elizabeth* that night, in his own peculiar style of French shorthand, men were still pouring ashore on three of his five attack points. None of the commanders were in touch with each other, however, and even the Commander-in-Chief had no notion of how desperate the situation was for the Anzac troops commanded by General Birdwood, whose two divisional commanders were recommending an immediate evacuation.

"It was just midnight when General Braithwaite went to awaken the Commander-in-Chief on the *Queen Lizzie,*" said Anthony, and yawned.

"Tell me about it, please!" said Anastasia. "You don't know what it's like here, waiting for news, hearing only what the wounded men can tell us. They don't know very much, but you must have seen it all."

"No such luck," said Anthony sleepily, "but I'll tell you what I can, then I want to go to sleep."

They were sitting on a soft carpet of pine needles on the hill overlooking Mudros Bay on the island of Lemnos, ten days after the landings. It was the first time they had been together since the abrupt curtailment of their honeymoon, an occasion neither of them had wished to prolong. By tacit consent, they avoided any reference to their wedding night, and Anastasia would have been glad to forget they were married at all. But the well-meant efforts of the other nurses to free her from duty while Anthony was on the island had made this impossible. The problems raised by their honeymoon were still unresolved, but for the moment Anthony was too weary to tackle them.

Anastasia had awakened on the morning after her wedding to find herself curled up in a corner of the bed. She dreaded the long day ahead. But a sudden change of weather during the night had altered all Anthony's plans. The high winds which had delayed the start of the Allied landing on Gallipoli had died away at last, and to her profound and guilt-stricken relief her husband of a single day and night was obliged to leave the *dahabeéyah* at once and rejoin his general aboard the warship *Queen Elizabeth*.

A husband in name only! She was glad to see him go, and gladder still when, on her return to the hospital, she was summoned by the matron who offered her the chance to join a nursing unit being transfereed to the island of Lemnos.

"I know you don't see eye to eye with Sister Price, and over there you'll stand a better chance of catching a glimpse of your husband now and then," she said kindly. Beneath her pristine apron beat a romantic heart full of pity for this young bride abandoned on her honeymoon. "I can send either you or Nurse Dunwoody, who is far more experienced, of course, but I think it's only fair to send you. You are recently married, after all and the staff officers are always popping across to the islands for one reason or another. I'm sure you'll work very hard to make up for your lack of experience. You have the makings of a fine nurse, my dear."

"Thank you, I would like to go to Lemnos," said Anastasia. Matron, she thought, would be shocked to know that the chance to see Anthony hardly ranked as an attraction in her eyes. But she longed to leave Egypt and Lemnos seemed to offer her a challenge in her nursing career.

"It always makes me sad to see young people torn asunder by the cruel hand of War," said Matron with a faraway smile. "I know just what it is to lose a loved one to battle's martial call. Now I can only do my poor best to reunite wives and husbands when the opportunity arises." She heaved a sentimental sigh. "So do your best, Nurse Khark—Nurse *Mills,* I mean to say. Remember all that Sister Price has taught you, and try to justify my faith in you."

"Yes, Matron." She left the hospital with a light step and a lighter heart, delighted to have escaped from the Welsh Dragon's thrall. Two days later—much to the chagrin of Sybil Dunwoody—Anastasia was on her way to Lemnos.

Hospital ships were already disembarking boat loads of weary soldiers from the Gallipoli Peninsula, and for the first time Anastasia worked with a will, doing everything she could to relieve their suffering. It seemed so different from Egypt. This was real: the chance to show what she was made of and help to win the war. This was why she had wanted to become a nurse. The sight of charred flesh and suppurating wounds no longer repelled her, nor did the long hours on duty tire her as they once had.

Scraps of news were brought back by the wounded soldiers, but they were meager and fragmented. Several of the landings seemed to have succeeded, though at heavy cost. Communications between the different bridgeheads were difficult, and few of the wounded had anything like an overall view. The only point on which all agreed was that it would be a long, hard struggle. Johnny Turk had dug himself in well; to dislodge him on that hostile terrain would not be easy.

Anthony's arrival on the island promised a more comprehensive view of the situation. The trouble was, he kept falling asleep when she questioned him. A little breeze sighed through the pines and cypresses, bringing the warm scents of thyme, myrtle and rosemary. The sea below them was peacock-blue between the gray sides of the warships, and far away the misty blue and lilac horizons of Imbros and Samothrace floated in a haze.

"The peace . . . the silence . . . it seems like another world," said Anthony. He lay back and closed his eyes.

She picked a sprig of juniper and tickled his neck above the khaki collar. "I won't allow you to go to sleep yet. I'm starving for news. We all are. We listen to the guns on the mainland, yet we know nothing. Rumors are everywhere, but nobody can tell us if we're winning the war or losing."

"It's hard to say. Probably more like a stalemate right now. What was I telling you about?...Oh yes, the message from Anzac..."

As he spoke a scene took shape behind his closed eyelids. Once again he was there at midnight in Admiral De Robeck's dining saloon aboard the *Queen Elizabeth,* watching the tall, thin figure of General Hamilton as he read the bleak message from General Birdwood on Anzac beach.

> Both my Divisional generals and brigadiers have represented to me that they fear their men are thoroughly demoralized by shrapnel fire to which they have been subjected all day after exhaustion and gallant work in the morning...If troops are subjected to shell fire again tomorrow morning there is likely to be a fiasco, as I have no fresh troops with which to replace those on the firing line. I know my representation is most serious, but if we are to reembark it must be at once.
>
> Birdwood

Slowly the general's eyes moved down the table's polished length, but the faces of the seated men revealed nothing of their thoughts. Other staff members were crowded in the doorway, aware that General Hamilton's decision might mark the turning point of the whole campaign. If the Commander-in-Chief ordered an evacuation of Anzac cove, he would be admitting failure. Even worse, the retreat might result in the deaths of most of the landing party.

He turned to Admiral Thursby, who was in charge of the naval side of the Anzac landing. "Admiral, what do you think?"

Thursby considered a moment before replying in his slow, deliberate voice, "It will take the best part of three days to get that crowd off the beaches."

Hamilton nodded. "And where are the Turks?"

"On top of them! I think myself that our men will stick it out if it's put to them that they must."

Hamilton said no more, for at that moment Commodore

Roger Keyes had been handed a message from the captain of the Australian submarine *AE 2,* announcing that he had successfully penetrated the Narrows and entered the Sea of Marmara. Keyes' monkey-like face broke into a grin, and he read the telegram out loud.

"Tell the men this," he said to the general, laying the captain's note on the polished table. "It's an omen! An Australian submarine has accomplished a major feat in submarine history. It is going to torpedo all the ships bringing reinforcements into Gallipoli."

The tense faces around the table relaxed. And in the silence that followed Keyes' words, Hamilton wrote his reply to General Birdwood.

> Your news is indeed serious. But there is nothing to do but dig yourselves in and stick it out. It would take at least two days to reembark you, as Admiral Thursby will explain. Meanwhile, *AE 2,* the Australian submarine, has entered the Narrows and torpedoed a gunboat at Chanak . . . Make a personal appeal to your men and Godley's to make a supreme effort to hold their ground.
>
> Ian Hamilton
>
> P.S. You have got through the worst. Now you have only to dig in until you are safe.
>
> Ian H.

"I think it was the postscript that did it." Anthony said, as he recreated the scene for Anastasia. "They dug themselves in with a will. They held their position. It's the weirdest front line I've ever heard of. Some of the Anzac trenches are literally only a few feet away from the Turkish ones. Our men have started calling the Anzacs 'Diggers,' and I expect they've dug themselves a foothold in history. The Turks won't be able to dislodge them now . . ."

While telling the story, he had temporarily shaken off his lethargy but now it threatened to overwhelm him again. As his eyelids drooped, Anastasia asked, "How did that submarine manage to enter the Sea of Marmara? Don't the Germans patrol the Narrows?"

"They certainly do," he said sleepily. "There were nets, mines, and guns blazing across the water, but somehow the submarine managed to dodge them all. There are two German battleships anchored in the Golden Horn, the *Goeben* and the *Breslau.* They've been there since the start of hostilities, and all our men are longing to blow them to hell..."

His eyes were closed and he seemed on the point of dropping off to sleep again. Impatiently she demanded, "Can't you stay awake for a few minutes longer? There are so many things I want to know."

Anthony smiled but he didn't stir. "You'll have to excuse my shocking manners, my dear, but we've all been short of sleep lately. What is it you want to know?"

"I want to know what you do?" she said in a rush. "Exactly what do you do on Sir Ian's staff? The other nurses ask me and I have to say that I don't know..."

He propped himself on one elbow and regarded her curiously. "This is very unexpected, my dear. Why the sudden interest?"

"It isn't sudden. I've always been interested. Why can't you share your career with me?"

"You haven't shown much sign of wanting to share, yourself." he said dryly. "I'll tell you this much. I'm in Intelligence work. That means that if I have any secrets, I shouldn't share them with anyone, not even my... wife."

Nothing had changed. The barrier was still there between them. Forlornly, she said, "Sometimes you sound like you hate me."

Anthony laughed, but without amusement. "How can you say that when I've come here today especially to see you?"

"But you keep falling asleep! You haven't asked anything about where I live, or how my work is going. You don't seem interested at all."

"All right. How *is* it going?"

"Oh, it's very much better away from Sister Price. The poor men! Their wounds are terrible, but they are so brave and don't complain. I can even help in the operating theater now..."

"So you've got over feeling sick at the sight of blood... Well done—some people never do." He put his arm around her shoulders. Instinctively she leaned back, enjoying the security, lowering her guard. This was more like the old times at the temple, when they would sit and talk about their work, and when no tiresome personal problems were allowed to intrude. Why couldn't it always be like this? Why must love and longing for the wrong person always cloud true friendships?

Anthony was saying, "You nurses are the real war heroes. To my mind, it takes a different and *much* rarer courage to patch up a man's shattered body than it does to storm an enemy-held position. It amazes me when I see girls like you and Sybil—who've never worked in your lives before, probably never touched anything dirtier than a garden spade—cleaning up filth that would turn the stomach of a Billingsgate fishwife. I've always wondered how you manage to get over the revulsion you must feel at some of the things you're asked to do."

So he did understand! Anastasia felt a small glow of pleasure at the praise. She said soberly, "You don't let yourself think about what you are doing. You have to put your mind somewhere else."

He looked searchingly at her. "Where do *you* put your mind?" he asked.

Without thinking, she told the truth. "I think about Valerian..."

"Damn Valerian!" said Anthony with sudden savagery. "You never let up, do you?" He removed his arm from her shoulders and stood up abruptly, grim-faced. "Sorry I can't stay to listen to any more of your soul-searchings, but you can probably indulge them more easily alone anyway."

"You—you're going? So soon?" Anastasia felt as if a bucket of icy water had been dumped on her body, leaving her cold and shocked. "When will I see you again?"

He shrugged. "I'll probably look in some time next week, but I can't promise anything. I'll be off now. I'm meeting a chap down at the harbor."

"Wait for me," she pleaded, but he was gone without a smile or a wave to soften the parting. She watched his fair head cross the path below and vanish in the pine trees, and tears of resentment sprang to her eyes. It was because she'd mentioned Valerian that he'd broken off their conversation so abruptly. Yet why shouldn't she speak of Valerian when he was constantly in her thoughts? Anthony had said he'd accept the risk that Valerian would always be between them. Why then couldn't he even tolerate the sound of his rival's name? There'd been so many things she wanted to talk about, and now she wouldn't get another chance for a week. It was unfair that Anthony should be able to go and come, apparently as free as a bird, while she was tied to her exhausting, demanding work. She felt disappointed as well as resentful as she picked pine needles from her skirt and walked down the hill.

On the way to the harbor, three of her nursing colleagues—Sally Scott-Ferguson, Fiona Brown, and sharp-tongued little Eileen Corrigan, whom nobody liked very much—were sitting at an open-air café. They were sipping from tall glasses and watching the sun set over the water. As she passed they asked her to join them.

"Where was your handsome husband off to in such a hurry?" asked Eileen at once, her dark eyes alert. "I thought he'd be staying overnight. Wasn't that why Matron changed the duty roster to suit you?"

"To suit me? That's the first I've heard of it." Though Anastasia's tone was cool, Eileen wasn't in the least abashed.

"He was walking as though the devil himself was at his heels. He went into that little house at the end of the street. It's where that woman lives, Ariadne Something-or-Other—the one with five brothers who're supposed to work hand in glove with the Germans." She paused, then said slyly, "I've heard that Ariadne is very beautiful."

Anastasia stared until Eileen's eyes dropped. "Anthony had an appointment to keep. That's why he was in a hurry."

The other girls exchanged glances, sensing trouble. "Well, sit down and drown your sorrows while you tell us all about it," said Eileen. "You may see him again when he's through with *la belle Ariadne*."

But Anastasia was too proud to sit and wait for her husband to leave another woman's house. She shook her head. "No, thank you. I'm going back to the home to rest. I'm on duty at ten o'clock."

"No, you're not. I just told you—Matron changed the roster so you could spend the night with your husband. Some people have all the luck."

"All the same, I think I'll go back."

Sally Scott-Ferguson, the outspoken, freckle-faced daughter of a duke, whose manners derived from the stableyard though her heart was the purest gold, finished her drink and rose. "I'll come with you." As they walked up the dusty hill toward the nurses' home, she said brusquely, "Don't mind Eileen. She's a nosy little bitch who always wants to know exactly what everyone had for breakfast. She's absolutely man-mad, and the sight of your handsome Anthony passing by without a glance at her was more than she could bear."

"She thinks I'm 'stuck-up' because I don't confide in her," said Anastasia unhappily. "What is this 'stuck-up'?"

"Just a stupid term. Don't let it worry you. She knows just as well as I do that your husband's in Intelligence, and you can't be expected to talk about that."

"*You* know this?"

Sally laughed, showing strong teeth. "I managed to figure it out . . . Oh lord, I nearly forgot! Matron wants a word with you."

"With me?"

"Don't look so worried. She only wants you to talk to that poor Senegalese soldier in bed thirty-four. He's convinced that his gods have deserted him, and he doesn't seem to want to live any longer. She thought you might be able to cheer him up since he'll understand your French better than hers. Apparently she never got much farther than *'la plume de ma tante.'*"

It was two weeks before Anthony returned, but at last Anastasia was summoned from the nurses' home by a message that he was waiting outside for her. She was so happy to see him that she quite forgot the coolness between them. That fortnight had seemed to be the longest two weeks she'd ever know—not only because of his absence, but also because the number of men in the hospital increased dramatically when typhoid broke out in another.

Her unit had worked day and night until they could hardly tell one from the other. And when she ran out into the street to meet Anthony, he was shocked to see how thin she'd become. The bones of her face stood out beneath her veil, and her green eyes were circled with dark shadows.

"What have they been doing to you?" he exclaimed, as she offered her face for his kiss. "You're nothing but skin and bones! Don't they feed you properly in that home of yours?"

"They do their best, but it's too hot to eat much. I'm thin

because so many patients are arriving that the days aren't long enough to look after them all. Today I'll be the one to fall asleep while you're talking!"

"I got permission from your matron and the loan of a car and I'm planning to take you up into the hills. Among the sheep and goats and wildflowers, you can forget all about the war and nursing for a few hours." He grinned. "I brought a bottle of wine, too, and I won't even complain if you want to sleep all afternoon."

"Oh, that would lovely!" She took his arm, conscious that Eileen's sharp eyes were observing from her bedroom window. Miss Corrigan would have no fresh tidbits for her fertile imagination today. If Anthony felt any surprise at her spontaneous gesture he gave no sign of it. Arm in arm, the picture of marital bliss, they walked down the street to the car.

That picnic set the pattern for many others. They ate, they drank and they lay in the sun, careful to avoid any subject that might start a quarrel. Sometimes they went alone; more often James Denny, who owned the car, and Sally Scott-Ferguson would join them. Slowly, Anthony's hopes rose that at last their marriage might become a normal one. Anastasia always seemed glad to see him, enjoyed his company, kissed him affectionately on meeting and parting, and no longer flinched if he tried to prolong the embrace.

He schooled himself to be patient, to give her time to forget Valerian, and as the long, hot summer wore on he began to hope that his patience might soon be rewarded. He didn't realize that she was still receiving letters from Valerian—letters which escaped the censor through devious channels known only to Andrei and his expatriate friends, and painted glowing pictures of the new Russia that was going to rise from the ashes of the old. He urged her to return to Russia as soon as she could and share in its glory. The political implications of his words were lost on Anastasia. She only knew that Valerian was happy and wanted her to share his happiness.

Though the idea made her dizzy with delight, she was careful to hide it from her husband. Meantime she answered the letters, making no mention of her own marriage, and assuring Valerian that when the war was over she would return to Russia. When the war was over... Would it ever be over? June, July, and August dragged by. The wildflowers withered in the parched brown hills, and the rows of crosses marking the Allied graves both on the Gallipoli Peninsula and on the island grew ever longer.

One hot morning in early September, when Anastasia was going on duty, she met Sally Scott-Ferguson just finishing her night's work. Her freckled face was tired and drawn.

"They're going to operate on poor Sam Horton again," she said. "Isn't it a pity?"

"Oh, Sally!" Anastasia looked at her friend in dismay. "Will he lose his other leg?"

"I'm afraid so. Once gangrene sets in there's nothing else to do. It makes you wonder, doesn't it? A kid like that . . . He's been asking for you all night. There's nothing, simply nothing, we can say to comfort him. He goes all to pieces, poor kid, begging them not to operate. We've had a hell of a night."

Anastasia had never seen her so upset. They were all used to death by now, but there was something different about Sam. He was the pet of all the nurses—a slight, rosy-cheeked youngster with curly dark hair and an engaging grin. He stoutly maintained he was eighteen and the recruiting officer must have accepted his story, though the nurses thought that sixteen was nearer the mark. He and his elder brother had enlisted at the outbreak of war.

He had fought in the parched, bullet-swept front-line trenches until he was the sole survivor of his original unit, and then his trench was blown up by a well-placed Turkish mine, burying him deep in the rubble. Someone had managed to dig him out before he suffocated, but his right leg was smashed beyond hope of repair, and before he arrived at the hospital ship gangrene set in. The surgeon had been obliged to amputate the shattered limb immediately.

The boy's cheerful courage in facing up to his loss had won the hearts of all the nurses on Lemnos. But a week ago the divisional surgeon had shaken his head over the condition of Sam's other leg, where wounds left by shrapnel were still inflamed and ugly.

Anastasia's heart was heavy as she went toward the bed surrounded by screens where Sam was being prepared for his second ordeal. She dreaded his frightened questions—questions to which there could be no comforting answer, but a single glance showed her that the boy was already delirious. His dark, curly hair was sweat-plastered to his skull and his glassy eyes were unfocused.

She laid her fingers lightly on his wrist and his hot hand caught at them, clinging with desperate strength.

"Oh, Mama, you've come at last," he said in the weak, querulous voice of a sick child. "I waited so long for you to come. Don't let the doctor cut off my leg so I can't walk any more. I'd sooner die than that—honest I would."

Anastasia caught Sister Warner's tired, worried eyes. "He doesn't know what he's saying," the Sister said. "He's been like this since I came on duty. Help me lift him onto the trolley now. The surgeon is waiting..."

Together they wheeled the soldier down the ward between the rows of beds. Anastasia noticed that many of the wounded men looked away when they recognized the figure on the trolley.

Throughout that long, stifling morning, Anastasia waited in vain for the oderlies to bring back the small, swathed figure, but when she went off duty the screened bed was still empty. Later, at the nurses' home, she tried to put him out of her thoughts, but at last, despairing of doing so, she went for a solitary walk along the cliffs. The peace and beauty of the wild coastline seemed only to emphasize Sam's tragedy. *"I'd sooner die* than that..." Perhaps he had known very well what he was saying. What kind of life awaited a sixteen-year-old veteran without legs...? A boy who had known the joy of running and swimming and climbing trees before this cruel, wasteful war dragged him away from his solid Yorkshire home and made him fight an enemy he didn't hate in a land he didn't know...?

All afternoon she walked along the cliffs, the cry of the sea birds in her ears and the sweet, warm scent of myrtle all around her. At four she returned to duty, unrefreshed, to find the ward in turmoil. Extra beds were being moved in to cope with the many new wounded from "V" Beach. Nurses rushed about, harried and overworked. The surgeons were tired and irritable as they worked through the stuffy afternoon heat.

"How's Sam?" she managed to ask Sally as they passed.

"He's dying..."

"Nurse Mills! Over here quickly, please. This patient needs a fresh dressing." Sister Warner's crisp voice prevented Anastasia from going at once to Sam's bed, but as order was gradually restored to the crowded ward, she seized her first opportunity to slip behind the screen. Sam was conscious, though his face wore the gray pallor they all dreaded—the pallor of approaching death.

"How do you feel, Sam? Are you comfortable?" The questions seemed meaningless. How could a youth whose leg had been amputated be comfortable?

"I feel nothing, Nurse," he said weakly. "They've taken off my leg, and I don't feel anything. Stay with me, Nurse, just a little while... It gets lonely listening to the groans."

"I'll be back in a few minutes, Sam, just as soon as I can."

She sat by him, holding his hand, while his breathing became weaker and weaker. When Sister Warner came to check his condition, she sighed. "Stay with him, Nurse Mills," she murmured. "I'll get Nurse Corrigan to attend to your duties tonight."

Later on, Sam said clearly. "When I'm gone, please write to Mama, will you, Nurse? Tell her I'm sorry... Tell her not to let young Terry volunteer. He's only a kid..."

Unable to speak, Anastasia nodded. She'd considered herself hardened to the dying of soldiers, but this gallant young man trying to spare his mother further grief was almost too much to bear.

Sam was silent for a long time then, and when he spoke again she had to bend down to understand his whisper.

"So long, then, Nurse. I'm going now..."

He broke off with a little gasp and his jaw sagged. A moment later the grip of his hand on hers relaxed and she knew he was dead. Her vision blurring with tears, she closed his eyelids and straightened the thin, mutilated body. Her shift had ended an hour before, but she hadn't wanted to leave little Sam to die alone.

Now she felt numb, drained of all energy. She walked home through the star-bright night, and when she opened the door of the bedroom she shared with Fiona to find Anthony stretched out on her narrow bed, reading, she was too exhausted even to feel surprise.

"Anastasia!" He stood, and she walked into his arms as if pulled by a magnet. Then the tears she had held back all day poured down her cheeks as if they'd never cease.

For a long time he held her close, murmuring endearments, while she sobbed out her grief over Sam. Only when the storm of weeping had died down did he ask: "What happened? Why are you so late? I've been waiting two hours. Fiona said you'd be back any minute."

"I wanted to stay with Sam, the boy who lost his leg," she said. "He died tonight. Oh, Anthony, it's so horrible... A boy like that—killed when his life was just beginning."

"War is a horrible business," he said. "I'm sorry about Sam. I should have realized that something important was keeping you. It's too late to go out to dinner, I'm afraid, but here's some chocolate and fruit."

She shook her head. "I'm not hungry. First I must write to—to Sam's mother. He asked me to." When tears began afresh, he realized how close she was to the breaking point. The long strain of nursing had undermined her defenses, and her nerves were badly strained. He longed to comfort her, but how could he when she shied away from all but the slightest contact?

"You shouldn't do that tonight. You're much too tired," he said firmly. "I have a forty-eight-hour leave. If you can square it with your matron, we'll go over to Rhodes together. It's high time you had a break. Things will look quite different when you get back."

Escape! Two days away from the smell of wounds and disinfectant, the flies, the germs, the losing battle with Death. It was an answer to a prayer.

"Only you and me?"

"Yes."

Slowly Anastasia shook her head. "I'm sorry. I can't go with you."

"Why not?" he said, impatiently, his eyebrows drawn together in a frown. "Would you go if someone else was coming with us? You'd go with anyone else but not with me, is that it?"

Her stubborn silence confirmed it. Savagely, Anthony said, "Yet you're glad enough to come to me for help if you think I can be useful! But when I expect you to keep your side of the bargain, you behave like a frightened virgin."

"I'm not a frightened virgin."

"Not frightened, or not a virgin?"

"You have no right to ask me that. I made no such bargain with you," said Anastasia, furiously.

"You married me. If that isn't a bargain, I don't know what is. You promised to love, honor and obey me, Anastasia, and for almost four months now you've done nothing of the kind."

"You're nothing but a bully! You forced me to marry you!"

Anthony pulled a crumpled piece of paper from his pocket, and held it in front of her eyes. She stared at her own words, scrawled on a temperature chart: *Yes, I will marry you. Anastasia*

"Do you remember writing that? It doesn't look much like coercion to me. No. You married me of your own free will, Anastasia, because you thought it presented a way out of your difficulties. And, God help me, I married you because I loved you. Because I wanted you. I still do, and I'm telling you now that I'm tired of waiting. I want you now."

Her tear-streaked face turned even paler, and she backed away until she stood against the door. "No," she whispered. "I'll go with you tomorrow. I promise I will! But not here . . . What if Fiona . . .?"

"Fiona is on night duty, as you know very well," he said. "I've had enough of your excuses and promises. If Valerian crooked his little finger you'd be happy to jump into his bed, no doubt. But Valerian is married to somebody else now and you're *my* wife, whether you like it or not."

"I *don't* like it!" Anger made her bolder. Surely no one, not even Anthony, would risk overpowering her here in the nurses' home, a well-built stone villa which had once belonged to a French millionaire. Although the walls were thick, a scream could be easily heard.

"Then I'll have to teach you to like it."

His hand shot out and imprisoned hers. He pulled her close to him. "What's the matter with you? Why are you so frightened of making love? I won't hurt you, I promise."

"You can't make love to someone you hate."

"Can't you? I'm not so certain about that. Why don't we give it a try? Besides, you don't really hate me. You only say that because you've clung to your silly romantic image of Valerian so long that you can't give him up, even though he doesn't actually exist."

"He does exist!"

"So you say." She caught the look of contempt he gave to Valerian's photograph, in its accustomed place on her dressing-table. ("My brother," she'd told Fiona, who had enjoyed fantasies of meeting him ever since.) "I think he is—and has always been—a figment of your girlish imagination."

As he spoke he was unbottoning her blue uniform dress unhurriedly, slipping it off her shoulders and hanging it over the chair. "Isn't it terrible how these lamps attract insects," he said in a conversational tone of voice, turning down the wick, pulling back the bedcovers with one hand while keeping a firm grip on her with the other. "Into bed with you now."

Unresisting, she let him slip one arm behind her knees and another around her shoulders and hoist her onto the bed. Struggling only made things worse, as she'd learned to her cost that night in Siberia. It was no use fighting a man as strong as Anthony. The best she could hope was that he'd lose interest in coupling with a dumb, passive zombie. All her maneuverings and subterfuges had been expended. Now she lay like a limp rag doll, unfeeling and unresisting as her husband took her in his arms.

She was grateful for the cover of darkness which made it easier to imagine that the hands caressing her were Valerian's, and that the mouth kissing her shoulders and breasts was his. When at last she felt the long-forgotten, easily remembered thrust that woke her body into involuntary response, her only surprise was that this time it was unaccompanied by pain. Rather the reverse. Despite her determination to remain frigid, loyal at least in spirit to Valerian while her husband forced his attentions on her, the physical love of which she'd deliberately been starving herself began to sweep her along on its turbulent tide. She struggled unavailingly against the warm flood of sensation, trying to derive no pleasure from it, but her treacherous body went on responding to his touch, shamelessly encouraging it and begging for more, inviting his caresses and reveling in his hard, muscular strength while she acquiesced in his demands.

This wasn't how she'd remembered that furtive, guilt-laden night in Siberia, which had wounded her mentally as well as physically. This has a meeting of equals, two bodies which were perfectly attuned though their owners' minds were miles apart. When Anthony rolled over with a sigh and cradled her head against his chest, she felt an overwhelming sense of well-being—a heavy, fulfilled drowsiness which lay like lead on her eyelids.

It lasted only a minute, and then the realization that she had enjoyed what she'd intended to suffer sent a stab of self-disgust through her body. Turning cautiously, she surveyed the sleeping face of the man beside her. His golden eyelashes glinted in the faint moonlight and his mouth was slightly curved in a smile. He had got what he wanted, and the knowledge filled her with unreasoning anger. She was deeply ashamed to find she had betrayed Valerian by responding to this crude, insensitive Englishman, who had taken her cynically, cold-bloodedly, gambling on her weakness after a day of emotional strain. He had demanded her submission like any caveman, and to her shame she had allowed it.

Never again, she vowed, lying stiff in his arms. She felt angry and defiled. She turned back to look at Valerian's photograph—and thought that the eyes reproached her. Gently she began to ease herself out of bed.

"What's the matter?" said Anthony, instantly alert. "Where are you going?"

"I want to find somewhere else to sleep," she said coldly.

Before she could move, his fingers were biting into her shoulders as he turned her to face him. "Oh no, you're not," he said grimly. "You're spending the rest of the night here in bed—with me."

"I won't! You can't make me." She jerked herself free and began to fling on her clothes. "Aren't you satisfied with your night's work?" she said, tying her shoes with trembling fingers. "Haven't you hurt and humiliated me enough for your pleasure?"

"Damned little pleasure I got from you tonight," said Anthony with brutal frankness. "The next time I feel like sleeping with an iceberg in the bed I'll let you know." He watched her finish dressing and then said: "Well, I suppose it's a fool who doesn't know when he's beaten, though it saddens me to admit that Sybil was right about you all along."

"What do you mean?"

"She told me you'd take everything I had to offer and give nothing in return."

As she remembered the guilty pleasure she'd felt in his arms, and the many times she'd run to him for help, a hot wave of shame washed over Anastasia and robbed her of all discretion.

"I hate Sybil and I hate you!" she cried. "I won't stay with you. I won't be your wife any longer. I shall go back to Russia and then you'll be free to marry your Sybil, if you think so much of her opinion." She paused and then added childishly, "I hope she makes you just as unhappy as you've made me."

Unconsciously she had reverted to Russian and he replied in the same language. "It hasn't made either of us very happy, has it? I thought that tonight we might be able to mend things. There was one moment when I hoped . . . when you seemed . . ."

She knew the very moment he alluded to. "I was pretending that you were Valerian." That wasn't altogether true but she hoped he'd believe her.

"So be it then," said Anthony with cold finality. "Nothing is going to change you, and I've waited too long already. I'm not prepared to extend the deadline. If you want your freedom I'll see that you get it. I'll give you grounds for divorce just as soon as you want them. You can consider yourself free of me as of now. May I ask how you're proposing to get to Russia—and what you'll do when you get there?"

"I don't know," she said lamely. "I haven't had time to decide yet." His sudden capitulation had taken her by surprise. She felt strangely lost and disoriented, vaguely chagrined to discover how easily he'd agreed to let her go. It was as if she'd imagined herself bound with rope which had turned out to be mere gossamer threads.

"Then leave it to me," said Anthony courteously. "I'll find a way to get you there. It may well fit in with a certain plan I've got at the back of my mind. And now I'll say good night to you . . ."

The door shut behind him. Anastasia, who had been promised everything she'd asked for, cast a look at the smiling photograph on her dressing-table and burst into tears.

Chapter Twenty

For ten days Anastasia heard nothing from her husband, and as she moved about the ward attending her patients, or leaned from her bedroom window to catch the evening breeze blowing across the harbor, she wrestled with the temptation to confide her troubles to Sally. At times she craved the Scots girl's forthright advice: at others she dreaded it. Living and working together as they did, it seemed incredible to her that Sally had not guessed at her inner turmoil. Surely, she thought, some hint of her misery must show in her face? But Sally, whose eye was so quick to detect the least change in the condition of a patient, remained strangely blind to Anastasia's agonized indecision.

Anthony or Valerian, England or Russia? Which did she want, and which wanted her? The hero of her childhood, or the strange, self-contained man whose love she had so blithely tossed aside? Anthony didn't want her now; he'd told her that plainly enough. How could she stay with him when he'd openly admitted that their marriage had been a mistake?

In her heart, she knew only too well what Sally's advice would be. Give Anthony another chance. Stick to your husband. Tell him you're sorry and try to patch up your quarrel. But Anastasia knew she couldn't do it. Before she apologized, her husband would have to meet her halfway and admit that she hadn't been the only one in the wrong.

If he had returned to her that night, he could have taken her in his arms and the rift between them could have healed without words. But as the days passed, his continued silence created an ever-increasing resentment, obliterating her memory of the good times they had shared. She kept remembering the inconsiderate way he had treated her, and the unflattering willingness with which he'd agreed to a separation. He's as glad to be rid of me as I am of him, she assured herself—and wondered why she felt like crying again. But surely it was better to separate now than to drag an impossible marriage on and on. At least the two of them were the only people involved.

In the bright morning, when she felt strong and resolute, that attitude was easy and the way seemed clear. But at night in the dim loneliness of the ward or restless at home, regret for the past and fear of the future made her long to forget their quarrel. It was not until early September, when the worst of the heat was past, that a sudden summons to the matron's office took matters out of her hands.

As she entered Anastasia noted that the matron's round pink face had lost its customary serenity. She looked puzzled and oddly flustered, pushing back straying wisps of hair as she stared first at Anastasia and then at a sheet of paper on her desk.

"You wanted me, Matron?"

"Yes, Nurse. It's about this message. Really, I hardly know what to make of it though the instructions are clear enough. I've been ordered to release you from your duties so you may return home to Russia. Another nurse is arriving tonight to take your place in our unit."

"Do you mean now? I'm to go now?" stammered Anastasia. Her heart began a slow, painful pounding. Go back to Russia? Surely this was Anthony's doing, but why—and how?

"So I understand," said Matron. She read the letter again, her lips moving silently as she did so.

"Please tell me how I'm to go to Russia?" said Anastasia. "How is this possible in the middle of the war?"

Matron sighed. "Your husband will be able to explain that to you better than I can. He's waiting now, aboard the hospital ship that docked this morning. You're to join him just as soon as you can. Oh dear," she smiled suddenly, "don't ask me how he got permission to run you through a blockade! Your husband is a very determined young man. Surely there aren't many people who could persuade the admiral to use one of his precious submarines for such a purpose."

Now Anastasia was thoroughly bewildered. "I'm to go in a submarine? But how . . . when . . . ?"

"My dear child, I don't have the answers." The matron put

the letter down on the desk. "I shall be sorry to lose you; indeed, we all shall. We're very grateful for what you've contributed here, and you'll be missed by the patients, there's no doubt of that. But of course it's only natural that you should want to help your own people in their time of trouble. I won't try to persuade you to stay with us now that you have the opportunity to go to them. Good-bye, my dear, and may God's blessing go with you."

Unexpectedly, Anastasia's eyes smarted with tears as she found herself pressed briefly to the matron's starched bosom. A moment later she was outside in the noontime glare, the sunwarmed cobbles hot through the soles of her sturdy white shoes. She followed the fresh-faced midshipman who'd been sent to escort her, and hurried toward the nurses' home. Neither Sally nor Fiona was there, so she scribbled a hasty note of farewell to each of them, then packed a single small bag.

Following her guide to the harbor, she boarded the hospital ship. On the deck, Anthony was talking to a dark, thick-set young man in naval uniform.

"There you are at last, my dear," he greeted her cooly, making no attempt to kiss even her cheek. His companion's dark eyes moved quickly from one to the other. "I thought you were going to keep us waiting all night."

"I came as fast as I could," she said defensively. "What's going on, Anthony? Why have you called me from my work?"

She had an obscure feeling that she was being rushed into some committment, some action, she wasn't prepared for. Why hadn't he talked to her first?

"Didn't the matron explain?" Anthony said. "That's surprising. Well, all in good time . . . First I'd like you to meet my friend Guy—Lieutenant-Commander Guy Rickard of Submarine *E 57*. My wife, Anastasia."

As they shook hands, Anthony went on, "Guy and I are taking a trip through the Dardanelles tomorrow, and he's been good enough to promise to extend it a little for your sake. He'll run you up the Bosporus as far as the Black Sea and put you on a Russian ship bound for the Crimea—at least, that's the general plan. Isn't that just what you want?" His gaze locked with hers.

"Door-to-door service, you might say." said the young commander cheerfully.

Anastasia's mouth was dry. *Isn't that just what you want?* He was challenging her to deny it. He was willing her to turn down this offer of a magic-carpet ride to Russia. To leave him.

"*Isn't* it?"

Both men were staring at her now—Guy Rickard puzzled by her silence, Anthony with that intent, watchful look, as if his whole concentration was focused on her reply.

The silence stretched out and Guy shifted uncomfortably.

"I'll leave you to talk it over," he suggested.

"Oh no," said Anthony quickly. "It's quite all right. I've arranged this with all the top brass, and I leave you to imagine how easy *that* was! No—I simply want to be sure that my wife isn't having second thoughts..."

He wants a witness, thought Anastasia suddenly. He wants Guy to hear me say that I don't want to go back to Russia. Well, I won't say it. I refuse to give him the satisfaction of thinking he's outmaneuvered me again.

Her chin went up defiantly and now the words came readily to her tongue. "But of course it is what I want! Thank you, Commander Rickard. You are very kind. I couldn't believe at first what Matron told me. I thought that perhaps it was one of Anthony's jokes... Yes, to return to Russia is what I want most in the world."

The tension seemed to go out of Anthony. He looked suddenly tired and drawn. He shrugged. "So I thought."

"All right then, let's go," suggested Guy. He picked up her bag and led them in silence to the upper deck of the hospital ship, alongside which the submarine was berthed.

From this vantage point, *E 57* looked longer and thinner than Anastasia had expected.

"Hurry," said Guy, "we haven't got much time. We go down a couple of decks and across that plank on *E 57*'s bridge. Follow me and watch your step."

Having negotiated the long, vertical steel ladder into *E 57*'s control room, Anastasia found the submarine's interior surprisingly large. Doors in the dividing bulkheads were open for'd and aft the length of the hull. The crew, dressed in overalls, shorts and underpants, was relaxing writing letters, playing cards, washing, cleaning and polishing.

Guy's first lieutenant, Patrick Donovan, a freckled Ulsterman with enormous hands, appeared from nowhere. He was wearing shorts too.

"Meet our guests," said Guy. "Anastasia—or rather Mrs.

Mills—a nurse, and Anthony Mills, of course, you know already. Find a corner for their gear in the wardroom, then I can spare you—" he glanced at the control-room clock—"ten minutes to show them around the boat. Then we'll shove off. Meantime I'll be with the navigator."

"Very good, sir." said Patrick. He turned briskly to his guests. "Let's start for'd. This is the Fore End—the torpedo space—and herein," he slapped the rear doors of the torpedo tubes, "lie four eighteen-inch torpedoes, minnows, as we call them, charged up and rarin' to go. We also have one beam and one stern tube loaded likewise. Now we'll move aft." He turned and squeezed past them to lead the way again.

"Above us," he said rapidly, "the fore hatch, kept shut when away from home. Beneath us a storage battery, starting about here—" he pointed—"and running aft to the control-room bulkhead, supplying the juice for the motors when we dive. This—" stepping into the control room—"is the brain center. Those two large steering wheels on the starboard side are the for'd and aft hydroplane controls. Depth gauges behind 'em. The for'd planes keep the depth ordered; the after planes keep the boat level."

Anastasia stared around her, trying to take it all in. Patrick took a deep breath and continued:

"On the center line, these are our two periscopes, now lowered, as you see, into their well. The for'd one, thin at the top lens, is the attack periscope; the after one, fatter, is bifocal. Wireless office: there. Heads—lavatory to you—over there. If you want to use them when we dive, better ask someone to show you the technique first."

He glanced at his watch. "These taps, valves, levers, switches on the starboard side control diving and trimming. Those bulges on either side—that you may have noticed when you came on board—are the saddle tanks, buttoned on the pressure hull, for diving only.

"Aft, the wardroom, crew space, galley, engine room, and right aft, the electric motors. That's the noisy end. It's hot and smelly now because we've been charging batteries all day, and that involves declutching the tail shafts with diesel engines running the motors as dynamos. Time's up, I'm afraid."

Anastasia was puzzled. "You said there were thirty-four in the crew? Where on earth do they all sleep?"

Patrick grinned. "You'd be surprised," he said, leading them back to the wardroom.

The sun was beginning to set as *E 57* nosed toward the southern entrance of the Dardanelles at twelve knots in a calm, oily sea. Guy, Anastasia, Anthony and a signalman lookout were on the bridge. At Anthony's insistence, his wife was wearing cut-down men's overalls. She looked almost as snug as the ship.

"A very sensible rig, if I may so," Guy surveyed her approvingly. "A high proportion of the female casualty list on submarines is due to their clothes getting caught up in this vicious machinery."

For a few moments they stared in silence into the sunset, then Anthony said quietly, "What's your plan, Guy, or do you want to keep it secret?"

"Not a bit. I aim to creep around the lip of the Dardanelles' entrance now; dive, sit on the bottom until first light, and face this thirty-five-mile-long obstacle course underwater, with a fully charged battery. According to others who've done it, we should make the Sea of Marmara with a pretty flat battery by dark. We'll hide somewhere and recharge. After that we'll play it by stealth."

As he spoke, Anastasia noticed that Guy was nursing a stopwatch and giving it occasional glances.

Suddenly—

"Alarm starboard!" he shouted.

The signal lookout shot past them like a bullet and dived down the conning tower.

"Down you go, you two, just as fast as you can or you'll have the Aegean Sea on top of you. Move!"

Anthony reacted like lightning and followed the signalman. Seconds later Guy was literally pressing the bewildered Anastasia's head down the hatch with his foot. From a peaceful appreciation of a lovely evening on an empty sea, she suddenly found herself almost falling down this vertical funnel, her whole body sucked down by the demand for air exercised by two powerful diesel engines below, with Guy's feet threatening her fingers on the rungs of the steel ladder. Added to the turmoil was the sudden screeching rattle from the diving Klaxon, the executive signal throughout the boat to crash dive.

A short pause, and then the thump of the upper conning tower hatch being shut and clipped above brought sudden excruciating pain to her eardrums, as the diesels drew their last breath before stopping.

As Anastasia landed in a dazed heap on the control-room floor, Guy brushed past her and stood between the periscopes looking at his stopwatch.

"Twenty-five feet, sir," reported Patrick, from between the diving gauges.

"Eighteen seconds from diving hooter to twenty-five feet," said Guy. He looked at Anastasia with a smile. "I'm sorry if you found that a bit shattering, Mrs. Mills, but in this life we can never afford to let our heels touch the ground. There are two kinds of submarines; the quick and the dead."

Anastasia brushed the dust from the seat of her overalls. "You mean that was a *false alarm*?" she asked indignantly. "Why didn't you warn me?"

"I wanted to preserve the element of surprise." Guy smiled. "Don't worry, you and Anthony did very well. I promise I won't play any more tricks, and there's a cup of coffee in the wardroom..."

Having lowered herself gracefully to ninety feet, *E 57* slithered gently along the seabed.

"Stop both," ordered Guy, and told Patrick to hold her there by filling the midship trim tank. "Keep one watchkeeper on the diving gauges; remainder fall out from diving stations and get all the sleep you can. Tomorrow's going to be a long day. Have you found a cozy corner for our guests, Number One?"

"I've fixed them up with a mattress under the wardroom table."

"Splendid," said Guy, adding aside to Anastasia, "it isn't exactly posh, but you can't beat the ocean bed for peace and quiet. No guns, no signals, no telephones, no rude letters from bank managers..."

His voice died away, and when she glanced up from beneath the table she saw that Guy Rickard was already in his bunk and his light was out.

"Coffee, sir? Coffee, madam?" The wardroom steward was stooping beside them. Anthony was already sitting up with a chart across his knees.

"Sleep well?" he asked.

She blinked and nodded, remembering where she was, reflecting that this was the first and probably the last time they would share a bed, and wake up in it together.

"We're well into the Dardanelles," he said, "and going deeper, by the sound of it." He could hear the sound of the hydroplane motors. "Guy says there are floating minefields across the straits all the way from Kephez to Chanak, but they move around too much to know exactly where they are. We're going to dive right under the minefields, keeping our heads down and relying on our batteries until we're through the Narrows. Are you warm enough?"

She was shivering, but more from apprehension than cold. "I'm all right—" she said, and suddenly there was a sudden fierce jolt that flung her hard against him, followed by a shuddering that shook the boat from stem to stern.

"We've hit the net," called Guy from the control room. "We'll have to cut our way through. Now, net-cutter, over to you."

He didn't sound unduly alarmed, but Anastasia had a horrible vision of the submarine floundering like a great silver eel in a fish-net. She tried to picture the floating buoys on the water's surface, which might of course, attract the attention of the German patrol boats and the gunners in the Turkish batteries at Chanak and Kilid Bahr, the two old forts which faced one another across the Narrows.

"Hold tight!" shouted Guy, as he ordered full astern for a few hundred feet, then charged the net again. The vessel plunged forward and hit the metal mesh a second time, but instead of shutting off speed after the impact, her captain increased power, and foot by foot the sleek sea monster barged and jerked her way through the unseen obstacle.

A muffled thud on the port beam told them that the Kilid Bahr gunners had opened fire on the disturbance in the water. But before any patrol boats with depth charges could be sent to investigate further, *E 57* slithered through the jagged hole she had torn in the net and sped up the narrow channel toward Nagara Point, rolling and wobbling like a rabbit shot in the head. At first Anthony thought her wild, zigzag course was a deliberate tactic to evade pursuit, but then he realized that Guy and his crew were doing all they could to steady the vessel.

"Sorry about—the—rough—ride!" Guy somehow found

time to shout to his passengers, who were huddled in their corner. Anastasia was clinging unashamedly to her husband.

"Oh, stop it—make him stop it!" she moaned, pressing her face against his chest. "I shall be sick."

"Not down my only clean shirt, you won't," he answered, holding her tightly and bracing his feet against the bulkhead to prevent them both from being flung headlong onto the deck. "What's up with the steering, Guy?" he shouted as the submarine raced ahead, still lurching drunkenly.

Occupied as he was in navigating his boat under extremely dangerous conditions, Guy looked perfectly calm. His answer was as untroubled as ever.

"Spot of trouble with the starboard hydroplane," he said thoughtfully. "It feels as if we're towing something—probably a piece of that metal fence and nothing to worry about... All the same," he added, as the lurches became even more pronounced, "I think I'd better come up and take a look. I advise you to sit tight in case we have to go deep in a hurry."

Anthony's curiosity was too strong to follow the skipper's advice. Leaving Anastasia huddled in the corner, he stood behind Guy and watched as he peered for a long time through the forward periscope. Then he whistled soundlessly, turned, and noticed Anthony's look of inquiry.

"Take a peek," he invited.

Anthony grapsed the handgrips and pressed his eye against the rubber-sheathed lens. About twenty feet away on the starboard bow, he saw a large gray rounded object—a mine, hanging with its mooring wire obviously caught in the starboard hydroplane.

The vessel was bucking and plunging with a mine tied to its tail! At any moment the vibration alone might be enough to explode the mine.

"That looks bad. How are you going to get rid of it?" he said.

"We might shake it off, if we retire gracefully astern."

"We'd have to be lucky."

"Keep an eye on it while I have a word with Number One," said Guy. He quickly explained the situation to Patrick Donovan as Anthony continued to watch the horned monster through the periscope. It swayed from side to side with the vessel's movement, trailing by its moorings with languorous, deceptive grace. Gripping the periscope, Anthony found that his hands were slippery with sweat. After each lurch of the submarine he hardly dared to move, in case the tiny extra shock should snap a horn and detonate the death-dealing charge of TNT inside the mine's hard gray carapace.

Suddenly he felt the nose of the submarine dip sharply as the after ballast tanks were blown. Then, with a jerk that made him clamp his arms around the periscope, *E 57* went full astern. When Anthony put his eye back to the lens, he saw to his immense relief that the jerk had shaken loose the mine, which was being dragged down through the murky water by its mooring to settle once more on the bottom.

"All serene," he reported to Guy, wiping his sweating forehead as he joined him at the bottom of the steel ladder. "Well steered, sir."

The submarine had immediately resumed her normal course and Anastasia finally looked up from her corner.

"Are we there?" she asked hopefully.

Both men laughed and shook their heads. "No such luck," said Guy. "Never mind, it'll be easy sailing from now on, I hope. We're approaching the Sea of Marmara, and we'll be able to go up for a breather pretty soon. Perhaps you'd like to help me look for a suitable stalking-horse, Mrs. Mills?"

She was glad of an opportunity to stand up. After the buffeting of the last ten minutes, the submarine's progress now seemed rock-steady. "Oh, I can see the land!" she exclaimed delightedly, when Guy had positioned her by the after bifocal periscope. "Have we surfaced already?"

"No, we're still at twenty feet, but the periscope's clear of the water. Now, Mrs. Mills, I want you to look for a nice, juicy little target. Sail or steam, not too big, and the heavier laden the better. Just see what you can find."

Mystified but obedient, Anastasia spent the next hour at the periscope, pointing out the craft she spotted to Patrick Donovan, who stood at her elbow ready to call the captain for anything which looked promising. Commander Rickard seemed hard to please. Ship after ship appeared—and was rejected after careful scrutiny. Some were too big and some too small. Some were empty, and on their way back to reload in the Golden Horn. Some were going in the wrong direction, and one or two carried guns camouflaged on deck.

"Lovely targets," said Patrick regretfully, "but not what

we're looking for just now."

At last, when she was growing tired of straining her eyes against the glare of the water, she saw a stubby, twin-sailed cargo boat which the captain said would have to do.

"Our batteries are nearly flat and it's time we all had a blow-through. I think that little lady will suit us fine." Guy altered course toward her. "Stand by to surface!" he shouted. "Boarding party, gun crew, stand by!"

The mahogany faces of the Turkish crew aboard the little twin-sailed boat were a study in surprise and terror when they saw the sleek hull of the submarine surface alongside them. Several jumped into the water immediately and headed for the shore; others rushed to defend their cargo with long knives and rusty flintlocks.

"Tell them to calm down. Say we're not going to hurt them," said Guy, handing Anthony a megaphone. "Go aboard, Number One, and throw those guns overboard before they blow somebody's hands off, then make her fast amidships."

Quickly the Turkish boat was secured alongside *E 57*, so that the submarine was hidden by her bulk from any curious watchers onshore. The Turks who had jumped overboard were picked up and deposited on deck. Reassured by Anthony, who spoke in their own language, they soon became more friendly and haggled good-naturedly with *E 57*'s crew for the fruit and vegetables they carried.

All day the two ill-assorted craft sailed eastward, the submarine invisible behind the hull of her prize, helping to propel the cortege with one engine while charging with the other. Lying at her ease on the deck of the Turkish ship, a scarf on her head in the manner of Turkish ladies, Anastasia watched the submarine's crew splashing and swimming in the limpid blue waters, recharging the Turkish ships batteries just as *E 57* recharged hers. The sailors' white bodies were in startling contrast to their weathered faces. Only Guy and Anthony were tanned below the neck, while the sandy-haired Ulsterman's skin had turned a fiery pink in the strong sunshine.

As the concealing darkness fell, the captain ordered his men to set free their Turkish stalking-horse, and all through the night *E 57* cruised gently east, never far from the coast, until in the pearly gray mist before dawn she hoved-to in the lee of the Princess Islands, within sight of the city of Constantinople.

Anastasia awoke from an uneasy sleep to the sound of a muttered argument.

"We can't go past without taking so much as a crack at her," Guy was urging.

"We can and we will. You can have all the cracks you want at the *Goeben* and *Breslau* on our way back but not before," insisted Anthony.

"All right, but we must take a look at her. That won't do any harm. 'Time spent in reconnaissance is never wasted,' remember?"

"Is *seldom* wasted," Anthony corrected. "As a general rule I'd agree with you, but not when my wife's aboard."

"Come on, Anthony! Show a little sporting spirit. Let Mrs. Mills see a bit of the fun."

"Fun?" said Anastasia, sitting up and rubbing her eyes.

"Sorry, I didn't mean to wake you up," said Guy. "We're sitting outside the Golden Horn with two big German battle cruisers at our mercy, and I'm trying to convince your husband that it's our positive duty to take a look at them, at least. Not a shot, you understand—just a look."

Anthony shook his head. "On your way back," he repeated.

"Don't be a spoilsport," Guy pleaded. "Mrs. Mills, can't you persuade your husband?"

Guy Rickard's quiet voice and gentle eyes gave no clue to his reckless, mercurial temperament. The previous afternoon she had been aware that he was growing restless, as target after target in the shape of Turkish military transports and storeships passed by them unmolested, and she realized that her presence aboard was preventing the captain from fighting. Partly because she was grateful to him for providing the magic carpet to Russia that she had almost despaired of finding, and partly because she wanted to prove that she was no coward, she smiled at Guy and said, "Of course we must go and see where the German ships are hidden. It's a golden opportunity. So it's two to one, Anthony. Now give in and let the captain do as he wishes."

"Bravo!" cried Guy. "Mrs. Mills, your word is law. We won't listen to what your husband says."

Anthony grinned. "I'm outnumbered, by God. Contradicted by my own wife. All right then, have it your way. I wouldn't mind a look at the *Goeben* myself."

"Well done, Mrs. Mills. Forward to the Golden Horn!"

It was still barely light when the submarine dove at the end of Seraglio Point—where the golden domes and spires of Topkapi Serai, the Sultans' former palace, lay wrapped in morning mist—and headed into the Golden Horn. The whole harbor was crowded with ships and it took Guy a while to locate his prey. He prowled to and fro in the murky waters where the sacks containing discarded wives had once drifted gently in the current.

At last, on the far side of the Galata Bridge, he located the splendid armored length of the German battle cruiser *Goeben* which, together with her sister ship the *Breslau,* had shaken off the pursuit of Britain's fastest cruisers in the Adriatic and, by entering the Dardanelles, had precipitated Turkey's entry into the war on the side of the Central Powers.

Conscious of her value as a prize for the Allies, the *Goeben* now lay well protected by chained barges and heavy nets.

"Thar she blows!" said Guy reverently, as he scanned the warship's majestic bulk towering above them. "A sitting duck—a big fat blooming sitting duck. What a chance! Anthony," he said, and the fanatical light in his eyes made Anastasia wonder why she had ever thought them gentle, "not even for you or your beautiful wife am I going to pass up this chance at immortality."

"I knew it," said Anthony. "I knew you wouldn't be able to resist a crack at her once you had her in your sights." He turned to Anastasia. "You'd better curl up somehwere safe below until Guy's had his fun. The Golden Horn will be no place for noncombatants in the next few minutes..."

Chapter Twenty-one

Anastasia watched the crew prepare to fire two torpedoes from the submarine's for'd tubes.

"There's a heck of a lot of explosive in those fishes' front ends," said a sailor with a face as seamed and wrinkled as an old leather glove. "You won't 'alf wake the Huns up from their beauty sleep, eh m' darlings?" he said, as he patted the sleek metal monsters affectionately, and withdrew the safety pins from the pistols in their noses.

Carefully the crew slid the torpedoes into their tubes and clamped home the rear doors behind them.

"Now we can open and report the watertight bowcaps at the other end of the tubes," her self-appointed mentor continued. He seemed anxious that she should appreciate the miracle of modern science she was about to witness. "We flood the tubes with water from special tanks inside the sub before we fire. That stops a lot of sea water from coming in, see? Then, when the fish are on their way and the bowcaps are shut again, we pump that water into compensating tanks to keep the trim, like."

"I must see them go!" exclaimed Anastasia. A heady excitement gripped her as she watched the dials being set to control the torpedoes' speed and depth.

"You won't see them, but you'll feel 'em go," said the wizened sailor. "Best go and stand behind the captain, but keep out of his way, no offense, ma'am. He can get a mite touchy during an attack, and you might hear some funny language no woman ought to hear."

"I don't mind that," Anastasia said, but she was nonetheless careful to make herself as small and unobtrusive as possible as she stood behind Guy. Patrick Donovan gave her a cheerful wink, but the skipper was far too absorbed to take his eye from the periscope.

"If only there was a gap," he was saying. "She's tucked up so tight behind those damned barges that the fish can't reach her. I'm getting two fish ready. Our only hope is that the first will blow a hole in the net and let the second one through. Here goes . . . Stand by number one and two tubes. Number one tube, fire!" He glanced at the stopwatch he held. "Number two tube, fire!"

"Number one and two tubes fired, sir," reported the forward voice. The shock of the air charge speeding the three-quarter-ton missiles on their missions shook the submarine from stem to stern.

"Down periscope," Guy ordered, and stood back as the periscope dropped into its well. "Twenty seconds to go . . ." he said, eyes still glued to his stopwatch.

Aboard the *Goeben*, they saw the lookout's mouth open wide, as his arm pointed to the telltale disturbance in the water at the spot from which the torpedoes had been fired.

"Wait for it," breathed Guy.

Seconds later there was a brilliant orange flash between two barges, closely followed by another, but alas, the *Goeben* still lay majestically at anchor, untouched.

"Damn and blast!" said Guy bitterly. "The second fish never got through. Bang goes my decoration! Now we'd better make ourselves scarce."

The double explosion had caused a ferment in the Golden Horn. Boats were weighing anchor as fast as they could in order to put distance between themselves and the blazing barges, which sent showers of debris and chunks of flying metal sizzling into the water. Capsized by the sudden turbulence, small caiques and open boats floated bottom up, together with bobbing nets of fruit and vegetables, and stunned fish and fishermen who had dived overboard into the harbor.

Cutting through the panic and debris like a shoal of hunting sharks came a flotilla of swift, German-manned patrol boats to pounce on the marauders who dared to cause such havoc.

The crew of one patrol boat was actually grappling with a boathook, trying to seize the periscope of the submarine, as *E 57* dived under the Galata Bridge, narrowly avoiding the great underwater chain stretched from side to side of the harbor. She dodged between two river steamers, dived to sixty feet, and headed up the Bosporus at her best speed.

Guy was inconsolable. "What a chance—and I missed it! She'll never present such a perfect target again. Next time anyone tries there'll be a string of mines all the way up to her mooring," he lamented. "I thought we had a two to one chance, at least. Blast those bloody barges!"

The crew did their best to cheer him up, pointing out that the torpedoes might well have damaged her. In any case, they had given the *Goeben* the shock of her life. Guy's gloom persisted, however, throughout the rough and uncomfortable passage up the Bosporus.

In this narrow channel, cold water from the Black Sea and warm water from the Mediterranean formed two separate layers of differing density, a freakish water condition which caused the submarine to bob about like a cork in a washerwoman's tub, despite Patrick Donovan's efforts with the trim. Anthony was unaffected by the turbulence, and laughed and joked with the young lieutenant, but Anastasia was miserably seasick again and Guy still mourned the loss of his chance to sink the *Goeben*. His spirits didn't recover until they were clear of the high rocks known to the ancient world as Scylla and Charybdis—which marked the exit from the Bosporus—and surfaced again in the calm, sparkling waters of the Black Sea.

The submarine rocked gently at anchor half a mile from the rocky Crimean coastline, and the hum of recharging batteries filled the air belowdeck. It was time to go.

Guy held out his hand, smiling. "I'll say good-bye now, Anastasia, and ask you to excuse me if I don't see you off my boat. I've got one or two things to do. Anyway, I wish you the best of luck." Then he was melting away, the soul of tact, to let the couple take leave of each other.

"Thank you for bringing me here," Anastasia said with an attempt at gaiety. "Just like a magic carpet in a fairy story. *Au revoir*, Guy. I wish you a safe journey back."

"Oh, that's the last thing we want . . . It's been a pleasure to have you aboard," he assured her gallantly. "You didn't upset the trim nearly as bad as some of the fat colonels I've had to ferry here and there."

Anthony frowned. "Come on," he said impatiently. "I'm going to row you ashore." He wanted to get the parting over with as quickly and cleanly as possible, and frustrate her instinct to play up the drama of the moment.

Perversely she sought to detain him. "Wait a minute, Anthony, I'm not ready. I want to talk to you. I haven't had a chance to tell you what I—"

"What more is there to say?" he cut in roughly. "You've had your chance—dozens of chances. If you've changed your mind, it's too late, because I've taken you at your word. This is what you asked for: a one-way trip to Russia and freedom. There's no return ticket. I know you're not very good at facing facts, but this one is inescapable."

"But—but *you* are going back?" she protested, shaken by his harshness. Suddenly the rocky coastline of her homeland seemed menacing—a prison whose gates were about to close in on her.

"I've got work to do. This joyride wasn't arranged entirely for your benefit, you know. We'll have to do enough damage to the Germans on our way back to justify the risk of getting you here. *That's* why there's no return ticket for you."

No one could have told from Anthony's voice how much he hated having to part from her this way, but the habits of a lifetime warned him to hide his feelings from her. He'd known Anastasia long enough to realize that if his attitude softened she was quite capable of begging him not to leave her, and promising him anything so long as she could evade the need to face reality. Without of course, any real intention of keeping her promises. No. Anthony's jaw tightened. He couldn't go through this a second, a third or an unspecified number of times—always hoping, and always having his hopes destroyed by her stubborn, unreasoning loyalty to the myth of Valerian Radek.

He mustn't give in now, merely because she looked small and frightened and lost. Like a long-caged bird who finds the cage door open but fears to fly through it, she was clinging to him for security, not because she truly loved him. Anthony was sick and tired of being regarded as a refuge and nothing else. This time he'd opened the cage door; she was going to fly through it whether she wanted to or not.

"Hurry!" he said. "We don't want to attract attention by staying here too long."

Only a few early-rising nursemaids and their sun-hatted charges were on the beach to watch the dinghy skim toward the shore. Anastasia sat in the bow, watching the muscles strain beneath Anthony's shirt as he rowed. He seemed altogether silent and unapproachable.

He wants to get rid of me, she thought dully. He doesn't even want to talk to me any more. He will go back to his Sybil Dunwoody and tell her how happy he is to be free of that Russian girl who took everything and gave nothing back. If only he'd turn and smile at me! If only he wanted to kiss me...

But when he put her ashore Anthony risked neither a smile nor a kiss. "Good luck, Anastasia," he said, and held out his hand.

The cold formality of the gesture hit her like a blow. She gazed at him through a veil of tears, unable to speak, then caught his hand and pressed it to her lips. Gently Anthony pulled it away.

"No drama, please. We've gone beyond all that." He fished in his pocket and pulled out a stiff white envelope. "I almost forgot to give you this," he said, trying to speak lightly. "I can't leave my wife entirely dependent on the bounty of Valerian Radek."

"Is it money?"

"Go on, take it."

"I—I can't take your money," she whispered.

"Don't be ridiculous. How much have you brought of your own? Ah, you forgot all about it... I guessed as much. Well, you won't get far without money believe me." He tried to push the envelope into her hands, but she threw it back, and it lay on the little dock between them.

"I tell you I don't want your money. I can manage without it."

"All right. It's entirely up to you. Everything, now is entirely up to you."

He got back in the dinghy and pushed away.

"You're... going?" she said, with panic in her voice, unable to believe that the moment had actually arrived, that he was leaving her to face the harsh, cruel world alone. "Oh, Anthony, please come back! Don't go away—I've made a mistake. I don't want you to go!"

Already he was out of earshot, rowing with strong, steady strokes toward the slim gray silhouette of the submarine on the horizon.

"Come back!" she called again.

He shipped his oars for a moment in order to wave farewell. Seconds later the dazzle on the water hid the dinghy from sight.

Slowly she bent and picked up the envelope. She couldn't leave it there for the first beachcomber to pocket. Besides Anthony was right; she was bound to need it. Then, with dragging steps, she stumbled up the beach toward the nearest hotel.

The coffee they brought her was an abomination—her first real taste of wartime Russia—and she wished she had ordered tea. Looking around, she thought the customers seemed shabby compared to the well-dressed men and elegant women she remembered admiring on childhood visits to Yalta and Sevastopol. The Russians now staying in such once-fashionable resorts were apparently trying to forget the war for the duration of their holidays, but no one could ignore the telltale signs. Very few men sat under the striped awnings or strolled along the flower-bright esplanade, and those who did wore slings and carried crutches. Many of the women were dressed in black, and all the waiters were boys too young to serve in any army.

Nasty though the coffee was, it cleared her mind. Tentatively, hesitantly, like an invalid relearning to walk after a long illness, she began to plan ahead.

First she must make her way to Ostrovskoye. The servants there would have news of Valerian, and she would send him a message announcing her return to Russia. Picturing his surprise and pleasure, she began to feel more cheerful, and the shock of parting from Anthony abated somewhat. Susanna would still be at Ostrovskoye, of course, together with Valerian's son, but this didn't worry Anastasia. After all, such newcomers could hardly turn her away from her childhood home. Then, in a few days, when she had discovered where Valerian was living, she would take the train to St. Petersburg... She was free! She could do what she liked, when she liked. Neither her father nor the Countess, nor Nurse Price nor Matron nor Anthony Mills, could give her orders now. For the first time in her whole life she was her own mistress. It was an intoxicating feeling.

Suddenly lighthearted, she bought a dark-red rosebud from a little flower girl and pinned it to her lapel. Then she paid for her coffee and strolled slowly through the holiday crowds in the direction of the railway station.

* * *

"Now for some fun," exclaimed Guy, as Anthony came back on board. The submarine's engines caused the deck to tremble. "Cheer up, you'll see her again soon—or so I hope. And I'm not going to badger you with a lot of questions," he added shrewdly. "It's none of my business if your wife wants to run through an enemy blockade just to pay a visit to her second cousin once removed... or whatever. She's a brave girl and I admire her spirit."

"I wish I could tell you more," said Anthony with less than his usual ease. "But—"

"Don't dream of apologizing! I know you Intelligence men can't tell the truth to save your lives—it's what they call an occupational disease. But get this clear: I don't mind who I take where, so long as it gives me the chance to hunt Germans."

"We'll go Hun-hunting as soon as you like," said Anthony. "There are one or two little bays we might scout on our way down the coast, then we'll take a look at the railroad. I know just the place. I remember thinking when I was there last year, what a perfect place for an ambush."

Guy gave the order for full speed ahead.

They returned directly to the Sea of Marmara, with no further incursions into the Golden Horn. For ten days they enjoyed excellent hunting, spreading alarm and despondency among the Turkish military transports and vessels carrying food and ammunition.

When all of *E 57's* torpedoes had been fired, and a dozen enemy vessels added to the wrecks littering the bottom of the Sea of Marmara—among them a destroyer and three steamships, Guy declared himself satisfied... for the moment.

Their destructive operations had left neither the submarine nor her crew unscarred. A Turkish shell from one of the shore batteries had opened up a seam of rivets which leaked badly enough to necessitate keeping air pressure in the conning tower to prevent water drawing into the battery and producing the fatal fumes of chlorine gas. Patrick Donovan had severe face and neck burns from an explosion in the hold of a captured steamship, and three of the crew were suffering from dysentery. Nonetheless, morale was high.

"Now for the railroad," said Guy, as they anchored one night in the lee of a small island just east of Kara Burnu.

"The last lap," agreed Anthony thankfully. He felt cramped

and out of shape after so many days aboard a small craft, and was longing to stretch his legs ashore. He and the helmsman, a carpenter in civilian life, spent an enjoyable day designing and constructing a small raft, which they loaded with a bale of gun cotton, wire, fuses, a detonator and other equipment Anthony would need on his mission of destruction.

The chosen stretch of railway line ran halfway up a steep cliff overlooking the sea, about five hundred yeards from a station. Anthony hoped that by blowing up the track he could produce a heavy rockfall from above which would make the line impassable for at least a week. Two additional submarines were due to rendezvous with *E 57* within a few days, and since the Turks would be obliged to switch entirely to sea transport while the railroad was out of action, this would give the submarines a fine opportunity to inflict further damage.

"I wish I was coming with you," said Guy quietly as he maneuvered *E 57* close to the overhanging cliffs just after midnight. The sky was moonless and the waters still. Even small noises seemed to carry across the shining surface of the bay.

Armed with revolver, bayonet and torch, his face and hair well blackened with soot, Anthony presented a fearsome appearance. "I'll wish you were, too, when I'm lugging that load up the cliff," he said. "But aren't we overdoing the fireworks?"

"You won't have a chance to come back for more," Guy pointed out. "Better take it all. Now remember, if you get into any kind of trouble, fire two shots close together, and I'll open fire on the railroad station to give them something else to think about. You should be able to return under cover of the bombardment. If you're not back by dawn, I'll return to the island and come back for you again at nightfall. All right?"

Anthony nodded. "All clear."

"Well then, off you go, and the best of luck."

Anthony slipped quietly into the warm black water. Pushing his little raft in front of him, he swam for the shore, careful not to splash or cause more than the faintest of ripples on the smooth, inky surface. He found a narrow cleft between two big rocks, and beached his raft. Then he gathered together the bale of gun cotton and the rest of his equipment. Staggering at first beneath the awkward burden, he made for the cliffs.

It was hard to climb quietly, encumbered as he was. Several times he slipped on loose shale and saved himself from plunging to destruction only by grabbing at the tough roots of thorn bushes, which lacerated his hands but kept him alive. After each slip he could hear the telltale rattle of small stones bouncing from rock to rock and finally falling into the sea. He prayed that this section of railroad was unguarded.

At last he heaved his burden over the crest and saw the dully gleaming metal tracks stretching into the distance. So far, so good. For a few minutes he lay still, listening intently as he got his breath. Then, satisfied that he hadn't been observed, he hid half the gun cotton behind a rock and searched for a place to cut the tracks. He figured he had enough explosives to mine the tracks in two places simultaneously. If he could time the explosions right, he would catch a troop train in his ambush.

With this in mind, he placed his first charge on a bend in the track where a heavy overhang of rock promised a certain landslide, and carefully measured off a slow-burning fuse that would take ten minutes to reach the explosive.

After walking briskly down the track, for ten minutes, watch in hand, he sited the second charge and wired it to a battery. Then he returned to the fused charge and stooped to lay his ear to the track for the singing in the metal that would herald the approach of the train. He would give himself until daylight. Then, if the train still hadn't come, he would simply explode the charges and return to the submarine. He hoped the train would come. Intelligence reports indicated that troop trains ran regularly at night.

For over two hours he heard nothing at all. He was stiff and cold, and beginning to suspect that his vigil was in vain, when at last the lines began to hum with the unmistakable sound of a fast-approaching train from the east.

At once Anthony lit the fuse of his westerly charge and then ran back along the tracks. He flung himself down beside the battery-operated charge just as the train rumbled past. Its windows were blacked out, but sparks were belching from the engine's funnel and Anthony caught a glimpse of the engineer and the stoker, their faces glowing from the orange-red glare of the boiler. He counted two and raised his right hand to press the plunger, but his hand was caught from behind in a grip of steel. Anthony, taken completely by surprise, threw himself backwards instinctively, trying to break his assailant's hold, and grabbed for the bayonet stuck in his belt. The train rumbled safely away as Anthony and his attacker grappled beside the tracks, fighting in what each recognized as a life and death struggle.

With a great effort, the Englishman got hold of his bayonet, but the Turk kicked it from his grasp with a force that nearly broke his wrist. Anthony realized very quickly—and with dreadful certainty—that his opponent was heavier, more powerful and in better shape than he was, and although he fought gamely, he could make no discernible headway.

The Turk grunted and pulled out a knife. Spread-eagled across Anthony's squirming, heaving body, he stabbed viciously downward. Anthony gave a desperate twist—and the blade missed his heart and penetrated his shoulder. With a curse the Turk tugged it free. He was about to strike again when there was a flash that lit up the sky above them, and the roar of an explosion shook the rocks they were lying on.

The slow-burning fuse had found its target and detonated the charge of gun cotton right in the path of the troop train. Engine and cars jacknifed into the cliff wall and were helplessly caught up in the avalanche that followed. Rumbling and roaring, half the mountainside vanished into the sea below.

The startled Turk had turned his head toward the noise, and that instant's inattention gave Anthony the chance he needed. With one mighty heave and a twist, he was on his feet. He ran, blood streaming from the knife wound, his breath coming in painful gasps.

Down the railroad he fled, light-footed in rubber shoes, fear lending wings to his heels. Meanwhile, the Turk slipped and lumbered over the crossties in his heavy Army boots; the weight that had given him an advantage in hand-to-hand fighting proved a drawback in pursuit.

Anthony ran until dizziness forced him to slow to a walk. Here the cliffs were too sheer to attempt to climb down. Dawn was not far away. Pink and turquoise streaks already lightened the sky in the east. Down on the rocks where he had landed, he could see a line of torches. Apparently the avenging Turks had guessed where the raider had landed. Anthony prayed that Guy had taken the submarine away before they arrived.

His head was swimming from loss of blood. He knew he must find a hiding place soon before he fainted, or was caught by the Turks.

Leaving the railroad and dropping down on his hands and knees, he clawed his way up the steep cliff. He fell at last, half-fainting, into a narrow cleft overgrown with scrub and thorn bushes, which concealed him completely. It was deeper than it appeared. When he hit the bottom one leg had doubled under him and he heard the crack of a broken bone. Piles of small, dry bones and a strong feral smell indicated that four-footed predators had also used this place for a lair. Anthony's last conscious thought was a hope that they were foxes and not wolves.

Anchored in the bay, Guy and his crew heard the troop train speed past and waited hopefully for an explosion to follow. When it came, far away to the left instead of directly above them as they expected, the officers looked at each other in consternation.

"That's odd. He had to go a long way to plant his charge," said Patrick. "Perhaps they put a guard on the line."

"If so, we may have to move off in a hurry," said Guy. "We'll trim down and stand by to pick him up, but be prepared to dive at once."

For the next half hour, Guy anxiously watched the lightening sky, and the first lieutenant's binoculars scanned the cliffs down which they hoped Anthony would return. After the noise of the avalanche had died away, they heard shouts and screams from the scene of the crash. Far above them, lanterns still flashed. They heard a single shot.

"That can't be him," said Guy, frowning. "We agreed on two shots. Keep a close eye on the beach, Number One. It sounds as if someone is coming our way."

"More than one, sir. Look!" Patrick pointed to a long line of lanterns moving down toward the beach.

Guy cursed. Though he knew it was tempting fate to stay within rifle shot of the beach, he waited nonetheless, certain Anthony would appear at any moment. When the lanterns were only a hundred yards away, he realized it was hopeless to wait any longer and gave the order to leave.

"He must have holed up somewhere," he said, as the submarine headed for her island refuge.

"Yes, sir." Donovan hesitated, and then added, "That is, if he hasn't been caught."

They stared at one another. That was unthinkable! The stories about how the Turks treated their prisoners were anything but reassuring.

"We won't assume anything yet," Guy said briskly. "Let's give the men a day's break, and we'll return to the beach tonight. Until then, keep your fingers crossed."

For three long dark nights, *E 57* kept a vigil, but when at the end of that time Anthony still hadn't been seen, Guy was obliged to admit defeat. As a final act of defiance, he bombarded the Turkish railroad station with his remaining shells and reduced it to a pile of smoking rubble. Then, heavy-hearted, he returned to report that Captain Anthony Mills was missing, captured or killed in the hills above Kara Burnu.

Chapter Twenty-two

The wagon jolted to a halt and Anastasia clambered down, valise in hand, in front of the wrought-iron gates of Ostrovskoye. Weeds had pushed their way through the once-immaculate gravel around the lodge-keeper's hexagonal house, and no one ran out with a bow or a curtsy to welcome the new arrival and open the gates, as in the old days. But although a massive padlock and chain now fastened the main gates, the narrow side entrance stood open.

"Ochen spassibo! Do svidanya!" she called out gratefully to the wagon's bearded driver. He grinned and clicked his tongue. Never before had one of the family begged a ride from the station in his old market-cart. There had always been carriages and coachmen and grooms aplenty to meet the special train from St. Petersburg. Recently, on his rare visits Count Radek had sometimes driven himself home in that devil's invention, a car—which had caused his horses to snort and plunge off the road as the car sputtered by in a cloud of white dust.

This tall, slim woman with golden hair must, he thought, be the gangling little girl he remembered riding around the countryside with the young *barins* when they visited Ostrovskoye each spring. Wasn't she the old Barina's adopted daughter? It all came back to him now. There was some old scandal: everyone said she was really Count Kharkov's own child—but who cared, anyway? She'd certainly grown into a fine-looking woman, even if she had spent too long in foreign parts, as you could tell by the Frenchified way she spoke Russian. He wondered if he should call out a warning at what she would find at the end of her long walk.

Tugging at his gray mustache, the driver dreamily watched the swing of Anastasia's hips as she strolled up the drive in the sweltering sunshine. Then, sighing, he tore his eyes away from that slim, graceful figure, and flicked his whip over the horses' backs. She would find out soon enough.

It was noon and very hot. Anastasia had never in her life carried a suitcase any distance, and though she had set off at a good pace her arms soon tired and her feet were dragging. She shifted the case from one hand to the other but it made little difference. The weight grew heavier every moment.

Surely the drive was longer than it used to be? Surely she ought to round the last bend any moment now and see the house with its two wings of fretted white woodwork waiting to welcome the weary traveler? As a child she had always fancied that the building looked like a motherly white hen, with her wings outspread to gather in her chicks. It hadn't occurred to her before she set off on this walk how great a difference there would be between walking and being driven.

It was well over an hour before she caught her first glimpse of the house, and then she hardly recognized it. The welcoming white hen now looked more like a dowdy gray peafowl. The clock-tower had fallen down, and the once-white woodwork was cracked and peeling. The lawns, formerly so smooth, were patchy and rough. Weeds covered the flowerbeds, and the borders of the lake were overgrown with brambles. The roof of the ballroom wing had actually caved in, leaving the stucco walls open to the sky.

"Oh, no!" she kept repeating to herself. Surprise and disappointment stopped her in her tracks. The image of Ostrovskoye she had cherished for so long vanished away, to be replaced by this sorry ruin. Why was the house in such a state? Where were the servants—the gardeners, the grooms, the dozens of peasants whose duty it was to keep their lord's domain in perfect order? How had Valerian allowed his favorite house to slide into decay? A hundred questions clamored for an answer.

The closer she walked, the more deterioration she discovered. Dreading what she might find inside, Anastasia dropped her suitcase on the steps leading to the verandah and walked in the direction of the *izbas,* the peasants' houses behind the stables, to see if anyone was there. The single-roomed huts were surrounded by beds of watermelons, near which there had always been black-kerchiefed *babushkas,* smoking and cracking melon pips as they watched the play of children whose parents worked in the big house. There had been lots of them, with their pigs and chickens, goats and geese. Surely, they couldn't all have vanished.

But apparently they had. The huts were derelict and the stables empty, their doors sagging forlornly on bent hinges. There wasn't even the scurry of a rat to break the silence, or the coo of a pigeon from the deserted dovecot.

In spite of the sun, Anastasia shivered. It had been six months since Valerian had written begging her to come to him. How much could happen in six months? The life of a Russian soldier in Galicia averaged six weeks, she'd been told. But Valerian was attached to the staff of the Tsar's uncle, the Grand Duke Nicholas Nicholaevitch, commander-in-chief of all the armed forces. Surely he would be in no danger?

But Anastasia didn't know of the recent upheaval that had shaken the already shattered Russian Army to its roots. The Tsar, egged on by his wife and Rasputin, who hated the Grand Duke, had sent his uncle packing and himself assumed supreme command.

The possibility that Valerian had been killed, and would never return to Ostrovskoye, seemed all too real in this deserted and melancholy courtyard. Anastasia felt a great weariness settle on her as she realized that her efforts to get home had been in vain. Home? She had no home. She had never belonged anywhere or to anybody. Throughout her whole life she had lived in other people's houses, off other people's charity. Now even Ostrovskoye, which she'd thought of as Home, offered no refuge.

What should she do? Suddenly she felt a treacherous weakness, an overwhelming longing for Anthony. He would know what to do, where to go, whom to ask for news of Valerian. "You're glad enough to ask me for help when you think I'll be useful to you," he had said contemptuously, and she realized that what he had said was true. She stiffened her spine: there was no point in thinking of Anthony now. He had gone out of her life and from now on she was going to fend for herself. She tried to revive the morning's pleasure in independence but, tired and depressed, she found herself incapable of planning the simplest move.

One thing was certain: she couldn't stay here. She had no food, and the prospect of a night alone in this haunted ruin was forbidding. But the thought of carrying her valise back to the park gates and begging for a lift to the station, was even less attractive. Although the sun slanted lower, the thin dress she wore was plastered to her back.

I'll wash at the pump in the barnyard and change my dress, she thought at last. Perhaps that will clear my mind. But having reached this decision, she continued to sit listlessly in the deserted courtyard, stunned by heat and disappointment, too depressed to move.

She heard a sharp metallic click which roused her to full alertness. The click was repeated. Her suitcase! Someone must be trying to steal her belongings.

She ran across the courtyard toward the house and suddenly stopped, afraid. She was alone and unarmed. Might not a thief, surprised in his crime, decide to silence any witness? Yet she couldn't stand by without protest and let her possessions be stolen. Anastasia looked around for a weapon, but all she could find was a lump of broken marble, the arm of a carved cupid which once had adorned the courtyard fountain. Clutching this, she moved stealthily around the house until she could see the front steps.

Fear vanished at once, to be replaced by indignation. A child was kneeling beside her suitcase, and flinging its contents onto the steps. His rapid movements suggested desperation.

"What are you doing?" she called. "How dare you open my bag!" She stormed toward the steps in righteous indignation, the cupid's arm raised.

For an instant the boy froze, his back still turned, both hands clutching her possessions.

"Who are you? Why are you handling my clothes?"

Slowly, the boy rose to his feet and turned toward her. At the sight of his face, she gasped.

The child was painfully thin. The raggic tunic and trousers he wore hung on his emaciated frame like rags on a scarecrow. His black hair tangled over his forehead, and his jaw and cheekbones stood out sharply through skin that seemed almost transparent. But it was not the dirt or his half-starved condition that made Anastasia's heart pound with shock; it was his face. There, gazing up at her with mixture of fear and defiance, was Valerian's son. There was no mistaking him.

"I—not steal. I want food. I am Valentin Radek," he said in broken Russian.

She scarcely heard the words. So this, she thought, this wild, dirty, half-starved creature, is Valerian's son. She felt suddenly dizzy and sat down on the balustrade. The lump of marble dropped from her hand, and as it did the boy's wary attitude relaxed a little.

"Where is your mother?" she asked gently in English, and at the familiar sound a shudder of relief passed through the bony, childish frame.

"You speak English!" he exclaimed, and then the words poured out in a torrent. "I thought you were going to kill me for opening your bag but truly I didn't mean to steal. I only wanted food. My mother is sick. She won't eat anything I give her, and only lies in bed all day saying she wants to die. Please help us. The peasants have taken all the corn and pigs and chickens. They took the cattle and sheep before we arrived. Then Boris and his friends took everything in the garden back to St. Petersburg. He said they needed it more than us, we have nothing to eat and no money to buy food."

"Hungry . . . ?" she said stupidly. She found his information hard to take in. What was Valerian thinking of to allow his son to go hungry? "No . . ." she said regretfully, "I have no food . . ." She realized how foolish she'd been to assume there would be food at Ostrovskoye. War had wrought many changes in this land of plenty. Most men had gone to serve the Tsar, their work left to the women and children. And here, it seemed, even women and children had moved away. But surely, she thought, there must be food somewhere—if only she knew where to look. She had never known real hunger. Even when the Countess had punished her with a bread-and-water diet, there had always been plenty of bread. Now she began to realize what it meant to be without food.

"Is there no food at all?" she said. Not in the pantry, the cellar, the dairy, the apple shed, the ice-house, the greenhouses—all the places where food had once been stored in such abundance? She would search them all. The peasants, however hungry, couldn't have taken everything.

Valentin shrugged. "No, there is nothing. Boris told the peasants that all our food belonged to them. They sold some back to Mother, but now we have no money."

Boris! Anastasia felt another spurt of anger at him, and a lesser but still distinct anger at Valerian for the casual way he had abandoned his son. Then, with a wave of thankfulness, she remembered the money Anthony had given her.

"I have money, Valentin," she said, and the boy's thin face lighted up.

"A lot of money?" he asked eagerly.

"I think so."

"Then we'll be able to buy food... That is," he added, "if you'll lend us the money, until Mother can work again. She's a doctor, you know. She could work in the hospital here if she was strong enough. She used to have her own hospital, only Yuan Chen and his bandits burned it down because his baby died there."

She asked gently, "Was that why you came here?"

"Yes." The boy's face screwed up, as though he was fighting to hold back the tears. "I wish we hadn't. I wish we had stayed with Martha and Elias. I hate it here. My father's gone off to the war and I can't understand what people are saying, and Mother is ill..."

Anastasia had the sudden experience of *déjà vu*. She seemed to have lived this moment before. She knew what it was like for a child to be uprooted and dumped in an alien environment at the mercy of unknown adults, and she was suddenly determined that this boy—Valerian's son—should not suffer if she could help it.

"I'll pay you back, I promise." he said.

She was touched by his dignity. "Never mind about that. We'll share what we've got, Valentin. Will this be enough to start with?" She handed him ten roubles, and saw with what difficulty he restrained himself from grabbing them as a hungry dog snatches a bone. Then he flushed scarlet.

"It—it's too much. The peasants will steal it if they know I have so much."

"They wouldn't dare! Where are these peasants?"

"In the village. They used to live here but Boris told them they were fools to work for a master who would never return, so they went away. Yuri stayed because he's got a wooden leg and can't walk far." Valentin added, "Boris was lying, wasn't he? Father *will* come back . . . ?"

How typical of Boris to inflict such mental torment on a child. "Of course he will," she said. "Now take me to your mother, and then we'll see about finding some food." She laid her hand on the boy's shoulder, shocked to feel the sharp bones beneath the rough fabric. "Cheer up, Valentin," she said. "Now you've got help. You must be wondering who I am. My name is Anastasia, and I've known your father a long, long time. We used to live here, sometimes, when I was a little girl . . ."

How often she had pictured this meeting. Anastasia gazed down at the angular, freckled face of the woman sprawled on a bed among moth-eaten blankets in one of the attic rooms. This emaciated woman was Susanna—her rival, the woman she had hated since she first heard of her existence. She had been bitterly jealous of her hold over Valerian, in spite of his protests that he didn't love her.

The child was proof that they had shared a bed, and who could guess what else? What secret knowledge of Valerian might Susanna possess; what shared memories, to which she alone held the key? Consumed with burning jealousy, Anastasia had considered every weapon in her armory, trying to choose the most effective to use against Valerian's wife.

She had bombarded herself with questions: Should she tell her everything, or nothing? Beg her to disappear as quietly as she'd come, or threaten her with physical violence if she didn't? Should she be stiff, haughty, cold and patronizing—or give full rein to her passions and flame with fury, attacking the pallid Scotswoman with her bare hands, tearing out her hair and scratching her face to a bloody pulp unless she swore to renounce her claim to Valerian?

These and many other scenes she had pictured, but never in her wildest fantasies had she imagined that when she finally came face to face with Valerian's wife, her dominant emotions would be pity and disgust.

She is old—quite old and ugly, Anastasia thought. Wizened

dried up, thin and dirty. She doesn't look much like a doctor, or the kind of woman to attract Valerian.

A sickly, cloying smell permeated the whole room.

"What's wrong with your mother?" Anastasia whispered to the boy. "Can we wake her up?"

He hesitated. "I don't know. She's taken some opium—she always does when things get bad. She may not wake up for hours."

"Then why don't you go to the village for food while I look after her?" suggested Anastasia. A faint gleam beneath the woman's eyelids told her that Susanna was awake and listening. If there was to be a trial of strength between them, it might be best for Valentin to be away.

"All right. I'll get tea and bread—and sugar if I can. Oh, and eggs . . ." He left, the money tightly clutched in his fist, but a moment later he was back.

"Anastasia . . . ?"

"Yes?"

"You won't—you won't go away before I come back?"

She saw the lonely fear behind the question and gave him a friendly shove. "Of course I won't! This is my home—didn't I tell you that? Don't worry so much. Everything is going to be all right . . ."

He left again and she bent over the bed. "Susanna! Are you awake? Can you hear me?"

There was no reply. Anastasia thought for a moment, then went downstairs to the filthy, comfortless kitchen. After a search she collected a bar of coarse soap, a rag, and a pail of cold water.

As she set them down by Susanna's bedside, the puffy, slitted lids flashed open and regarded her with plain hostility. "So you have come at last, Anastasia," said the woman, in a slurred yet venomous tone. "They told me that vultures will gather even before a corpse is cold, and I see that it's true. Go away, Anastasia! Isn't it enough to steal my husband, without coming to gloat over me as well? Leave me to die in peace. I need no help from you—and neither does my son."

Far from being intimidated by this curt dismissal, Anastasia felt an invigorating spurt of anger. She wanted to shake Susanna by the shoulders.

"How do *you* know?" she demanded. "Just because you have

chosen to die, you need not assume that your son wants to do the same. You should be ashamed—you, a doctor, lying there in a pile of filth while that child struggles to feed you both. Get up, woman! Stir yourself out of that drugged sleep and wash yourself—or had you rather I did it for you?"

Susanna gasped. She was so used to playing on Valentin's sympathy that his sudden attack astonished her. "Don't be absurd," she said. "I can't get up. I'm too weak. I've had no food since..."

"Whose fault is that?" Anastasia pointed to the pathetic collection of scraps with which Valentin must have tried to tempt his mother's appetite. Bowls of gritty gruel. Molded hunks of blackish bread. A couple of hard green plums. Unpalatable, certainly—but enough to keep body and soul together if you wanted to live.

"I've been deserted by my husband and stranded in a shambles of a house without food or fuel," whined Susanna. Anastasia noticed that already her diction had sharpened perceptibly. There was nothing wrong with this woman that couldn't be cured by food and fresh air, she decided. If only she could be jolted out of her drugged self-pity. Anger appeared to be an excellent stimulant.

Anastasia said with deliberate scorn, "I was told that the Scotch were fighters, not given to surrendering because of a little hardship..."

"That's easy for you to say. You've never known hardship. You don't know what it's like to be alone and unloved, your hopes gone and your life's work ruined."

"Then you must build your life's work up again," said Anastasia—and almost laughed. Was this her self speaking, or Anthony? Hadn't he said exactly the same thing to her when she tried to cry on his shoulder the night she learned of Valerian's marriage? It seemed absurd that she should now be advising the selfsame technique to Valerian's wife.

"Why are you laughing?" asked Susanna suspiciously.

Anastasia shook her head. "Never mind." She took a deep breath; she had managed to rouse Susanna from her torpor. Could she succeed in getting her on her feet?

"Now listen, Susanna. You may not want my help, but you're going to get it anyway. Not for your sake—you can starve to death for all I care—but for the sake of your son. I know what it's like to be abandoned by everyone you trust, and I'm going to see that he doesn't suffer as I did."

"So you're planning to steal my son as well as my husband?"

Anastasia shrugged. "If that's what you want to think, I can't stop you," she said. "But if you have any sense left at all, you'll see that we have a better chance of surviving here if we work together. I'll leave you to think about it."

"I won't let you take my son away from me," said Susanna.

"Then you must do something to stop me. I'm going downstairs now, but if you haven't bathed and dressed yourself in an hour, I'll come back and do it for you. It's time you started to live again."

Without another glance at the stunned and furious woman in the bed, Anastasia walked out of the room.

Valentin's delighted and astonished face when his mother walked downstairs an hour later, fully dressed, quite stilled Anastasia's pangs of conscience. Guilty she might feel for bullying a woman unable to defend herself, but there was no doubt that shock tactics had worked where sympathy would have been useless.

"Mother!" he cried, holding out a chair with a cushion. "How do you feel? Are you better? Now everything's going to be better, with Anastasia here to look after you."

The two women exchanged a long look. Rivalry was in it—rivalry, suspicion, and veiled dislike of everything the other stood for, but there was also the beginning of complicity. Valentin must be protected, on that they were agreed, and for this reason alone they were willing to declare a temporary truce.

"Of course things will be better," said Anastasia firmly.

During the following months, Anastasia frequently wondered if those words had tempted fate, for despite all her efforts, by Christmas things were far from being all right at Ostrovskoye.

The letter she had written to Valerian, informing him of her return, had prompted an immediate though not very helpful response.

My darling,

How wonderful to know that you are safe at Ostrovskoye after your dangerous journey. I'll come to you as soon as possible, but I am very busy in Petrograd just now. As you may have heard I am now fighting a new kind of battle. After being invalided out of the army, I have decided to stand for election to the Duma. Affairs are moving fast these days—watch out for amazing news soon! Look after yourself, my darling, and wait patiently for the return of your adoring

Valerian

Not a word about his wife and child. No anxiety whatsoever over how she was managing to run Ostrovskoye without its army of servants. She found it hard to banish the suspicion that Valerian was enjoying himself too much at the center of events to bother with affairs at Ostrovskoye. Yet she could hardly leave Susanna and Valentin to cope with the ramshackle household while she pursued Valerian in the capital. Apparently his new enthusiasm for politics was absorbing all his attention. She felt hurt and resentful to be ranked so low in his estimation that he couldn't even pay them a fleeting visit. How differently Anthony would have reacted to the news that his wife was ill and his child hungry.

Still, disappointed as she was not to see him, at least she knew that Valerian was alive and well. That knowledge gave her fresh strength to tackle the many things that must be done if she and the woman and child now dependent on her were to survive the winter.

A careful search of the house and grounds revealed resources which neither Valentin nor the pillaging Boris had discovered. A cache of potatoes, slightly moulded but otherwise undamaged; carrots stored in sand in a garden shed; a half-cured pig encrusted in salt on a cellar slab; and, best of all, the rubber-tired governess cart in which the Countess used to drive herself around the estate, together with a harness.

"Now all we need is a horse," exclaimed Anastasia jubilantly, examining this treasure.

Valentin looked thoughtful. "The army has taken all the horses."

"I know. They call it 'requisitioning,' but it's no better than stealing," she said. "They take what they want and march off with it—I only wish we could do the same. We can't walk all the way to Simferopol every time we need supplies."

Valentin nodded and said no more. He was by nature an assured, self-contained child. Now that he was certain that Anastasia wasn't going to vanish in a puff of smoke, he adopted the role of man of the house so naturally that she often had trouble remembering how young he was.

Frequently he left the house at first light and stayed out till dark, visiting the snares old Yuri had set in the woods, or catching fish in the trap he'd constructed from a piece of tennis netting. One evening, it was not until Anastasia realized that it was after ten and he had not returned that she began to worry.

She waited until eleven o'clock, twelve, one... there was no sound in the dark house except her anxious pacing from room to room, while the samovar grew cold and her heart with it. Where could he be? Her imagination ran riot, picturing the horrors that might have befallen him. Roving Cossacks frequently rode through the countryside in search of forage. She pictured the fierce wild men demanding Valentin's catch... the boy refusing... the sweep of a saber...

Why hadn't she asked him where he was going? Should she rouse Susanna from her drugged sleep with the dismal news that her son was missing? Anastasia paced back and forth, unable to decide. Never before had Valentin failed to join her for the evening ritual of the samovar. He seemed to appreciate instinctively how much the little ceremony meant to her—the last vestige of the civilized life the house had once known.

At half past two in the morning, when she had almost given up hope, she was astonished to hear the crunch of hoofs on the gravel outside. Snatching up a candle, she ran to open the door. By it's flickering light she saw Valentin seated on a pony, swaying with fatigue and grinning from ear to ear.

"I've brought your horse," he said, and slid down from its back.

It was a sturdy, shaggy pony of the type most favored by the Cossacks, long and low, standing four-square on strong, clean legs, with its nose jutting boldly below the long forelock, and its tail sweeping the ground.

Anastasia's hand flew to her throat.

"Oh, Valentin, did you *steal* it?" she said faintly.

"No, I requisitioned him." Valentin's grin became wider than ever. "I had to, Anastasia, there was no other way. Don't worry though, they won't look for him here. I took good care of that. I cut him loose from the back of a cart while the drivers were eating. I had to follow them all day before I got a chance to get near enough—that's why I'm so late. They had three other horses. Why shouldn't they spare us one?" He ran his fingers through the long, tangled mane. "I'm going to call him Khan, after my Manchurian pony... I cut all the other horses loose too, and they went off in different directions. That should keep the Cossacks busy!"

She couldn't scold him, but her blood ran cold at the thought of the risk he had run.

"Oh, Valentin!" she said weakly. "What if they had caught you?"

"They'd have shot me, I expect. Don't look so worried—I told you I was very careful," said the boy cheerfully. "Now I'll put Khan in the stable. It's all ready for him. We'll keep him hidden for a few days, but after that he'll be able to take us wherever we want to go."

A week later they made their first visit to Simferopol. Isolated as they were at Ostrovskoye, it was difficult to get news of how the war was progressing. But as Khan trotted briskly along the flat white road, the deserted villages and uncultivated fields told their own story. Russia was being driven back on every front, and her armies were now composed of boys and old men. Peasants who had never held a gun before were being flung into the path of the German juggernaut—while their families died of starvation.

Susanna went outdoors as infrequently as she could, and had refused to go with them today. But she had grudgingly agreed to prepare a meal for their return. Cooking, she implied, was beneath the dignity of a doctor, but given a choice between cooking or working in the garden, she had opted for the former. Anastasia found it a strain to put up with her complaints and imaginary ailments, but for Valentin's sake she endured Susanna's company, and there was no doubt that in the last few months her general health had much improved.

"Mother is so much better now," confided Valentin, in his curiously unboyish voice. "If only she'd make the effort to go outside sometimes, she'd see what a beautiful country this could be. Then she might not mind living here so much."

"It was beautiful once," agreed Anastasia sadly, "but now..."

The fair and smiling land she remembered from her childhood was no more. The few peasants they met trudging along the road with baskets on their arms waved no cheerful greetings as in the old days. Anastasia shivered and carefully counted her dwindling store of roubles. Anthony's money wouldn't last forever. When, oh, when would Valerian come?

They spent almost half the money she had left on provisions and clothes, for Valentin's pants were in tatters, and the few clothes Anastasia had brought from Egypt were almost worn out. With considerable difficulty she persuaded a doctor to sell her Susanna's one requirement—a few ounces of opium—and then they set off for home.

It was almost dark when they reached the park gate, and Anastasia clicked her tongue to hurry Khan. He'd had a long day and needed his stable. If only we had better food to give him, he'd have more energy, she thought. Then they rounded the bend in the drive and saw the white wings of the house outspread before them—and something else.

Three flat carts were drawn up in front of the door, and men were loading them with boxes and furniture. Anastasia's heart suddenly leapt with hope—had Valerian come home at last?

She glanced sideways at Valentin: in the gloaming his face looked deathly pale. "It—It's Boris," he stammered. "He's come back... he'll take Khan away with him. Oh, stop! Stop before he sees us."

Bewildered, she halted the pony and Valentin sprang out. He pulled Khan on to the grass, where the sound of the wheels was muffled. Then, with hasty, trembling fingers, he unhitched the traces, unbuckled the reins and led the pony out of the shafts.

"Hide the cart in the bushes," he whispered to Anastasia. "I'll take Khan—I know where he'll be safe." Before she could protest or question, he had hoisted himself onto the pony's back and kicked him into a reluctant trot in the opposite direction from the house. Boy and pony faded into the twilight and Anastasia was left alone.

Lights blazed from every uncurtained window. Rage at the intrusion made her forget her fear of Boris, and she strode toward the house, determined to protect Valerian's property from the marauders.

"What are you doing? Robbers! Stop it—put those chairs down, you thieves! Leave that carpet alone!" she stormed at the peasants as she approached. They stopped uncertainly, lowering their burdens, looking over their shoulders for instructions.

There was a roar of laughter form the hallway, and she entered the door to confront Boris, who stood with hands on hips, thumbs hooked under his wide leather belt, his booted feet set well apart. He looked more massive than ever, a peasant reverting to type, she thought, and the thin layer of sophistication that his city clothes lent him had vanished entirely. The broad face tapering to a bear's long, mean snout was split by an unpleasant smile. His small, piggy eyes were gleaming with malice.

"So the ice maiden has returned at last," he growled. "You haven't changed, have you, little ice-queen? You still like to give the orders, and see the men jump to obey you." He turned to the idling peasants. "Get back to work. Fill the carts and drive them to the station. Don't mind the lady . . . I'll deal with her."

Anastasia stepped hastily back, but she was too late. Boris reached out and imprisoned both her hands. "Come here, damn you! You didn't want to play with old Boris when he saw you last, but he'll have his way with you this time."

"Let me go," said Anastasia, trying to free her hands. In answer, he jerked her toward him with a force that made her wrists crack, crushed her against his chest. His brutal face, alight with cruel pleasure, was only a few inches away from hers.

"You'll have to ask more politely than that," he said softly. His breath made her senses reel.

She tried to control her panic. "Please, Boris . . ."

"That's better. That's more like it. In fact, I might even consider letting you go if you'll give me a little kiss."

"Never!" She strained away from him with all her might. Over his shoulder she saw Susanna standing in the doorway that led to the kitchen. Her freckled face was wan, and she clung to the door frame for support. Faintly her whisper reached Anastasia:

"Be careful—don't make him angry. He's dangerous."

Boris swung around, his head lowered, his shoulders hunched like a bull ready to charge. "What did she say? Speak Russian, damn you! Isn't Russian good enough for you?"

"She's English, as you know very well," said Anastasia, with undisguised scorn. "She can't speak Russian." The momentary distraction had steadied her. She knew that she must dominate him somehow. She must not give way to panic or anger, no matter what he said or did. She must be cool and wary, as with a dangerous wild beast, and give him no chance to attack. Then—and only then—might they all survive. "Susanna was telling me that . . . that supper is ready. Will you eat supper with us?"

"Yes, my lady!" The idea seemed to afford Boris great amusement. He released her and bowed mockingly, his hand touching his brow in a feudal salute. "Since you graciously invite me to sit at your table, I'll do you the honor of accepting. How fortunate that I brought the keys to the wine cellar with me!"

The cellar door had resisted all their efforts, and the sturdy oak panels still bore the marks of Yuri's ax and Valentin's crowbar.

The two women watched silently as Boris drew a jangling bunch of keys from his pocket and strode toward the cellar. Then Susanna whispered urgently, "Where's Valentin?" Her thin hands were twitching convulsively.

"He's gone to hide the pony."

"He mustn't return while that beast is here. Last time—oh, it was terrible—he tried to make me dance for him." She shuddered.

"Hush, he's coming back."

They went quickly down the passage to the kitchen. Boris followed, a bottle in either hand. His boots clumped loudly on the bare stone floor.

The black iron pot over the fire gave out the appetizing smell of boiled bacon as Susanna's shaking hands ladled steaming brew into three wooden bowls.

"Where is the silver? Where are the candles? Don't tell me you eat out of bowls like peasants," growled Boris, raising a bowl to his nose and sniffing like a dog. With an exclamation of disgust he sent it spinning across the room to spatter its contents against the door. "Ugghh! That garbage is too strong for my stomach. Bring me some wine. Go on, knock the top off the bottle."

Trying to hide her disgust, Anastasia did as he asked. From outside, she heard the crunch of wheels over gravel. Boris' men had finally stripped the house of all they could carry and were going away with their stolen loads.

"That's better." Boris drank deeply and long, and set down his empty mug with a crash. "Come here, ice-queen. I want to take a good look at you. You're not so plump as you used to be, but that won't matter if you've learned some manners. Come closer, I say, closer . . ."

With a quick lunge he pulled her close enough to imprison between his knees. Susanna gave a little moan and turned away, her shoulders shaking. Boris lay back in his chair, the cruel smile on his lips again as his eyes moved slowly over Anastasia's body. She stood rigidly, held by his knees, fighting her fear and disgust.

He was breathing heavily. Before she realized what he meant to do, he took hold of the collar of her dress—one heavy hand on either side of her neck—and ripped downward. Suddenly, cold air struck her naked flesh. "Ah," said Boris, running his hands like great hairy spiders over her skin, "now you're learning, ice-queen. Be kind to Boris and he won't hurt you—too much."

Anastasia struggled to break free, hitting his hands in a frantic effort to cover herself. Her resolve not to resist was forgotten in the sheer panic of finding herself naked and at his mercy.

"Now I'll show you who's your master," said Boris. He ran his hands over her shoulders, pressing her breasts and laughing as she flinched. "Not so proud, are you, when a man does *this* to you. How many men have done it before? Watch this, you old crow," he said over his shoulder to the trembling Susanna. "You needn't be jealous, your turn will come. I've been waiting to melt this little icicle for a long time now, and by God, I'm going to enjoy it."

In a frenzy of fear, Anastasia twisted and turned, but her struggles only excited Boris more. Her skirt was still caught at the waist, but now he stripped it off and held her at arm's length in front of him, gloating. Red marks where his fingers had pressed stood out vividly against her white skin.

"Go on, fight me," he invited, fumbling to undo his breeches. "I don't care—I like it. That's how the peasant girls used to try to escape, but they all gave up in the end. Ah, you mustn't bite, that's nasty." Casually he slapped her face. Through the tears that sprang to her eyes, she saw the door begin to open.

Susanna saw it too, and moved swiftly to put her back against it. "No, Valentin. Go away!" she whispered.

Instantly Boris was on his feet, releasing his victim, who caught up her tattered dress in a vain effort to cover herself.

"So the young gentleman has returned in time for the fun?" he said. "I wondered where he was hiding himself."

Boris shoved Susanna roughly aside and jerked open the door. He caught Valentin by the collar and propelled him into the room. Then he hoisted the terrified child onto the table.

"Stand up there and watch me," he ordered. "I want to show you what to do with a woman."

"Don't look, Valentin," said his mother in a shaking voice, and after a single, terrified glance at Anastasia, the boy screwed his eyes tightly shut.

"Watch, I said," growled Boris, grabbing Anastasia around the waist and pulling aside the final remnants of her dress. She tried to hit him with the poker, which she had snatched up from the fire, but he twisted her arm behind her back with one hand while his other hand fastened on her breast. He flung her to the floor, then brutally forced her thighs apart with his knee.

"What am I doing now, boy?" he demanded of Valentin. "Tell me what I'm doing now, or you'll get the same treatment."

"You're . . . you're . . ." Valentin choked.

In slow motion, as if in a dream, Anastasia watched Susanna pick up the long, slender knife, one of their few remaining kitchen utensils. Oh, please God, please give her strength, she prayed. She's a doctor: she must know where to strike, if only You give her strength . . .

Boris' thick, hot lips were against her mouth, his tongue forcing entry while his hands pried at her legs. All of a sudden he gave a queer, deep grunt that was almost a cough, and his whole frame jerked convulsively. His hands reached over his shoulders, trying to find the handle of the knife which stuck out between his shoulderblades like the key of a clockwork toy.

"You bitch! You Goddamned bitch . . ." he groaned.

Chairs crashed down as he strode around the room, and when he reached the corner where Susanna was cowering, he seized her from behind. "I'll break your neck for that," he growled, and crooked his elbow around her throat. His knee came up to the small of her back and he jerked viciously. Susanna's spine bent backward and there was a sickening crack.

"Mother!" screamed Valentin.

He flung himself on his knees beside the limp body as Boris let it slide to the floor. "He's killed her..." Valentin cried.

Boris was bellowing like a bull, his enormous fists locked round the handle of the door, but he no longer had the strength to turn it. Suddenly he slumped to his knees, a gasping whistle came from out of his punctured lungs and a rush of bright red blood poured out of his mouth. A moment later he lay lifeless beside his victim, equally dead, stabbed through the heart with the long kitchen knife. Now the only sounds left in the kitchen were the steady, relentless ticking of the clock and Valentin's heartbroken sobs.

Chapter Twenty-three

A shadow fell on Anthony in the hollow where he was lying. Squinting painfully into the sun, he saw a gaunt dog standing above him, its tail wagging gently.

A moment later, its owner appeared, a tall man carrying a shotgun casually, as though used to its presence. Anthony's eyes fastened on the gun. He isn't a soldier, he thought, perhaps a shepherd. Had it not been for his shoulder and leg, he could easily have overpowered the man. As it was, he could only lie there helplessly, too weak to move.

For three days now he had lain in the hollow, unable to climb out, roasting by day and freezing almost stiff at night. He could hear the boom of heavy guns across the Narrows and, much closer, the shouts of the workmen repairing the railroad.

When at last he had somehow found the strength to sit up, a wave of dizziness combined with the agony in his injured shoulder to make him slump back on the rockbed, groaning. His left leg was completely numb, but he could hear the sinister grating of a broken bone. His water flask was empty, and he knew that if he remained there much longer, he would become delirious with fever and thirst. His only hope was to reach the beach and attract the attention of *E57*, but from where he now lay the beach seemed as inaccessible as the moon. To get there he would have to cross the railroad, and even if he succeeded in doing that unnoticed, there remained the precipitous climb down the cliffs—a notable feat for a fit man. Quite apart from his broken leg, he was suffering from dehydration and loss of blood.

It wasn't until he heard the owner of the dog speak that

Anthony realized that his discoverer was in fact a woman. An old woman, with a proud, aquiline face that must once have been beautiful, and diamond-shaped black eyes above the muffling *ferajeh.*

She squatted down beside him, the gun across her knees, and spoke with the authority of one used to command. "So you are the English soldier, the one those fools down there are searching for?"

Anthony nodded; there was no point in denying it. "Water," he croaked.

"So there's life in you still, is there, Englishman?" She pulled out a goatskin flask and carefully trickled a little into the corner of his parched mouth. "Steady now, don't be greedy. A sip at a time—that's the way. I want to know what you're doing up here on the cliffs? Why didn't you go back to the beach where your friends were waiting? Oh yes, I saw them, though no one else did. They've gone now, and left you behind. I suppose they gave you up for dead, though the Germans haven't, you know. The Germans want to catch you and put you in a dungeon full of rats, as they did with your friends from the other submarine. They're still down below on the beach, as thick as plums in a fruitcake. Now the question is, how are we going to get you past them? You're on the wrong side of the Sari Bair mountains, and even if you're another Hercules I don't think you can cross those hills with a broken leg and a mangled arm. Here, let's take a look at it."

The water was warm and tasted strongly of goat, but to Anthony it was ambrosial. As the life-giving liquid trickled down his throat, his wits began to clear and he realized that this talkative old lady was no peasant, nor did she appear to be an enemy.

"You're not going to turn me in, then?" he asked hoarsely.

"Surrender an Englishman to those strutting German pigs? I should say not. Let them do their own dirty work," she exclaimed. "If they can't locate what's under their noses the way my Grip can—" she stroked the dog's head—"I'm not going to do it for them. They've done too much damage already, and they'll ruin the whole country if we let them."

A German-hating Turk! Anthony could hardly believe his luck. He knew that the ruthless, power-grabbing Enver Pasha, who had dragged Turkey into the war on Germany's coattails was regarded as a dangerous upstart by many Turks of the old regime. And although his savior was dressed in the roughest homespun and a man's boots, she spoke with natural authority. Was she, he wondered, a lady of quality fallen on hard times? There was no opportunity to speculate further, because he felt her hard old hands probing his wounded shoulder, pulling the bloody cloth away from the skin and then patting it back into place with a little hiss of dismay.

The pain made Anthony faint.

When he next opened his eyes, the old woman was trickling water over his face and into his mouth again. The eyes in her seamed brown face were sharp. "I'm sorry, I shouldn't have done that," she said. "The wound is—very bad. I have some medical skill—just a little, but a wound like that is beyond my power to dress. Perhaps you'd be better off with the Germans after all—at least they have doctors."

Anthony tried to smile. "I don't think it's . . . all that bad," he said with an effort. The Turkish words kept floating away before his mind could grab them. "If you can help me . . . to walk . . . to get out of this hole . . . I'll be all right. I'll trust your . . . medical skill. I don't want a German doctor."

The old woman considered, staring at him with unblinking black eyes. She appeared to be listening intently, though he himself could hear nothing but the distant bleating of goats and the irregular pounding of his own heart. The dog cocked his head and whined softly.

"Yes, it's your master," she said softly, and pressed her water flask into Anthony's good hand before standing up. "Wait until dark, Englishman," she said, and left him.

At nightfall she came again, and with her a man as short and fat as she was tall and lean. As she guided him carefully down the slope, Anthony realized that the man was blind. He ran his short blunt fingers over Anthony's face by way of greeting. He was very strong, however, and between the two of them they hauled Anthony to the top of the hollow and hoisted him onto the back of a donkey. Steadying him one on either side, they set off on a long march, following goat tracks that wound through the contours of the hills until they reached an old stone house, standing in a walled garden high above the Sea of Marmara.

Somehow, Anthony endured the crude surgery that followed, as the old woman whispered assurances that blind Mehmet was the best bone-setter in Anatolia. Sweating and shivering on a trestle table, he tried not to scream as the man's blunt fingers did their work...

"You are fortunate that Sevinc Hanum found you, *effendi*," he said gravely, when he had finished. "By morning you would have been dead."

"I am fortunate indeed," Anthony said, before thanking them both.

He wondered how long his luck would last...

Valerian was far too absorbed in his own affairs to dream of leaving Petrograd in order to please any woman, even Anastasia. Since the Tsar had dismissed his uncle, the Grand Duke Nicholas Nicholaevitch, from supreme command—at the instigation of the Grand Duke's sworn enemy Rasputin—Valerian had been convinced that the only way to save Russia from ruin was to destroy the Siberian monster, whose baleful influence on politics had become intolerable to every right-thinking Russian.

Sinister rumors that Rasputin was giving the Tsar drugs, which affected his judgment and led to further military reversals, now circulated freely in the capital, and so did obscene cartoons showing the Empress locked in the arms of the black-robed *starets*. Everything that went wrong in the winter of 1916, from ammunition shortages to strikes in the factories, was blamed on Rasputin, whose power over the Tsar and Tsarina seemed to grow daily stronger.

Now a group of young aristocrats—headed by the Grand Duke Dimitri Pavlovitch, nephew to the Tsar, and Prince Felix Youssoupov, one of Russia' richest heirs—planned Rasputin's murder. They found in Valerian a willing recruit to their ranks.

"Every recent political appointment and dismissal can be traced directly to that meddling *starets*," he exclaimed in disgust to Andrei one afternoon in late December. "Have you heard that Sturmer is to replace old Gorymekin as Prime Minister? It's a scandal. Sturmer is well known to be nothing but a German agent. And as for Protopopov, that scatter-brained syphilitic couldn't direct a flock of sheep, let alone the Ministry of the Interior. Something has to be done."

"Then why not *do* something, instead of merely talking about it?" snapped Andrei. His temper had noticeably deteriorated since his colleague Boris, on whom the success of their underground paper depended, had vanished on a visit to Yalta. Andrei suspected that Boris had probably been too outspoken in his contempt for the Romanov dynasty and was languishing perhaps in some Crimean jail. But none of his careful inquiries had elicited Boris' whereabouts, and Andrei was forced to struggle on with the paper alone.

'Don't worry. I'm going to do something," said Valerian.

"I'll believe that when I see it." said Andrei contemptuously. "Rasputin may have more enemies than any man in Russia, but he's safer than most. People are too scared of what he might do to dare lift a finger against him. And he has a police guard wherever he goes. Lots of people talk about getting rid of Rasputin, but talk is all it amounts to."

"Don't be too sure of that," said Valerian, tossing aside the newspaper he'd been reading and going to the window. The dim light of the short winter afternoon was already fading, and the slush-filled street was empty except for a few shabby women, bundled up against the cold and hurrying home—or hurrying somewhere... Valerian frowned as he watched them. Where were all the elegant carriages with their fashionable occupants who used to throng this street in winter? How many sons and grandsons had those bent *babushkas* lost to the war and the terrible machinations of Rasputin?

He glanced at his watch with a twinge of excitement. Six hours to go... Felix Youssoupov's conspirators were meeting tonight at his sumptuous house on the Moika Canal for a final briefing. Tonight was the night. Rasputin had agreed to attend a small and select party *chez* Youssoupov. It was the chance they had been waiting for. Nothing must go wrong with their plan to destroy him.

A fluffy white bearskin rug had been spread in the corner of Felix Youssoupov's basement apartment, the carefully designed stage for the evening's drama. In front of it stood an antique cabinet of inlaid ebony, filled with tiny mirrors and secret drawers—a child's dream. Valerian played with it idly, pressing hidden knobs to make the drawers fly open, as he listened to the Prince's final instructions.

"I will bring him here at eleven o'clock," said Felix. Tall, dark, and elegant, his eyes heavy-lidded and his movements graceful, he used an amber cigarette holder to point out the luxurious trap prepared for his victim. Niches in the walls held red Chinese porcelain vases, and the red granite mantelpiece was adorned with antique plates and bowls. The bare cellar Valerian had seen on his last visit here had been transformed.

"Won't he think it strange that Irina isn't here?" asked the Grand Duke Dmitri, the Tsar's handsome fair-haired nephew. He prowled restlessly around the room, his footsteps muffled by the beautiful Persian carpet. He picked up a crucifix of Italian rock crystal and held it admiringly up to the light before placing it carefully on top of the ebony cabinet.

"No, that shouldn't worry him," Felix said at last. "I'll say that Irina is upstairs with my friends and that I often use this room to work in."

"To work in!" Dmitri snorted with derisive laughter.

"I do work," said Felix stiffly. "Colonel Vogel was tutoring me only this afternoon. He says I'm certain to pass this time. Now listen! I want you all to stay upstairs and play the piano while we're down here. Make it sound like there's a party going on. Where's the poison, Lazovert?"

The military doctor, his rubber-gloved hands unsteady with excitement, lifted the tops off half a dozen small cakes and sprinkled the insides with crystals of cyanide of potassium, as the other conspirators watched in silence.

"Good! Now for the wine," said Felix. "Push back the chairs We want it to look as though we all had supper here."

They proceeded to simulate a finished meal with the materials at hand. Valerian upset a glass of wine on the tablecloth and allowed the stain to spread across the table.

"That looks very realistic," said Felix. "Now remember! We mustn't do anything to arouse his suspicions, so stay upstairs until I call you. May God be with us."

Valerian seconded the prayer. He wished there were fewe conspirators in on the plot, and that Felix hadn't chosen poiso as his weapon. Poison was tricky stuff; it had a nasty habit o ending up in the stomach of the wrong person. Besides, Feli was volatile and highstrung. Could he cooly sit by with a smil on his face as his victim swallowed cyanide of potassium?

Felix shepherded the group upstairs, where they settled dow to wait while he went to pick up Rasputin from his home. Hour seemed to pass before the click of the side door told them that Felix had returned with his quarry. As their footsteps echoed on the stairs leading to the basement, Vladimir Pureshkevitch opened the study door a crack and peered through.

"The *starets* is wearing all his finery tonight," he reported. "A white silk blouse and boots you could see your face in. He's obviously determined to make a good impression on his hostess. How disappointed he will be when she doesn't appear!"

Then quickly he strode to the piano where he began to play a rousing polka, as his fellow conspirators, shouting and laughing, started to dance.

For two hours they simulated the sounds of a rollicking party. Finally, when there was still no word from below, Dr. Lazovert said, "What can be happening down there? He should be dead by now. He *must* be dead. I put enough poison in those cakes to kill two men."

"That monster can smell danger like an animal," said Vladimir. "Rasputin may have refused to eat." The strain of waiting was beginning to tell on him.

"But the wine!" protested Lazovert. "A drunken sot like Rasputin couldn't spend two whole hours surrounded by wine bottles without drinking."

Dimitri looked at his watch. "It's after two," he said. "I'm going to see what's happening down there."

"I'll go with you," offered Valerian. The long wait was fraying his nerves, too. He felt that the plot must have gone wrong somehow.

Before they could even reach the door, Felix burst into the room, wild-eyed and disheveled.

"What shall I do?" he demanded. "He wants me to take him to the gypsies and I don't see how I can refuse. The poison didn't work! At first he wouldn't touch the cakes, but once he started eating he couldn't stop. He ate the whole plateful. We can't kill him—the man's bewitched."

"Calm down, Felix," said Dimitri, putting an arm around his shoulders and forcing him into an armchair. "We've got to go through with it now. Bewitched or not, Rasputin must not leave this house alive. If the poison won't kill him, I'm going to see what a bullet through his head will do."

Captain Soukhotin had another idea. "A bullet's too noisy," he said. "Someone's bound to hear the shot and ask questions.

How do we know the secret police didn't follow him to the house?"

Felix groaned. "Then what do you suggest?"

"Let's strangle him," said Soukhotin at once. "It's six to one—he won't have a chance."

"No, no!" said Felix. "If he sees you all approaching, he'll get suspicious. Besides, he's strong as a bull. You won't even be able to hold him. Our best chance is to catch him unawares. Give me your revolver, Dimitri."

The Grand Duke hesitated. "You really think you can do it?"

"I—I've got to."

"Good luck, then." Dimitri clapped him on the shoulder. "Remember! We'll all be here if you need us. Just give a shout."

The revolver hidden behind his back, Felix left the room.

Five minutes later, the men upstairs heard a single shot, followed by a scream like that of an animal in pain.

"He did it!" said Dimitri, incredulous. "Quick, let's go!"

They rushed downstairs and flung open the basement door. As they crowded through, Valerian was pushed against the light switch, and the room was plunged into darkness.

"Turn on the light! For God's sake, turn on the light!" shouted Felix. Someone bumped into him and swore, and in the darkness all was confusion. Then Soukhotin turned on the switch.

Writhing and twitching in agony, Rasputin was lying face up on the white bearskin rug. His eyes were wide and gaping and his fists clenched spasmodically. He arched his back in a final convulsive heave, then keeled slowly over sideways and lay still.

"He's dead," announced Dr. Lazovert.

The conspirators stared down at the body of the man who, only seconds before, had wielded more power over Russia than the Tsar himself.

"Are—are you certain?" asked Vladimir.

Lazovert felt for a heartbeat—a pulse. "Nothing," he announced, letting the limp hand drop. "The bullet struck him in the region of the heart, as you see. He is completely dead."

A mood of wild jubilation swept the conspirators, as they crowded around Felix, laughing, clapping him on the shoulder, congratulating him.

"We'll have to move him before he ruins your bearskin rug,"

said Dimitri, grinning. "Here, Valerian, give me a hand. He weighs a ton."

Together they laid Rasputin's body on the bare stone floor. Blood was oozing through the fine silk blouse embroidered with blue cornflowers. "Put on his hat and coat, Soukhotin," said Dimitri. "You're closest to his size. Then we'll pretend to drive you home in the open car. You'd better act drunk as you cross the courtyard in case the police are watching. They'll recognize the symptoms because that's the way they're used to seeing Our Friend. Valerian and Vladimir can stay here with Felix until we get back, just in case there's any trouble. Later on we'll take the body out to Petrovsky Island in my car and drop him through the ice. It'll take a lot of time for them to find him there. All right, let's get moving." He turned to the Prince. "Felix, you have saved the Romanov dynasty from ruin—singlehandedly. You deserve a drink more than any man ever did. Now leave everything to us."

Felix eyes were glittering with triumph. "I did it." he said. "He was playing with the little drawers in that cabinet . . . He had his back to me. I—I couldn't shoot him in the back. But then, when he turned—"

"You've saved us all. You've saved Russia. Now go and have that drink . . ."

Dimitri put his arm round Felix and led him out of the room. The others followed, closing the door behind them.

As they did so, Rasputin groaned and stirred.

He was lying on a stone floor in the dark. What had happened? He tried to move but pain struck him sharply: pain in his head and stomach, and pain worst of all in his chest. Every breath was a torment.

Then slowly, Rasputin's wits cleared and he began to remember, piecing together the events of the evening. Obviously he had been lured into a trap. Felix Youssoupov, whom he trusted, had set up a trap and tried to kill him. Now he understood his nervousness, his wary eyes as he had offered the cakes and wine.

"Yes, Felix had tried to kill him, but he hadn't quite succeeded. Bullets were powerless against Rasputin, the immortal counselor of princes and healer of human ills. Now the *starets* lay quietly, hoarding his strength, vowing that Felix should pay for his treachery.

Time passed, and then a dazzling light shone into his eyes. He heard a low, tense voice. His arm was seized and violently shaken, sending shockwaves of pain through his chest. Summoning all his strength, Rasputin rolled over and got to his feet. He recognized Felix's white face and panic-stricken eyes.

"Felix!" cried Rasputin in a terrible voice. He seized the younger man by the shoulders, shaking him like a rat, his hands moving inexorably nearer the Prince's throat with the firm intention of squeezing the life out of him.

Half-crazed with fear at seeing the grim living face of the *starets*, risen from the dead, oozing blood and contorted with hate, Felix struggled like a madman in the grip of a nightmare. With a wrench which tore the epaulette from his tunic, he managed to free himself from those terrible hands and bolted from the cellar, leaving the door wide open. Gasping and groaning, Rasputin crawled after him on hands and knees, up the steep steps. There was a door... He remembered seeing a door... If he could reach that door and break into the courtyard—if he could call the police, who followed him everywhere...

Snatching up a rubber truncheon, Felix rushed back to the head of the stairs just in time to see the bleeding figure of the *starets* pull the handle of a door Felix believed to be locked. To his horror, it opened. Rasputin stumbled through, clutching at his stomach, reeling like a drunk, and blundered straight across the courtyard toward the open gate.

"After him!" Felix shouted. "Quickly—he must not get away. I'll cut him off by the canal. Valerian, guard the street!"

Revolver in hand, Vladimir ran after the *starets*, as Valerian ran to block the street exit. A moment later two shots rang out, quickly followed by two more.

"I got him!" shouted Vladimir brandishing his revolver like a flag. He was wild with excitement. The others ran back to the courtyard where they stared in fresh wonder at the crumpled figure of Rasputin, his body lying motionless at last against a bank of snow.

"He's dead this time!" said Vladimir, poking the body with his foot. "What should we do with him now?"

"Hide him, in case the shots were heard," said Valerian quickly. Questions were bound to be asked, and the sooner they got rid of the body the better.

But Felix's nerves now threatened to desert him. "I—I can't touch him again," he said, shaking all over. A servant who had followed them across the courtyard now plucked at his sleeve.

"Yes?" he said to the servant.

"The—the police," the man stammered. "The constable heard the shots from the street. He wants to know what's going on. I—I had to let him in."

"Oh, God!" Felix made an effort to pull himself together, then assumed a noncommital expression and went to face the constable.

"It's nothing to worry about, officer," he said. "One of my guests became a little excited after dinner and decided to take some target practice."

"All right then, sir," said the policeman. "So long as no damage was done. I'll have to make a report, of course."

"A report? That's nonsense! I tell you, no damage was done, none at all." Felix tried to hustle the man away, but suddenly Vladimir, who had joined them, exclaimed:

"I've killed a mad dog—the maddest dog in all Russia!"

The constable stopped in his tracks. "Will you repeat that, please?"

"Oh, don't mind my friend—he's talking nonsense," said Felix. "He's had far too much to drink, poor man." Felix took the constable's arm, adding confidentially, "Don't worry, officer. We'll put him to bed to sleep it off and he won't remember a thing in the morning."

"It's morning now . . ." Undecided, the policeman looked at the Prince, then shrugged. "Very good, my lord. But you understand it's my duty to report any disturbance. I'll have to make my report."

"But that's ridiculous! Surely you don't need to concern yourself with a trifling matter like this?"

Felix tried to slip a coin into the officer's hand but he wouldn't take it.

"It's my duty, sir," he repeated . . .

"Hell and damnation!" said Felix, watching the constable walk stiffly away. "That clown is going to ruin everything. Why can't you control your tongue, idiot? He would have gone away if you hadn't butted in."

Vladimir looked stricken.

"And let me do the talking in the future," snapped Felix. He turned to Valerian. "Get the—the body indoors. Make the servants carry it. Put it on the landing until the others come back with the car. We must get rid of it soon."

Rasputin still lay where he had fallen, but Valerian thought his position had changed slightly. Fighting his revulsion at touching that ruined and bloodstained corpse, he helped two servants wrap it in a length of heavy linen and hoist the gruesome bundle into the back of a car.

Felix, who had done most of the evening's work, was left behind as the other conspirators drove the car to Petrovsky Island. There, they began to cut a hole in the ice large enough to admit the swathed body of Rasputin to the frozen river. They worked in silence, gripped by a kind of superstitious horror that stilled even Vladimir's tongue.

As they shoved the long bundle through the hole, the linen wrapping caught on the ice and for a moment the *starets'* ghastly face was exposed again, his beard matted with blood and his pale lips drawn back from his teeth in a snarl of hatred. Although one eye-socket was no more than a gaping hole, Valerian couldn't rid himself of the impression that the other deepset eye was still glaring with revenge, as the body slid quietly beneath the ice and out of sight.

Thanks to blind Mehmet's nursing and the old woman's refusal to betray him to the German, Anthony's body began to heal. For weeks, as autumn turned to winter, he lay listening to the dull boom of guns far away south at Cape Helles, wondering how to get back to them across the Turkish-held peninsula. Often he dreamed of Anastasia. Where was she now? Had the stubborn streak that parted them carried her safely to the arms of Valerian? Had he been a fool to let her go?

His mind could give him no answers, but at last his restlessness became so acute that Sevinc Hanum reluctantly agreed to let him rejoin the Allied forces. Mehmet would guide him as far as the Turkish trenches, and from there he must make his way to the Anzac-Suvla bridgehead in the north.

"It grieves me to lose you, my son," the old woman said sadly.

"Four sons had I once, and now the army has taken them all. Will you not stay and keep me company until the spring?"

Anthony shook his head. "I am a danger to you, and I've accepted your hospitality too long already. I must go back to my own people and help them win this war. But I thank you from my heart for what you have done for me, and I promise to return. Then you can make me laugh again with tales of the Khoja Nasr-ed-Din. Truly it was laughing that cured me, as much as Mehmet's skill."

She clicked her tongue and smiled, but her black eyes were sparkling with tears. "Allah go with you, my son," Pulling her veil tighter about her face, she watched Anthony limp carefully up the stony track to the mountain. A blind man leading a lame one, she thought. What chance had they of reaching the Allied lines?

Sightless Mehmet might be, but he knew the winding goat tracks like the lines on the palm on his hand. Anthony followed him slowly, marveling at the instinct that led Mehmet to avoid shell holes, booby traps and landslides as they worked their way forward to the very edge of the Turkish lines. A bitter wind full of tiny snowflakes stung their faces, but it had its uses, too, for the half-frozen men in the Turkish trenches scarcely looked up as the two men passed by. To all questions, Mehmet stolidly repeated that they were carrying rations to the front line—Sanders Pasha's orders, and one after another the sentries let them go by.

As darkness fell, the firing from the Australian trenches in front of them slackened off perceptibly. There was a single ragged volley all along the front line, then silence.

"That must be it," said a bearded Turk with knowing, slanted eyes in the trench they were following. "They've used all of today's ammunition. The Christians always stop firing about now."

That's odd, thought Anthony, picking his way forward over broken ground littered with craters and the carcases of mules. Why should the firing stop as darkness falls? Surely the Allies couldn't be all that short of ammunition? Perhaps it was a ruse designed to cover the movement of troops before an attack. But the Turks were apparently used to such a schedule, because they began to leave their trenches like a colony of ants bent on taking the air. Yawning, stretching, smoking, they strolled around seemingly convinced that no sniper would shoot at them now.

Very odd, thought Anthony again.

Then a rifle from the Australians suddenly spat flame, and automatically a Turkish gun answered it.

Silence fell again. Mehmet turned and tugged at his sleeve. "I can go no further, *effendi*. From now on you must travel alone. Allah go with you."

Anthony wanted to thank the man once more, but before he could speak there was the sudden whistle of a mortar overhead. The blind man flung himself flat, but it was too late. Anthony was left staring at a crater not six feet away, into which Mehmet had vanished. All along the Turkish line, an angry volley of shots peppered the spot from which the Unbelievers had broken the early night truce.

There was nothing for Anthony to do but wait until the firing died down and then go forward alone. He crouched in an empty trench where mining operations had been recently interrupted. At the end nearest the Anzac lines he found a tunnel down which he crawled, ears alert for any sound of Australian voices. He wondered if the Anzac troops knew quite how close their enemies lay during the daytime.

Two more shots sounded close overhead, giving him the exact location of the Austrialian trench. The Turks replied, and once more there was silence, with only the rain to break it.

It was now or never, Anthony decided. He must try to break through into the Anzac trench above him and convince them of his identity before they shot at him.

Grabbing a pick which the mining Turks had abandoned, he cautiously hacked at the clay at the end of the trench, keeping a sharp lookout for Turkish soldiers returning to duty as he did so. Within ten minutes he was streaming with sweat at the unaccustomed exercise, but the sound of the pick had a sharper note. After two hours of work, the pick struck timber and he knew he was almost there.

Again he listened. If there were soldiers above, they were keeping abnormally quiet. Perhaps there was a man lying above him, his rifle trained on the spot where the pick would break through. Perhaps someone waited there, his hand poised over the plunger that would detonate a mine to blow Anthony in his tunnel sky-high. There was no way of telling.

Gently, carefully, Anthony loosened the boards of timber that separated him from the Australian trench, and peered through the crack into the inky blackness above.

Putting his mouth to the hole, he said quietly in English. "Is anyone there?" Again a rifle cracked close overhead.

"Don't shoot—I'm a British officer!" He spoke louder now, but as he did so the very feel of the air coming through the crack suggested that there was no one to hear him. The trench was probably empty.

A dreadful suspicion filled his mind. Less careful now, he pulled at the barrier, breaking through the hole he had made. When he flashed his tourch around the trench he had entered, his suspicions became a certainty. Rows of rifles and homemade self-firing devices were propped against the sandbags lining the trench, their muzzles pointed skyward. Otherwise, the whole length of trench was empty. From its desolate look—so different from the affecting home-away-from-home appearance of an inhabited trench—it was clear that its late occupants had no intention of coming back.

At some time during the night, the Anzac troops had been silently withdrawn, leaving their self-firing rifles to spit flames at the Turks and conceal from Liman von Sanders, the German commander, the fact that an army was slipping away from under his very nose.

But the mortar that had killed Mehmet had been real enough, Anthony reasoned. It was triggered by a human hand. The Australians could not have been gone long. That last ragged volley of shots had probably signaled their departure. If he hurried, he might still catch up with some stragglers.

Anthony limped as fast as he could through the labyrinth of deserted trenches, guided only by his sense of direction. Sometimes he was obliged to retrace his footsteps when he encountered tangled wire or high explosives. But it was all deserted; the invading army had melted silently away.

Savage stabs of pain seared through his newly mended leg as he reached the cliffs above Anzac Beach at last. He limped down the path up which so many soldiers had tramped to their deaths. A faint light already glimmered on the deserted beach. Row upon row of dead horses and mules, their throats slit, lay amid huge piles of food, tents, clothing and timber. Anthony's gaze rested briefly on this evidence of evacuation before it went beyond to the sea.

Far out on the horizon, the shadowy shapes of departing boats packed with troops seemed to mock at him—the only living Allied soldier left behind with the dead at Anzac Cove.

For a long time he stared out to sea, suddenly it was all over—there was nothing to hurry for now. When wild whoops behind him on the cliff told him that the Turks had discovered the deception, and were running down to speed the enemy on their way, he moved a little to one side. He watched them run like madmen down to the beach and fling themselves on the treasure the Allies had been forced to abandon. He felt curiously detached, as Turkish soldiers in tattered uniforms seized all they could grab of their loot—their manna from heaven.

His leg was hurting. He sat down on a rock, stretching out the injured limb as he waited for the inevitable. It was not long in coming. Soon a young German officer was standing before him, speaking in slow, careful English.

"You are a British officer, yes?"

"Correct."

The German laughed, showing perfect white teeth. "I think your comrades have left you behind when they departed. Give me your weapons, please, and follow..."

His bid for freedom had failed. His luck had run out at last. Anthony stood up to obey, knowing as he did so that there was no alternative now to spending the rest of the war in a Turkish jail.

Chapter Twenty-four

When she learned that the body of her beloved friend—the *starets* whose constant intercession at the Divine Throne was all, she believed, that kept her hemophiliac son from bleeding to death—had been pulled from the frozen Neva at Petrovsky Island, riddled with bullets yet dead by drowning, the Tsarina's rage and grief were terrible. Valerian's fears that the conspirators had let too many people in on their secret was soon justified.

Within hours of Rasputin's disappearance, a rumor that he had been murdered at the home of Prince Felix Youssoupov, by the Prince's own hand, was everywhere. Nothing Felix could do or say dispeled the suspicion which now fell on him. On the first of January, 1917, after an intensive search, the body was recovered from the river. The Tsarina would have had the principal conspirators executed at once if the Tsar hadn't intervened hastily.

The Grand Duke Dimitri Pavlovitch was banished to Persia; Prince Felix Youssoupov to his estate at Rakitnoye, and in mid-January Valerian, after two weeks under house arrest in Petrograd, was exiled to Ostrovskoye in the Crimea. His arrival took Anastasia by surprise. She and Valentin returned from a drive one winter afternoon to find a fleet of army cars parked on the gravel drive, and lights blazing from every window.

"Father has come home!" shouted Valentin, and flew indoors. Anastasia followed more slowly, hardly able to believe that the long wait was over. There had been so many disappointments—so many times when she dreamed he had come and awakened to find it was only a dream. At the insistence of Yuri, the slit-eyed Tartar with a wooden leg who was now their only servant, she had concealed the truth about Susanna's death, and guilt had lain heavy on her conscience.

"Say nothing, barina," Yuri had urged, standing squat and strong in the kitchen from which he'd eradicated all traces of the night's violence. From the creases of his face, his tilted eyes surveyed her anxiously. "The English lady was sick. You must explain that she slipped and fell when her mind was bemused. Boris Ivanovitch was an evil man. If it becomes known that you killed him, his friends will return to seek vengeance."

"He's right, Anastasia," said Valentin, white-lipped, clinging to her hand.

"But I *didn't* kill him."

"Who will believe you?" Yuri shook his head. Mistrust of those in authority ran deep in his soul.

"But people must know he was here last night. Those men with carts . . . and Andrei."

"Andrei has long been bewitched by that evil man," said Yuri, "but he will not come here seeking him, so long as you are silent."

"Oh, *please* say nothing. Telling the truth won't bring Mother back. Instead it will put us in danger," said Valentin gazing at her with haunted dark eyes. And because the child wa still in a state of shock, and Yuri had worked all night to concea the evidence, she had finally agreed to the story. But whe Susanna had been decently buried and prayers read over her b a shabby, mournful old priest, Anastasia was still haunted by th thought of that unshriven body, dragged away to rot in som secret corner known only to Yuri.

Shivering at the sudden rush of memories, she pushed ope the front door and was immediately enveloped in light, warmt and noise. It was like stepping into another world. There stoo Valerian—an older, stouter Valerian than she remembere perceptibly thicker in the waistline and heavier in the jowl wearing a plain suit and cravat, although the men wh surrounded him were all in uniform. In the few moments befor he saw her, she gazed in dismay at the new lines on his face, an the bitter, sardonic twist to his mouth. Never before had th resemblance to his mother, the Countess, struck her so forcibl His cheekbones were flushed, in sharp contrast to the rest of h face. One hand held a glass and the other gripped Valentin's th shoulders as he talked.

Her glance traveled to Valentin's face. There she saw a loo

of dazzled hero-worship which gave her a shock of recognition. That was the way she used to look up at Valerian. On how many other features, mostly female, had she seen that selfsame expression when Valerian conferred his attention? How many others had known his warmth, and his interest, only to see it quickly dispeled when he dismissed them and moved on to someone else?

"My dearest Stanya!" he exclaimed when he saw her, his voice only slightly blurred with drink. "You're more beautiful than ever. Allow me to present to you the officers of my escort: Major Voikov—Lieutenant Kosygin—Captain Gortchakoff."

"Your escort?" she cried, bewildered, as she smiled and shook hands.

Valerian poured her a glass of wine. "Drink to the future of Russia, free at last from the Siberian monster!"

"To Russia!" chorused the officers. They threw their empty glasses over their shoulders to smash on the marble floor.

Anastasia felt a heightened sense of unreality. These laughing, cheering soldiers, with their loud voices and wine-flushed faces, seemed to belong to a world she had forgotten. Valerian saw her bemused face and smiled.

"Haven't you heard, my darling? Rasputin is dead. Russia is free from his vile machinations and a new era is beginning."

"Long life to the saviors of Russia!" shouted the soldiers, then drank another toast breaking more glasses.

She struggled to understand. "But why have you come back now?"

"Haven't I been away from you long enough?" he teased. "I'll tell you why, though you'll hardly believe it. Our gracious Tsar in his wisdom has rewarded my loyalty by sending me and my friends into exile."

"It's a terrible shame, and I don't care who hears me say so," shouted Major Voikov. "You're one of the saviors of Russia. You should be honored, instead of banished to your estates."

"If the Tsar can't tell his friends from his enemies, there are others who can," declared Lieutenant Kosygin.

"Our time will come," agreed Valerian.

Again, she was struck by the change in him. This wasn't how loyal officers of the Tsar usually spoke about their sovereign. This sounded more like the conversation of radicals—even revolutionaries.

But later that night, when the noisy soldiers had left in their cars and Valentin had gone to bed, she and Valerian sat over their wine at the table he had ordered his servants to set for dinner by the library fire. Logs crackled merrily in the hearth, and the unaccustomed luxury of caviar and champagne which Valerian had brought from St. Petersburg were making Anastasia pleasantly dizzy.

"At last, my darling," he murmured, and his dark eyes glowed with the old special look of admiration he reserved for women he hoped to win. "At last! I thought they'd stay here drinking toasts all night."

"Toasts to you. How does it feel to be the toast of the Russian forces?"

He shrugged. "You wouldn't understand. We hoped for so much... but nothing has changed. Everything goes on as before, in spite of all we risked. The Tsar is throwing away his last chance to save the dynasty. He's a child where politics are concerned, and the German woman still rules. What's the good of trying to explain? All our dreams are tarnished now, and I've been banished to cool my heels here for the rest of the war."

"Is that such a hardship?"

Valerian smiled. "My only comfort is that you're here at last. There's no one between us now. Not Mama, not Susanna, not—"

He shouldn't have mentioned Susanna. Anastasia glanced involuntarily toward the library table on which her makeshift coffin had rested, seeing again her closed eyes and waxen features. Valerian would not grieve for Susanna, nor would he understand her guilt. She hadn't liked the woman, yet Susanna had died to save her. Anastasia knew it was too soon to usurp her husband.

In a low voice, she said, "There's something I must tell you, Valya, something you have to know. There *is* someone between us still: my husband. In Egypt I married an Englishman, Anthony Mills."

To her surpirse he laughed, putting his hand beneath her chin and tilting her face up to his. "Did you actually think I didn't know? Poor little Stanya, how could you imagine I was ignorant of your dark secret? Even in wartime letters fly back and forth in this wonderful new world of ours. Kadya told Andrei of your marriage long ago. You can imagine what pleasure it gave dear Andrei to pass the news on to me!"

He was teasing her, his dark eyes alight with amusement. Suddenly she felt foolish and flustered, as if she had leaned on a prop which had collapsed beneath her weight. Of course her father would spread the news among the family. She said hesitantly, "You mean—it doesn't make any difference?"

"Why should it?" he said, shrugging. "I'm not the jealous type—I find it far too exhausting to be jealous of other men. You've apparently tired of your Englishman, since you've come back to me. A little wartime romance isn't important; it happens to everyone now and then. Forget your Englishman, just as I shall forget all the other girls I've loved. Give yourself to me . . ."

"It doesn't matter to you?"

"Had you rather it did? Stanya, I think you're still living in a bygone age! Virgins have never held much attraction for me, as you know. It's always puzzled me that any man should prefer a rough diamond to one which has been cut and polished—or an unbroken horse to one which is well-trained. Your Englishman—what was his name, Anthony?—yes, Anthony's unlikely to have been a great lover. Anglo-Saxons lack the dedication to master the art of love. But he must have taught you something, and if he's done no more than awaken your passions I shall be grateful to him. Virgins are very boring in bed, my dear."

Anastasia felt confused. It would never do to show indignation at this slighting view of Anthony's capabilities. Besides, how could she judge? She had never allowed him the opportunity to show his skill as a lover. All the same, she couldn't help resenting Valerian's confident assumption of superiority. She picked on something she could reasonably object to.

"Are you comparing me to a horse?"

He smiled. "A well-schooled one—you ought to be flattered. In the world of horses, there's a world of difference between a well-trained mount and nature's raw material.

"I still don't care for the comparison."

"Ah, but the diamond," he said, his voice low and caressing. You surely don't mind being compared to a precious jewel?"

Strangely enough, she did. She wished he would think of her as a person, rather than an object—even a precious object, to be admired, displayed, flattered, perhaps made love to, but never talked to or treated as an equal. Trying to steer the conversation away from the personal, she asked about the war, about politics, but gently he headed her off.

"I had my fill of politics in Petrograd, Stanya. Two weeks under house arrest is a trying experience, you know, even if my friends did manage to smuggle in news to me. Now all I want is to relax and enjoy your company. I've done my best for our poor, troubled country. Now it's up to others to make the most of the opportunity we've created."

"The opportunity to depose the Emperor?" she asked boldly, remembering the officers' open discontent.

"That is the first step, naturally. After that, we have our plans . . ."

"What plans?"

"Nothing you need to trouble your head about," he said, as she half expected. "It won't be long before they relax this stupid exile, and when I can move about more freely again we'll see. Until then—"

"Yes?"

"I intend to make the most of my enforced holiday. With your help, of course." He rose and walked around the table to stand behind her chair. Gently his hands slid down her shoulders until they cupped her breasts. He bent and kissed the nape of her neck. Anastasia repressed a shudder, as shocking to her as it was unexpected. There was something so practiced and mechanical about his gestures. She couldn't help wondering how many women he'd held like this as a prelude to lovemaking, confident in his power over them, knowing precisely how many endearments, how many caresses were necessary to guarantee their surrender.

But she knew that if she obeyed her instinct to break away, he would think her gauche and inexperienced, not worth the attention of a connoisseur of women. She imagined his voice, resigned, regretful: "I see you're just the same. I had hoped you'd be grown up by now, but obviously I was mistaken. Is this how your Englishman liked you to be?"

She sat as if frozen, feeling his hands move under her blouse, willing herself not to scream. It's got to work this time, she told herself with a kind of desperation. I can't—I simply can't—be wrong again. I do love Valerian, and I must make myself forget that he's used these words, these gestures, on a hundred other women . . .

"Little Stanya, my darling, you're so beautiful."

She closed her mind to the tired old phrase—and tried to respond to his kisses as he led her into the bedroom where a wide fourposter with a blue silk canopy had suddenly materialized. Valerian had always traveled with his own bed. When he picked her up and carried her over to it, she had a sharp memory of Miss Louisa's pale, plump arms locked around Valerian's neck beneath that same blue canopy, seen so many years before—and herself, a leggy, pigtailed child, staring at them in dismay. Suddenly Anastasia felt goosebumps all over her body. Miss Louisa must be over forty now, fair, fat and foolish. Yet Valerian had loved her in this same bed. Would she, Anastasia please him as much as Miss Louisa?

At dinner she'd drunk her champagne sparingly. Now she wondered if that had been a mistake. With half a bottle inside her, she might have been able to deaden her memories and let her senses respond to his lovemaking. He mustn't know!, she thought with a kind of panic. I must never let him guess what I feel. Surely it will be better next time...

Then, with infinite relief, she realized that Valerian was finally satisfied. He relaxed across her with a groan, and the lamplight showed her what she hadn't noticed at dinner—that his dark glossy hair was thickly streaked with gray. It doesn't matter, she thought fiercely. I don't mind if he's getting older, everyone gets older. I love him and I don't care what he looks like or what his politics are. I don't care if he does depose the Tsar: Nicholas probably deserves it. *It's got to work this time.* I won't think about all the other women he's loved, I'll make him love me. And I won't ever think about Anthony Mills again.

A moment later Valerian raised his head from where it was pillowed on her breasts. He leaned over her, smoothing her eyebrows with a forefinger as he murmured: "Well, little Stanya, wasn't that better? Wouldn't you say that was an improvement?"

Puzzled, she gazed up at him. "An improvement?"

She thought he was referring to their night together in Siberia, but he explained impatiently, "An improvement on your experiences with that Englishman. Wasn't it?"

"Oh. Oh, yes. Of course."

She couldn't let him down, and anyway, it was true. It had been better than her wedding night, and better than those edgy, emotion-torn hours in the nurses' home. That was all she had to compare it with, but sadly she was aware that tonight had shown her neither fire nor ice, neither heaven nor hell, ecstasy nor despair. Perhaps she'd been wrong to expect them. Perhaps it was always different for men...

For a long time after Valerian fell asleep, Anastasia stared into the dark with hot, aching eyes, fighting her sense of guilt and confusion, fighting to convince herself that all her dreams had finally come true.

The old Turkish fort where Anthony and a hundred other Allied prisoners were incarcerated lacked any kind of comfort, ancient or modern. In winter the cells where the prisoners slept were dank and chill, and the walls ran with water which dried in summer to become an evil-smelling slime. Rats and mice shared their unappetizing food, and fleas abounded in their thin straw pallets, but the prisoners knew that their living conditions were little worse than those most Turks considered normal. They were hardly surprised when their protests about food and sanitation fell on ears that were not only deaf but uncomprehending.

Better treatment? Impossible. They were prisoners, weren' they? They'd made the mistake of being caught—now they mus pay for it. Why should Christian dogs be lodged in luxury whil so many Believers were ragged and starving? They were lucky t be fed at all.

As the months dragged by, those prisoners who didn' succumb to typhoid and dysentery acquired a certain immunit to disease and forgot what it felt like to have a clean skin and full stomach. The company was good—if nothing els was—inside the Chanak Hissar, and by the late summer of 191 no one believed the Turks would remain in the war much longe

"They'll sign a separate peace before Christmas, mark m words," predicted Rory O'Connor, a Dublin Fusilier who'd ha the misfortune to be captured the day after the landings a Gallipoli, and now resembled a walking skeleton. "I've bee over three years in this hellhole, and I can smell change in the ai Our guards are getting jumpy, right, Badger?"

"Maybe so. Abdul Aziz hasn't had any fresh horror stori for weeks now," agreed Badger Burles, ex-schoolmaster, who classical education stood him in good stead with the priso commandant, who could speak Greek. Anthony's fluency i

Turkish was envied by all, but he found it a mixed blessing to know exactly how badly the war was going for Russia. The guards took a simple pleasure in tormenting the prisoners with stories of Allied reverses. Even allowing for exaggeration, there could be no doubt that the news from Russia was very bad indeed.

To all intents and purposes she was now out of the war, totally preoccupied with a bloody internal struggle which furnished the Turkish guards with plenty of gruesome material. Her Tsar was deposed, and many said murdered. Her government was in chaos, and mutiny ran like wildfire through the armed forces. Her new rulers the Bolsheviks, headed by Lenin and Trotsky, had signed a separate peace with the Germans. Only the White Army, as it was called—the dwindling band of Russian diehards who refused to recognize the Bolsheviks—continued to fight them with Allied support. Recent reports suggested that the White Army was being driven back on all fronts.

It was hell knowing all this without being able to lift a finger to help. Far worse for Anthony than his physical discomfort was the knowledge that Anastasia was in danger.

As a Russian aristocrat whose family had long been notorious for its high-handed extravagance, she was a natural target for the Bolsheviks, and Anthony couldn't escape the fact that it was largely his fault that she was within their reach. If he hadn't allowed his wretched temper to get the upper hand when she refused to sleep with him; if he hadn't been determined to show up Valerian as he really was; if he had been patient with her foolish whims... If, if, if!

Anthony twisted uncomfortably on his thin straw mat. He heard the dry rustle of a rat's feet scurrying along the wall, then the crack of the stone Taffy Williams threw at it.

"Steady on, Taff," grumbled Badger Burles. "That was too damn close to my head."

If, if, if!

If only he hadn't been captured. He'd intended to do several more runs up the Bosporus to the Black Sea. He could have landed at Novorossiysk; he could even have offered her a chance to return, if she'd wanted to. In his heart he believed she would have wanted to then... but now, two years later, that hope had become a mockery. Worst of all was the memory of how nearly he'd won her that night in the nurses' home. He'd thought he *had* won her—and then she'd flung Valerian Radek in his face again. In a black temper he had vowed to take her at her word and show her what Russia—and Valerian—were really like. There was no point in regretting it now, but he knew she'd been frightened when he told her he was taking her back to Russia. He'd hoped she'd capitulate aboard Guy's boat, and admit she didn't really want to leave him. It seemed to him that she'd been within an inch of doing so. Then her chin had gone up and her green eyes flashed defiance... There had been no hope of reconciliation after that.

He was well rid of her. He wished Valerian joy of her fads and fancies. Valerian, now... What kind of a man lay behind that smoothly handsome face? Would Anastasia find in him the tower of strength she craved, or did the man she loved exist only in her imagination?

Turkey might be about to sue for peace; freedom might be at hand for him and all the other prisoners, but Anthony knew he could not go back to England with these questions unanswered.

"Do any of you men fancy a trip to Russia before going back to England?" He broke the silence in the heavy, fetid darkness.

It took a moment for the men to respond. Then...

"If you'll stand me caviar and champagne at the Hotel Splendide!" said Badger Burles.

"Filet mignon with mushrooms!" said Rory O'Connor.

It was an old and well-loved game. Other voices chimed in from cells father away.from cells farther away.

"Absinthe frappé!"

"Hot apple pie with ice cream!"

"A feather mattress, dear heaven! and no fleas in it either."

"Disallowed," ruled Anthony. "You've got to be able to eat it."

England... Sybil... he thought. He closed his eyes and visualized her sitting beneath the cedar tree on the smooth lawn at Bishop's Glebe, wearing a linen dress, a wide-brimmed hat. A child—their child—played near her feet. The image was so real he could almost reach out and touch her. Then the dream girl raised her head, and under the wide-brimmed hat he saw that it wasn't Sybil but Anastasia.

"Damn you, why won't you leave me in peace?" he groaned.

And Badger, who thought he was addressing the fleas, offered him half a vile-tasting cigarette, which the prison commandant had given him in exchange for a lesson in colloquial English.

For centuries Yildiz Khan's watchtower had leaned across the abyss which was the boundary to the Ostrovskoye estate, but as Anastasia and Valentin rode toward it on a crisp morning in autumn, she thought that the angle had become more pronounced than ever. Surely the steps were less steep now, and the platform even more tilted than when she had climbed it as a child?

"This is where Uncle Andrei had his accident, isn't it?" said Valentin. "Yuri told me all about it."

"Yes." She could sense the old tower's attraction beginning to tug at the boy's sense of adventure. *Why do you have to climb it? Because it's there, of course!* To distract him, she said, "What was it you wanted to tell me, Valentin? No one can listen to us here."

Reluctantly he dragged his fascinated gaze away from the tower. "Did you know that Father is one of the Reds?" he asked.

"What nonsense! Of course he isn't."

"But he is."

"Don't be silly, Valentin. How could he be a Red when he's—"

"A nobleman?"

"Well, yes. And all his friends are fighting in the White Army. You know that as well as I do."

"Then why isn't Father fighting with them? And why hasn't Ostrovskoye been searched and the furniture taken away? Why haven't guards been stationed at our gates? They have at all the other big houses around here. Tell me that."

"I don't know. Because we're not all that important, I suppose," said Anastasia, though for weeks she'd been asking herself the same questions. "What would be the point of guarding us? We're not trying to escape. Where would we go? It's much safer to stay where we are until all this trouble is over."

"Do you think so? Do you really believe it will even be over? Will we still be safe if the Bolsheviks come here looking for Boris?" asked Valentin.

Her feart gave a nasty lurch. Valentin had not mentioned

Boris to her since the night of his mother's death. "Why do you ask that?" she whispered, though no one else was within earshot.

Suddenly, Valentin looked much older than his years, but his voice was steady as he replied: "One of the men who came to see Father last night was the commissar from the Sevastopol Soviet. He told father that he'd found a witness who could swear that you asked Boris to eat with us the night he disappeared. He thinks you poisoned him."

"Oh, no," she said, feeling sick and dizzy. Not after all this time—surely no one would look for Boris now?

"They asked Father's permission to search the grounds. Stanya," he said carefully, "Bolsheviks don't ask permission when they want to search. They just come and do it. That *must* mean that Father is one of them—and pretending not to be. You know how he spends all day talking on the telephone to Prince This and Countess That? I think he's betraying their secrets—his friends' secrets—to the Reds. Who's trying to leave the country, for example, and where have they hidden their jewels? Who's engaged in counter-revolutionary activities? . . ."

"That's a terrible thing to say, Valentin."

"It's a terrible thing to do."

"*If* he's doing it. You don't know for sure, you're only guessing." But to her horror she found herself believing what he said. So many little things seemed to fit the picture: casual remarks by Valerian; the way Ostrovskoye alone among the large estates in the district had partially escaped the pillaging Bolsheviks—and had no restrictions whatsoever on the movements of its occupants; the suspicious swiftness with which Valerian's requests for a new telephone, or the use of a car or whatever were always granted.

She pushed those thoughts aside and said, "But Boris was a thief—a murderer! Why should they care what became of him now?"

"From what I could hear through the door last night, Boris was special. He was a friend of Lenin's. When he vanished, the Bolsheviks thought he was in the hands of the Tsar's police. But they've checked all the prison records and found no trace of him, so they're beginning to investigate his movements just before he disappeared—and the trail stops here."

He paused and then added, running his fingers through

Khan's rough mane, "They want to question us all, Stanya. They know that Father wasn't here then, but you and I must tell the same story."

"And Yuri."

They stared at each other. Their safety would depend on Yuri. He alone knew where Boris' body was hidden, but his temper was unpredictable. He hated the Bolsheviks with a bitter loathing. He might say what Anastasia told him to, or he might refuse to answer any questions at all. It was possible that his love of fantasy might lead him to relate some extravagant tale which would excite suspicion rather than dispel it. Suddenly Yuri was a dangerous unknown quantity.

"What shall we do?" It no longer seemed odd to Anastasia that she could speak to the boy as an equal. Already he was strangely adult and, after all, the peril was equally theirs. Her mind searched for possible courses of action. Should they admit it? Deny it? Should they confide in Valerian?

"Perhaps we'd better tell your father the whole story," she said.

"No!" Valentin said. "Don't do that. Father won't help us—he'll only take the easiest way out. You know what he's like."

Did she indeed? After a surprised glance at her companion, Anastasia was suddenly far from certain that she knew either Valerian or his son. She had thought that Valentin worshipped his father. Was it possible that the boy's shrewd eyes had seen so quickly through Valerian's handsome exterior to the shallower, more fickle soul within? It had taken her two years in his company, sharing his bed, to recognize how far he fell short of the ideal she had cherished so long, and she still found it difficult to admit to herself how empty were his promises of devotion. Novelty was the spice of life to Valerian. He could no more remain faithful to one woman than he could resist an invitation to a party, a new fashion—or a new creed.

She had tried hard not to notice the way his eyes lit up at the sight of pretty, elegant little Mathilde Tchernichev, when her father brought her to visit, nor mind when Valerian insisted on showing her the rose garden after supper, while the old man droned on and on to Anastasia. Alone with her, Valerian was frequently moody and withdrawn, but as soon as a pretty newcomer crossed his path all his charm and gaiety revived. She had thought he was like that all the time. How could I have been so naive?, she wondered.

"Promise you won't tell Father," Valentin said urgently.

"I think we ought to..."

"Then how will you explain why you didn't tell him before?"

"Oh, Valentin," she said helplessly, "I really don't know what to do."

"Do nothing," said the boy firmly. "Let me warn Yuri, and if we're ever questioned by the Bolsheviks we must all say that Boris went away with the carts after stealing our food and furniture—and that was the last we saw of him."

"But the men who were driving the carts know he stayed."

"We'll say they're lying." Now his train of thought was changing. "Wait a minute... I want to climb up the tower... I'd like to see if Khan will do it..."

"Do you want to have an accident too?"

He grinned. "No. Just to see if we can do it."

The unmistakable hum of a car motor came faintly to their ears. Anastasia turned to see the car moving up the long drive toward the house. She exchanged a glance with Valentin. Could the Commissar be returning so soon?

"You stay here," said Valentin quickly. "I'm going to find Yuri. If it's those Bolsheviks again, don't talk to them. Tell them you're ill or something..."

He clapped his heels into Khan's fat sides and cantered away in the direction of Yuri's *izba*. Anastasia turned her horse's head toward the house. She wanted to be alone, to think. Could Valentin be right, and his father in league with the Bolsheviks? Why hadn't Valerian told her? Because he doesn't trust me, she thought. And then with sudden clarity she thought, No: it doesn't matter to him what I think. He doesn't believe I *can* think. I'm still Little Stanya; no more important to him than a glass of good wine or—what was his phrase?—yes: a well-schooled horse. He told me so himself. He doesn't think of love as I do, as something deep that lasts forever. For him, love is merely one of life's pleasures; for me, it's the whole of life. Ruefully, she allowed the reins to slide through her fingers, and wily old Katinka, Valerian's retired charger, dropped her head to pick delicately at the grass.

Then she had a brainstorm! I'll make a life of my own!,

Anastasia thought with sudden excitement, I'm not tied to Valerian. I can earn my own living as a nurse. Hospitals still need nurses, even if the war is over. I may find a good use for Sister Price's training yet! The decision invigorated her. She gathered up her reins and trotted back to the stables.

In the past year Ostrovskoye had regained much of its former beauty. Now the estate had a prosperous, well-ordered appearance. Roofs and outbuilding had been repaired, and the estate was adequately staffed, both indoors and out. Now she gave Katinka into the care of a smiling stable boy and hurried indoors to change from the boots and breeches which Valerian hated to see her wearing.

Through the hall window she noticed that the car was still parked in the driveway. She could hear the murmur of men's voices from the library. Trying to make as little noise as possible on the marble floor, she tiptoed past the library door, but as soon as she started up stairs, the door swung open and Valerian called out: "Anastasia!" he said. "I've been waiting for you."

Sunlight was streaming into the hall, and suddenly Anastasia was very conscious of her disheveled appearance, her dusty boots and windswept hair. In the gloom of the booklined library, she saw the vague form of a man standing behind Valerian. His face was in shadow, but he seemed to be watching her with curious intensity.

It's the Commissar, she thought. He wants to question me.

Valerian moved toward her. His dark eyes seemed to glow with a special excitement. "You have a visitor, my dear," he said. "Someone who's very anxious to ask you a few questions."

Her hand went to her throat, and all the color drained from her cheeks. "I—I don't want to talk to him," she said faintly.

"But, he's come such a long way to see you," said Valerian smoothly. "Won't you spare him just a few minutes?"

Suddenly she was very frightened. "Please, Valya . . . ask him to excuse me," she said in a trembling voice. "I—I'm not feeling well. Katinka threw me. My head . . . I can't talk to anyone right now."

"*That* sounds familiar," said the man behind Valerian. He moved forward through the doorway.

With an icy shock, she recognized Anthony Mills!

Chapter Twenty-five

For a moment, she was speechless.

She gazed at Anthony, noting the differences. His hair was cropped and his face seemed to have a prison pallor. His coat hung from his shoulders as loosely as a peasant's smock. He looked almost like a phantom. But this was no mirage or dream: this was her husband, real and solid, sprung from heaven only knew where just when she needed him most. He had come to rescue his errant wife . . .

The wave of thankfulness that swept over her left her almost lightheaded. She felt as if she'd been drifting through a fog, uncertain of when she had been, uncertain of where she was going. Now, suddenly the mist had rolled back to show her a single safe and familiar haven.

"Anthony!" she exclaimed, finding her voice at last. "Where have you come from? What are you doing here? Why didn't you tell me you were coming? I never thought—never realized—"

"That you'd ever be faced with me again?" To her dismay he sounded harsh, almost forbidding. "I must apologize for bursting in on you without warning, and disturbing your idyll, but I had an odd feeling that if I'd told you I was coming you might not have been at home to receive me. I couldn't have gotten in touch much earlier, however, because I've been stuck in a Turkish jail. *Incommunicado,* you might say. Still, it's clear that you've fallen on your feet—I really needn't have worried. The present political climate seems to suit you amazingly well."

"Oh," she said, "you were captured by the Turks!" How terrible! That explained why he was thin and pale, with those deep hollows beneath his cheekbones. But it didn't explain why he spoke with such anger, as if he hated her. Didn't he realize how glad she was to see him—how much she needed his help? She smiled, but his eyes remained hard and cold.

"Strangely enough," he continued, "a husband doesn't just vanish in a puff of smoke, however convenient that might be for you. There are still a few formalities to be arranged before I leave you for good."

"What do you mean? I don't understand." Before he left her for good? Just when he'd come back to her? Anastasia blinked; the fog seemed to be rolling back in, clouding her vision. Why did Anthony insist on remaining so stiff and formal?, she wondered. Was it because Valerian was present, and observing the Englishman with barely veiled hostility. She wondered what he Valerian might have said to Anthony before she arrived, poisoning his mind against her.

"I think it's time we agreed to a divorce," said Anthony. "Valerian tells me you've decided to stay in Russia for good, and it's the only sensible course to take. With your consent I'll make the necessary arrangements. Then—"

"No, no! Not a divorce!" She struggled for words. "Anthony, I haven't thought about it. I haven't decided."

"Then it's high time you did, as Captain Mills suggests," cut in Valerian smoothly. "Come, Anastasia, even you must admit that the present situation is far from satisfactory. No doubt Captain Mills wishes to marry again. You did desert him, remember? You hardly have the right to stand in the way of his happiness now."

Was that how Anthony thought of himself, as a husband deserted by a faithless wife? She sought in vain for the words that would tell her husband that she had been wrong; that Valerian's love was no more than a will-o'-the-wisp, a welcoming fire that flickered from a distance and turned to gray ashes the moment it was reached. By making that mistake, she had forfeited her own happiness, and now Valerian was telling her that she had no right to stand in the way of Anthony's right to his. Happiness? Yes, she wanted Anthony to be happy. But with Sybil Dunwoody? The thought of Anthony married to Sybil brought a sharp and bitter pain.

"These questions you want to ask me—what are they?" she said.

"I think you've answered them already," said Anthony bleakly. Valerian nodded.

"But I've said nothing!"

"That's what I mean."

"Do you want to marry someone else? Do you want to marry Sybil?" It was a body-blow to her hopes: he hadn't come to rescue her but to free himself in order to marry Sybil.

Anthony frowned. Valerian said lightly, "Isn't that the captain's business rather than yours, little Stanya?"

"No," she cried passionately, "it's mine! I must know. Answer me, Anthony!" If only Valerian would go away and leave her alone with Anthony. If only he would let go of her hand, which he seemed to have taken possession of. But Valerian did neither of these things. He had no intention of relinquishing her to this intrusive upstart Englishman, whose challenge for Anastasia's love he believed he had beaten off long ago.

"Why should you care who I marry?" asked Anthony.

Why indeed? But she did care, more than she would once have believed possible. However illogically, she hated the thought of Anthony married to anyone else, and the vision of a triumphant Sybil taking her place in Anthony's heart filled her with bitter jealousy. Yet, as Valerian had pointed out, she had no right to protest. She herself had preferred another: why shouldn't Anthony do the same? In front of Valerian, she could hardly declare that she had been wrong, and that she had loved her husband almost ever since they had parted. Besides, even if Valerian believed her, Anthony wouldn't

"I—I can't . . . tell . . .," she began, then faltered.

Anthony shrugged. "Since you're obviously too shaken from your fall to discuss the situation now, why don't you come to my hotel to talk it over later this week? I won't impose on your hospitality any longer, Count Radek, since this is a personal matter between Anastasia and me. I'm at the Hotel Splendide until Thursday."

Her heart leapt. He was offering her a chance to be alone with him—it might even be a chance to win him back! "Oh, yes," said Anastasia eagerly—too eagerly.

Valerian's eyes narrowed and he shook his head. "Impossible, I'm afraid. I don't think you quite understand the present situation here in Russia, Captain Mills. Certain restrictions are placed on our movements. Yesterday the Commissar instructed me that no one from Ostrovskoye is to leave the estate without an escort from the local Soviet. I'm afraid a tête-a-tête with Stanya is quite out of the question." He gave the Englishman a charming, mock-rueful grin. "These days, unfortunately, we have to respect the orders of our new masters whether we like it or not."

You hypocrite!, Anastasia wanted to shout at him. Why drag in the Soviet? Why not say straight out that *you* won't let me leave Ostrovskoye? Suddenly she hated Valerian's blandly smiling face, and knew instinctively and with certain conviction that Valentin's accusation had been right. Valerian *was* betraying his friends and neighbors to the Reds whenever he could, and they repaid him by leaving Ostrovskoye unharmed. She knew it!

She decided to be reckless. "I will go, Valya, and you can't stop me."

"My dear girl, it isn't I who would stop you, but the guards at the gate. They were stationed there last night."

"Yet you yourself seem to enjoy excellent relations with the Soviet?" suggested Anthony, watching him closely. Anastasia was silent, but she was thinking hard. There had never been guards on the gate before; why had they suddenly been put there?

"That's from necessity, not choice, I assure you. I'm deeply sorry about it, but surely you can see that to flaunt the Soviet's orders would jeopardize that whole relationship—as many of my unfortunate neighbors have learned to their cost. Besides, since you're both in agreement about getting a divorce, surely there's nothing further for you to discuss?"

His tone was cool, but Anthony saw his fingers tighten so hard on Anastasia's wrist that she winced. Obviously Valerian Radek had no intention of leaving them alone, which caused Anthony for the first time to have doubts. Was Anastasia really as happy as Valerian made her out to be? Was there a hint of the jailer in his whole attitude?

If only she would say something either to confirm his suspicions or deny them! One thing seemed certain, however: whoever else sank beneath the wave of the Revolution, it was clear that Valerian Radek intended to float on its crest—even if he had to drown old friends and loyalties in order to do so. The prosperous appearance of the estate was evidence that he had come to terms with Russia's new masters, by what means Anthony could only guess. Whether Anastasia approved of, or was blind to, his political leanings was impossible to ascertain unless she gave him some clue.

He turned to her directly. "Do you agree to a divorce, then?"

"Naturally," said Valerian, making no attempt now to conceal his impatience. "Go ahead with your plans."

"I want to hear it from Anastasia. It's her decision," insisted Anthony. He moved to stand in front of her, but she still wouldn't meet his eyes.

Will you take this man to be your wedded husband?

Will you divorce this man from being your wedded husband?

Her head seemed to swim and a vast weariness overwhelmed her. If she refused, Anthony would continue to argue until she agreed to divorce him. He didn't love her any more; she had forfeited his love when she ran away from him.

"Will you agree to a divorce, Anastasia?" Anthony's voice was insistent.

"If it will make you happy," she said painfully at last, and felt Valerian's fingers relax on her wrist as Anthony took his leave.

"A dangerous man," said Valerian, as he watched the open-top car speed away down the drive, clouds of white dust in its wake.

Anastasia tried to come out of her private misery. "*Dangerous?*"

"Captain Mills is an English spy. I know that he's worked for their Secret Service for years. Those fools on the gate should have known better than to let him in. I'll have to see that it doesn't happen again."

"But he only came to see me. To get my consent—" Her voice choked on the word, and Valerian turned to look at her curiously.

"You surely didn't believe *that* absurd excuse? Captain Mills had other reasons for forcing his way in. Perhaps he thought he might pick up some interesting data for the Allied Interventionists, meddling fools that they are. I managed to anticipate every move he made, however. Your arrival provided a timely distraction, my dear." Valerian was smiling, pleased with himself.

Anastasia said, unsteadily, "You mean, he *didn't* want to talk to me, that his visit was just an excuse for spying?"

The smile vanished. "Don't you listen to a word I say?" Valerian snapped. "Really, Stanya, I sometimes find your naiveté extremely hard to take."

"And I find your secrecy intolerable!" she said. "Why must you think the worst of everyone? Why can't you ever tell the truth?"

"So the handsome captain's visit has awakened our Sleeping Beauty from her trance!" Valerian eyed her speculatively. "It doesn't pay to tell the truth," he said. "I've learned that the hard way."

"Not even to me?"

"Least of all to you—not until a little more political awareness penetrates that lovely head of yours," said Valerian cooly. "Although perhaps it's beginning to at last. Andrei told me it never would, but I was more optimistic—I usually am. Well, so long as it's the right kind of awareness, it will suit us very well, me and my friends."

"Who are your friends, Valya—the Bolsheviks?" she said scornfully.

Valerian laughed out loud. "You mean you didn't know? I swear to God. Even young Valentin realized it before you did!"

"Tell me about the guards on the gate. Why were they put there? Why won't they let us leave Ostrovskoye?"

"Those guards are for our protection, my dear—to keep unwelcome visitors out, rather than to keep us in."

"Then why did you say I couldn't go to Sevastopol?"

"Do you think I want you blurting out everything you know to that interfering Englishman? He's not interested in you in any case. He has adequate grounds for divorce with or without your consent—but he'd be very interested in what you could tell him about me."

"You flatter yourself," said Anastasia coldly, but she couldn't disbelieve him entirely. "How long have you been a Bolshevik, Valya?"

For a moment, he seemed to consider whether or not to tell her, then he shrugged. "Why shouldn't you know? A good many years now—since Andrei introduced me to Boris Miliukoff. You remember Boris?"

He was looking at her with a curious light in his eyes, as

though he was asking a different question. Suddenly all the earlier fears returned. She shook her head. "I—I don't think so."

"We'd certainly like to know what finally became of Boris," Valerian said softly, "Oh, I suppose some people might have called him rough. He was never very appealing, in terms of pretty manners, but Boris was quite brilliant in his way. A magnificent speaker—he could get a crowd howling for blood quicker than anyone else I ever heard. And he was a friend of our great leader's, of course."

Anastasia remained silent.

Valerian continued, "You're certain you don't recall an occasion when Boris made—ah—advances to you? In Petersburg? I wasn't there, of course, but Andrei told me what happened."

It was useless to deny it. "Oh, *that* Boris!" she said, as blithely as she could. "Yes, I do remember him. Now, if you'll excuse me, I think it's time I changed..."

She tried to leave, but his hands were suddenly on her shoulders, forcing her to look at him. "Can you throw any light on his disappearance perhaps? Think carefully, Anastasia. Your answer could be important—to you and to Yuri..."

"What do you mean?" she whispered.

"I believe you can guess if you think hard enough. Certain evidence seems to indicate that Boris paid a visit here just before he vanished, a visit which coincides very closely with the time Susanna, my unfortunate wife, met with the accident that led to her death." He added softly, "I think the two events are connected. You've never really given me a full account of that... accident. One might almost think there was a conspiracy of silence between Yuri and you. He won't talk about it either."

She clasped her hands tightly together to prevent them from shaking. "That's absurd!" she said indignanty. "Poor Susanna fell down the stairs, as I wrote you. What more do you want to know?"

"Perhaps Commissar Yakovlev will have more success with Yuri," said Valerian blanky. "The Soviets have their own ways of extracting information from unwilling witnesses. Their methods are not for the squeamish, but they're highly effective."

She stared at him with horrified revulsion. Could this actually be Valerian, gloating over the suffering poor old Yuri might have to undergo at the hands of the Bolsheviks? "You're wrong, it wasn't Yuri," she said urgently. "He had nothing to do with Boris' death, I swear it."

"So you admit that he's dead!" Valerian pounced on her slip. "If Yuri didn't kill him for molesting you, or Susanna—am I right?—that doesn't leave many other candidates for the crime. Because if either you or Yuri must take the blame, I'd infinitely prefer it to be him. Boris was Lenin's good friend, you know, through all the dark days of exile, and the Petrograd Soviet is out for someone's blood to avenge him. I think it had better be Yuri's—rather than yours."

"But Yuri is innocent. You can't allow an innocent man to be punished for something he didn't do! Yuri didn't kill Boris, I tell you!" she said wildly.

"Then why—after a little *persuasion*—was Yuri able to lead Commissar Yakovlev to Brois' grave this morning?" asked Valerian, his voice like silk. "You couldn't have done that, could you, my dear?"

"You—you devil!" She spat the words at him, her green eyes blazing in her sheet-white face. "That old man is innocent. He did his best to protect *your* wife, *your* son, *your* property—yes, and your mistress, too! He's done nothing more disloyal than risk his life for you, and now you're allowing him to be tortured as a scapegoat. You revolt me, Valya—you make me sick. Take your hands off me! Let me go. I don't want you near me again—ever."

She began to cry. Valerian watched her without emotion, a cold, clinical interest in his alert dark eyes.

"Just one more question, and then I'll let you go and get out of those clothes." He eyed her dusty boots with disfavor. "You've told me everything I want to know, except this. If Yuri didn't kill Boris, *who did?*"

"Susanna killed him," said Anastasia reluctantly. It could do no harm to tell the truth now; it might even help poor Yuri. But Valerian threw back in head and laughed.

"Oh, Stanya, you can't expect me to believe that! That strains my credulity too far. I could believe that *you* stuck that long knife into Boris. You're a strong girl, Anastasia, and you've got a temper, too. You could have done it—but not Susanna. She hadn't the strength, poor woman, nor the courage. No; if that's the best you can do, I'm afraid old Yuri must face the consequences alone. The Commissar will want to question you, no doubt, when Yuri eventually confesses. He probably won't hold out very long. That's why I thought it wise to have this little discussion with you first. But don't, I beg of you, ask Yakovlev to believe such a story! These Bolsheviks take themselves very seriously, you know. They don't like a joke at their expense. That story might have unpleasant consequences for all of us."

"It's the truth," insisted Anastasia, but Valerian shook his head.

"Go change your clothes, Stanya. It's clear that you're still shaken from your fall and hardly know what you're saying. I think you'd be wise to rest until luncheon, at least."

"I can't find Yuri anywhere," said Valentin, entering her bedroom after knocking. "Where on earth can he be?"

He looked at her closely as she lay on the chintz-covered bed. "What's the matter, Stanya? Why didn't you come down to lunch? And why are you crying?"

Anastasia rubbed her eyes and sat up. "I'm not—I mean, I was, but I'm not any more. Valentin, something dreadful has happened. The Bolsheviks have taken Yuri away. They're going to force him to confess that he murdered Boris."

There was no way of softening the news, though the sight of Valentin's horrified face made her wish she'd broken it to him more gently. "But he didn't!" he whispered. "He—he only tried to help us . . . to hide what Mother had done. Stanya, we must stop them. If he says he killed Boris, they'll shoot him. Can't we tell my father to stop them?"

"I've tried, but he won't believe me," she said flatly. "You're right, Valentin. Your father has gone over to the Reds. He won't listen to anything I say." She paused and then added, "I've decided that I can't stay here with him any longer. I'm going to escape."

As she put the unspoken, only half-acknowledged plan into words, she felt a sudden lightening of mood. She was going to leave Valerian, and leave Ostrovskoye. There was no other course open to her.

Valentin stared at her solemnly for a long moment, then he nodded. "*We* are going to escape," he corrected. "Did you know that guards have been put on the gate?"

"Yes. That makes things more difficult, but I'll get past them somehow."

"*We'll* get past them . . . Look, Stanya," he said, and his voice slipped unexpectedly from a boy's treble to a man's bass, "you're not going off on your adventures and leaving me behind, because I won't let you. I'm coming with you, and I can assure you that we won't be able to get past the guards at the gate. They're not letting anyone in or out. But there is another way."

"Oh, Valentin! Not the watchtower . . . ?"

"Why not? If we creep out very early and take Khan and Katinka, they won't miss us for hours. We could get to Sevastopol, where there's a British ship in the harbor. Then we could sell the horses and buy our passage to England."

"Stop! You're going too fast for me," she protested. "How do you know there's a British ship in the harbor?"

"Sergei told me when he brought the car back."

So that was how Anthony had come! Against all reason her spirits were lifting rapidly. Valentin's enthusiasm was infectious, but she tried to think cooly—to look ahead to all the possible dangers. Even if they succeeded in jumping the boundary ditch, it would take them four or five hours to ride to Sevastopol—which was ample time for Valerian to realize where they'd gone and pursue them in the Delaunay-Belleville. He could even telephone ahead and have them stopped . . . and dragged back in disgrace . . .

Nevertheless, though many pitfalls loomed, the prospect of action made her feel more alive than she had for months. "I'll have to think it over," said said. "We wouldn't be able to take much—just the clothes we're wearing and some food. D'you really think the horses will jump that big ditch? Do you really want to come with me? You don't have to, you know."

"Just try to stop me," said Valentin cheerfully. "I'll get the horses ready. The stable boys are used to seeing me hanging around the stables, but they might be surprised if you did it. We'll take Khan and old Katinka. Father's charger is faster, but he tends to be nervous and highstrung. Katinka is much more sensible and that counts more than speed." Suddenly his face clouded, "Oh, poor Yuri! Isn't there anything we can do?"

She shook her head, unable to trust her voice.

"Then we should leave tomorrow morning."

Could it really be so easy? She looked at Valentin blankly. For hours she'd been lying here wrestling with her decision, and suddenly everything seemed simple and obvious. She wondered why it had never occurred to her before today that she might leave Ostrovskoye and go elsewhere. Her dependence on Valerian had bound her to him for so long, but now it was finally broken. She felt strangely rudderless. Valentin, however, had no such qualms. To him it was simply an adventure. He was tired of being cooped up at Ostrovskoye: he wanted to see the world.

"Get as much sleep tonight as you can," he advised. "I'll wake you up very early—about five o'clock. That's when it gets light. And don't..." he hesitated, suddenly embarrassed, then plunged on, "don't let Father sleep here tonight—that could spoil everything."

But to her relief, Valerian made no attempt to come to her bed. At dawn, after hours of sleeplessness, she was up and dressed long before the soft tap on her door signaled Valentin's readiness. Together they crept out through the kitchen into the pearly dawn mist that lay like a blanket over the sleeping buildings and rolled away across the dew-spangled park.

The boy had muffled both horses' hoofs with rags, and they trod like ghosts across the cobbled courtyard and through the park gate. No words were exchanged until the rags were removed; both Anastasia and Valentin were too afraid of hearing a sudden shout calling them back. But all was silent in the muffling mist as they mounted the horses and started to move away.

"We've done it!" whispered Valentin, and gave Khan his head. The pony cleared his nostrils with a cracking snort and broke into a canter.

"Hush!" said Anastasia, with an anxious glance back at the house. Nothing moved, but she felt an overpowering urge to get away from it as fast as she could. Valentin was right: the first part of their escape had succeeded. Now there remained only the hazard of the watchtower and its gaping abyss. If they could cross that safely, the way to Sevastopol lay clear.

It was the pony's snort that roused Valerian. He had drunk far more than usual the night before, partly to stifle his guilt over what must be happening to Yuri, and partly to still his suddenly-aroused desire for Anastasia. He couldn't forget how she had looked at Anthony Mills—or the Englishman's arrogant assumption that he had the right to interfere in the affairs of others.

The Englishman had said enough, in his oblique British

manner, for Valerian to realize that he was being threatened. Many people—Anthony had hinted—were talking about Ostrovskoye's miraculous escape from the Bolshevik depredations. They were beginning to suspect Count Radek of Red leanings, and to be correspondingly wary in their dealings with him. What, Anthony had demanded, would his value be to the Sevastopol Soviet, which had protected him so far, when he could no longer feed them information? They would toss him aside like a cast-off shoe, and then the Red tide would break over Ostrovskoye amidst burning and plundering, and all the friends he had betrayed would be avenged. His machinations and maneuverings, his switching of political allegiance, might have bought Ostrovskoye a little peace, for a little time. But then it would count for nothing. The message had been clear. Renounce your Bolshevik friends now. Support the White Army and Allied Interventionists before it's too late.

Damn him! thought Valerian again. Why should he tell me what to do? Still, he knew it wasn't really the threat to his property that had made him drink vodka until he was oblivious; it was the way Anastasia had looked at the English intruder—with that spark of green fire in her long, tilted eyes that had once been reserved for him alone. She had never been able to hide her feelings. They were transmitted direct from her heart to her face without any attempt at censorship. Once, this had seemed to Valerian both funny and touching—it gave her a kind of vulnerability at odds with her elegant clothes and cool sophistication. But now this transparence was a source of irritation.

Why can't she pretend, as other women do?, he thought angrily. What use to me is an overgrown child who shows her innermost thoughts to everyone? Deep down, however, the fear of losing her outweighed all his other anxieties. She was the one worshipper he had left to remind him of the days when everyone had worshipped him. It was the subconscious realization that she might already be slipping away that brought him out of a dream-haunted sleep when the pony snorted.

He threw back the covers and went to the window. Gray shapes were moving in the mist-wreathed park—shapes that resolved themselves into the figures of two horses cantering away from the house. Valentin and Anastasia were going for an early ride.

There was nothing in this to alarm him, except the extreme

earliness of the hour. Why should they leave their warm beds at six o'clock of a November morning? Why not wait until the winter sun could clear away the mist that would soak their clothes before they had gone half a mile? There was something odd—something furtive—about those muffled figures, and Valerian's hair-trigger suspicions were instantly on the alert.

Hastily putting on his shirt and breeches, stamping into his boots, he made for the stables. Two stalls stood empty, but in the next one Timur, his big bay charger, whinnied his anxiety at being left alone. He was restive, swinging his hindquarters across the stall as Valerian struggled with the girth.

"Stand still, damn you!" he growled, his fingers clumsy with haste. He led the horse into the yard and mounted, as the sleepy heads of grooms poked out from the haylofts, fearing they had overslept.

Sergei came running up. "Master, is anything . . . ?"

"Who saddled the other horses? Where have they gone?"

"I don't know, Master, The young barin . . ." faltered Sergei, but Valerian rode out of the yard without waiting for him to complete the sentence.

A pile of rags inside the park wall caught his puzzled eye; then he realized their purpose and spurred Timur forward. So his instinct had been right! There was something furtive about Anastasia's early departure. He could think of no other reason why she had gone to the trouble of muffling her horses' hoofs. He gave Timur his head and the big bay stretched out at a gallop across the parkland turf. It wasn't hard to guess at what point the fugitives planned to escape. The main gate was shut and guarded: the only alternative was Yildiz Khan's watchtower. Valerian cursed himself for failing to have a guard put there too. That young scoundrel Valentin: no doubt he'd persuaded Anastasia to attempt the yawning abyss. If she should break her neck, Valerian told himself, he would never forgive himself. Why had he driven her to such desperate measures? What demon in him insisted on frightening her, and accusing her of killing Boris? Even if she had, it would have been in self-defense. He had only been trying to assert his superiority over her once more, to retie the bonds of dependency that seemed to be loosening since the visit of the English captain. No doubt she was deluding herself now with visions of his sheltering arms awaiting her at the Hotel Splendide. And to reach them she was prepared to face anything—even that terrifying abyss.

* * *

"Someone is following," said Valentin suddenly, as they alted at the base of the watchtower, their horses blowing hard.

Anastasia listened. "I can't hear anything."

But Valentin's sharper ears had caught the rhythmic tattoo of ursuing hoofbeats. White-faced, he turned Khan's head toward he steps. "Come on," he said tensely. "When I reach the second light, follow me. And for God's sake don't look down."

It might have been the echo of Petya's own voice from long go. Suddenly petrified with fear, Anastasia sat huddled in the addle as Valentin's pony lowered his sensible head and began to scend the steps, placing his hoofs with caution. Yildiz Khan iust have climbed, to survey his domain from the watchtower's eight in the very same way, Anastasia thought, as she watched iem.

Then she heard it too—galloping hoofbeats approaching ist. Katinka pivoted to neigh a greeting to her stable ompanion. The newcomer was still at the edge of the clearing, ome forty yards away in the mist, instinctively she knew it could e no one but Valerian.

"Quick—it's Father!" Valentin called urgently from above er. "Hurry up! I'm going to jump..."

It was no time for memories, no time to have her ears ringing ith Andrei's screams and in her mind's eye the image of his aring horse, its great black body twisting as it hit the ground. he glanced up at the sloping platform high above her head and w Khan gather himself for an instant and then launch into othingness, a gray blur in the air stretching out across the black ulf and landing with a thud on the far side.

"We've done it!" shouted the exultant boy. "Come on, anya—it's easy."

"Come back!" yelled Valerian, from the edge of the mist, and e sound galvanized Anastasia into action.

Unhesitatingly, Katinka picked her way up the first flight of eps, and then the second, but when they reached the ownward-tilting platform at the top, Anastasia gathered up the ins, holding the mare back with hard, unyielding hands as she ood poised on the brink of the abyss.

"Come back!" Valerian's voice was stern.

"Come on!" Valentin entreated.

"I—I can't!" she whispered, and was certain she couldn't.

Like a diver who realizes too late that the parapet is higher the water farther away than dreamed, she stared down into th gaping pit below, her mind and body paralyzed, unwilling t retreat yet quite unable to nerve herself to take the plunge.

"Don't look down!" shouted Valentin in agony. He wheele Khan and start to gallop away down the track, and Katink shook her head free from her rider's restraining hands—sh didn't intend to be left behind. Her quarters bunched like tw great springs; for a second her hoofs scrabbled sickeningly o the platform as they sought for a grip, then she floated over th yawning gulf as easily as if it had been a culvert, and rockete down the track after her companion without a break in he stride.

Anastasia felt a wild elation. "We've done it!" she shoute just as Valentin had, and the boy turned in his saddle to grin a her.

"That was wonderful!" he shouted back. "I thought for minute you were going to lose courage."

"I... nearly... did." she said, somewhat breathless. The they galloped on into the mist.

"Come back!" Valerian cursed as he stumbled up the wor old steps, his boots slipping on the uneven treads, knowing h was too late to stop the fugitives. When he reached the top, h stared down into the sea of mist, hearing the hoofbeats thuddin faintly in the distance. His jaw tightened: he wasn't beaten ye Anastasia and that crazy boy might think they were free, b they'd soon discover their mistake. He would alert the guar and have a car speeding after them long before they reached th nearest town. They had a choice of routes; the track forked a fe hundred yards from the watchtower, and both roads l eventually to the coast. He wondered which one they wou choose, the twisting mountain track to the right, or the longe more frequented road that followed the valleys? Would it be le or right at the fork? The muffling mist seemed to thro reverberating hoofbeats back at him from both sides. Listenin straining his eyes to see, Valerian moved farther and farth down the sloping platform. He had to be sure...

As they reached the fork, both Anastasia and Valentin hea the dull rumble of collapsing masonry behind them, but neith guessed its cause—nor did they turn back.

* * *

When Anthony returned to the Hotel Splendide after a hasty visit to White Army headquarters, the young clerk at the desk refused, with some embarrassment, to give him the key to his room. Instead, he summoned his superior.

The manager, a thin, balding, middle-aged man who had spent half his life in France and spoke French more fluently than Russian, popped out of his office like a rabbit in a conjurer's sleeve. A frightened rabbit, ruminated Anthony, observing the twitching nose and uneasy eyes glancing constantly toward the revolving door that led to the street.

"Monsieur, I regret so very much," he murmured. "But tonight all rooms are full, and we cannot give accommodation to you."

"That's very interesting," said Anthony, with a glance at the numbered keys hanging in unbroken rows behind the young clerk's head. "Very interesting indeed. Perhaps you'll be good enough to explain this sudden invasion of your very empty hotel? Why is there no longer room for me?"

"We have a large number of unexpected bookings, monsieur," improvized the manager unhappily. "A conference of important delegates, arriving within the hour. We are obliged to prepare extra accommodation... Believe me, it is not my choice."

No, it certainly wasn't the wretched man's fault, reflected Anthony. Running a hotel these days, when a word from the local Soviet might compel you to evict paying customers at a moment's notice, was no one's idea of a cinch. Under whose orders, he wondered was the manager acting?

Whose toes had he stepped on hard enough to warrant this treatment? The answer was staring him in the face: Valerian Radek's, of course. Valerian hadn't been pleased by that invitation to Anastasia. Eviction from his room was Valerian's way of making sure that she didn't pay any visits to her ex-husband in the Hotel Splendide.

"You'll allow me to enter my room to collect my baggage, at least?" he said, and again held out his hand for the key.

"Your baggage is here, monsieur." The manager, visibly relieved that the Englishman wasn't going to make trouble, pulled two leather bags from behind the desk. "I took the liberty of packing your possessions before—"

"Before anyone made off with my belongings? I'm most

grateful to you." Anthony took a bill from his wallet and tapped it thoughtfully on the counter. "Can you suggest where I might find a bed for the night? I plan to leave tomorrow."

The manager's eyes were riveted on the bill. He was beginning to sweat. "Monsieur, I regret, there is nowhere. Nowhere at all. That is the order."

"What do you mean?" asked Anthony sharply, but the manager wouldn't reply.

He hadn't expected to find all hotels barred to him. The wires must have been humming between Count Radek and the local Commissar. Obviously Valerian was determined that Anastasia shouldn't see him again. Anthony sighed. You couldn't save someone who was so determined not to save herself. Why had he believed it might be worth visiting Ostrovskoye? Had he hoped to make her leave Valerian? If so, he was a fool, he told himself. Her refusal to speak to him—her whole attitude—had said more plainly than any words that she didn't want to return. His foolish hope had been destroyed for good, and it was time he faced the fact. She had never loved him; she had simply made use of him. Now that he was no value to her any longer, she wished to be rid of him. The marriage had been a bad bargain from the start, founded on mistrust and misunderstanding. He should have realized long since that it could never succeed while Valerian Radek still held her heart. Now was the time to cut his losses, put her out of his mind and try to forget she had ever been his wife. Russia and Anastasia would have to work out their own destinies without more help from him.

Suddenly, he laughed, and the manager eyed him nervously. Was the Englishman going to cause trouble after all?

"If a lady should look for me here this evening," Anthony said, "Tell her I've come to my senses at last?"

"Come to your senses, monsieur?"

"That's right. She'll know what I mean. Tell her I've gone back to England. I won't be bothering her again."

"Very well, monsieur." The manager bowed and smiled, glad to be rid of this foreigner in whom the Soviet was taking such an uncomfortably close interest. It was because of Count Radek, of course. He wondered for an instant if he should mention Count Radek's fatal accident, so soon after the Englishman's visit to Ostrovskoye, but decided almost immediately against it. The less said the better. Besides the news might delay Captain Mills' departure.

"I wish you *bon voyage, mon capitaine*," he said, and gestured to a porter to pick up Anthony's luggage.

The *Wakefield Princess* was already crowded with Russian refugees, mostly aristocrats with despair in their hearts and the last of their family treasure crammed into cabin trunks. They had come from Moscow and Petrograd, Omsk and Tomsk and Kiev and Ekaterinburg. They were leaving Russia, most of them forever, escaping before the Red tide finally swept them into oblivion, engulfing their lands and destroying their possessions.

With some difficulty, Anthony had obtained a first-class cabin on the upper deck, where he now lay reading on his bed, resolutely refusing to allow his thoughts to return to Anastasia until the horn blew to signal the ship's departure. She had haunted him far too long already, but any habit could be broken, he told himself grimly, given sufficient willpower.

Not until the ship was far out of sight of land did he surrender to the impulse to go up on deck and look toward White Russia for the very last time.

The November breeze was strong and sharp-edged, with the hint of a wintry bite. Only two other people were standing at the stern rail. In the dim light, he saw a thin dark-haired boy and the tall figure of a woman, cloaked and hooded, who stared down at the ship's foaming wake as if mesmerized.

For a moment or two, he watched them idly, speculating on who they were and whither bound. Mother and son? No; the woman looked too young, the boy too old for that relationship. Brother and sister perhaps—the last scions of some noble family, setting out to seek their fortune in a new world. The boy looked happy, excited; his mop of dark hair blew across his forehead as he talked eagerly to his companion. But she gazed silently at the waves going by, apparently oblivious to his chatter. Something in the boy's clearcut profile stirred a memory. Anthony frowned, trying to capture it. Where had he seen that face before?

He heard the boy say triumphantly, in English, with the air of concluding an argument: "My mother's family, then!" Intrigued to discover that they weren't Russian after all, Anthony moved closer. Then he saw—with a deep sense of shock—with the feeling that he'd stepped into, not out of, a dream—that the woman was Anastasia. He stood there stockstill, watching her, trying to understand, while his pulses raced and all his careful resolve to forget her evaporated like mist in the evening air. How and why she was there didn't matter. She was present, here, aboard this ship, and this time he wouldn't let his chance to win her slip away.

"It's cold up here. I'm going to turn in," announced the boy, and then with a hint of anxiety: "You *are* all right, aren't you, Stanya? You're not—too sad?" His voice suddenly broke. "You know, it might be... for the best—best for him, I mean."

"I know. I'm all right," she said in a remote, abstracted voice, as if battling with some inner turmoil. "Don't worry, Valentin. I know exactly what you mean. Only I can't help think of what he was like, long ago. I can't help remembering..."

"People change," said Valentin, with the wisdom of adolescence. "Mother changed a lot. I try to remember her when I was little, before the hospital burned. Laughing with Martha in the orchard. Telling me stories about her home in Scotland. That's how I like to remember her."

With a sudden impulsive gesture, she put her arm around his shoulders and hugged him. "Off you go to bed now. I won't be long."

When the boy had gone she continued to stare fixedly at the waves. Anthony watched her, his mind in whirling confusion. The hope he had been so determined to obliterate had sprung to incredulous new life. At last! She had left Valerian Radek! His visit to Ostrovskoye had not been in vain—it had apparently triggered the reaction he had hardly dared to hope for, and she had left Valerian of her own free will. He was puzzled by the boy's presence, however. Why should he be returning to his mother's family in Scotland?

"Anastasia," he said softly, stepping forward from the shadows.

She turned sharply, then gave a startled exclamation, and before Anthony could stop her she picked up her skirt and began to climb over the rail.

"No!" he shouted, springing toward her. The reason for her mood was suddenly horribly evident: she meant to drown herself. He ran to the rail and caught her, struggling, in his arms.

"No," he said. "No, not that way."

"Let me go," she demanded, striking out at him, straining with all her might to reach...

He hoisted her back bodily onto the deck. "You little fool! What the hell did you do that for?" he shouted, his heart still thundering with shock. A moment later, a roll of the ship, and she would have disappeared into the waves.

"Anthony!" she said in amazement, staring at him with eyes as round as a startled kitten's. "What are you doing here? Why did you try to stop me...?"

"Why shouldn't I stop you?" he said in consternation. "You were about to jump to your death."

"Jump to my—? Oh, my God!" Unexpectedly she began to laugh, wild peals of merriment that held more than a trace of hysteria. "You thought I wanted to drown myself? Oh, no!"

"Well, you won't get a second chance, that's for sure." Still carrying her, Anthony elbowed his way through the swinging door and down the deserted passage to his cabin, where he dumped her unceremoniously on the bed. "Now you can share the joke with me," he said. "What's so funny about trying to jump overboard?"

She stood up and wiped away her tears—though whether of laughter or sorrow it was impossible to tell. "I wasn't trying to jump overboard. I thought I was alone. And when I heard your voice so suddenly, so close, I dropped the ring I was holding—Valerian's ring. It was the last thing I had of his, and I dropped it on the other side of the railing. I could still see it shining, so I tried to climb over to pick it up. Then I saw it slide into the sea..."

There was a long silence.

"I'm sorry, said Anthony, "sorry for your loss."

"I'm not," said Anastasia.

"You're *not*?"

"No. I think, after all, that I'm glad. The last link of the chain is broken and now I am free. Truly free." She paused and then added, "That ring has always been between us, Anthony. When I was married to you in Egypt, and in Lemnos, I used to look at that ring and think how much Valya must love me. But he never really loved me; he only loved himself. When I left him, I knew I must throw that ring away before my life could begin again. So I took it off my finger and tried to let it fall, but suddenly I seemed to be throwing away all my past. And I couldn't do it..."

"I've been trying to forget the past, too," said Anthony.

She looked up in quick surprise. "You, too?"

"Yes," he said deliberately, his eyes never leaving her face.

Anastasia suddenly discovered that she was having difficulty in breathing. She had forgotten that look of his—the narrowed, intensely blue gaze that made her wonder if she'd forgotten to put on her clothes, the gaze that told her she was a beautiful, desirable woman and he was desiring her. With a shiver, she drew her cloak closer around her, trying to ignore the racing of her heart and the fierce, overwhelming compulsion to feel his arms hold her once more. It was difficult to concentrate on what he was saying, when his eyes told her so much more than his words.

With only a telltale suspicion of breathlessness, she said, "Did you—succeed?"

"Very nearly," he said slowly. "I almost persuaded myself that I could forget you. I thought if I tried very hard I might be able to stop thinking of you every moment of every day." He paused, then said simply, "I was wrong. I simply can't do it. I still love you, Anastasia—will you come back to me?"

"Oh!" Her cheeks burned like fire, and she took a hasty step backward.

"What does that mean?"

He tried to put his hands on her shoulders, but she continued to back away, shaking her head, talking rapidly, as shy as if no man had ever touched her before.

"Oh, Anthony, you mustn't ask me that. Don't make it more difficult. You think I'm running to you for help once more, but this time you're wrong. I'm going to make a new life now—my own life. I don't need help from you or anyone..."

"But I need yours," said Anthony. She stared at him, her torrent of words, of thoughts, abruptly dammed. "You hadn't considered that, had you?" he asked softly.

"You—you're joking?" she said uncertainly.

"I was never more serious."

"But why? I don't understand. You called me an iceberg in your bed. You said you didn't love me—that you were going to marry Sybil Dunwoody."

"*You* said I was. I said nothing of the kind. Besides, Sybil is already married. I think she realized even sooner than I did that my feelings for you were never going to change. Now will you come back to me?"

"Oh, Anthony!" Then her resistance broke completely and she was in his arms, clinging to him fiercely. "Don't ever send me away again," she whispered, her mouth close to his. "I can't live without you any more. I knew it long ago, but I couldn't tell you when I thought you didn't love me. So much time has been wasted!"

"We'll make up for it," he promised, and carried her to the bed. As his mouth found hers, the restless plunging of the ship seemed to change to a faster, more urgent rhythm, and the hum of the engine was drowned in the tumultuous singing of her own blood.

"Fire and ice, heaven and hell, despair and ecstasy," she murmured. Anthony stiffened suddenly, his arms so tight around her that they hurt, but Anastasia didn't flinch.

"Who said that?" he demanded.

"Valerian said it," she responded steadily. "Long ago, Valerian said love would be like that when I found it, and I didn't believe him. Now I know he was telling me the truth."

"Valerian . . ."

For a moment the handsome smiling image of the young Guards officer seemed to hang between them, as it so often had in the past. Then it faded like an over-exposed negative.

"He'll never come between us again," she said with certainty, and Anthony could detect no lingering trace of regret in her voice. The image of the Russian nobleman blurred and dissolved into nothingness.

Alone in his cabin a few doors away, Valentin stirred and smiled, dreaming of a land of hills and lochs, a land he'd never seen.

Anastasia smiled too, although she wasn't dreaming. She was lying in her husband's arms, hearing the steady beat of his heart in counterpoint to the throbbing motors of the *Wakefield Princess*, ploughing through the dark seas toward England.